Sarah Barnwell Elliott

John Paget

A novel

Sarah Barnwell Elliott

John Paget
A novel

ISBN/EAN: 9783337000455

Printed in Europe, USA, Canada, Australia, Japan

Cover: Foto ©Andreas Hilbeck / pixelio.de

More available books at **www.hansebooks.com**

JOHN PAGET

A NOVEL

BY

SARAH BARNWELL ELLIOTT

AUTHOR OF "JERRY," "THE FELMERES," "A SIMPLE
HEART"

"To man propose this test—
Thy body at its best,
How far can that project thy soul on its lone way?"

NEW YORK
HENRY HOLT AND COMPANY
1893

THE MERSHON COMPANY PRESS,
RAHWAY, N. J.

DEDICATED

TO THE MEMORY OF

My Father,

THE RT. REV. STEPHEN ELLIOTT, D. D.,

FIRST BISHOP OF GEORGIA.

JOHN PAGET.

I.

" The branches cross above our eyes,
    The skies are in a net ;
And what's the thing beneath the skies
    We two would most forget ?
        Not birth, my love, no, no,—
        Not death, my love, no, no,—
The love once ours, but ours long hours ago."

"I SENT for you, Claudia, because——" then he
hesitated.

"Because you could not help yourself," suggested a voice that anyone, man or woman, would
have listened to until its last cadence faded.

"Yes," the man answered, "I would not have
troubled you else."

"No. I was outlawed. John had ceased to
be my brother, and his children had none of my
blood in their veins. Nothing but the circumstance of their being twins would have let you
turn to me for help."

"You are quite right."

"Alice did not want me? To put it gently,
Alice did not care for me; and yet, I might

have helped her in all these months of her illness."

"She had everything that was necessary."

"Alice had been accustomed to luxuries."

"The war had cured us of luxuriousness."

"And my Northern money could not have
been digested?"

"Some of Alice's Northern friends were very
kind to her."

"It was only *my* money then; and *you* declined it. Alice loved money; she would have
taken it. You are angry? Pardon me, but I
never believed in my brother John's wife. Did
John bear me ill will to the last, Carter?"

"We never spoke of you."

"Do you *think* he bore me ill will?"

"You caused him the greatest sorrow of his life."

"If my marriage was all his sorrow, my brother
was fortunate. Am I a disgrace because I married a Northern man on the eve of the war?
Nonsense!"

"And you did no more than that, Claudia?"

"In the letter—no. In the spirit——" looking up at the man who had crossed the room and
now stood close beside her.

"In the spirit, how was it, dear?"

Her look faltered. It was the thrill in his
voice, maybe, or the "dear" of old days that
made things about her seem to waver. "I hurt
you, Carter—you! And I——" She stopped
and turned her face aside.

Carter waited. The soft curve of the cheek was so near him ; and she had been his once—this woman. The bitterness of years overwhelmed him suddenly, and he cried: " And you—what *can* you say?" bending to look in her eyes. The old love his tenderness had wakened, turned and stung itself to death.

Moving a little she answered, " I was wise."

"And happy? Made happy by your exceeding wisdom?"

" Not perfectly—not as happy as I expected to be, perhaps, but happier than I should have been under any other circumstances."

For a moment they stood looking hard at each other; then Carter went away.

The room in which Claudia was left was large and well proportioned ; but the walls were defaced, the floors were bare and charred in places, as if fires had been built elsewhere than in the broad fireplace, and the wainscoting was battered and hacked. The furniture it contained was heavily carved, and on the table, where lunch had been served for one, and where the remnants still stood, were odd pieces of exquisite china. In front of the hearth there was a square of worn Turkey carpet; the faded curtains that draped the windows were of silk damask, and the pitchers and bowls that stood on the mutilated sideboard were of heavy beaten silver.

Outside there were further marks of past wealth. The side windows, opening down to a broad piazza, looked out on curiously designed gardens where the camelias, grown into trees, were covered with perfect flowers; where the roses were opening under the warm March sun, and where the yellow jasmine, running wild, had climbed to the tops of the great magnolia trees. In front was the stately, solemn vista of the live-oak avenue, draped with sweeping gray moss, and meeting overhead so that the yellow sunshine could seldom reach the white shelled road beneath. About this circle of cultivation the untouched pine forest kept guard, swaying and murmuring, sighing and whispering in an eternal monotone.

To Claudia, alone in the desolate house, the cry came strangely. At first her listening was unconscious, for her thoughts were busy. Perhaps it was this call from the stately pines that disturbed her—that took the tones of voices she had loved; for old laughter sounded faintly—old footsteps echoed through the empty halls. She walked hastily to the open window. The fresh wind swept by her, swaying the old curtains, and bringing in faint whiffs of garden sweetness. She paused a moment, drawing in a long breath.

"I will go to the landing," she said aloud, and the old phrase startled her.

A quick walk in the sunshine would help her. She looked about for some other head-covering than her traveling bonnet that still lay on the chair where she had placed it on her arrival. It seemed an absurd thing in the light of this Southern sun, and going back to an old habit, she turned into the hall and looked up to the remnants of deer-antlers, still screwed to the paneling, for something more useful. And there, as if swept back like her memories, was a broad-brimmed hat that she could have sworn she had left there six years before.

"Carter's," she said, reaching it down and turning it about; then she put it on and left the house. Through a well remembered side gate she went, turning her face away from the deserted outbuildings, and entering quickly the dim gloom of a long cedar walk. A raised path or dam it was, for the land was low, with gnarled old cedars growing along one side, and wild myrtle making a dense brake on the other. Overhead the pines met across the path; under foot the shining brown needles; on all sides the golden jasmine; and far in the depths of the wood, where the pine-barren turned into swamp, stood the great magnolias, and the solemn cypress trees on their knees in the still, brown water.

Claudia knew every step of the way, every turn of the path, and waited a little before she passed the last curve, where she knew she would see the brilliant flash of the river. There it was! Time nor war could change that; and she ran as she had not run since her girlhood, swiftly, gladly, down to the water's edge. The broad rush of waters—how wide—how wide it was to the far-

away dim line of woods on the other shore!
And between the blues of wood and water the
low stretch of brown rice fields, with a storm
house standing in the midst like a sentinel. The
blue sky shone and sparkled as one looked, and
the sunlight fell in a deluge of glory.

Close about her feet the brown rushes; the
line of foam and broken sedge left on the low,
shelled bank; the rotting, barnacle-covered posts,
scarcely showing above the water, where the
boats used to be tied; the old oak bending low
over the stream. Beyond, bunches of wild myrtle,
ending in a cane-brake. Nothing was changed.
She stood still and looked and listened.

The wind came across the river, making a little
white shiver as it came; it trembled in the dry
rushes, then stole away to the swaying pines—a
cry—a sob. The water swished up softly to her
feet. There came the sharp rat-tat-tat of a wood-
pecker, and far away in the dark woods the cry of
a dove.

She had been mad to come back! She lifted
her clasped hands above her head—she wrung
them together, then reached them, palms upward,
to the sky, with an expression on her downcast
face that told more than torture could have
dragged from her lips.

She laughed, and dropping her hands at her
sides, sat down on the bare roots of the old oak.

This had been a favorite seat of hers and
Carter's. It was here that she had told him of

her decision to marry Mr. Van Kuyster. His first look of contempt had been withering, and her cheeks burned at the memory. This morning Carter had given her that same look.

In every line of the letter he had sent her, and which had brought her South, she had read defiance, and in so many plain words was the assurance that "only the starving necessity of others could have driven him to her." That had seemed natural, but his bitterness, as she had realized it this morning, seemed immeasurable. How had he ever appealed to her? The letter had hurt her. The difficulty of winning from her husband permission to come had been great, and surrounded by hard conditions. She had suffered much humiliation in order to help Carter.

She shied an oyster shell into the river, smiling when she found that she had not lost the art. So many things the boys had taught her. The smile died from her lips, her eyes grew brighter and harder. She leaned back against the tree, and looked out across the shining water. She had not been the only one to blame. Alice had made her life miserable; John had taken his wife's view of things, and Carter had seemed to look on Alice as perfection. Between them they had made her desperate. A young, sensitive thing is easily driven to desperation.

A step sounded near. She rose quickly, and confronted Carter.

"It is not safe to come so far alone," he said.

" Safe ! Must I be afraid of the negroes ? "

" Not of our own," Carter answered, " but there are many strange negroes about."

An uneasy silence fell between them, while Claudia thought, " I have betrayed weakness in coming to this old haunt," and Carter thought, " She remembers, at least ; " then he said: " The little boys have waked from their nap if you wish to see them."

" I wish to see them very much," Claudia answered formally, and they turned their steps toward the house.

" The war has made no difference in this walk," Claudia went on, preferring talk to silence.

" It was entirely overgrown when we came back."

" It does not look as if it had been touched," she answered, then the silence came again.

To Carter the silence was nothing. The woman beside him was so entirely the cousin of bygone days, even to his old hat that she had put on and had forgotten, that to make talk—to do anything but feel, through every fiber of his being, would have seemed monstrous to him. How prettily the old hat drooped about her softly rounded face, where scarcely a tint or a line was changed. The years that had made him an old man seemed not to have touched her. He wondered if she would ever grow old—if the light would ever fade from her changeful eyes and face, the music from her voice. He and John had helped to bring her up and educate her; had taken entire care of her after her father's death—the wild, pretty child they had found it so hard to discipline. He had no wish to talk as they sauntered over the brown pine needles. His life was past, and in that past his mind and heart were busy. He might live a long time yet, but he had no hope in store for that possible future.

"What are the names of the children, Carter?"

"The names? oh, yes! why John and Claude, of course."

"Claude?" looking up quickly. "Claude, after——"

"Your mother."

Her look held his for a moment, then she turned away.

"I had forgotten," she said, "for I never knew my mother." The momentary hope that she had been remembered by her brother had made her glad. Carter had not let this gladness draw one breath; but he had not known that to kill her joy would hurt him.

There was silence after this until they entered the hall, and, as of old, Claudia swung her hat to cast it up to the stag's horns. She stopped with her arm poised, while her cheeks burned, and her eyes met Carter's like the eyes of a guilty child.

"My bonnet would not have served," she said.

It was not in man to withstand the look, and Carter took the hat from her gently. "You al-

ways liked our hats better than your own, dear,"
he said.   "It was only an old habit."

Old habits? Of one thing she was sure, she
must get away.   She went into the dining room
like one in a dream. Children's voices greeted
her, and she stopped just inside the door. She
could not see them, for they were playing under
the great, old-fashioned table, but she had not
moved a step forward before she was clasped so
suddenly about the knees that she would have
fallen but for Carter, who followed close behind.

"Old Tenah," he whispered, his mustache
brushing her cheek, and Claudia looked down
into the wrinkled, black face of the old negress
kneeling before her.

" Mawmer!" she cried, and put her soft white
hands tenderly about the small old face.   " I was
afraid you were dead, Mawmer—I was afraid to
ask."   The old negress was standing now, scarcely
reaching to Claudia's shoulder, and kissing over
and over again the little hands she held.

"Me chile—me missus—me little chile!" she
murmured in her soft, flat voice, " I nebber tink
to see *dis* day—old Mawsa chile come back—teng
Gawd—teng Gawd!"

This was the first remembered voice of Claudia's
childhood.   These old hands had cared for her;
these old eyes had watched her lovingly; in these
old arms she had found comfort for all her child-
ish troubles.   And now this faithful heart had
given her the only welcome she had found,

She drew one hand away, and laid it about the old negress's shoulder.

" You love me, Mawmer ? " she asked wistfully.

" Dawter ! " and ceasing her caresses the old woman looked up reproachfully ; "*you* ax me dat ? Who I got in dis wull 'sides you an' Mass Cahter an' Mass Johnny chilluns ? Fahder in heben, *who* I got ? " her voice breaking into a wail, and seating herself on the woodbox near the hearth, she rocked back and forth repeating : " Who I got—who I got ! " There was a scrambling rush, and from under the table the children came, crying out, " Mawmer, Mawmer ! " and clung about her.

Claudia looked with swelling heart on these last sons of her father's house—on the old servant still clinging to their fallen fortunes—on the signs of careful poverty that were everywhere. The short-waisted jackets and old-fashioned long trousers of the little boys ; the homemade woolen shoes ; the colorlessness of the old woman's frock, and apron, and head handkerchief—all so faded, so darned, so clean.

Carter watched her. He, who for years had loved and studied her face, could read every thought and feeling. She had shown herself strong, and hard, and cold in the years that were gone ; this morning she had betrayed some heart —what would she do now ?

One moment longer Claudia stood aloof, then with a hasty movement she knelt beside the little group. "I am your child too, Mawmer?" she pleaded, and her face went down on the old negress's lap, and her tears fell once more where so often they had been shed. It was Carter's turn now to suffer, and leaving the house he walked fast and far until the sun set and the soft red light that came with the death of the day spread over the level, moss-draped, solemn land.

And when he reached home some magic seemed to have changed the place. The curtains were drawn; the fire burned brightly; the pitifully thin homemade candles were lighted; flowers made a sweet radiance on the table; the children were playing on the floor, and Claudia and Tenah were arranging supper.

He paused just within the door—had his old dream come true?—and a cruel sweetness said:

"You look so weary, Carter!"

"I am," he answered, crossing the room and sitting down near the fire; "I am very weary."

When supper was over and the table cleared, old Tenah came for the children. Two little boys—one fair, and strong, and beautiful; one dark, and plain; and Claudia, watching, saw Carter kiss the fair one lightly, but the dark one he took into his arms. "He loves little John best," she thought, "the other boy has *my* name." When the door closed she said, "I must go to-morrow, Carter."

"To-morrow!"

"Yes, I am sorry that I cannot take both the

boys, but I cannot." A burning color stained her face. " My husband is an old man, you know, and two children would annoy him."

"Yes," Carter answered, looking steadily into the fire. Why did she mention her "husband" to him? Then he added, " My object in writing to you was not to burden you with either of the children, but only to arrange for their maintenance until I was in a position myself to support and educate them. I am sorry that I had to trouble you at all."

" I know that ; but in any case I should have claimed one. I have no children, and one will be a happiness to me."

There was silence for a few moments, then Carter said with an impassible look on his face, " Which one will you take ? "

" Claude," Claudia answered, and saw the whole man relax.

" That is best," he said quickly. " He looks like you ; I thought you would prefer Claude for his good looks."

He had misjudged her. John's great, steadfast eyes had won her too, they were so like her brother's. But she had seen that Carter loved John best.

"John has the ancestral name too, John Paget," Carter went on. " Then Tenah understands John, and will go with us."

" You leave the old place ? "

" Yes. I cannot bear it now, and it would

be bad for John to grow up here among traditions of lost things. We shall go West; to
Texas, I hope; I am in correspondence about a
place called Corpus Christi."

" What will you do there?"

" The ministry."

Claudia turned away. This choice of a profession had been a long battle between them in
the olden time.

" I was ready for ordination when the war
came, you remember, and deferred it only until
that struggle should be over. If Alice had lived,
I should have put it off still longer in order to
plant this place for her; but now as I have only
John and can go away, I shall be ordained as
soon as possible."

" And the old place?"

" Is mortgaged. Only to satisfy Alice would
I have tried to pay the debts. The silver will be
sold, and I will send Claude's share to you."

" To Mr. Van Kuyster," Claudia corrected,
with a new bitterness in her voice, "he adopts
the boy."

Carter bent his head. For a moment he was
still, then the words, "Will he change the child's
name?" seemed to break from his lips against
his will.

The pain in his voice was very clear to Claudia
as she looked thoughtfully into the fire. But
why should he not suffer? She herself had felt
the bitterness of her husband's condition that a

Paget should be made to perpetuate the name of Van Kuyster. Carter would feel it doubly, but why not hand it on? He had been willing to give up the ministry for Alice, but not for her. He disliked little Claude because the child looked like her and had her name. He had no belief in her; no respect for her; no mercy. He was as hard as steel save where his pride was touched; and he would have done more for Alice than for her, and she used to beg him so. Why need she trouble to mitigate any truth for him, or soften any fact? And she answered:

"Yes, Mr. Van Kuyster wants the boy to be as much his as possible."

There was a sound like the echo of a sob, and Carter turned his face away.

"If you had given up the ministry for civil engineering, as I tried to persuade you long ago, you could have kept both the boys, could not you?" Claudia suggested.

Carter did not answer, and she went on.

"Of course it is too late now, for I claim Claude. He shall keep Paget as his middle name, and Claude because it is my own."

Carter got up and went to the window. Very still he stood looking blindly on the moonbeams that, not satisfied with the broad sweep of the garden, strove vainly to pierce the dense shadow of the avenue. Presently he turned and looked to where Claudia sat in the red circle of fire-light. He drew a short, sharp breath; had necessity been his only motive in sending for her ?

"Do you realize that little John will be the only Paget left ?" he asked harshly.

Claudia looked up. "The last Paget," she repeated, "so he will. I always forget that you are a cousin and named Wilton."

"And still you take Claude's name away?"

At last he was pleading—pride at least could move him.

"Mr. Van Kuyster is the last of *his* name," she said quietly, "and he adopts a son of good blood in order to perpetuate *his* name." She knew how Carter's eyes would flash and burn, and she looked to see. Like a mortally wounded man he flung up his arms, and she heard a bitter, inarticulate cry! Transfixed, she gazed at him leaning against the window with his face half hidden in the curtain. He was hard enough for anything; why had he not turned on her— poured the bitterest reproaches on her—done anything but give that cry?

Carter Wilton was hard. His love and trust trampled in the dust, he had gone out into the bloody mist of war, and groped for death as the only hope left in life. Ruined and defeated, he had touched that round of suffering where one is thankful when those they love die. He had a right to be hard.

He came back to his chair by the fire, asking Claudia if she would mind his pipe.

"It is not a necessity," he said.

"No," she answered; "no, I will not mind." She scarcely knew what she said, she was so longing to tell him all the misery of her life—to tell him how bitter her punishment was. It might help him, and she would give her life to help him.

"Will Mr. Van Kuyster educate Claude for any profession?" Carter asked presently from out a cloud of smoke.

"There will be no necessity; he will be Mr. Van Kuyster's heir."

"I had forgotten—" and Carter blew out a ring of smoke. "I hope that you and the boy will be very happy, Claudia."

"Thank you."

"And however much I regret the necessity for separating the brothers, I think I am doing the best thing in my power. I will educate John myself; it will be an object."

"And Claude shall have every advantage," Claudia rejoined, casting about for some method of stopping this foolish babble. "What time will I have to leave in the morning?"

"The train passes at eleven, and the steamer sails at four."

"That will give me time in town for a little shopping."

"And to see some friends," Carter suggested.

"Scarcely."

Carter cleared his throat. "I forgot; you

must not blame us too much. The South feels her failure very bitterly, and even old friends must forgive a little coldness if they come from the North. In a little while it will be different."

"Doubtless; but I will have no call to come back; even the old place will be in strange hands." Then a sudden thought flashed into her mind; so sudden, so simple that she uttered a little exclamation.

Carter looked at her suspiciously. "What is it?" he asked.

"Nothing—nothing," but a new expression was on her face, and she said good-night in a preoccupied way.

When she was gone Carter dashed his old clay pipe into the fire and covered his face with his hands.

"She will buy the silver and the place," he groaned.

But he made not a sign the next day when she asked who held the mortgage on the place, and where the silver would be left for sale. He had himself well in hand by that time; he even smiled when old Tenah said with joy: "Miss Clauddy is gwine left awl Mass Cluddy cloze fuh Mass Johnny."

What he had been able to provide was not good enough. Of course not, but it hurt him.

To Claudia that day was like a dream. Old Tenah's tears and blessings, and John's pitiful cries as they drove away from the old place.

The slow journey across the wide rivers and level rice fields—through the dim swamps and into the old dreamy town. The worried shopping ; the settling in the steamer; the last farewell to Carter; his mute acceptance of the package she sent back to John and Tenah. And at the last she looked into his deep, sad eyes—so weary—so lonely.

"God keep you," he said, then hastily turned away.

The great steamer moved slowly, leaving the beautiful old town sleeping beside her tawny river.

II.

"This is a spray the bird clung to,
  Making it blossom with pleasure,
Ere the high tree-top she sprung to,
  Fit for her nest and her treasure.
  Oh, what a hope beyond measure
Was the poor spray's, which the flying feet hung to,
  So to be singled out, built in, and sung to!"

CLOSE in the curve of a crescent of chaparral, that grew on the side of a dip in the prairie, there stood a small group of buildings. A low, unpainted frame house of two rooms; a smaller outhouse of the same material, and one or two huts built of mud and brush after the Mexican fashion. From point to point of the protecting crescent of chaparral there was a high fence or hedge of cactus, filled in, where the cactus failed, with thorny brush, the combination making a most effective barrier. The entrance to the inclosure was by a winding path through the chaparral at the back of the houses. The place was known as "Marsden's" when known at all, which was seldom; for it was not easy to find. There were no landmarks anywhere to guide the seeker, and it was so cleverly screened that even in winter when the foliage was gone the low, weather-stained houses were not easily descried.

No actual crimes could be traced to the Marsdens, but they were not considered safe, and many prophecies were afloat in the surrounding country, to the effect that startling revelations would be made some day. It was many years since Marsden's first appearance; indeed no one knew very clearly the date of his advent. But when he first became differentiated from the surrounding country, it was as a lone man living somewhere out on the prairie, with only a tiny girl for companion. He came into Corpus Christi sometimes to buy supplies, and the baby was always hanging over his bridle-arm, and the women said that of course his wife was dead. Then he disappeared for several years. Not that anyone thought of him as appearing or disappearing, or thought of him at all, for that matter, but after a while, when a gaudy creature came to buy provisions, who called herself Mrs. Marsden, people remembered Marsden and the baby, and that they had not seen them for years. The loud-voiced woman had two small boys with her who called her mother. A day or two later Marsden rode into the town; the little fair-faced girl was with him still, but she was big enough to ride alone; at least her father thought so, and her saddle was a sheepskin strapped on the horse.

Then the women made sure that her own mother was dead and the present Mrs. Marsden was her stepmother. After this the Marsdens seemed to be permanent features in the landscape ; and a place, somewhere out on the prairie, came to be called "Marsden's." Where they had come from, and how they lived, was their own affair, and in those days, in Texas, it was considered the better plan to mind one's own business, and to attend to one's neighbor only when he got into a difficult position and asked one's help. So the Marsdens lived their own life in their own way. The little girl grew to be a big girl, and had a saddle when she saw fit, and the small boys grew to be very hard cases, and very skillful cowboys. From the time they were ten and twelve, they were in great request in the driving season, the only young fellow who could compete with the Marsdens, father and sons, as a shot and as a rider, being John Paget, the young cousin of the Reverend Carter Wilton, the clergyman in Corpus Christi.

But John Paget held a very different position in the community from the Marsdens. It was perfectly well known that he made his living as a cowboy in the busy seasons ; but to obtain his services was difficult. There were only certain people for whom he would drive, and then only if he had complete control. His terms were always accepted, however, as he was universally wanted, and as popular as he would permit himself to be. He seemed to enjoy, as the rest did, the recklessness of a cowboy's existence, but once his time of service expired, and he was back in

Corpus, his life was as secluded as a nun's almost, and report ran that he was never seen without a book in his hands. He had a little boat; and old Calavaros, a Spaniard ranchero, gave him a steady job of horse-breaking and training, which placed many beasts at young Paget's disposal. He and Mr. Wilton were close companions; indeed, Mr. Wilton had no other, for his married life with a young Spanish girl had been of very short duration, and after his wife's death, which happened when John was a young boy, he had sent his baby girl to a convent down the coast where his wife had been brought up. A truly pious parish in a truly Christian community would have wondered, not to say flared up, over the little Beatrice being placed in a convent, but there was no sewing society in Corpus at that time, nor any altar guilds, nor any other female centers in which the flare could begin. In truth, out on those borders the fight was between heathenism and Christianity, and not between creeds. Besides, Mr. Wilton was a dreamer, and his only wish was that his daughter should be trained by a good woman and a lady, which he knew the Mother to be. Added to this, it was the last and only request of his child-wife. He had married his wife out of pity, and felt sorry for her still; so, though he was a good Protestant, the child went to the convent, and he and John Paget lived on together with old Angela, who had succeeded old Tenah, for housekeeper, and maids, and cook, and boot-black, everything, in short, and were eminently comfortable.

One afternoon a wild horse of old Calavaros', a beast in every sense of the word, had taken young Paget many miles farther out on the prairie than he had dreamed of going, and riding back in the dusk, he was halted from behind a large bunch of cactus and mesquite. John drew rein, then obeyed the further order to dismount and give up his valuables. He looked over the prairie, however, and saw that for miles there was not another hiding-place for man or beast—and listening, he heard that his captor was a Mexican. Deceived by John's obedience, the robber lowered his pistol for the space of a breath as he pushed John's money and watch into his pocket. But that second was enough, his pistol was struck from his hand, and he was in a grasp like a vise. It took John about two minutes to disarm his assailant, and to tie his hands behind him. When he finished he said :

"You are Manuel Planco ; you live at Marsden's. I will put the bridle of my horse around your neck so that you can lead him, but you had better not try to run. You know the horse ; he is Calavaros' horse Black Eagle ; he bites when he is provoked. Is it Marsden's horse you have tethered there behind the brush ? "

" Yes."

"Then I will bring him. Now lead the way to Marsden's. Remember, I have your pistols

and mine, all loaded—and the horse bites."
John felt the Mexican tremble, and knew that if
he could see him he would look gray, for that is
the way with Mexicans when they are cold or
frightened. Once Manuel had turned off the trail,
there was seemingly nothing to guide him, but
though going carefully, because of the beast
behind him, he went steadily in one direction,
and after a while a line of chaparral crossed their
line of march. Into this Manuel went, and John
followed without any hesitation. Presently they
entered an inclosure and Manuel stopped.

"Marsden's," he said.

"All right," John answered, "you and the
horse wait here until I see."

His knock on the door of the main house was
answered by a young girl, who looked very much
surprised.

"Is this Mr. Marsden's house?"

"Yes."

"Is Mr. Marsden at home?"

"Yes." Then a tall, lean, gray-headed man,
with a face like an eagle, came to the door.

"Good-evening, Mr. Marsden," the young man
said; "Paget, you know."

"Yes, of course," opening the door wider.
"Come in. How did you find me?"

"Out on the trail, Manuel Planco tried to rob
me. I have brought him in, and your horse. You
will find my watch and money in Manuel's pocket.
He will get you into trouble, Mr. Marsden."

With a deep oath Marsden closed the door and stepped out into the yard where John stood. They found Manuel just where John had left him, and could hear his teeth chattering. It is not necessary to give old Marsden's address to Manuel, save to say that it finished with certain blood-curdling threats and a kick that sent the creature rapidly in the direction of the house door.

"May I put up for the night?" John asked, as he restored his money and watch to their places.

"Of course; I'll send the boys out to attend to your horse."

"I think I had better do that," John answered; "I am riding Calavaros' Black Eagle."

"You are not afraid of that devil?"

"No. But I put the reins round Manuel's neck as we walked here. Manuel did not try to run." There was a low laugh, then old Marsden opened the door of the outhouse that was empty. "Put him in there—the other horses we leave out in the yard." After this they went into the house. Within, everything was as rough as possible, but the food and drink were clean and plentiful, and the young girl seemed to be the presiding genius. Mrs. Marsden could be heard quarreling with Manuel and one of her sons in the next room. Her language was not choice, and, as her utterance was thick, John drew the very correct conclusion that she was drunk;

and that as no one seemed to mind, it must be a common occurrence.

Up to this time John had known the two Marsden boys, who were much younger than he, only as boys whom he never employed on his drives; the old man he knew only by sight. He had felt some curiosity about these people because he had heard them talked of mysteriously and carefully; because everybody seemed to distrust them, yet have no specific charges against them; because nobody could ever tell him exactly where they lived, and because, as a little boy, he remembered seeing old Marsden ride into the town with the baby over his bridle-arm. To his knowledge he had never seen the girl since, though now that he met her face to face, he recognized her as a person whom he had seen sometimes in church. That old Marsden's girl should go to church was another complication.

Mrs. Marsden and Manuel did not come in to supper, seeming to prefer to quarrel and drink in peace in the next room. Old Marsden and the two boys and John sat down, and the girl, Elizabeth, waited on them. After supper the boys disappeared, and two or three men whom John knew well as desperadoes, came in. They seemed a little disconcerted on seeing him, but sat down, and Elizabeth bringing in glasses and bottles and pipes, the night began. Elizabeth took her seat in a low chair near the fire, for it was winter.

As the evening wore on, John heard some strange revelations, and talk that made his cheeks burn for the young girl near the fire. Once after an awful story from the old man, their eyes met. Her look did not waver—her color did not rise—and after a moment in which her eyes told him that she understood his feeling for her, and that such feeling was a waste of sympathy, as she was quite used to this kind of thing, she returned quietly to the reading of a book that lay open on her lap.

John drank very little. In the first place he did not care for it; in the second, it would not be safe to drink much in such company. Gradually speech got thicker, and the talk less coherent; then Elizabeth laid her book on the floor and came to her father's side.

"You had better lie down now, father," she said. After a few oaths the old man essayed to rise; it was difficult, but with John's assistance he succeeded, and tottered toward the door of the next room.

"George is usually here to help me," Elizabeth said, as between them they piloted the limp, lurching, swearing old man to a low bed, "but to-night he and Jim have gone to a Mexican dance."

On another bed Mrs. Marsden was snoring, and Manuel, on the floor by the fire, was also asleep. John followed Elizabeth back to the kitchen, and watched her with some curiosity as she spread three piles of hides and blankets in three corners of the room, and ordered the other men to go and lie down. They seemed to be accustomed to it, and did as the girl told them.

"Now I will show you a place to sleep," she said.

"And you?" John asked, "you cannot stop in here."

"Oh, no! My place is in a loft outside; but I must clear all this away first."

"I will help you."

When all was done, and the fire made safe, she led him to one of the huts outside, which evidently had been prepared for him.

"The boys sleep in the other cabin," she said; "they will not disturb you when they come; and I live up in that loft," pointing to the top of the shanty where John's horse had been put.

"But my horse is in the lower part; will he not disturb you?"

"No, horses are often put in there."

"And are you not afraid?"

"No, I have a pistol and a Winchester; I am quite safe. Often and often I am the only sober creature on the place; but I am never afraid." Then she said good-night and went away, and John turned into the little hut with much to think of.

The next morning he was up at an early hour, to find Elizabeth arranging the breakfast table out in the yard.

"Those people are still asleep in the house,"

she said, " and as it is not cold I think it will be pleasanter out here."

By daylight her face seemed fresher and more appealing. She was not handsome perhaps, but there was something that attracted John strongly. It might be only the contrast to her surroundings, but she struck him as being so undefiled. Purity was an unmistakable thing, and her clear steadfast eyes must look out of a pure heart and mind.

" I saw you reading last night," John said ; " what was it ? "

" ' Ivanhoe,' " was answered, to his great astonishment.

" I have very few books," she went on ; " only a remnant of what father used to have, and one or two that belonged to my own mother. Mrs. Marsden is not my mother."

" Of course not ; and the boys are only your half-brothers."

" Yes, but they have Marsden blood in their veins, and maybe they will do something some day." John stirred his coffee slowly, as he pondered on the words " Marsden blood"—what was there in the old reprobate to be proud of ?

" And you are fond of reading ? " he went on.

" Yes. When Mrs. Marsden is herself, she manages everything ; then I have little to do except ride and read, and I read whatever I can find. We stayed a long time in San Antonio once, and father let me go to school."

" Perhaps I can lend you some books," John

suggested. "I am a horse-breaker and a cowboy, but between the busy seasons I do a good deal of reading and studying. My cousin, Mr. Wilton, you know, has spent a great deal of time on my education. Perhaps I can help you."

"I know all about you," Elizabeth answered quickly, "and several times I have been on the point of stopping you and asking you a favor. But I was afraid that, when you heard who I was, you would not listen to me. Last night, when I opened the door for you, I thought—'God has sent him here to help me.'"

"And the favor?"

"That you will be kind to my brothers. They admire you; you can do them good if you will."

"I will," John answered promptly.

So it was that John Paget came to know the Marsdens. After this he often carried books to the girl, and kept faithfully his promise to befriend the boys.

When it was observed that these young fellows were constantly with him, and when later it came to be known that Paget went constantly to Marsden's, it aroused much interest; far more than the sending of little Beatrice to the Convent had done, because it seemed a stranger, and a far more dangerous thing. It was a dreadful step down for young Paget. Few comments were made, however, for manifestly Paget and Mr. Wilton were old enough to manage their own affairs; and neither Paget nor the Marsdens

were safe objects of criticism.   So events moved
quietly.

The gray prairie stretched without a break out
to the far horizon, where it met the gray sky.
Down in the west a long red gash showed that
the sun had set.   The low, steady wind, that blew
straight from the north, had a relentless sound
that promised length, and strength, and at last a
touch from the polar seas.

At the beginning of the path that led through
the chaparral into the inclosure, Elizabeth waited,
with a red setter puppy at her feet.   Her arms
were crossed, and she leaned against one of the
small, gnarled trees.   She was facing the north
and the wind, but her head was turned, and her
eyes were fixed on the red bar down in the
west.

Presently, far off, she heard the thud of a
horse's hoofs; the ground was so baked by
drought that the sound traveled a long distance.
She moved as she heard it, and calling the dog,
withdrew into the woods by the little path.   She
did not want to be found waiting and watching
save by one.   Her surroundings demanded great
circumspection.   Presently she saw the horseman
silhouetted black against the gray sky; for a
moment she watched him, then she and the
puppy she called " Wamba" came back to where
they had been waiting, and took position as
before.

The horseman was not riding very rapidly, and when he saw the girl he did not seem to hasten at all. Evidently it was the usual thing to find her waiting there. Dismounting, he put the horse in the path, and struck him slightly ; this seemed to be a habit too, for the horse trotted quietly through the chaparral into the inclosure. Then the horseman stooped and touched Elizabeth's brow with his lips. Elizabeth put her hands on his shoulders, and looked up into his face.

" I am a tall woman, Jack," she said, " but you are so much taller that I cannot kiss you unless you will."

Then John stooped and kissed her on the lips.

" You are late," Elizabeth went on ; " I began be be afraid that you would not come. To-day is my birthday—don't you remember ?—and *the* anniversary. Three years ago to-day you came here first, and I have always looked on you as a birthday gift."

John's eyes grew gloomier as she spoke. " I ought not to have forgotten," he said, " but——"

" You did ?"

" I am afraid that I did."

There was silence for a moment while Elizabeth turned her eyes again to the red gash down in the west ; but she did not move her hands from where they were on John's shoulders, nor did he move his arm from where it rested about her waist—loosely, but still it was about her waist.

Elizabeth sighed a little, but there was a smile on her lips when she spoke.

"As it is the first time you have ever forgotten," she said, " I suppose I must forgive you. Three years is a long time, Jack, and to-day I am twenty. It is hard to realize."

"I don't know," John answered; "it seems longer than that since I came here first—it seems ages."

"Counting by the strides in my education," the girl went on, " it seems ages to me too. You have been very good to me, and have taught me a great deal. You believe in my gratitude, don't you?"

"Yes, I suppose so; but you ought not to be grateful."

"I think I am the best judge of that," Elizabeth answered, "and you have been good to the boys too. But what is wrong this evening—are you ill?"

"I believe I am ill. My head has been dull for days, and now it aches dreadfully. As for wrong—everything is wrong, and has been wrong from beginning to end."

Elizabeth looked up with a slight start, as one who had been struck unexpectedly.

"My cousin came nearer to lecturing me to-day," John went on, "than ever in my life before; and he was right."

"What did he say?" Elizabeth asked, and moved as if to leave the circle of the arm that scarcely touched her. It did not tighten its hold; instead, it was withdrawn. Then, as if she had intended to move, Elizabeth took her original position, leaning against a tree with her arms crossed. John put his hands in his pockets.

"He did not say much," he answered, "that is not my cousin's way; but what he said drove home."

"Does he know anything about me—about your coming here?"

"I do not know what he knows. We seldom talk of our private affairs. What he said was to the effect that I was wasting my life—and I am."

There was a moment's silence, then John went on. "He said that he had, after educating me, left me free to choose my own path, hoping that as the last of the name, I would choose a worthy one. That so far I had drifted; making my own living, of course, and paying my way—a gentleman could do no less; but did I intend to be a cowboy and a horse-trainer all my life. It is a just question, for I am nearly twenty-six and no choice made yet."

"What does he want you to be?" Elizabeth asked quietly.

"I do not know."

"Civil engineering, or law, or medicine?"

"Medicine would finish me; civil engineering I do not fancy, and the law—would take too long."

"That does not matter," Elizabeth said; "you

have plenty of patience—I have tested it. You would make a good lawyer, I think."

John looked at her a moment. "And you?" he asked.

"I have nothing to do with it," she answered steadily. "I have loved you, that is all. If 'everything is wrong, and has been wrong from beginning to end,' it must stop."

"Has it not been wrong?"

"You must answer for yourself. For me, I have loved you truly and purely—there has been no wrong in *my* love. I——" She stopped abruptly

John moved restlessly.

"Perhaps a cup of coffee will help your head," Elizabeth went on.

"And the family?"

"Were perfectly quiet when I came out. But you need not go into the house unless you like; I can bring it to you in the loft."

"Oh, no; one riot more or less at the end of things should not matter. Come on."

"Was your cousin angry?" Elizabeth asked, as she followed down the path.

"No, but there was an infinite scorn in his voice, which he made worse by trying to hide. I felt more than he meant, I suppose, because I knew how true it was, but I had not realized it fully. I know now, though, how far down I have gone."

It was bad that he could not see the girl's face

as each word struck her. She lived a long time while they walked through that little wood.

John turned aside when they reached the inclosure, to unsaddle his horse; and Elizabeth went into the house. Alas, for the quiet she had left! They had finished supper while she and John talked, and now the old man had his bottle beside him, while Manuel Planco, Mrs. Marsden, and the younger boy, Jim, were having one of their many squabbles in the next room. George was cleaning a gun near the fire. The air was close, and the mingled smells of food, and whisky, and gun-cleaning were not pleasant. It was no worse than it had been on the evening when John first came there, but Elizabeth knew that it would seem infinitely worse. Then it was new and strange, and there seemed to be possibilities—now, he said, 'One riot more or less at the end of things should not matter;' and if it were the end, it *did* not matter. She left the door partly open to freshen the air a little; and pulling out some coals, she put the coffee down to get hot. She straightened the table as well as she could on such short notice, and put the chairs in their places.

"Paget come?"

"Yes, father."

The old man laughed a little. "What are you good for, Bess," he said, "if you can't make Paget go with us to-morrow night. I think we will make a good job." Elizabeth went on with her preparations silently.

"You think he is too good? If he is too good for your father, he ought to be too good for you."

"He is," the girl answered.

"I'll be damned if he is! do you know who you are?"

"Your daughter. But do not let us quarrel; Jack is sick this evening." She spoke hurriedly, for she heard John coming.

John paused a moment in the doorway, and the look on his face as he stood there would have hurt Elizabeth, if the words he had said outside had not benumbed her. As it was, she smiled a little as she took the coffee-pot from the hearth.

"Things are not as quiet as I represented them," she said. Then, John sitting down, she poured out his coffee. He took it without a word, and, stirring it slowly, said a short, "No, thank you," to her offers of food. Having done all that she could, Elizabeth took her seat near George, withdrawing from John, as it were, and the old man spoke.

"I tell Bess, Paget," he said, "that she ought to make you go with us to-morrow night. Manuel has been to find out, and he knows what will be in that stage. It will be an easy and a paying job, and it is so far away that no-body will connect it with us. We will leave in the morning before day, and, by riding pretty hard, we can make the place where the road skirts

the bayou by nine o'clock to-morrow night.
There is good cover there, and if George and
Jim, and Manuel and I, are willing to run the
risk, your going will reduce the risk to nothing,
and will only divide the spoils by one more."

Elizabeth watched John closely. Somehow, he
seemed to have drifted so far away from her
already that she could look at him with critical
eyes. But he neither looked up nor answered.

" It will surely pay you better," the old man
went on, " than breaking old Calavaros' horses ;
and besides, to do the one, you need not give up
the other. These little expeditions come in very
well in idle times. Manuel there," looking up to
where Manuel stood in the doorway between the
rooms, " is making quite a fortune. And he
takes precious good care to get behind me or
George when the fight is on ; but, as he does all
the sneaking and lying beforehand, in order to
find out the valuable stage-loads, he is entitled to
his share. I could not do that part, but the rest
of it is fun. Will you go?"

" No."

" Damn it, then, you needn't, " the old man
answered sharply, as John, rising from the table,
pushed back his chair roughly.

" He too good," Manuel said, " too good. What
you think, Mees Eleesabet—what think the loft—
yah !" Something bright glittered in John's hand
that Elizabeth clung to as he sprang toward
Manuel.

"George!" she cried, as John tried to fling her off; and John was pinioned from behind.

"No murder here, Paget," George said quietly, as John, struggling like a madman, tried to free himself. "Get out of here, Manuel—you fool!" George went on. But Manuel was just drunk enough to be reckless, and stood laughing softly until Jim, pushing him aside, came to George's assistance.

"Tie him," Elizabeth said, seeing that the struggle was going against her brothers. "Here is a lariat," bringing it quickly, while John swore that, if they tied him, he would kill them all. Nevertheless, the boys managed to hold him while the old man tied him skillfully.

It was not a pleasant or elevating sensation that John experienced as he lay helpless on `the floor; and in the mad rage that possessed him he swore that he would never forgive this insult and would some day murder Manuel. But Manuel's time had come; for George, who loathed him, now collared him, and reaching down a cowhide as he went, dragged him outside. "Cur" was the mildest epithet that George used as he flogged the creature, and the blows and curses rained down relentlessly until the old man, remembering the next day's work, went out and stopped it. Then Manuel crept away.

Presently Elizabeth kneeled down by John, and he felt the cords loosening. "George has

beaten Manuel, and sent him away," she said.
"Will you come?"

John rose and went in silence to the loft, where
Elizabeth followed with a bucket of water. She
put it down, with some clean towels, near the box
that held the basin.

"It would have been murder, Jack," she said.
"I could not let you do it; that would have been
worse than all the rest." Then, without further
speech, she left him, closing the door after her.

Wrapped in a *serape* she seated herself on the
lowest round of the ladder. John thought that
she would hold him. He seemed to have
wakened suddenly to such a loathing of himself;
and he thought that she would hold him! She
felt a great pity for him. She knew, for she knew
him better than he knew himself, that to a man
of his temperament all that he had done was
irrevocable, but *he* did not realize this, and she
would not tell him. She would let him think
that it could all be wiped out quite easily; she
would let him go without one remonstrance.
This would do until he could take a fresh grasp
on life; by that time she might be dead and he
be really free.

"He *has* loved me—yes, he has loved me."
She whispered it over and over. "He loved me
once—once!"

The gray sky was starless, and the steady wind
blew a little stronger and a little colder each
hour. By dawn it would be very cold. She

must get John into Corpus, for she felt sure that he was going to be ill, and she could not make him comfortable. Besides, in his present state of self-abasement, the further humiliation of being found in such a place by the physician would be death to him almost.

Her face burnt in the darkness. For some time she had seen that John was growing rest-ive, but she had not said anything one way or another. She had been afraid of losing him. Now she called herself a mean-spirited coward.

She heard a twig snap. She did not move, but she listened intently. Something was moving very cautiously, but moving, and in her direc-tion.

Presently a shadow stole from out the chapar-ral, pausing to make observations, then came for-ward quickly.

"Manuel!" she said, rising, and the figure stopped. "Go and make the fire in the house—go quickly." Her voice was very low, but it did not quiver. "Go; one shot will kill you and rouse everybody."

There was a second's pause, then with a low oath the figure turned, muttering to himself, "To-night he make you stay outside—dog to him now——" and Elizabeth drew a long breath; she went over to one of the cabins and roused her brothers.

"It is time to get up," she said, "and you had

better get Manuel away quickly." Then she went back to her watch at the foot of the ladder. It would be an easy thing for Manuel to slip up to the loft and stab John.

When the party was gone she went into the house and made fresh coffee; then, after eating her breakfast, she fed and saddled John's horse and her own. It was bright enough now to be called day, and she went up to rouse John. She felt instantly that he had fever, and became more anxious than ever to get him into town. It would be almost a day's journey, going at the pace a sick man would have to ride, and they must start at once.

John did not want to go—did not want to move at all until she bathed his face, and persuaded him to drink a cup of coffee into which she had put some whisky.

"I will ride with you to the edge of the town," she said. "It will be better for you; indeed it will be, Jack."

It took some time to persuade him, but at last they started. The wind that now was blowing cold revived John somewhat, and they rode more rapidly than Elizabeth had ventured to hope; still it was late in the day when they reached the town.

"Good-by, Jack," she said, drawing rein behind a clump of huisachie trees within a stone's-throw of Mr. Wilton's house, "remember, you are free; good-by."

"I don't know what you mean," John answered. "I have never gone to your father's house against my will. But my head aches too much to talk—good-by." He held the hand she extended, for a second, then rode up to the gate of his house.

III.

"Stand still, fond fettered wretch! while Memory's art
    Parades the past before thy face, and lures
    Thy spirit to her passionate portraitures:
Till the tempestuous flood gates, flung apart,
Flood with wild will the hollows of thy heart,
    And thy heart rends thee, and thy body endures."

"A YOUNG woman is here, sir." Old Angela stood outside Mr. Wilton's study door; a brown, shriveled, little old woman with great gold hoops in her ears, and a scarlet cloth about her head. These things struck one first; then the pathos in her soft black eyes made one wonder if her heart were as old as her body looked, for her eyes were bedded in wrinkles, and her figure was much bowed.

Mr. Wilton came out quickly. "Do you know her, Angela?" he asked.

The old woman shook her head. "She is young, she is strong," she answered, "that is all I know. She waits in the kitchen."

"You are sure you can get no man, Angela, who could nurse?"

"Those who will take money are low—are dirty and will drink, and you will have none except you pay them. You give kindness, but you will not take it. I have tried for three days.

45

This woman is clean, and young, and strong, and she will take the money."

"Send her here, then."

And the old woman disappeared down the hall.

Mr. Wilton, with his hands clasped behind him, and his head bowed, was thinking very deeply. He did not hear the light steps, and started when a low, clear voice said, "I am here, Mr. Wilton."

He looked at the tall, slight girl who stood beside him, in silence for a moment.

"What is your name?"

"Elizabeth Clare Marsden."

"Marsden?"

"My father is Reginald Marsden, an Englishman, and lives many miles out on the prairie. My brothers are cowboys. Mr. Paget has been very good to them, and has made them better men. When I heard that you needed help to nurse him, I came. I know a good deal about fever."

"You look very young."

"I am twenty by the count of years, but my life has been hard and rough; full of dangers and experience, and I have been a woman a long time; you may trust me to do my duty, and nothing but my duty. I can give you no references, however, for I know no one in the town. I have kept away from the people—I do not like them."

"I have seen you in church."

"Yes. My father was a gentleman once, and

my mother was a lady, brought up in the Church of England. She died when I was born. I have her prayer-book, and I go to church because I think she would like it if she were here. I have brought you one of my father's books, the only proof I have of my story "—handing him a much worn, but handsomely bound volume. " His name is in it, and his coat-of-arms. He was dismissed from the English army, and disinherited. He forged the name of a brother officer. Now I have told you all. I would rather nurse Mr. Paget because I am grateful for his kindness to my brothers, but if, as your servant says, you will not permit this, I will take the money."

" You need not take the money, Miss Marsden."

" Call me Clare, if you please."

"As you will," Mr. Wilton answered, closing the book he had been examining; "and now I will take you to my cousin's room."

He had listened to John's ravings; they were incoherent and unconnected, but "Elizabeth— Elizabeth—Elizabeth," came with monotonous certainty at the end of every storm of words. Was this the Elizabeth? Her request to be called Clare made him almost sure.

Old Angela sat by the bed where the young man lay; his eyes brilliant, his lips parched, his tremulous fingers picking, picking, always picking at the coverlid. He did not see them, and Elizabeth, approaching from behind, laid her hand on his forehead.

"Tie me—tie me! how dare you!" he muttered; then his voice sank into a whisper, while he struggled as if to free his wrists.

"You are not tied," Elizabeth said quietly; "see, I have loosed you." At her words a perfect stillness fell, and the sick man seemed to be listening for her voice again.

"You may go, Angela," Mr. Wilton whispered; "Clare will take charge of things now," and the old woman went away.

Elizabeth turned to him. "What are the doctor's directions?" she asked.

Mr. Wilton handed her a sheet of paper, then showed her where everything was.

"Elizabeth, Elizabeth!" John called; but the girl did not turn from reading the paper.

"If you want me," Mr. Wilton went on, "I am in the room just below; strike on the floor."

"Yes. And when does the doctor come again?"

"At nine this evening. Do you know him?"

"No; we are our own physicians."

"Elizabeth!" John said again, but again she did not answer.

"Does the doctor have any hope?"

Mr. Wilton shook his head. "He has not said so, but I think he fears the worst."

"Elizabeth!" This time she turned and laid her hand on John's that were so restless, and looked into his eyes that were so bright, and yet so weary. "All that I have done has been of my own free will," he said.

"And all the future shall be according to your will," she answered.

"And I am not tied?"

"No."

"Then I will be quiet—I will try." He lay still after this, and Elizabeth kept her hand on his. When Mr. Wilton left the room, she bent over John—bent low until her cheek touched his forehead.

"Jack," she whispered, "Jack, you know me—you are glad to see me?" But his mind had slipped away, and he looked at her vacantly.

For days they fought death. Sometimes John was raving, sometimes in a stupor, and, though never seeming to know Elizabeth, he was always submissive to her word or touch. At last the crisis came, and he fell asleep. The doctor said that he would watch himself for his waking, and Elizabeth went downstairs. She met Mr. Wilton in the hall, and asked if she might speak with him in his study.

"If Mr. Paget wakes up himself," she said, "I will go without seeing him again, for his recovery will then be sure. If not, I will stay until the end. But in view of my going, I want to ask a promise of you. It is that you will never tell Mr. Paget that I have been here, and never ask him any questions concerning me or mine. If he tells you anything of his past life that is in

any way connected with us, do not let him know
even then that I have been here. It is for his
good that I ask this, and you will believe me
when I tell you that you will do well to heed this
promise."

"I promise."

"And I am going to ask something else of
you," Elizabeth went on. "Will you lend me
something to read that will make me a better
woman? I am weary with the struggle of my
life. Sometimes I feel that I must let go and
drift. Life is not so glad a thing to me that I
can return thanks for my 'creation and preserva-
tion.' I am not needed anywhere, and I am
lonely."

There was a moment's silence; then Mr. Wilton, walking slowly up and down the little room,
with his hands clasped behind him and his head
bent, spoke, almost as if to himself.

"It helps us sometimes," he said, "to know
that we have helped another. That the character
we have been building for years, through pain
and hindrances, has reached a point where it
strengthens others without knowing it—without
effort. You have helped me. You have made
me see in a different light a woman who long
ago trod on my life." He stopped and held out
his hand. "You are sure that what you ask is
best?"

"I am sure," and Elizabeth put her hand in
his. "What is really mine will come to me; I

will wait. About the books. Outside your back
gate there is a large huisachie tree, hollow, surrounded by bushes. Every fortnight, beginning
with next Monday, I will come there and take
what I find, and leave what I have finished.
Now, I will go and listen outside his door until
he wakes. Put the book you will lend me to-day
on the hall table, so that, if I go, I can find it. I
may not see you again. Good-by."

"Good-by. God bless you, child."

She went upstairs and into the sick room,
where she stood for a moment looking down on
John, then took up her position just outside the
door. After a while—a long while—she heard a
movement and a sigh. She held her breath;
then a weak voice asked:

"Have I been very ill?"

She did not wait for the answer. She found
the book on the hall table, and her small bundle
where she had placed it at the back door. She
did not say farewell to old Angela, even, but
took her way through the back gate out to the
prairie.

"What is really mine will come to me," Elizabeth had said; but as far as could be seen,
nothing came. She had answered the family
jeers concerning John by silence, until about six
weeks after John's recovery, when the fact became
known that John Paget had given up his old life
entirely, and was studying for the ministry.

Then, out at Marsden's things threatened to become serious.

"Paget preaching!" the old man roared. "I'll go preach myself, Bess; and you are not good enough for him now? I'll break every bone in his hypocritical body—damn him!"

Elizabeth laughed softly. "It does seem rather funny," she said; "but you need not trouble him, nor yourself, father, nor be so quick to take it for granted that it is his fault that he does not come here any more. It may be my doing, you know."

The old man looked at her doubtfully. "You are sure about it?" he said. "We will put a bullet in him any time you say so."

"I do not say so. I do not want him shot. I could do it myself if I wanted it done, and I would."

"Good for you!" was Jim's comment, but George looked at her earnestly. "I should hate to kill Paget, sister," he said, "and so would you."

"Of course I would, especially as there is no need. I nursed him when he was ill, to pay off all old scores, and now we are quits. Jack is a good fellow; he could make a great deal of trouble for us if he chose to talk."

"He would be sure to get his bullet then, and he knows it," Mr. Marsden said.

"If he wanted to talk he would not stop for fear, and *you* know it. He keeps silent simply because he is a gentleman, and has accepted our

hospitality, such as it is. For me, I am surprised
that he came here so much; we are not very
desirable acquaintances. I wonder that he did
not loathe us and our life long ago."

The old man looked at her thoughtfully.
"You have never known any other life," he said.
"What do you mean by loathing this?"

"My blood has known a better life," she
answered, "and I am thankful that Jack Paget
has turned from this sort of existence while he is
still young enough to choose another."

"It is your own business," her father said at
last; "do as you please. I am sorry you loathe
us, though; I might have sent you across the
water to a respectable life when you were a baby,
but you were all I had—and—well, I loved you."

Elizabeth laid her cheek against his hand.

From that day the jeers ceased, and John
Paget seemed to drop out of the life and memory
of Marsden's.

For three years neither John nor Mr. Wilton
had seen Elizabeth. If she came to church she
managed to sit where she would be hidden from
them. But in all that time she had not failed
once to go to the huisachie grove for her books.
Sometimes there would be a note from Mr.
Wilton—a few kind words, but she never answered
them.

One afternoon toward dusk she went to get
her books; she heard voices in Mr. Wilton's
garden, and listened. John's she recognized, but

a new voice, and a woman's voice, answered him.
It was a short way from the shadow of the
huisachie grove to the shadow of the garden
hedge, and in the gathering dusk it was easily
crossed without detection.

With one arm resting on the low branch of
a fig tree, John stood looking down on a girl
swinging in the hammock. He addressed her as
" My dear child," once or twice, then he called her
Beatrice, and Elizabeth knew that she was Mr.
Wilton's daughter come home from the Convent.
She went back to the huisachie grove and got
the books, then walked out to the chaparral
where her horse was tied. It was well that he
was fresh, for she put him at his best speed and
did not let him flag for a moment until she
reached home.

Once more she kept a long night's vigil seated
on the lowest round of the ladder to the loft,
where she had watched three years before. To-
night the moon was full—the ragged shadows
were clear cut and black as ink, and the wind was
a low whisper. In the other vigil the sky had
been gray, and the wind had been wild. How
long ago it seemed ! In what a fool's paradise
she had lived while John Paget had loved her.
How had she dreamed, even, that that life could
continue?

And yet she had not been all to blame in
grasping whatever she could get of happiness.
She had been so lonely.

Once she had seen a half-starved dog find a bone; an old, dry bone it looked, but the poor beast seized it hungrily. Suddenly he dropped it and fled, howling piteously. Curiosity made her look closely, and she found that the bone was filled with small red ants.

She laughed a little at her parable.

She had thought that in the three years just gone she had learned what suffering meant, but now the lesson seemed just begun. She shut her eyes and saw her lover—the curve of his throat, the poise of his head, the movement of his hands, so slim and tapering, so firm of grasp. And who so tall and straight as he, and who could ride or shoot so well? How brilliant and fearless were his eyes—how deep and dreamy! And the tones of his voice—how she knew them every one!

He had loved her—yes, he had loved her. And now it was dead.

She had thought some bitter things when she saw John Paget ordained deacon, but she had fought against them, and had reasoned with herself until she could see things from John's standpoint.

He had gone down into the shadow of death, and life had come to seem a different thing. He had lived for weeks with no influence near him but Mr. Wilton's, in the light of whose pure life John's past must, indeed, seem dark and loathsome. She was a part of that past—she was connected irretrievably with all that would make him miserable for years. If she had let him murder Manuel, he would have been committed to outlaw life. If she had chosen to keep him through his illness, he could not have withdrawn then. If she had chosen to stay by him in his own home, Mr. Wilton would have thought her justifiable. She *could* have held him, but she had not fallen low enough for that!

Now, how could she live? To let him go had been agony—to yield him to another was torture unspeakable. Perhaps, after a little while, the pain would destroy itself; there was a limit to pain.

For the next fortnight she did not go near the town; her rides were all in the opposite direction, and she went on some wild expeditions with her brothers; a thing she had begun to do since John's desertion.

At the end of the two weeks she rode to the huisachie grove early in the morning and deposited the books. This time she left an unsigned note saying that she would not come again, and thanking Mr. Wilton for his past kindness.

That evening Mr. Wilton asked John if he knew where the Marsdens lived. John said yes, but that there were no landmarks by which one could be directed to the place. This was all. He asked no questions in return, and gave no opening for further explanation, and Mr. Wilton, remembering his promise to Elizabeth, did not push his inquiries. But he asked in the town,

first one person and then another, something of
the Marsdens, intimating, as his reason, that the
girl came to church. No one seemed to know
anything at all about the girl, but all spoke of
the family as low and bad—hopelessly bad;
generally adding that they had been so glad
when young Paget dropped the acquaintance.

After this Elizabeth had no further communication with Mr. Wilton, but she kept an unfailing watch on John, and her reward was the
certainty that he loved his cousin, the little
Beatrice. She watched him in his walks and in
his rides with his cousin, hiding skillfully, and
hearing his talk when he thought nobody near
but Beatrice. Such innocent talk as it was!
Sometimes her eyes would fill with tears for the
very simplicity of it. How pure the girl was!
So she herself should have been, so it was her
right to be, and not the hardened, life-tired,
deserted thing she was. And John—how really
true John was at heart. At night, through the
open windows, she watched him busy with his
books, and she would see him stop, when alone,
and a cloud come over his face. She knew what
that meant. Dressed as a boy, both for disguise and protection, she dogged him day and
night. Her people gave up expecting her at any
given time, and it was very seldom now that she
would go on expeditions with her brothers and
father.

The months went by; then, before the first

year of Beatrice Wilton's life at home was past, Elizabeth heard of the illness of the rector. It was a grief to her. She went constantly to listen and watch for news of him, until her own father was brought home badly injured, and her time and strength had to be spent on him.

Then the news came of Mr. Wilton's death. Once more Elizabeth donned her disguise and went to the rectory. The moon was full and brilliant, and the shadows were black. Elizabeth, keeping close to the hedge, drew very near to the open windows of the study. The lamp was dim, but the moonlight pouring in, she could see the coffin on the bier, and John sitting close to the window, looking out over the water.

How motionless he was—how broken-hearted his expression. If she went straight up to him and took his hand, would he send her away? would he look at her with that loathing she had thought so much about? If she told him she had come only as a friend, asking nothing—if she told him how she had learned to love and reverence the dead man, would he look at her still with that loathing?

How she loved him—how she loved him, sitting there so still and sad! How she loved him! Would anyone in all the world love him as she had done—as she did?

John left the room, closing the door after him. She heard doors shutting and keys turning. He was locking the house for the night; he would not be back for a little while yet, and if he should come on her suddenly she would take the consequences.

She moved swiftly toward the house; to step in at the low window was the work of a second, and she stood by the open coffin.

"Death was sweet to you," she said, laying her hand on the hands of the dead man. "It is best to be good;. that is what your face says. I know it, and I will try. Your life had been trodden on too. You were lonely yourself, so you understood me. If I could have confessed, you would have absolved me, but it was Jack's story too. You know all my story now. You lived for others. I will try—I promise you. Good-by. Wherever you are, pray for me." There was a movement in the room above. Her whisper stopped, and she listened. A step, and it was not John's; no one else must find her here.

"Good-by—pray for me"—and she stepped from the window. From under the shadow of the hedge she watched.

The door opened and a woman, a stranger, tall, slender, beautiful, came in. She did not look at the coffin; she looked at the bookshelves, at the floor, at the desk, out of the window, any-where but at the coffin. She came to the window and stood there as if thinking, and Elizabeth was so near that she could almost smell the huisachie flowers the stranger held.

She was not afraid of death, or she would not

stay in that room alone; she must have some
deeper feeling. Yet love would go straight to
the coffin. Was she the woman who had "trod
on the life" of the man lying dead behind her?
Foolish woman! She need not be reluctant to
look; she would find only peace and gladness.
She had no more power to hurt him. She was
going to the coffin now. Ah, it hurt her! How
still she was—how deathly white! What pain,
—what dreadful pain was on her face! Poor
thing! The stranger went away, then John
came again. He lowered the lamp, and took his
seat by the window as before. He was going to
watch; so would she; they would keep this vigil
together.

The night waxed and waned. Through the
long, slow hours the moonlit waters of the gulf
washed back and forth on the glittering sands;
the flowers flung out their perfume to the warm
wind, and the woman sitting under the hedge in
the darkness looked and looked as if her eyes
would never get their fill.

Hovering about the next day, she learned that
the strange woman whom she had seen would take
Beatrice Wilton away, and that John would go too.

Then Elizabeth waited at home. Surely John
would not go without some last word to her.
But he did not come; and on the day of his departure, disguised, with a sombrero pulled well
down over her face, and a *serape* hiding her figure,
she rode to the railway station.

She stood quite close to John in the crowd; she relieved the party of their bags and wraps; she followed them into the train and stowed the things away. When she finished John gave her a half-dollar, but he did not look to see who it was that had helped him.

She stood outside on the railway platform, and as the train moved she laid her hand on the edge of the open window. She said softly, "Good-by, Jack." Low as it was he heard it, and the color left his face.

IV.

> " Is all our fire of shipwreck wood
>   Oak and pine ?
> Oh, for the ills half understood,
>   The dim dead woe
>   Long ago."

"YOUR letter has made you grave, mother."
Mrs. Van Kuyster looked up in a startled
way from where she sat behind the glittering tea-
urn.

"Yes," she answered slowly; "it is from John,
your brother."

"And the contents?"

"Carter Wilton is dying."

"Dying!" Claude repeated, his blue eyes
clouding.

"Yes, and you must get a ticket for me," Mrs.
Van Kuyster went on as she rose—"a ticket to
San Antonio."

"Have they sent for you?"

"Yes. Carter is the last who belongs to me.
He asks me to take his daughter. He married
out there—a Spanish girl. I think we should have
written to each other in all these years; but Carter thought not. Your brother John will come
too. Get one ticket, Claude; I prefer to go
alone, and shall leave to-night."

"You will not need me, then?"

"No. But remember they live in Corpus Christi"—looking at the letter. "Perhaps you can get a ticket farther than San Antonio. Find out all about it."

"And all your engagements for the next month?"

Mrs. Van Kuyster frowned. "You will have to make my excuses. Write to the Slaters at once; their dinner is this evening."

"And your lunch on Thursday?" Claude went on; "I shall have to hire a secretary."

"Write to the Slaters, and get my ticket," Mrs. Van Kuyster answered, "then you will find on the study table a list of commissions," and she left the room.

"The highest civilization gives way sometimes," Claude soliloquized. "The mater is marvelously civilized for an impulsive person, but she fails sometimes. Sometimes temper, sometimes affections, but both marks of the Beast. And these Philistines she will import! I am afraid my own civilization will be tried. A cowboy and a—a cowgirl! But a Spanish mother promises eyes—eyes shake me. After all, they may be interesting studies. Redfern can make the girl over, and John can go to my tailor. Poor Dechard! a cowboy will tear his delicate nerves to pieces; nevertheless, he must clothe him. I suppose this 'long-lost brother' will advance on me habited in very light trousers; a low-cut evening waistcoat; a red cravat, a black frock coat longer in the front than in the back—a sombrero! his boots very short with very high heels. Ye gods! I have seen one or two of the things in Chicago," and he poked the fire as if his own civilization were shaken. " I must suggest to the mater to stop in Philadelphia and get him an ulster—a blanket—anything to hide him from the servants. I do not believe that I could stand the pity I should see in Waters' eyes."

The said Waters entering to remove breakfast, Claude ordered the coupé and his overcoat, then went away to the study.

It was a long journey to Corpus Christi ; the biting wind growing softer, the world growing greener as Mrs. Van Kuyster went. The sweeping prairies burst on her sight ; the sunshine became hot glare ; then in the dawn a shadowy town that seemed to spring from the desert sand. A muddy stream, the Rio Grande, and foreign figures from the Mexican side. All seemed a dream to the weary woman. The desolation depressed her, and the voices of the few people that were about had a slow, tired sound. Time meant nothing to these people, and Carter was dying. Five hours would have done the remaining distance, even in most parts of the South ; here they said it would take twelve. Carter had been so patient always, perhaps he would wait for her even now.

Three times in her life Carter had sent for her. The first time he had sent a messenger on horseback to fetch her from a neighbor's where she was calling. She was sitting in front of a roaring wood fire, talking to a friend of her grandmother's, an old lady who looked like a delicate ivory carving. She remembered the fine lace of her kerchief, and the careful tying of her cap-strings. Strange that she should recall it here in this border town, sitting on a railway platform in the chilly dawn. And she had put down the cake and wine and had gone away quickly from her old friend, because Carter had sent for her, and in those days she belonged to Carter. They seldom agreed, for she craved excitement and gayety, and he was stern, and grave, and years older than she. She could remember the sound of the carriage wheels in the sand, and the voice of the old coachman as he called to the footman behind to get down and open the gate. And she had laughed at his grumbling about "dese good-fuh-nuttin young niggers dat sleep awl de time." Her last careless laugh. Carter had met her at the gate, helping her out of the carriage. "I had to send for you, dear," he said; "I needed you." And his eyes were so full of love—clear, sweet eyes, so tender and so true. The last love she had had. Since then she had lived without it, as the desert lives without water.

In the drawing room she had met a stranger; handsome, thoroughbred, but beyond middle life; further beyond than appeared, and she a girl in her teens.

"Mr. Van Kuyster," Carter had called him, from New York, with letters to her brother John. Had a cold wave touched this almost tropic dawn that she should shiver? Was it the memory of that first clasp of her husband's hand?

John had gone to take Alice to her own people and could not be back until night, so it fell to her lot to make the stranger welcome.

Again Carter had sent for her when the war was done, and the land was desolate, and she had hurt him. She had not dared to do anything else. She would explain it to him now when she should meet him. Would he wait for her—stop one day longer in this worn-out world for her sake?

After that visit there, she had bought the old place, and the silver too ; and Claude had been down often, but not she. It must go to this nephew John, who was the only Paget. He had been trained by Carter, he would have all the traditions of the race—all the old ideas—all the old-time breeding. Claude was essentially modern. She had not been allowed to train him, and she had been held up to ridicule so systematically in his presence that she had scarcely been able to keep his respect. Claude had been trained by Mr. Van Kuyster, who seemed to have cast away traditions. He ridiculed everything—nothing was sacred—everything was a fetich. She had been trained through Claude.

And now Carter sent for her again. Death was too strong for him, and he sent for his old love—the child he had helped to rear. She remembered once she had run away from old Tenah to follow him to the rice fields. Such a long way it was, and she had fallen into a ditch and got wet, and had lost her sunbonnet, but at last she had found him. She remembered how he looked, sitting so straight on his horse, with his gun across the saddle in front of him, and the sunshine all about him. And Romp, his red setter, had rushed up to her and licked her face in his delight. Dear old Romp, were ever any eyes in all the world as beautiful as his? Then Carter caught sight of her and came quickly, giving his gun to a negro standing near. He had swung her up in front of him, holding her close and wiping away her tears. "How did you come, little one?" he asked, half laughing. "I wanted you," she sobbed, "I wanted you."

How was it that she had changed so much after she met that strange man? She had seemed bewitched. And Alice had worked against her, had made the first unhappiness in her life. Alice always made her appear wrong in John's eyes, and had made Carter hard on her too. Alice, who was much older, and should have known better, had spoiled the home. Still, she must have been bewitched. That worldly tongue had fascinated her, those wicked eyes had charmed her as a snake would charm a bird. She shuddered, they were closed forever; now she must not call them wicked.

Soon Carter would know all. She had never explained anything to him, for he, himself, had taught her that explanation showed weakness of cause and character.

A bell rang; at last the train was ready. Twelve hours, and Carter was dying. The world would seem empty without him, and where would he be?

She nodded a farewell to the little town. The paper she had read the day before said that it had a great future—a future down here in the desert. And how dreary to have a future! She would almost like to agree with Claude and Mr. Van Kuyster about this future: laugh at the suggestion and live in the present. But Carter would know, for he hovered now in the border-land between life and death, and he would tell her.

It was a hot day, and the way was long and dusty, and the train was slow, and the prairie was endless. It was a dreary country in spite of the sweeps of wild flowers, and she would never forget it. The snow she had left in the North seemed more sympathetic.

How would Claude and John get on, and what would Carter's daughter be like? Beatrice, a pretty name: and the story of Carter's marriage was strange. A Spanish lady, in dying, gave him her little fortune and her daughter, praying him to save both from a rapacious uncle who had a dispensation to marry the girl. And Carter had married the girl at once. They had had one daughter, Beatrice, who was now just seventeen; brought up in a convent ever since her mother's death. Carter had been such a stanch Protestant, how had he consented to this? Or had his young wife managed him? Her nephew John was studying for the ministry. That would have annoyed her in the old days, but now, if one could reach the point of being absorbed and fanatical about anything, she deemed it a blessing.

The people she lived among were absorbed in many ways. One man had a fancy farm, and could talk of nothing but weeds. Some women were daft about Church embroidery, some about art, some about dress reform, prison reform, hammered brass, woodcarving, refuges for women, cruelty to animals, etching, orphan asylums, gymnastics, Christian Science, Russian cruelty, anything to quiet the conscience and the craving for reality. No doubt good was done as well as time killed, but reality seemed to be missing.

They were all in earnest, these people; the man who talked of weeds spent hundreds, that his acres should be guiltless of one dandelion. All the rest were in earnest too, only the work did not seem to have come to them as the duty of life. They seemed to have created a great deal of it in order to satisfy a restless energy by which they were possessed. She had no restless energy, and any of these things would have seemed playing at work. She gave money, but she could not give herself. For generations her people had lived in a hot climate, owned slaves, and been filled with repose. Work was a serious thing to such people, and had to be a solemn duty before they would do it. These Northern people had lived in a cold climate, where life was a battle, and so had been energetic for generations. As long as they had nature to conquer, and fortunes to carve out, this energy was a necessity, a boon; but now it had become the gadfly that goaded them into rest-cures and lunatic asylums. For herself, she spent her time on books and the study of her kind. The world called her icy; Claude said she was thoroughly civilized. To analyze thoroughly, one must put one's heart out of count; thus, to her, analysis of her kind was an easy thing. It had become a second nature; but she could remember the time when she hated herself for this power of moral dissection. Once when she analyzed her brother John because he was unjust to her, once when she had analyzed Carter, it had seemed to harden her heart. In her analysis of Carter, she had left weakness out, but weakness had come and he had sent for her. When she should come to die, there would be no one to send for. A trained nurse, for it was not civilized to trouble one's friends with illness and pain and death throes. All the eyes that would look into hers at the end would be calm and resigned; no hardly restrained

agony, no passionate pain, but Christian resignation changing into resigned cheerfulness as she
passed the point where she could change her
will.

She laughed a little. She had not weighed all .
this when she made her choice.

She smoothed her soft dress. She had gone
"clothed in purple and fine linen," and had
"fared sumptuously," but that had not been the
temptation to her, for she had never known anything else—she had been bewitched, that was all.
The glamour of the world, the mocking light in
those wicked eyes that had made the simplicity
and peace of her past seem contracted. And
Carter had insisted on going into the ministry.
The day seemed endless. Would Carter wait for
her?

Poor Carter! He had been richer than she.
His wife, his child, his peaceful life full of small
duties. How the thought of quiet day succeed-
ing day had irritated her in her youth, when she
longed for the "kingdoms of the world." She
had grasped the mirage, and regret and longing
had made the warp and woof of her life; a
"might have been" had been her only dream.

Again she smoothed her soft dress. She had
always loved luxurious things, and missing them,
she would, without doubt, have been miserable.
Traveling alone to the death of her one love was
making her maudlin. How Claude would have
laughed—how Mr. Van Kuyster's eyes would

have glittered with cynical amusement over her
train of thought. His nostrils would have contracted, and his face have drawn into many tiny
wrinkles, because he had found a point on which
.to attack her.

He was dead, but she often seemed to see his
face, and hear the clear metallic sound he called
a laugh. The ridicule she had undergone was a
bitter recollection ; under it she had become what
Claude called " civilized." The same civilization
as the Red Indian's, whose lips no agony can
open—as the old Spartan civilization ; only in
these modern days the Indian must smile as the
fire crisps his flesh ; and, while the fox gnaws, the
Spartan must wax enthusiastic about the preven-
tion of cruelty to animals.

She laughed. She must gather herself together
before she reached her journey's end ; whatever
she might reveal to Carter, the young people,
John and Beatrice, must see nothing.

The evening fell, the air grew cooler with a
freshness in it "like the sea winds at The Oaks,"
she thought.

"What is it that smells so sweet?" she asked
a fellow-traveler. "Huisachie," was answered ;
" we are at Corpus."

The train stopped at the edge of the bluff, and
before her eyes was spread a glory of moonlit
waters, and the air was filled with a sweetness
strangely familiar. Huisachie, what was that?
Then a tall young man—and more than the

magic perfume, he took her into the past. She
went up to him. "John," she said, "John
Paget."

"Aunt Claudia," he answered, and stooped
and kissed her. Surely she was dead and gone
into the other world!

He held her hands, and she looked up into his
face, so clear-cut, so stern. Was it not the same
face that had condemned her when she went
away years ago with the man of her choice?
And the same voice that had said "God help
you"—but never once, "God bless you."

"Carter is dead," he said, then dropped her
hands and turned to gather up her things. "He
died this morning at dawn—at the rise of the
wind."

In the gray dawn, when she sat shivering and
dreaming, his spirit had come to her—had led
her back to the still, old days. She said nothing,
but followed to the vehicle that was waiting below the bluff.

There stretched a white-shelled road that ran
very near the water; then the wide sweep of the
bay that went out to the gulf—that went out to
the wandering sea.

"How beautiful," she said, "and how sweet!"

"Huisachie," John answered. "Opoponax,
Carter called them. All these trees are either
huisachie or fig."

"Opopanax; that is the reason it made me
think of home."

"The old plantation?"—it was a deep, sweet voice. "Carter has often told me about it."

"You called him Carter?"

"He liked it because my voice was like my father's. He wanted you very much, Aunt Claudia."

"You should, have telegraphed," she answered quickly.

"When we wrote the physician said he would live for weeks; at the last it was very sudden."

"And his daughter?"

"Beatrice has been away from her father all her life almost, she scarcely knew him. For me "—he stopped for a moment. "For you, Aunt Claudia, Carter had a great longing. He talked of you incessantly. At the last he wandered a little." John paused, and the woman beside him scarcely breathed. "He seemed to have gone back to when you were a little child, and laughed because you were so droll, he said. His last words were to you. 'I had to send for you, dear,' he said, 'I needed you.' Then his mind came back, and he looked at me and whispered, 'The wind has risen, and my soul will go out with it— tell her I tried to wait.' And I heard the long ripple on the sands, and his soul went with a sigh."

He ceased, but no answer came. They had driven the length of the town by this, and stopped on the beach, where a small house stood with some trees about it. In front was a garden reclaimed from the sand—then the beach—then the curving bay. It was only a short way to the piazza where a figure in white stood, and John said:

"This is Beatrice, aunt," and Mrs. Van Kuyster scanned the young face from which the soft dark eyes looked dreamily, as if the soul behind them were sleeping still.

"You have come too late," the girl said simply.

"She knows," John answered, "and is very tired. I will take her to her room, and you send a cup of tea, dear."

"So? well then, I will," and she turned away.

"She is such a dreamer," John explained as he led the way up the stairs, "I have to tell her always what to do. I think the training at the Convent was a mistake, but Carter said a girl needed women about her. This is your room, aunt, and when you want to go down, he is in a room to the right of the hall. I shall send Beatrice to bed presently; she is a gentle creature." Then he shut the door and went away.

Mrs. Van Kuyster looked about her mechanically on the plainness and barrenness of the place; but through the open window shone the moonlight, and the bay, and the long waves rippling softly on the sands.

In the same mechanical way she took off her bonnet and bathed her face. Then a little, old, brown woman came with a tray, putting it down and courtesying, and Mrs. Van Kuyster ate and drank with scarcely a realization of what she did. When the servant and the tray were gone, she

heard the sound of muffled steps and closing
doors, then all was still. Was the town asleep
too? How plainly she heard the waves and the
wind that stirred in the opopanax trees outside
the windows! She reached out and gathered
some of the little yellow balls; how sweet they
were! The old lady she had been seeing, that
first day Carter sent for her, kept them among
her caps and laces. How merrily the fire had
crackled, how nice the lightwood had smelled as
it burned—how blue the sky was; how sweet the
orange blossoms that looked in at the open window! How oppressive the steady heat of the
Northern houses had been to her, after the open
windows and roaring fires of her home! The
careless, spendthrift, comfortable, arrogant, beautiful South—what a wonderful life the "upper
ten thousand" had led—how sure they had been
that the world had been made for them! Swept
away! And now it was becoming a money-
making, and money-saving, conventional country
like any other! She smelled the little yellow
balls once more. She had found some in Egypt
when she went there on her wedding tour. Some
of the bitterest realizations of her life had come
to her in that beautiful Cairene garden.

As a child she had learned to climb on an
opopanax tree, because the branches were near
the ground. It had been destruction to her
frocks, but what Southern child ever hesitated
between fun and clothes! Once she had fallen

from the top of the tree, and had caught by her skirts on the stump of a broken branch. It was not a tall tree, but it had seemed an awful fall to her. At her cry, her father had come from where he was smoking on the long piazza, to find her dangling. What a stout little flannel petticoat it must have been to hold her safe while her father laughed! How furious the laughing made her! Then Carter came and lifted her down. He was laughing a little himself; she saw that when he brushed her curls back, but not much, and he had carried her off in his arms that she might weep away her anger and mortification with only him for witness. Carter—Carter—Carter! How all the days of her life had been woven in with his!.

How still it was! John had meant that if she went down she should be alone. Carter lay there dead. Not the Carter of her youth, not even the Carter she had last seen, but an old man. Did she want to see him? Living, she would have found his heart and soul as they had been; the body would not have mattered! Would not she rather remember him?

She would hide the little flowers in his coffin *in memoriam;* he would understand what they meant. She would bury her remorse with him; it was not needful that it should live now that he was at rest.

He *had* come to her in the dawn—where was he now? She opened the door softly and stole downstairs. She paused with her hand on the latch. It was an old man she would see, not her lover.

All the available space in the little room was filled with bookshelves, and a shabby desk was pushed against the fireplace to make way for the coffin. The windows opened down to the floor, and the dim lamplight mingled strangely with the moonlight that poured in. Here, apart from human kind, he had lived the real life of all these years. He had had a way of walking up and down with his hands clasped behind him. Up and down *this* little hole !

Carter dead ! It was a stranger she would see when she turned to that coffin. The fine dark hair would be white; the delicate, sensitive features would be a little thickened and marred by time; the grave, sweet lips would have grown thinner and sterner; the eyes would be closed.

She shivered a little. The moonlight had grown so cold, and the winds and the waves so still !

The white priestly vestments lay in straight folds, the fine hair shone as a silver crown, the slim, folded hands were marble—the calm, strong face was radiant ! What vision had his vanishing spirit seen that left such light in every death-fixed curve and line? What use her little flowers, what use her remorse, her earthly love and sorrow? The light from that glorified countenance destroyed the flimsy dream that through all these years she had been in his life ; and past and future were left empty. He had lived above her—above the world. A conquered life, a free spirit seeing the unseen, touching the infinite.

There were such things. In the world one doubted them, but the glory in that face swept one out to the central calm where faith keeps guard. What use her remorse, her love, to this strong saint of God?

She closed the door softly, and went away upstairs. No fear now of betraying anything, and she would impress it on John that all the longing for her, and all the wanderings, had been but a sick man's fancies.

Very matter-of-fact she was the next morning while John studied her. Very quiet through the funeral service, showing annoyance when Beatrice broke into sobs as the earth fell on the coffin. The man's dead face had struck her such a numbing blow at the last. What use that she should feel and remember?

And when the little flowers drooped, she flung them into the sea.

V

" She hath fair eyes ; maybe
  I love her for sweet eyes, or brows or hair,
  For the smooth temples, where God touching her
  Made blue with sweeter veins the flower sweet white ;
  Or for the tender turning of the wrist,
  Or marriage of the eyelid with the cheek ;
  I cannot tell ; or blush of lifting throat,
  I know not if the color get a name
  This side of heaven—no man knows ; or her mouth,
  A flower's lip."

BEATRICE thought that she had never seen anything as dismal as New York. The weather was very bad, and Mrs. Van Kuyster lived in a fashionable part of the town, so that an occasional omnibus or coal wagon or cab was the only thing to be seen. Ever since morning sleet and rain and snow had taken turns in falling, and a horrible homesickness came over the girl as she remembered the roses of Corpus Christi and the blue waves washing on the shore. How could one live in a climate like this from choice? The house was warm, with a dead, still heat for which the fires could not account ; a heat that oppressed her, but did not drive the cold from her bones.

They had arrived very early, with nothing to meet them but servants and a telegram from her cousin Claude in Washington. He would be at home for dinner.

After lunch she was told to lie down until the maid should come to dress her; then her few dresses were taken away. She was dressed now in her Confirmation frock; a white wool thing which she remembered as being unsufferably hot that Southern winter day, but that seemed noth-. ing in this climate. Would she ever be warm again?

She satin a deep chair close to the drawing room fire, feeling more comfortable than she had done at any time since her arrival. This seemed a strange life, and John now left her entirely to Mrs. Van Kuyster. A very handsome woman she was, looking scarcely older than John, and dressed so beautifully; but why should middle-aged people care how they looked?

All the long afternoon she had rested; still, she was sleepy. Why not go to sleep? No one seemed to be coming, and dinner would be in the middle of the night, probably, for it had been dark for so long.

So this was the " cowgirl," and, leaning against the mantelpiece, Claude looked down on Beatrice sleeping in the big red chair. He had come into the fire-lighted room quietly, and now stood very still. What an extraordinary frock it seemed! but such a throat, and such hands and wrists— ye gods! Tailor-made clothes would spoil her. Was her hair arranged at all, or did it grow in

those waves and folds about her head? Was it
the firelight that made the girl such a picture?—
and her lips! A pomegranate flower. A cheap
old simile, but it suited her. Would her eyes be
beautiful? How heavy the lids were, and the
lashes lay like shadows on her cheeks. Would
her teeth be good—and her voice—and her English? His dream seemed to fall into dust and
ashes. If the mother had been half as lovely
as this girl, it had been no hardship for Carter
Wilton to marry her.

Mr. Van Kuyster had so often twitted his wife
with the name of Carter Wilton that Claude had
decided that an old love story lived behind it,
and Mrs. Van Kuyster's explanation that her
cousin had married for pity had confirmed his
belief. He raised his eyes from the fire where
they had been fixed while he thought, to find
the girl's eyes open. They did not look startled,
perhaps hardly awake.

"Is dinner ready?" The voice was so soft and
slow that each syllable seemed to be a matter of
thought. "Not quite," he answered, then waited
while the dark eyes, questioning like a child's,
looked at him quietly.

"Are you John's brother, the one who changed
his name?"

"Yes."

"I would not have done that."

"Nor I," Claude answered glibly; "it was done
for me."

"How is it you are so fair?" was the next question. "John is dark; are not you twins?"

"Yes, we are twins," pulling his mustache to hide a smile, "and I do not know how the difference came."

"And John is bigger than you."

"Is he?"

"Have you not seen him?"

"No, I only had time to dress for dinner."

"So? I should have gone to see my brother first."

"You have been better trained than I."

"Yes, I was trained in the Convent, and the Mother is a saint, I think."

"A Frenchwoman?"

"No, the sisters were French, and the priest; the Mother was English."

"Ah, yes; I believe some English people have been saints."

"But French people also. Oh, there have been lots and lots of saints! We used to read their lives all the time. Poor things, they had such trouble. But that little while of suffering does not matter now, you know, for they have reached eternal blessedness. They had not to go to Purgatory for a day even." She was leaning a little forward, and her eyes were shining.

"Are you a Catholic?"

"What do you mean? I called the Sisters Catholics, and they called themselves so, but John got vexed and gave me a long explanation about it all. He called them Romanists; is that what you mean? No, I am not a Romanist. John lectured me a lot, but father did not bother me; he only said we must be good, that we must fight for Christianity, and not about different creeds."

" And are you going to fight for Christianity?"

" Oh, no; I have not got sense enough. The Mother said that woman's work in life was obedience; so while father and John studied and puzzled, I swung in the hammock under the fig trees."

" And are you obedient?"

" Yes, when anybody tells me what to do."

" And when they do not?"

" Then I don't do anything."

" You go to sleep, perhaps."

" Perhaps. John always told me what to do until Aunt Claudia came; now he seems miles away. John is so good he frightens me. He is a deacon, you know."

"The devil!"

" Yes," nodding her head. " He makes me think of Father Michael who used to come to the Convent to confess us. Sister Thérèse said *he* was a saint. He was an Englishman. She said the father used to lash himself on his bare skin until he bled, and then he put on a stickery hair shirt and a belt with spikes in it. Once he had been very wicked. He frightened me; his eyes used to burn like fire. Do you think he did all that?"

"No," Claude answered promptly. "But is John like that?"

"Old Angela said not; she was the servant, you know, my grandmother's and my mother's servant. She cried when we came away. She said John should have married me and gone on living there—that my mother had been married so—that a motherless girl should be married very soon and asked no questions. The Mother thought so too. I wanted to be a nun, it was so peaceful. I put on a habit one day, and showed myself to the Mother. She smiled and blessed me, and hoped it would be so some day."

"And was the dress becoming to you?"

"Yes, only all my hair was covered, and everybody says that I have very pretty hair. Sister Thérèse used to take care of it, and she said I could cut it off and lay it on the altar of the Blessed Virgin, and then in heaven I should find it all again, and turned to purest gold. But I like dark hair best, don't you?"

"I believe I do," Claude answered, turning to where Waters was lighting the lamps. "Light them all," he said, then watched to see how the girl's beauty would stand the light.

"I love light," she said, "and here it is so dark and cold. In Corpus the roses are blooming, and the sky and the water are so blue. And the jackdaws! There are thousands of them, and they are so funny and so clever. I loved to see them steal the figs. Do you know jackdaws?"

"Only what I have read."

"I wish you had come to Corpus. At the Convent we had a pet crow—old Corvus—he used to steal dreadfully, and when the cat would be asleep in the sun, old Corvus would nip his tail, then look away as if he had not done it ; and the cat would be in such a rage—and the dog too. Once Corvus was nearly killed. Father Michael found him on the altar in the chapel, and said that he must die, and shut him up in a cage to kill him after vespers. How we cried—Marie, Antoinette, and I, and prayed the Mother to save him, and she did. She talked to Father Michael, then brought Corvus to us."

" How many girls were in the convent ? "

"Only the three of us. It was not a school. It was away off in the country, down by the water. The Mother and six Sisters lived there. It was a farm that sent things to Convents in towns, and took care of sick Sisters and girls from other Convents. The Mother never let us see the town girls; she said that town mice were not good for country mice. I could just talk when I went there. My grandmother was Spanish and found out this convent for a place to educate my mother. So it was my mother's home and mine. Marie and Antoinette were orphans and given to be nuns. I wish I had been, but John gets into a rage when I say that. Yet, when he talks to me he makes me long more than ever to go back, for it makes me tired even

to think of all the things he says a [Christian
ought to do." Suddenly she rose and stood as
if on drill, and Claude turned to see Mrs. Van
Kuyster entering.

"So you have come," as Claude kissed her
lightly on her cheek, "and have made friends
with Beatrice. Sit down, dear," to the girl, who
was still standing; and Beatrice sitting down
primly on a very straight chair, Claude felt a
little at a loss. He had thought she was afraid
of being caught sitting carelessly, and talking
familiarly to a stranger, even though he was a
cousin, but Mrs. Van Kuyster's words made him
abandon this conclusion. Perhaps it was respect!
He had seen such respect in other countries, and
had fallen in love with it rather ; but the average
American girl, if she observed her elders at all,
granted them only a condescending patronage.
Then he remembered that this girl could scarcely
be called American.

"You are quite well, mother?" he said meanwhile.

"Quite well, thank you : and you?"

"Quite well. I should have been at home to
meet you," he went on, "but did not dream that
you could get here so soon."

"We left immediately. Have you seen John?"

"No, but here he is," and Claude went forward
to meet his brother. How different they were,
Beatrice thought, as she watched the meeting.
Claude was slighter and shorter than John, and

so very fair. There was something grand about John—too grand; he frightened her.

And Claude said lightly, "What a whale you are, Jack." John seemed to wince a little, then he smiled. His smile was beautiful—if only he would smile oftener, the girl thought.

"I remember you perfectly," he answered, putting his hand on Claude's shoulder and looking straight into his eyes, "have you no recollection of me?"

Claude shook his head—"I remember old Tenah, and remember what we played, and how we played, but your looks made no impression on me."

"And our mother?"

"Only as someone always sick, and Carter as always taking us out that we might not disturb her. I remember him as a sort of lovely giant."

Then dinner was announced, and Claude turned to Beatrice.

"Dinner at last," he said, and put her hand on his arm. "John frightens me too," he whispered as they followed into the dining room; "he is quite awful."

"But he has a better voice than you. I never knew until now what made me listen always when he spoke—it is his voice. You call Aunt Claudia mother?"

"Yes, I was adopted. Your father sold me, and now you tell me it was wrong."

"Not if father did it. I wonder how much they paid him for you."

"Hush!" Claude answered, laughing, "another time."

As dinner went on Claude's spirits rose. To him the girl was charming; and John, though a trifle solemn, was most distinguished looking. He was terribly in earnest, and was talking about the slums now.

"Carter suggested that I could provide for my course at the seminary by assisting in some church," he was saying; "is it possible?"

"I suppose so, but there is no necessity."

"I want the experience," he answered a little stiffly, "and I suspect that they need slum-workers—'slummers' you call them?"

"The best antidote for the slums is Black-well's Island," Claude struck in, "with Sing Sing for the extras, and electricity for the hope-less."

"Perhaps," John answered; "but even with all these antidotes working busily, wretched crea-tures still swarm in the slums. What shall be done with, or *to* them, if you like that better?"

"'To them' is better. I think transportation to Alaska and New Mexico would be good."

"Then form a society for the prevention of poverty and sin and slums?"

"Poverty and sin are synonymous. Preven-tion of poverty would be sufficient."

"What is poverty?"

Claude shook his head. "It is as hard to define as wealth. I should say it is not having what one wants. You ask dreadful Pilatinous questions. What is poverty, Beatrice?"

"The Mother said not to have what one *needed* was to be poor."

"*Needed*—not wanted. I think I must hunt that Reverend Mother up and go to school to her. What do you think?"

"She would teach you a great deal," Beatrice answered, and Mrs. Van Kuyster laughed.

"What made her tell you that about poverty?"

"There was a bad man with a big ranch who used to come to the convent for medicine, and Sister Thérèse called him rich, and the Mother called him poor. He was not a Christian, she said, and so did not have the only thing that one absolutely needs." She looked deprecatingly at John. "He asked me," she said; "I had to answer."

"Does not John allow you to talk?" Mrs. Van Kuyster asked, smiling.

"Yes; but the Mother said that I was too young to speak unless I was spoken to, and John looked so surprised."

There was silence for a moment, then Claude looked at Mrs. Van Kuyster. "Don't you think," he said, "that the government should import a Reverend Mother for every girl baby born in the land, and send them off to lonely prairies? Think of it, women who would listen!" and he gave

Beatrice a meditative look which she did not see, being busy with her dinner.

"And you and the Mother, Claude, agree with a difference," John said. "She says sin is poverty; you say poverty is sin."

"I understood that the Mother holds unbelief to be the only poverty, not sin. Am I not right, Beatrice?"

"Of course; for unbelief is sin, is it not?"

Claude smiled. "*I* don't know," he said; "for the Mother would call Jack a heretic, and Jack would call the Mother a schismatic; and when saintly Mothers and Reverend deacons begin to vituperate, what must lay folk think?"

"I fancy that the Mother and I agree on the fundamental truths," John answered, looking at his brother thoughtfully; then he added, "But to whom shall I apply for work?"

"Why, yes"—and Mrs. Van Kuyster seemed to bring her thoughts back with an effort,—"to Mr. Ratcliffe, our rector, of course."

"And his churchmanship," Claude suggested. "What is the rhyme—

"Broad and hazy,
Low and lazy,
High and crazy—

"What is your fad, Jack?"

"Carter advised me not to be a party man if I could help it," John answered. "In these days everything Christian had better stand shoulder to shoulder against everything anti-Christian."

"Quite true," Claude answered. "The creeds ought to decide where the best stand can be made, and make it at once. And any scheme of religion on which they agree as being the best moral sanitary measure, ought to be supported, and would be, I think, by all respectable people. Don't swear, Jack," laying his hand on his brother's arm as if to stop the words he saw on his lips. "The sooner we understand each other, the better. We must talk it over. Meanwhile, I think that you and Beatrice are most docile young people. She declares herself a reflection of the Mother, and you seem to reflect Carter Wilton."

"I wish I could reflect Carter, for even that would be a great light."

"Why did he not come out into the world, then? why did he not head a crusade?"

"A crusade takes a strong heart," John answered, "and I think Carter's heart was broken." Then he rose to follow Beatrice and Mrs. Van Kuyster.

Later, Mrs. Van Kuyster and Claude were in the study together; Mrs. Van Kuyster looking over bills, and Claude smoking.

"I hope you are not going to have tailor-made clothes for Beatrice," he said unexpectedly.

Mrs. Van Kuyster looked at him a moment, then returned to the bill she was studying.

"She is too picturesque for rectangular clothes," he added.

"On the contrary, absolute plainness and simplicity will greatly enhance her beauty. A beautiful woman can dare any style of dress if she cling to two things—trimness and freshness; and a plain woman can always be *chic*. Who ever remembers that Marjorie Van Kuyster is not pretty."

Claude clapped his hands softly. "Positively you wax epigrammatic," he said; "but Beatrice has a style of her own."

"And will always have. Besides, Beatrice is a schoolgirl, and for one year will be in mourning."

"The devil!" and Claude walked to the fire. "The folly of it, putting that child in black: sacrificing her beauty and my pleasure to a vile old custom that must have been invented by idiots—it's scandalous!"

"My dear Claude, you are foolish. The only question to be asked is, 'Ought one to grieve?' if the answer be yes, then one must show some semblance of grief. It is the proper thing, and heretofore I have looked on you as the Apostle of Propriety."

A change came over Claude's face as he listened, and when Mrs. Van Kuyster ceased, he was looking at her as one who was realizing her for the first time.

"And one thing I must beg of you," she went on more coldly, if that were possible; "it is that you will not disturb the child's religious faith. Women ought to be religious."

Claude took a turn up and down the room, then, throwing his cigar into the fire, faced Mrs. Van Kuyster. "I am going to astonish you," he said. "I announce to you as guardian, that I am going to marry Beatrice."

Mrs. Van Kuyster looked at him a moment. "Love at first sight," she said; "you who laugh at love?"

"Call it what you please, but you cannot object. From a worldly standpoint you can ask nothing better for the girl. It is quite out of line with all my plans of life, still I am going to do it."

"And John?"

"All I ask is a fair field."

"Will you tell him?"

"No. I tell you because the girl was left to you. If, as you seem to say, John loves her, he will realize my attitude before many days."

"Do you not agree that he loves her?"

"If he does, the girl does not know it, and has only awe for him. But you are free to do as you please in the matter. I *know* I will win her." Then Claude left the room, and Mrs. Van Kuyster sat looking into the fire.

Carter Wilton's daughter to be Mrs. Van Kuyster!

VI.

"For some ships safe in port, indeed,
        Rot and rust,
        Run to dust,
All through worms i' the wood which crept,
Gnawed our hearts out while we slept;
        That is worse."

"HOW do you do?" and dropping the *portiere*, a woman entered who would impress the most casual observer as being perfectly finished. Nobody who knew Marjorie Van Kuyster could ever think of her as having a button off her glove or shoe, or her bonnet-strings awry, or with an umbrella that was not the perfection of smoothly rolled slimness.

"Don't let me disturb you"—holding out her hand to John, who had risen. "You are Mr. Paget"; then, touching Claude on the shoulder, she went round to Mrs. Van Kuyster. "I thought I would step in, cousin, and see your condition."

"Thank you, Marjorie," Mrs. Van Kuyster answered, while a place was arranged for Miss Van Kuyster; "and this is my cousin, Beatrice Wilton; I am her guardian, you know."

"Yes, Claude told me. You find New York dreadfully cold, do not you?" to Beatrice.

"Yes; I think my frocks are too thin."

"How nice of you," Marjorie answered, "to blame your gowns and not the climate!" Then to Claude: "How are you after your Washington outing?"

"I had a frightfully stupid time. But then *you* know, Marjie, that only one place in Ameriea is thoroughly civilized, and that is New York."

"I don't know it at all. I *adore* both Washington and Philadelphia."

"And I am devoted to Boston," said Mrs. Van Kuyster.

"After a life spent in training you two," Claude said, "is this my reward—to have you adoring such provincialisms and crudities as those names suggest?"

"Washington is so spontaneous and unique," Marjorie said, "and Philadelphia is so conservative and self-contained, and altogether so different from any other place in the world."

"Thank God for that!" Claude answered fervently. "I suppose the mater will repeat all that and tack it on to Boston, and Jack can say it of any wilderness or prairie in the far South. I think I must begin to train Beatrice; I am sure she will make me a better return."

"I will like any place that is not cold," she answered.

"Then you are safe against any of these places. As for Washington," Claude went on, "I always think of it as a great menagerie where every idea of the 'Eternal Fitness' is shocked. I suppose

that is what Marjie means by 'spontaneous.'
Fancy Buckingham Palace or Marlborough House
with towels hanging out of the windows!"

"The simplicity of a great Republic," John
said. "Given the window and the sun, and what
more fit than that a towel should be hung there?"

"Exactly," Claude answered, "and the Royal
family wash in the shrubberies."

"Eminently practical," John returned.

"And supremely simple," Marjorie added, "and
quite the correct thing in this country, where all
are free and equal, where any Bridget or Sukey
can say to a member of the elect 'Four Hundred,'
'Are you the woman who want a lady to cook
for you?' We shall have to do our own laundry
work presently, and you may be sure, Claude,
that I shall hang my things out of the front
window, as that is the sunny side of the house."

"If there had been an English general with
any sense on this side the water," Claude went
on, "the miserable little sixpenny Revolution
would have been ended in a jiffy, and we should
have been under a respectable government still.
As it is, we have demoralized the world, and all
that I see ahead of humanity is abject slavery."

"You are talking nonsense," Marjorie said.
"This is the freest country in the world."

"On the ground that there is no freedom save
in obedience," John said, "Claude is right."

"That is not my ground exactly," Claude
answered ; "but all know that there is no such

slavery as mob rule. In a country where caste
is recognized, so many laws are not necessary,
for each man knows his place, and the friction is
immensely reduced."

"But there are blacker slums," Marjorie suggested.

"America can show slums with any country,"
Claude answered. "And think of the freedom
where there are States in which a gentleman
cannot have a glass of wine on his table, and
of other sections where a man may have twenty
wives, and more, if he likes; where Marjorie can
have me arrested for managing my horse, and I
can have her remonstrated with for wearing bird-
wings in her hat. We are so free that training
has become obsolete, and everything, living and
dead, has to be protected by a thousand laws."

"This excited tone, Claude, almost proves
your theory of the lack of training," Mrs. Van
Kuyster said; "I have not seen you so animated
in years."

Claude laughed. "You are quite right, and
there are very few things in life worth an extra
beat of the pulse."

"There are things that I would die for," John
answered. "I am interested in this talk, even.
I think you have touched on the poisoning evil
of these days—the lack of training. All are
allowed to develop; hence, principle is almost
unknown, and law has to come to the rescue.
And this age seems to be extremely sensitive,

and a maudlin sentimentality is going far to pauperize about half the nation. 'If a man do not work, neither shall he eat.' I believe in hanging for murder; the penitentiary for *all* kinds of stealing; ducking and flogging for drunkenness; stocks for scolds, and whipping for children. I go so far," he went on, looking at Marjorie with a smile, "as to shake hands with the old law that still obtains in South Carolina, which forbids divorce, but permits a man to whip his wife, provided the stick be no bigger than his thumb."

"You are a barbarian," Marjorie said, "and I thought from the cut of your coat that you were a benevolent clergyman who would want us to give all our goods to feed the poor."

"Need clergymen be sentimental?" John asked. "Will you not allow us to be men with common sense?"

"With pleasure; but the type is new to me, that is all."

"Maybe your search has not been very extended."

"Perhaps I have not put the same zeal into it that I would put into the search for a good dressmaker," she answered, laughing, "but I have known a good many clergymen. The religion of to-day seems to me to be degenerating into a sort of kindergarten arrangement, with athletic attachments to the churches. It is not good. When you have to pamper and pay people to

come to church, the system must be very rotten.
I think the old times, when people were burned
because they went to church, were much more
wholesome. At least it was genuine."

"Immensely so to the victim," Claude said.
"Suppose it had been you?"

"Never, my dear Claude! I am one of Mr.
Paget's unprincipled Americans—threaten me
with an attack of neuralgia, and I would give up
anything. The 'correct thing,' 'The fashion,'
'expediency'—these are my principles, and I
flourish."

"I have seen you torture yourself for the 'correct thing,'" said Mrs. Van Kuyster.

"Of course, but it pays; and when it ceases to
pay, I let it alone. For instance, I am tired of
dancing, so am ceasing to exert myself for dancing acquaintances; meanwhile, I cultivate the
dinner and lunch people. I used to be a Sun-
day-school teacher, it looked well in a young girl;
in an old maid that sort of thing looks lonely,
and I have stopped it."

"Do you call yourself an old maid, my dear?"
Claude asked.

"If I did not, other people would, and I worry
some of them by taking their stings out."

"Why not spoil their fun by marrying?"

"You always say such nice things, Claude,"
looking at him with a twinkle in her eyes. "Of
course because I do not want to. All the same,
I am going to write a love story in which the

woman, in a moment of temporary insanity, casts away the love of her life! The rest of the book will be a harrowing picture of her regrets. And, Claude——"

"Well?"

"Many men will embalm that book, each thinking himself the hero. I will immediately loom into 'a masked life'—a 'mysterious wreck.' All this from the men; do you see how I revenge myself on the women?"

"What an awful fraud you are," Claude said, while the company laughed.

"But successful; what deadlier blow could I deal a woman who after a long chase has bagged her game, than to have this game look sentimentally at a *passé* old maid?"

"A truly fiendish revenge."

"But why so down on your own sex?" asked John.

"Woman is woman's natural prey," Marjorie answered, and, as they left the lunch table, she put her hand through Mrs. Van Kuyster's arm and led her to the study.

"Your girl is beautiful," she said, "and Mr. Paget most effective."

"Yes; only I think John is handsome."

"He is, but the strength struck me first. His eyes are fine; so grave, don't you know, yet not solemn."

"They are like his father's," Mrs. Van Kuyster went on, "my brother, who brought me up."

"And you left him for Cousin Jacob?" and Marjorie looked at the elder woman with a gleam of amusement in her eyes.

"Yes. But what about the sewing woman?"

"She will come in the morning, and you may leave everything to her."

"Thank you, that is just what I want. The child's clothes are not nice enough even to go to the tailor in, so something must be done first at home."

"Exactly; but I am in love with the child, and so are your young men. I have never seen Claude as animated as he was to-day, but he was never so much interested as to overlook her slightest want; and she so exquisitely unconscious."

"It promises to be interesting," Mrs. Van Kuyster answered.

Marjorie looked at her keenly. "So?" she said, and rose. "You may look for me often; your household is pleasant."

"Always glad to see you. We are in half-mourning, you know?"

"Yes, Claude explained. He was upset—he did not know what to expect."

"Claude is immensely selfish," Mrs. Van Kuyster answered, "and I do not think that he will ever realize it, for he has money enough to gratify every whim."

"Let us hope he will desire something that money cannot buy: there are such things."

" I know : I have always had money, and never had anything I really wanted. Food and rai·ment of course, and loads of other non-essentials; but the real wants are things that no wealth can compass."

Miss Van Kuyster looked thoughtful. " That has always puzzled me," she said. " If you had married for money—but you did not."

" No, I did not "—opening the study door for her guest.

"And you had position, and beauty, and youth," Marjorie went on cautiously. " What did you lack ? "

" Sense," the elder woman answered with a smile.

"Good-by," Marjorie said.

"Good-by," and with the lightest of cheek touches and a little sound of the lips made in the air, they parted.

"What has happened ? " Marjorie wondered as she drove away. "I have never dared mention her miserable life to her until to-day. I have always likened her to a fire in an ice box. Something has frozen the fire. And will she lift no guiding hand to that play beginning in her house—will she watch it as a play ? "

VII.

"Alas, poor soul possest!
Yet would to-day when courtesy grows chill
And life's fine loyalties are turned to jest,
Some fire of thine might burn within us still!
Ah, would but one might lay his lance in rest,
And charge in earnest—were it but a mill!"

"WILL you walk down to the club, Jack?"
They were standing near the fire in the drawing room, the only other occupant of which was Beatrice.

"Yes, I should like to," John answered; "I will get my gloves."

"And what are you thinking of?" Claude asked, approaching the silent girl, who looked very doleful.

"Home and the roses," and the eyes she lifted were suspiciously dewy. "Then all are so clever, and talk so fast, that I do not understand the half that is said; of course I am stupid, too."

"Poor little cousin," and Claude lifted her face still higher by putting his finger under her chin. "We did chatter like magpies, and with about as much point. I will tell it all to you some day. As to home and roses"—taking her two hands and putting them together in his—"you must not cry about them, you break me all up."

Beatrice shook her head hopelessly.

"Crying will spoil your eyes. If you will be very good, I will give you all the roses you want. I will bring you some to-day. Better still; there is a conservatory to this house, which the mater shut up for some inscrutable reason. It shall be done over for you."

"You are very good to me; but—it will be so much trouble."

"A pleasure. There comes Jack, and I must go: watch for me and the roses. If no one has given you any orders, I tell you to go to sleep," and nodding, he was gone.

"Shall I put your name up at the club?" Claude asked as they walked briskly down the street.

"I scarcely think it worth while, thank you; I will have no time. Besides, I do not know that it would be wholesome for the club to have a slummer, or the slummer to have a club."

"Oh, the clergy patronize the clubs, I assure you," Claude answered, "and find them very respectable, not to say fascinating."

"Doubtless, but where do they find the time?"

"They are systematic and have all sorts of machinery; assistants, and superintendents, and readers, and brigades of women in various capacities. I have studied the church question," he added; "I wanted to find out where the weakness lay—I was curious."

"And where is the weakness?"

"In humanity, I think."

"Whose humanity—clergy or laity?"

"Both. The laity are so human that they do not enjoy being bored to death, so they put their hands into their pockets and make religion as inviting as money can, with handsome churches and beautiful music, and, if possible, an eloquent man, who is also a gentleman. For he must be a person whom they can ask to dinner."

"If that is all," John asked, "why do you have any religion?"

"Well," Claude answered, as if thinking, "it does seem a little pointless, but it is the custom, and violent revolutions are troublesome. I do not remember any that have been great comforts or successes."

"That depends on the point of view. But to return; how does the clergyman's humanity come in?"

"Why, he likes it and wants to keep his comfortable position. To do this he must keep his church full of paying people, for even in the free system the expenses must be paid. To accomplish this he must keep his mind and body in good order to preach the eloquent sermons, and must have time to keep up with the world and its fads. So he organizes a system of assistants, and readers, and superintendents, and women."

John struck his stick sharply on the pavement.

"Why, my dear fellow," Claude went on, "there is as much competition among the churches as among the shops. They rush after customers in the same manner, and they look the other way when a brother clergyman has to advise his people to sell the church and move farther up town in order to pay expenses. So you see all this organization is necessary; they are in a sense 'drummers' for the different parishes."

Again John struck his stick on the pavement. "If they would only realize," he said sharply, "that one man who killed himself with over-work would be worth a hundred well organized parishes."

"Rather heroic treatment, especially for the dead clergyman, and I am not sure that it would do any good. The world is grown cheerfully cold, and practical, and critical. Civilized, in short, and enthusiasm and heroics are not good form."

"It is not heroics I mean," John answered. "An earnestness that means death, and an enthusiasm that means crucifixion, would be bound to have an effect. A man who would give his *life*—not sell a portion of it for so many dollars and cents, but give his very life for the love of the Christ, could make this city, you think so cool and critical, burn with a fire of enthusiasm. Work day and night, if need be, anywhere that work is to be done, and when the time came to preach the soul would speak; and always soul answers to soul," and the eyes that looked into Claude's were burning.

. Claude looked away. "And kill himself in a year," he said. "I had a friend, we were classmates; he went in for that sort of thing. He broke down in six months."

"Well?"

"He lives in Europe now for his health."

"He should have died between the plow-handles! So many look on themselves as being necessary, that they think they must take care of themselves. If they have any faith at all, they ought to believe that the Almighty will take care of his own tools. It reminds me of the old woman who said when her horse ran away—'I trusted in Providence till the breechin' broke, then I jumped out.'"

Claude laughed. "And you intend to kill yourself?" he asked.

"God helping me, I will die in harness. But do not think"—turning quickly to face his brother —"do not think for a moment that I hold myself worthy to do it. I would not have you dream such a thing! My life has been absolutely misspent; evil in every direction. There is no sin, save perhaps lying and stealing, which a gentleman cannot do, you know, that I have not committed. Murder; aye and worse," lowering his voice. "I did my best to commit murder, but a woman made them throw me down and tie me. I take no credit that my hands are not bloodstained, for I did my best. You see," looking into Claude's face wistfully, "I grew up on the border. I was poor, and at certain seasons I could make a good deal of money by going on cattle drives as a cowboy—they were a hard lot. Between the seasons I studied, and at the last Carter's life overcame me."

"My dear fellow," and Claude's voice had lost its slight drawl, "I understand perfectly, and I like you infinitely better. I systematically avoid young clergymen; they are—well—clammy; and I beg your pardon, but I had a dread of you. Now——"

"Now that you find me to have been a licentious, blasphemous ruffian," John struck in, "you have more faith in me. It is always so, but why?"

"Because a man is a man, and a woman is a woman, and a tough is a tough, and you can classify them, but I'll be hanged if you can classify a clergyman—I mean the usual run of them. For the different parties seem to mean different things, and few of them seem to mean—I scarcely know what to call it."

"A consecrated life," John suggested.

"Exactly. Some make it ridiculous by looking as much like early Christian art as possible; but they are more logical than the other party who try to secularize themselves. Men of the world don't respect that sort of thing, far from it; but we do ask that whatever a man is, or thinks himself, let him be that thing really. I would like much better a bigot who tried to burn me for my unbelief, than these men who offer a compromise on every point. Your man who would kill himself all the week in the slums, and poke hell-fire at us on Sunday, would have some grit at least."

"And yet you say that such a man would do no good."

"Maybe not, but at least we would know what he would be at. We could classify him; a great thing in a scientific age. Further, we could believe that he believed what he preached. Bad as we are, we outside heathen have an ideal of priests, filled with divine joys and visions— living far above this world, save as they come down to minister to sorrow and pity sin. Think of an early Christian martyr playing billiards in a cutaway coat, or smoking in a club. They smoked, but differently. You .cannot better a thief by helping him to steal, nor elevate a beggar by sleeping with him in the gutter. If the Church is anything, then these men are priests; and if priests they ought to be 'set apart.' They had better rise so high as to be out of sight than descend to our level. Take this from a man of the world, and I don't think that I am much off the average. You are the first clergyman to whom I have ever spoken my mind."

"Thank you," John answered. "I will remember. Now I must get the other side of the picture. There is another side, of course."

A few men were standing about in the club,

to one or two of whom Claude introduced his
brother, then watched a little anxiously to see
how he would demean himself in this new sphere;
for a fashionable club must be a new sphere to
John. In ten minutes Claude said to himself,
"He is clubable," and felt his spirits rise. A
man was talking now whom Claude had never
heard talk before. From weather to climate, to
health, to heredity they had gone, and in an
aside a listener said to Claude: "It's a beastly
shame your brother goes into the Church, he is
far too clever."

Claude laughed. "Don't you think the Church
needs clever men?"

"Awfully; but they can't get 'em. A clever
man can't believe all that stuff, don't you know."

"My brother believes it to the extent of fagot
and stake."

"Gad!" his friend said lightly. "But listen,
he's preaching now, and of all men, to Tilly."

Claude pulled his mustache with some speculation in his eyes, and a slight line gathering
between his brows.

"It is a terrific thing to realize," John was
saying; "it is hopeless, immutable. 'The sins
shall be visited on the children unto the third
and fourth generation.' You commit the sin, and
your children pay the penalty; it is in their blood
and character. It is a frightful thought, but we
cannot sin to ourselves alone, or bear all our own
punishment."

Claude took out his watch. "If we are to go to the tailor's, Jack," he said in the pause that followed John's words, "we have just time to make it in."

"Thanks, I do want to go," and they went away to the fashionable place where Claude's perfect garments were made.

"Remember," Claude said as they entered, "the mater has given you unlimited credit here, and this fellow can furnish you entirely."

"But I do not like this," John said, coloring slightly, "I am able——"

"Doubtless," Claude interrupted, "but you are the mater's heir. I tell you this to set your mind at rest. You are the last Paget, and she has bought the old place for you, and all the old silver, and everything that she could lay her hands on that ever was a Paget's. For me I am bound to perpetuate the name of Van Kuyster; but if I know anything, one of my sons shall take my father's name."

Having handed John over to the shop-people, Claude turned again toward the door, promising to be back very soon, realizing at the same moment how astonishingly eager he was to reach the florist's. Beatrice had bewitched him.

He got exquisite roses, and, late as it was, he gave orders that the florist should send his people at once to look into the condition of the conservatory, and to put the flowers in before lunch the next day. Then he returned to the tialor's.

He was immensely amused at himself. His ideal civilized man must be absolutely calm and rational; impulses, and emotions, and eccentricities were bad form. Matrimony and love, as usually practiced, were vulgar. A civilized marriage must be nothing more than an alliance made with calm, critical discretion, based on respect, equality, and forbearance. And behold! A simple child had thrown him completely off his balance. For nearly twenty-four hours he had been acting solely and entirely from impulse, and was discovering the most vivid emotions in every direction. It was his Southern blood that was to blame ; it could be nothing else. It was little short of absurd that after years of careful training of himself, after years of preaching to Mrs. Van Kuyster on the total depravity of impulse and emotion, he should come to this. To fall so low that his disciple laughed at him as she had done the evening before.

"And to-morrow," John finished, as the cab stopped, "I must see Dr. Ratcliffe, and arrange for work." Claude wondered if he had been talking slums all the way home. "Yes," he answered, "we can go before lunch," and looking up, as he turned from paying the cab, he caught the outline of a girlish figure behind the lace of the drawing room window. It would be wise to get John settled to something.

"A man has been here to look at the conservatory," Mrs. Van Kuyster said to Claude, when as usual they were having their last words by the study fire. "You sent him?"

"Yes, I want it rearranged for Beatrice. You have no objection?"

"None," with a smile that Claude did not think pleasant. "And you have not changed your mind since last night?"

"Am I so changeable?"

"Yes, or rather, you are contrary. You would go through fire and water for *anything*, if fire and water opposed you; but the thing once yours you begin to pick flaws in it. Beatrice has captured your fancy, and in John you see a rival. Let John leave the field, and Beatrice tumble into your arms, and——"

"What?"

"I should be sorry for Beatrice."

Claude laughed. "You are a clever woman," he said. "Why have you not done more in this world?"

"Environment."

"You chose your environment?"

"Yes, and you will choose yours. I envy those people who have been strong enough to let duty and not desire make their place in life for them. In the end they are better off. For you," tapping on the table with her pen-handle, "you seem to have no duty to direct you, unless you make this girl love you. I have always thought it fortunate that you had trained yourself into a perfectly practical view of life; not a high view,

but a safe one. Now, you are making a dangerous experiment."

" And yet you permit it."

" Permit it! opposition would determine you
as nothing else could. And •Beatrice will also
want to break her heart her own way; nothing
else ever satisfies humanity."

" And after the break?"

" Some have the sense to gather up the fragments and make a compromise. Some spend the
rest of their little span in breaking each fragment
separately. Some go to the bad."

" And Beatrice?"

" Will grind each fragment to powder, to the
refrain, 'dust and ashes all that is.' Her con-
ventual training will come in, you see, with penance and the rest as wheelhorses."

" You take a cheerful view of things."

" The truth is seldom cheerful. But remember, if you win Beatrice you must stand to it;
and as I have no doubt of your success, I will lay
before you my plans for her."

" Thanks."

" I have to-day engaged teachers for her in
French, German, music, and dancing—all women."

" Most wise."

" Of course. I could not spend my life keeping
guard over masters. She will exercise at the
riding club two afternoons in the week. Her
house dresses for the present will be white; her
street dresses, black. We will let her be seen a

little in Newport this summer; next winter she will come out. Finally, I have engaged an elderly woman as attendant."

"Admirable! And John?"

"Mr. Houston comes to-morrow to turn over to him The Oaks, and all the income that has accrued; when I die, I will leave him all that I can. For the rest, he has withdrawn all influence from Beatrice, apparently all interest. I do not understand him."

"I believe I do, and, accepting your parable, I think that he is now busy smashing all the fragments of a rather wild life, which he seems to feel called upon to repent. Why, God only knows; and is going to show his repentance by killing himself in the slums. If he loves Beatrice, I do not see how he intends working her into his plans unless they both join the Salvation Army."

VIII.

" Whose sad face on the cross sees only this
After the passion of a thousand years."

"IT is inhumanly early, Jack," Claude said, rising reluctantly from a deep chair in front of the study fire, "but as it is a clergyman it does not matter. Let us go and see the Reverend Ratcliffe."

"People used to come and see Carter from dawn until midnight," John said. "I suppose they all thought 'it does not matter with a clergyman.'"

"Quite so. One does not like to be formal with one's spiritual adviser. Suppose I should have a moral chill; must I wait until after lunch to have my morals doctored?"

It was the morning after the visit to the club, and Claude was carrying out his plan of putting John to work as soon as possible. John had had a long start of him in the affair of Beatrice, and though he did not seem eager in the pursuit, Claude knew that nothing made one so eager as to see another pursuing.

"You won't want the coupé before lunch, mother?" Claude asked, as he rang the bell.

"No, nor after lunch. Marjorie is to be here

to see me through some interviews. A sewing woman this morning; after lunch, Beatrice's teachers."

"What a day for you," Claude said, smiling down on the girl who sat near the fire. "Think of being pinned and basted all morning as I have seen the mater done, when as a small boy I used to go with her to her dressmaker. To go about with the mater was a liberal education. I learned my first installment of French oaths from that dressmaker."

"She was dreadful," Mrs. Van Kuyster admitted, "but she fitted one marvelously."

"I never saw her do anything but swear at the pale, nervous woman who did the work. I hope that woman is dead, she looked so tired."

"Madame died of absinthe; but in Beatrice's case Marjorie will direct."

"And if she swears, Beatrice," Claude said, "you must be sure to tell me. But, mother," he went on, "*I* want Beatrice after lunch. When will those teaching creatures come?"

"At half past three. By the way, have you a voice, Beatrice?"

Beatrice looked at John.

"She used to sing to the guitar," John answered.

"By Jove! what a find." And Claude sat down close to Beatrice. "Did you bring your guitar?"

"No."

"You shall have one by noon; then we will heat the conservatory to a torrid degree, and play that we are your Spanish ancestors singing down in the tropics. How distinctly precious!"

Beatrice looked at him curiously. "You are like a child," she said, "always wanting to play at something."

"Of course; if we do not play, we might be inveigled into work. I live in terror of Jack dragging me down to the slums. Fancy my going among those brutes. I have a theory, you know, that by the process of the survival of the fittest, all mortals with souls have risen and are clean; and all without souls have sunk and are unclean; and that is the reason why nothing can be done in the slums; they have no souls—are beasts. They ought to be put out on the plains in droves, and 'rounded up' every night by cowboys—clerical if you like—and put in stalls."

"There is too much truth in that nonsense for it to be funny," John said slowly.

"It is *all* truth. I think there is just as much sense in going out and living with a herd of cattle, as in going down into the slums; or in working on any low caste people."

"And yet, if it be true that suffering and pain live, and that pleasure vanishes," John said, "the lives of those 'brutes' are more immortal than yours. The teaching is that it is the experience gathered from the suffering of a generation that is handed on, and not the pleasures. That Father Damien's sufferings, for instance, will live and help people for generations ; but the balls of that year, the pleasures, the heaped up refinement of enjoyment—where are they ? "

Claude shook his head. " Where is the flame of last night's lamp?" he said. " I do not know ; but I would rather be the flame that vanishes, than the wick that suffers and lasts. I would rather have balls than leprosy, and Spanish songs than slums."

Then they went out, and Mrs. Van Kuyster and Beatrice went upstairs.

The rector of Mrs. Van Kuyster's place of worship lived in a handsome house on a fashionable street, and, admittance being gained, the interior was found to be handsome also. Dr. Ratcliffe had a guest in the front parlor, so the gentlemen were shown into the second parlor, which was dark save for the gaslight, which permitted chairs to be found without danger.

" Our senior warden owned this house," Claude said, when the maid had disappeared with the cards, " and when the church was moved up here, he sold it for a rectory. The improvements of his own house, which is next, shut up these two windows "—pointing to two heavily curtained windows—" but as the price was tremendously lowered, nothing was said."

" ' As it is a clergyman, it does not matter, ' " John quoted.

Claude laughed. "Very true," he said; "still, he is free to resign."

"If there is so much competition among the churches," John answered, "situations must be hard to get."

"'Situations' is good," Claude said, "and they are very hard to get until you have made a reputation. Ratcliffe is holding on to his tooth and nail, for some of the richest men in the congregation are tired of him, and he knows it."

"Poor fellow!" John said slowly, "how much better to have a place that no one covets, and do a work that only God pays for."

Claude looked at his brother curiously, then down on the floor. "I hear the parson," he said.

"Here is five dollars," came to them in a rather metallic voice, "and really I can do no more for you until next month, for there are many demands on the communion alms. And the books I bought of you for the reading room are not worth having."

"But, sir," a low voice pleaded, "I can only sell what I can get to sell."

"Very true; but I am responsible for the Guild books."

"And I am so old," the low voice said again, "and this little will not support life."

"I am very sorry, but really I have guests waiting. Bridget!"

There was a sound of shuffling footsteps and a

walking stick in the hall, a shutting of doors, then the rector entered with Claude's card in his hand.

"Ah, Mr. Van Kuyster?" and a glove seemed to have been drawn over the voice—"so glad to see you."

"You are very kind; this is my brother, Mr. Paget. We seem to have interrupted the visit of a 'dead beat,'" Claude said, when they had been taken into the front parlor and seated.

"No, only an incapable, the most difficult class to deal with. This man has 'seen better days,' and is quite willing to work, but knows nothing practical. Then he is old, and age is at a discount, Mr. Van Kuyster."

"Of course," Claude answered; "but of course you have plenty of work for a young man. My brother, here, is in orders."

"Ah?" looking at John curiously.

"Yes, and is madly anxious to go a-slumming. My mother desires to turn him over to you. We do not want him killed, however, because he is the only Paget heir."

Dr. Ratcliffe looked puzzled. "I did not know that you had a brother," he said.

"Yes, we go so far as to be twins," Claude answered. "I was adopted by my aunt, and took the name of Van Kuyster; my brother lived with a cousin in the far South, and kept the family name. As I say, he is the last of the Pagets, and must be handled carefully."

"I would like to say all that a little differently," John said, smiling. "I am very anxious to see the mission work in the slums; to assist, if possible. I hope you are not overrun with workers?"

"No, there is plenty of room in that kind of work—but——"

"I will not do for it?"

"Not at all; I meant to say that I could not assist you in that direction."

"What parish does the slum work, then?"

"Well, each large church has its mission chapel and its guilds. Then there are the City missions that do good work, and a brotherhood that potters about in various directions. But a quantity is done—too much, almost."

"I have told my brother that it will be a waste of muscle," Claude put in; "he could do just as much good in a menagerie. But I have an engagement," he added, while Dr. Ratcliffe looked a little shocked. "I will leave the carriage, Jack; lunch at one, remember." Then he went his way, and Dr. Ratcliffe looked a little uneasily at the stranger left on his hands.

"You have just arrived?" he began.

"Yes. I want to study in the seminary and do mission work."

"Of course money is no object with you?"

"No," John answered, as if regretting the estate and bank account turned over to him that morning. "No, I am not permitted to deny myself pecuniarily. I see what you think "—flashing a quick look on Dr. Ratcliffe, who had sighed : "that I am a young enthusiast. I am not very young, and I do not think my enthusiasm comes from a lack of experience. I was educated by a clergyman. His work was unheard of, but no saint ever lived a grander life. His people, a mixed and shifting population, loved him beyond expression, the worst reprobates honoring goodness for his sake. His life was lonely and, from your standpoint, comfortless, but he was so filled with faith that he seemed not to realize doubts and difficulties. He looked up so steadfastly that he did not see the trial that the next step might hold for him ; he walked as simply as a child walks holding by its father's hand." He stopped abruptly, and the light went out of his eyes. "I beg your pardon," he said ; "when I speak of my cousin I forget myself."

"You are very pardonable. You describe the ideal Christian life—a life that is seldom lived now."

"Why?"

"Why, life has grown so complex that simplicity is not understood, and enthusiasm drives people away. A bishop described one of his clergy to me, very much as you describe your friend, and finished with, 'he is the holiest, the most ideal Christian ; he is, indeed, impossibly good ; he belongs to the first century ; I had to send him into the rural districts.' You perceive,

Mr. Paget, that modern life cannot assimilate truth and enthusiasm in its crude form."

"Then I am sorry for modern life," John answered.

Dr. Ratcliffe smiled. "I will tell you an anecdote of this same man. He was trying to pay off the debt on his church ; one of his most influential vestrymen sent him a check for several thousand dollars, saying that it was a tithe from a lucky speculation. He asked this gentleman to tell him about this speculation ; hearing that it was railroad wrecking, he thanked the man and returned the check. He very nearly destroyed the parish."

"And the bishop sent *that* man into the country ?" John said, a tone of scorn creeping into his voice. "He had better have resigned his bishopric to him. I would ruin a dozen dioceses to establish a truth like that."

"Experience teaches the necessity of expediency," Dr. Ratcliffe said, smiling. "Must I decline the offerings of my people because the money was made by gambling on Wall Street? Almost every fortune in New York has been founded on lucky speculation."

"A man whose fortune is the result of his father's gambling, is not responsible," John answered. "But a man red-handed from a theft— sending a check wet, as it were, with the tears of those he has ruined, ought, it seems to me, to be shown his wrong in the clearest way, and to a man like that, declining his money would be the clearest way."

"And drive him from the church?"

"The money-changers were driven out of the Temple. .I may be mistaken," John went on, "but only yesterday a man of the world said, 'I would like much better a bigot who tried to burn me for my unbelief, than these men who offer a compromise on every point.' The man who declined the check would have pleased him."

"In theory, yes, but that simplicity will not work. Of course, I am talking to you now as a clergyman, and one who has evidently heard my order criticised. It is easy to criticise—to say, 'if our teachers were better, or the Church more at unity and more consistent, we would believe,' and perhaps, Mr. Paget, these people are not consciously telling an untruth; still, what they say is *not* true. They have no wish to believe, or to lead higher lives. They are corroded through and through with worldliness, vanity, selfishness, and luxuriousness. The supercilious stare that would be accorded the guileless saint, would go far to annihilate him. In a fashionable parish, such as I have, for instance, such a man would be impossible. Each day has a hundred things to be adjusted wisely, and a man has to meet them— come down to them, if you like—so that things may be kept in decent order. As parishes go, mine is considerate and kind. They make no difficulty about my getting away in summer; the offertories are good; they stand well on mission lists; they have guilds and missions, and spend much on the music; but they require a rigid account to be kept of all this kindness. For in these days we may not 'permit' our congregations: we have to ask permission, and have to make everything most attractive in order to persuade them to come to church at all. There must be no draughts; there must be no strangers allowed, except in certain pews; the decorations must be in the latest style; the sermon short and quiet; the service rapid, and the music perfect. Our congregations require all this, else they will not come to church. Then when the time comes that all moves smoothly and there is nothing to find fault with, they begin to realize that it is artificial and perfunctory, and turn and rend the church and the clergyman. They want reality, conviction, simplicity, they say. Let me assure you that they do not want anything of the kind; they are idle and pampered, and will *never* be satisfied. And not only in New York is this so, but *everywhere.*"

"In that case I would go my own way," John said, "and disregard their fads—musical and other."

"And be starved out, and your church sold for debt," Dr. Ratcliffe answered. "I often wish," he went on, "that Mr. Gladstone could be the rector of a fashionable American church for a little while; he would take a different view of disestablishment. Over there, if a man *is* in earnest, he can preach and teach as he thinks right ; here, a man may be desperately earnest, he is ruled by his congregation, and the ' divine call ' amounts to an excuse for Sunday concerts, and a weekly salve for fashionable consciences. The rector must truckle or must go. How to remedy all this is the problem. It is a luxurious age, a doubting age, an age that will have nothing but sugar-plums and persuasion. Sometimes I look about me, and ask, 'will any faith be found ?' Every other man you meet is at heart an agnostic, and the women are not far behind."

"If it is so bad as that," John said, "we had better stop persuading and begin to fight. If truth is with us, we *must* prevail. Throw over all nonsense, let the churches be sold for debt, and preach on the street corners. If they put us in prisons and lunatic asylums, men have died before this for truth and right ; why should not we? A luxurious, unbelieving age—grant it. But there has never been an age when men were more eager for truth—when men were more earnestly pleading for some firm place where they could cling ; never an age when humanity was so eager to help humanity ; never an age when people cried out more for reality ! It seems to me that there never has been a grander age in which to make the fight for truth ! Only, the champions must be *true*—must eliminate self, and live the life of the crucified."

Dr. Ratcliffe looked at his young companion sadly. "You almost make me believe that enthusiasm is better than experience," he said— "almost make me believe that youth only can grapple with the problems of this generation. The race is become so swift, the battle so fierce! When one is weary, one can but lag, and one must temporize with blistered feet and tremulous heart. As a vigorous young soldier, I used to feel the deepest pity for those who lay down on the roadside and let the column move on, and now I begin to look longingly at the roadside."

"Surely not yet," said John, looking at the hair that was just touched with silver.

"It is the pace that makes age, more than time," Dr. Ratcliffe answered. "But tired or old, I cannot drop out. There is no life that seems so pitiful as the life of a superannuated clergyman. They are so often dependent on the alms of the Church, and people are so apt to feel that money given in that way is wasted. You will see that all the tendency is to set the young forward in life. It is right; it is of the first importance; but as I get tired I begin to think of those who have to drop out. There are alms-houses and homes——" He stopped abruptly. "I cannot see why I should talk to you in this way, Mr. Paget; I beg your pardon. But when one has always to keep one's finger on the pulse of one's public, nervousness as to the fluctuations is sure to ensue. People who are stimulated all the week cannot do without it entirely on Sunday, and to play the part of stimulant is nothing short of death by slow torture.   Meanwhile, Mr. Paget," as John rose, " I hope that your enthusiasm will do good work, only it will be hard to keep."

Then John went away without having found the hard work about which Claude was anxious.

IX

"And some we loved, the loveliest and the best
That from his vintage rolling Time has prest,
Have drunk their cup a round or two before,
And one by one crept silently to rest.

"Ah, make the most of what we yet can spend,
Before we too into the dust descend :
Dust unto dust, and under dust, to lie,
Sans Wine, sans Song, sans Singer, and—Sans End !"

"DID Marjie swear?" Claude asked Beatrice, as they sat down to lunch.

"If there be a time when swearing is allowable for a woman," Marjorie said, "it is when she is struggling with a dressmaker."

"Were you polite and sweet-tempered through it all?" Claude went on.

"Yes," Beatrice answered; "but the sewing woman looked astonished at my Convent clothes. Cut and fit are nothing to the Sisters, you see."

"Fancy being such a saint as not to mind a baggy gown," Marjorie said, laughing. "Were they not a great trial to you—the gowns, I mean?"

Beatrice shook her head. "I never thought of them. I am afraid I just like to be comfortable."

"Very sensible, I am sure," Claude answered. "And women so seldom look comfortable."

"We are, though," Marjorie asserted; "and in a week Beatrice will wonder how she endured her Convent clothes."

"And when are we to judge of the difference between clothes made by saints and clothes made by sinners?" Claude asked.

"By Sunday," Mrs. Van Kuyster answered. Then turning to John: "How did you get on with Dr. Ratcliffe?"

"Speaking of saints brought him to her mind, you see," Claude said. "When I left, mother, they were looking at each other like two strange dogs."

"He was kind and civil, and talked to me quite frankly," John answered.

Claude laughed. "He had to be frank. Jack walked up to him as a terrier walks up to a rat he means to shake. About this time I remembered the proverbial horrors of religious wars, and left. Did you find out about the slums? Will he turn you over to the brotherhood that he spoke of so kindly as 'pottering about down there'? That was just like old Ratcliffe," Claude went on. "A different church party, hence the amiable detraction. Ratcliffe is finikin."

"He seemed very much in earnest this morning," John said.

"He could not help it, my dear fellow; when you come at a man with that life-and-death earnestness of yours, you compel the truth. I have never told the truth so straight along in my life, as I have done since your advent."

"I have been wondering what was the matter," Marjorie said. "You talk more and better, and your opinions seem to have crystallized with remarkable celerity."

Claude gave her a quick look of amusement. "Your criticism is quite just," he said. "As soon as I come in contact with truth and strength, my whole nature answers to the call. Meanwhile, I wish we would hasten to finish this abnormally protracted meal. I am in a hurry."

"Claude!" and Mrs. Van Kuyster looked at him in astonishment.

"Yes, mother, I know all that you would say if I had left you any breath. Still, I *am* in a hurry. I want to take Beatrice home to that delectable little Christi—what?"

"Corpus Christi."

"An extraordinary name for a heathen village."

"Oh, no, not heathen!"

"Why, it must be, unless you can convert jack-daws, water, and roses to Christianity, for I have not heard you mention any other inhabitants."

"Claude, you are positively silly," Mrs. Van Kuyster said, laughing with the rest, "systematically silly."

"Even so," and Claude emptied his wine-glass. "Still, the company looks ten per cent. better than when we sat down. The systematic idiot has done some good. *Have* you finished, Marjie? Your appetite makes me think of an Egyptian locust."

Mrs. Van Kuyster pushed her chair back. "You are hopeless," she said.

"Come," and putting Beatrice's hand on his arm, Claude led the way through the study to a door that had hitherto been hidden by a carved screen. This had been removed, and Waters stood waiting.

"All quite right, Waters?"

"Yes, sir."

"Come forward, dear friends," Claude went on, "and see the home of the lonely cow-girl who was captured and brought away by cruel friends to a cold and dismal land. Open!" and Waters rolled the doors back.

"Oh!" Beatrice cried, and held closer to Claude's arm. "All this for me?"

"All this!" he repeated, laughing. "I have done nothing but give a few orders. Come." And he led her down among the palms and flowers.

"It is beautiful," John said to Marjorie. "And how kind Claude is to the child."

Marjorie looked up at him curiously. "Why are you not kind to the child?" she asked.

"Am I not?" returning her look questioningly.

They were in the conservatory now, watching Beatrice as she went from flower to flower with Claude.

"And you may cut every one every day," he said. "Northern flowers are much superior to Southern flowers; they bloom all over every night."

"You talk to me as if I were a dreadful goose," Beatrice answered, laughing; "I shall be very careful."

"No," Claude answered, "you may be anything but full of care. You must behave as if the world were full of flowers put there for you to gather—promise me?" taking her hands. "Promise me?"

"But, Claude——"

"'But me no buts,' even if you are a cowgirl. Promise me."

"Yes. Oh, there is the guitar!" and drawing away her hands, she went to where a servant stood in the doorway with a case in his hands.

"Take it and open it for her," Marjorie said to John, and he obeyed her.

"O John!" Then, looking up wistfully: "It is such a beauty; must I take it all, John?"

"Yes, dear, just as you would from me." And Marjorie thought, "How grand and true his love will be. Claude will make a petted doll of his wife; John will make a living soul of his, and the girl will never realize this, never!" And an unreasonable anger sprang up in her heart against Claude, who was so clever to make and to take opportunities. "A great, true nature like John's was apt to blunder," her thoughts ran on, "and

could never learn how to handle these toy
weapons that Claude had used year after year
on as many flirtations as there were weeks in a
season. The weapons were old until they were
dingy; why was he burnishing them on this
child's heart that still slept?"

Mrs. Van Kuyster had gone back into the
study, and sitting there the tones of the guitar
came to her. She turned her face away, for
Marjorie stood in the door. The old Spanish
Fandango! It was like a dream—the fireflies
were tangled in the jessamine vines, and the
moonlight flickered up and down the dark
avenue. A voice that had been stilled on the
battlefield was singing low, and a hand that
death had clasped by the blue Southern waters
was holding hers. And now these—these also,
in there among the flowers, would break their
hearts their own way. Nothing else would content them—nothing else!

There was a sudden discordant twanging of the
strings and a sobbing cry of "Father!"

Mrs. Van Kuyster started up; Marjie still
leaned in the doorway; Claude had caught the
falling guitar, and John on the low, cushioned
seat had his arm about Beatrice, who was sobbing
bitterly.

"Take me home—please take me home! ' she
pleaded, clinging to him and burying her face on
his shoulder; "I want father—I want Angela—I
want my home! Let us go, John; let us go!"

Mrs. Van Kuyster beckoned. "Better leave her alone a little with John," she said, and led the way to the drawing room. "The first attack of homesickness," she went on, seating herself near the fire. "I knew it must come."

X.

"It's wiser being good than bad ;
It's safer being meek than fierce ;
It's fitter being sane than mad."

BEATRICE'S mortification over her breakdown
was very great, and she was thankful that the
interview with the four teachers came on that
special afternoon. She was very miserable
through it all, and when the hours, the methods,
the books had been arranged, and Marjorie had
gone, she donned her thick white frock and stole
downstairs in search of John.

It seemed to her that he was the one rock left in
the sea of misery which life had become since
lunch. She felt that she could not live another
hour in this New York—that she must go back
to her home. If not to Corpus Christi, then to
the Convent to the dear Mother. It was impossible that she should stay here. Perhaps if she
talked to John reasonably and quietly about it,
he would take her back, or send her back, it did
not matter which. She had been very foolish to
cry, she would not be such a baby again, and
maybe he would consent to her going. He would
have to consent, or she would die. He had not
refused positively when she begged him in the

conservatory, and it might be that now he would say yes. Indeed he had seemed very miserable himself. Maybe he wanted to go home—maybe he would! and she could keep house for him, and old Angela could cook.

Her visions grew rose colored as she stole through the hall and peeped into the drawing room. She made no sound, and Claude, who, ready dressed for dinner, sat staring into the fire, did not know of her nearness.

She scarcely breathed as she turned away. She did not want to meet him just then, for he seemed a part of this obnoxious new life—a possible barrier to her plans. She wanted John—John, who of late seemed to have slipped away from her—John, the only salvage from the wreck of her old life.

He must be in the study; and like a ghost she stole across the hall, and pushed open the door that was not latched. Yes, there he sat gazing into the fire, pretty much as Claude was doing in the drawing room. She closed the door softly, but as soft as the click of the latch was John heard it, and looking, up held out his hand to her. Quickly she came and knelt down at his knee.

" What is it, dear? have your teachers appalled you ? "

" No, I have not thought of them," she answered quickly. " I have gone through it like a dream—a bad dream; but I am awake now, and

I want to talk to you. John, do you remember when I was a little child, and came home from the Convent once, you were very good to me ? "

" Was I, dear ? "

" Yes; and when I came home last year a big girl, you were good to me. And when father was ill, John, all that long while," with a break in her voice, "you told me always what to do, and you promised father you would be good to me. You remember ? "

" Of course,"—looking into the fire.

" And, John," putting her hand on his face and turning it back again, so that she could look straight in his eyes, "all that goodness and kindness meant that you loved me—did it not ? "

" Yes."

" Loved me a great deal ? "

" Yes."

" And you wish me to be happy ? "

" Yes."

" Then you will do what I want? you will take me home again," her voice breaking with a sigh that was almost a sob, "take me home to old Angela; we will make you so comfortable, John, she and I ; and I will do everything you tell me. I will teach Sunday school, and read Church history, and do all the things that you wanted me to do and I did not want to do. I will do it all, and more, if you will take me back again. I tell you I will *die* if you keep me here—I cannot stand it—I *will* not stand it! John!" drawing closer to him, "I did not mean that; I did not mean to say that I would not obey you—only"—then her voice failed.

John laid his arm about her shoulder as she kneeled beside him. "If you will try to be happy," he said, "and will trust me, I will try to arrange it all for you."

"I will—I will!" an ecstatic light coming into her face, "I will study—I will practice—I will wear tight clothes and play the guitar for Claude. I will do *anything.*"

"Yes," John went on, "you must return their kindness by being as happy as possible, and I will do my best for you. You see I came here to study to be a clergyman, and I have not found out yet how long it will take me—but not long, I fancy. I promise you I will do it as quickly as possible. Then——"

"Then we will go home," the girl struck in, "and hang up my old hammock again—I left it with Angela, and my own old guitar, and the boat, and old Calavaros will let us have the horses as usual. Oh, I will be so happy! Only, father, John; it will be lonely without him,"—her voice faltering.

"Hush, we will not talk of that just now; but we will work hard and be good, and all will come right."

"We will; oh, you are so good to me!" and she pressed her lips on his hand that lay on her shoulder, "and I will begin by thanking Claude for the guitar. I did not to-day, you know; I cried instead, and begged to go away: now I will go and thank him. Don't you think so?"

"Yes, where is he?"

"By himself in the drawing room. I looked in there to hunt for you, and saw him, and, John—" pausing.

"Yes, dear."

"You will never go away and leave me here? To-day a sort of terror came over me that you might feel it your duty to go—and you and father always do your duty, and so you would leave me."

"I will never leave you without your full knowledge and free consent. I think you would let me do my duty?"

"You make life so hard," she answered slowly. John sighed.

"Life *is* hard, child; I do not make it so. All we can do is to obey—obey, if obedience brings the bitterest sufferings. Only so you will win the peace that no pain can touch."

Then she went away slowly, with thoughts in her mind that she did not seem able to grasp. Talking with John left her always with a troubled longing for something she could not define. What was it, this vague unrest he always roused, that made her look back so longingly to her life at the Convent. All she wanted in life was peace such as she had there. Why not let her go back?

And John, left alone, thought of the day rather
sadly. He was still full of enthusiasm for his
work, and would never let his enthusiasm go, but
things were very different from what he had expected. In the provinces New York was looked
on as the Mother Church, and he had thought to
find there, as nowhere else, a strong spiritual life
among the clergy—men working shoulder to
shoulder, with glowing faith and burning hope.
He had thought to find an environment and an
encouragement that would be a memory and
strength through all the coming years. His talk
with Claude had hurt him ; still, he had been sure
that there was another side to the picture. To-
day he had seen that other side. It was true he
had met only one clergyman—had had only one
talk ; but from that talk he had come away feeling himself an ecclesiastical Don Quixote, instead of having had his zeal and enthusiasm confirmed. He felt helpless when he remembered it.
How everywhere there was revealed the struggle
these men had to make against worldliness. The
fight against poverty and outspoken sin was
nothing compared with this war against luxuriousness and pleasure. How pitiful Dr. Ratcliffe's
talk had been ! Sometimes bitter, sometimes
sad, sometimes complacent, but never taking the
calm high note of perfect faith. How pitiful his
praise of his congregation—how pitiful his fear
of the future. And the old man who had begged
for a little more help. He could not forget the

sound of those shuffling footsteps. No wonder
Dr. Ratcliffe dreaded loss of wealthy favor, he
knew so well how alms were doled! To-morrow
he would send a check for the old man.

Mrs. Van Kuyster entered. "Dreaming all
alone?" she said.

"Yes," and as she came within the circle of fire-
light, John was struck afresh by her beauty, and
his thoughts went back to the old love story that
had come to his knowledge during Carter's last
illness. What had separated those two?

"What was it that came between you and
Carter, Aunt Claudia?" he asked quietly.

She started slightly, then, as she settled herself
in her chair, she answered in a voice as quiet as
his own, "Your mother."

"My mother!"

"Only that she showed him my faults day
after day," Mrs. Van Kuyster went on, "and in-
duced him and your father to begin a system of
reproofs; needed, probably, but that, coming
after a life of indulgent love, I could not understand. I was very young, not eighteen when I
married. Then I did not like the thought of
Carter's going into the ministry. I did not know
life then, you see."

"Now you would love his work."

"Now I know that to be absorbed in anything
—to believe in any work, or person, or future, is
the nearest we get to happiness."

"Aunt Claudia!"

" It is quite true. I do not forecast anything for you, for you have earnestness and enthusiasm to give away. You will have many disappointments—enthusiastic people always do ; but you will make excuses for those who fail you, and repeople your ' fool's paradise ' immediately. I do not mean to call you a fool ; on the contrary, I think you most fortunate to have a paradise of any kind. But you have not told me one word about Dr. Ratcliffe."

" I am sorry for him."

" How strange ! he is well paid—well fed—well clothed ; his wife has several of the best people on her visiting list ; his daughter was educated abroad ; his son is just come home from Harvard. Why pity him ? "

" Because of all these things ; because he is obliged to be so worldly that, in a measure, he has forsaken his calling."

" On the contrary, I don't know a man who poses better as the successful rector."

" Is Dr. Ratcliffe typical ? "

" Yes, of his school. He is really a good man, I think, and tries to do his duty, but he must be guided by the taste of his people. It would be a desperate job to live elsewhere, once having held such a comfortable position in New York. He was elected missionary bishop once, but declined."

" On what ground ? "

" Various grounds. He felt that a great city

parish was quite as important as a missionary
jurisdiction; then he loved his people, and did not
think his health could stand the climate. This
to the public. Mrs. Ratcliffe told a select few
that she had cried for a week, and had declined
to leave New York. That the salary as bishop
was small, and out in the wilderness there were
no social advantages for either Jessie or Horton.
She told Dr. Ratcliffe that if he went he would
have to leave her and the children."

"Why did he not do it?"

"My dear John, the wife of his bosom!"

"Ten of them, if necessary."

Mrs. Van Kuyster laughed. "He is at least
Christian enough to have only one. But I was
really sorry for him at the time, he seemed to be
so troubled. Of course it increased his value;
the people like to have a rector who refuses bish-
oprics—it sounds well. Don't look so ill, dear,"
Mrs. Van Kuyster went on. "I may be mistaken as to his being typical. And at last it is
all very natural. One cannot blame him for preferring a parish with a good salary, a rectory,
and a minimum of work to a diocese, a poor
salary, a tent, and work enough to kill two or
three men. Human nature must be considered."

"Excuses of human weakness have to be made
for us all, God knows," John answered, "but the
wrong lies deeper than that. You speak of them
just as you would of any paid dependent, and

you have a right to do this because Dr. Ratcliffe has put himself in the position of a paid dependent. He has shown how much his place and his position mean to him from a worldly standpoint. Why, in refusing a poor diocese in order to stand by a rich parish, he simply trampled on his calling and lay down like a hungry dog before his vestry. Do you suppose that a man who regarded the Church as she should be regarded—who believed in her as the mystical body of Christ—who honored his office as priest of the living God as he should honor it, could take any such position as that? Do you suppose that a man who believed that he was carrying on the work that the Son of God suffered and died to inaugurate, could stop for one moment to consider social advantages or money? Of course, if you look on the church as a sort of religious society, earth-born and-bred—what Claude calls a 'moral sanitary measure'—why then elect your officers for any reasons and in any way you please, and 'log-roll,' and truckle to any extent. No one expects anything else of earthly things. But the Church is not this—is not a republic subject to mob rule; it is a kingdom, with the Son of God for king—it is divine."

"My dear John, you should have lived a thousand years ago; to-day you are an anomaly, you are a phenomenon that only the remotest provinces could have produced. That you should come to light in this age of 'isms,' and smooth words and ways, is almost enough to make one believe in miracles."

"You are quite right," rising as dinner was announced; " my position is an old one, but it is the only one that is true or 'that can be held permanently. And after all our discussion may have arisen out of nothing, for we may have misjudged Dr. Ratcliffe."

"Who and what?" Claude asked, as he and Beatrice came into the dining room behind them.

"Dr. Ratcliffe and the bishopric," Mrs. Van Kuyster answered.

"And Jack is indignant? My dear fellow," he went on as he took his seat, "the mater and I almost came to blows about that. I said, 'What is the proposition? a thin salary and the glittering honor; we offer a fat salary and a rectory—he will pray over it and stay.' Don't murder me, Jack, I am only a plain-spoken black sheep, and that is the regular formula. Why, when I heard of a man who 'prayed' and then left the rich parish, I could scarcely believe it. I went to that man's consecration all the way to Philadelphia; I bought his picture and sought an introduction."

"Claude sends that bishop a box every spring and autumn," Mrs. Van Kuyster interrupted.

"Of course I do, and all the periodicals. If Dr. Ratcliffe had gone, the mater should have had that ponderous girl to stay here. I might even have gone so far as to invite the abominable son, but never the mother!"

John laughed. "What ails the mother?" he asked.

"Everything. She is scrawny and whiney, and has a bullet head. As you love your life, Jack, avoid women with bullet heads—they have *hides.*"

"Is Miss Ratcliffe nice?" Beatrice asked.

"Nicer than her mother; God forbid that *anything* should be worse; but she is red-headed and voluble in three languages. The son is pink-eyed and morose. By the way, mother, if that woman dares bring that son to see Beatrice——"

"Well," John said, "if she does?"

"I will sell him to a butcher for cat's meat. But, really, you will not permit that, mother."

Beatrice looked anxious. "I am afraid of strangers, Aunt Claudia," she said.

"You are only a schoolgirl, dear," Mrs. Van Kuyster answered, "you need not be afraid."

And everybody looked relieved.

XI

"Better men fared thus before thee;
Fired their ringing shot and passed,
Hotly charged—and sank at last."

ON Sunday morning, at breakfast, a note was handed to John, and as he read a troubled look came on his face. He handed it to Mrs. Van Kuyster.

"Dr. Ratcliffe wants me to help him in the service," he said; "both assistants called away."

"Of course, you cannot decline," Mrs. Van Kuyster answered.

"Why not?" Claude said sharply. "I call it cheek."

"You assisted Carter, did you not?" Mrs. Van Kuyster went on, giving Claude a glance of amusement.

"Yes, but this is not the kind of work I want. You will excuse me while I answer the note."

A frown gathered on Claude's brow. This would be more trying than the club; and, turning to Waters, he said: "I wish you to look to Mr. Paget's boots yourself, Waters." Then to the company at large, "I loathe dingy boots, but under a surplice they are unbearable."

"Have you vestments?" Mrs. Van Kuyster

asked when John came back. "You are taller than Dr. Ratcliffe or the assistants."

"Yes. A tall or a short man must always have. A clergyman has no right to look ridiculous."

"Decidedly not," Claude said so emphatically that John turned and looked at him. "You will take John in the carriage, mother; I will walk. Will Beatrice go?" Then, the answer being in the affirmative, Claude's face cleared a little, and he turned to the girl. "You must sit near my end of the pew," he said, "between me and Marjie."

"Suppose Marjorie is late?" Mrs. Van Kuyster suggested.

"Why, then, I will give Marjie a gentle push which she will understand. She knows that Beatrice can't find her places without help."

"Can you?" John asked.

"My dear fellow, I am as regular at church as Dr. Ratcliffe. I sing all that is singable, and respond in the most approved mumble. You do not know me."

"You may always count on Claude to this extent," Mrs. Van Kuyster said; "whatever is correct and proper, he will not fail in. Marjie calls him the Apostle of Propriety."

"A gentleman has no choice," Claude answered. "He *must* do the correct thing, no matter what his private fads may be. It is your own teaching, mother."

"And Carter's," John said.

Claude was not happy. He had not been happy

since the day before, when in the conservatory
Beatrice had turned to John. His sensations
under the circumstances had astonished and provoked him, the more so that both Marjie and Mrs.
Van Kuyster had seen his discomfiture.

Nor had his temper been improved when in the
dusk of the evening Beatrice had come to him in
the drawing room, to apologize for her tears. She
had looked very lovely as she stood by him in the
half-light, and he had started to his feet, pleased
and surprised that she should have sought him.

"You must think me very stupid and rude,"
she began, "when I cried. I have come to beg
your pardon ; it was the music did it, and I thank
you very much for the guitar."

"I understand perfectly," he said, leading her
to a sofa and sitting down beside her. "It was
silly of me to make you recall your home."

"Yes," her voice breaking a little, " but I should
not have made everyone so uncomfortable."

"You must not think of it any more"—and
Claude laid his hand on hers.

"I must think of it enough not to do it again.
John says that if I will study and be good, and
show my appreciation of all the kindness by being
happy, that he will promise to take me home again
soon as possible. John is so good to me."

"So it seems ! " and thrusting his hands into his
pockets, Claude took up his position in front of
the fire.

"And I shall be so happy ! " the girl went on.

" I will keep house for John, and old Angela to
cook. And the jackdaws, and the flowers, and
all the shabby old things just as they used to be.
You cannot think how happy we were. I did not
know it myself until now, and I did not know
that our things were old and shabby."

" And maybe when you go away," Claude said
slowly, " you will recall the guitar, and these
flowers, and that silly Claude, with regret; for
maybe you will have learned to care for this house
by that time."

" Oh, but I care for you now! No one has ever
been so good to me before ; but John, you know,
is a piece of my life."

" Yes," Claude answered, and after that he let
her talk with little interruption, and accepted her
plan that he should go to Corpus Christi too.

And now he was still more annoyed by John's
having to take part in the service, and Mrs. Van
Kuyster's smile at breakfast added to his anger.
Of course he must go to church; to stay away
would not be civil. But suppose John's vest-
ments were shabby—suppose he should fail.
Hang old Ratcliffe! And Marjorie and Mrs. Van
Kuyster would read him clearly, and laugh at him.
Confound it all !

None of this annoyance appeared, however, and
at a quarter before eleven he stood in the hall carelessly twirling a white rose between his perfectly
gloved fingers, and watching with approving, if furtive glances, Waters, who was brushing John's hat

in a truly scientific manner. In church he found
things arranged as he had ordered. Marjorie was
next to Mrs. Van Kuyster, and Beatrice looked up
with a very lovely smile as he entered the pew.
So far, so good ; but he caught a twinkle in Marjie's eye that made him long to fight. Of course
Mrs. Van Kuyster had told her that John was going to read, and of course Marjorie knew that he,
Claude, was miserable. His feelings were in some
degree soothed, however, when he saw that people whose opinions were worth having were looking at Beatrice with approval, not to say admiration.

But satisfactory as this was, the organ prelude
and the opening of the vestry-room door, made
Claude wince ; Marjorie's nerves were a little
strained too. But Mrs. Van Kuyster smiled, and
Beatrice looked up with a serene light in her eyes.

Many people looked, and some whispered "Who
is it ?" Claude would have asked himself if he had
not known, and he wondered that he had not
realized long ago how very commonplace Dr.
Ratcliffe was. After this his fears subsided, and
the service had a different ring to it.

In the aisles when all was done, people asked,
" *Who* is that young man ? " " What a *lovely* voice!"
" *How* handsome ! " " *Such* hands, I could not
take my eyes off them. " And Claude heard Mar-
jorie answering, " Mrs. Van Kuyster's nephew, Mr.
Paget," and Mrs. Van Kuyster answering,
" Claude's brother, Mr. Paget," and Claude an-

swered many times himself, " My brother, Mr.
Paget. "   John was a success, and Beatrice was a
success, and a calm settled on his spirit.

" You read so well, John," Mrs. Van Kuyster
said at lunch.   " It seemed no effort to you."

" It was not ; the acoustics of the church are
good."

" You would not think so," Claude said, " if
you could hear little Dorkins shriek the lessons
at us."

" You created quite a sensation, Mr. Paget."

" You are laughing, Miss Van Kuyster."

" I was never more in earnest in my life," Marjorie answered.   " Am I not right, Claude ? "

" Quite right ; the buzz began before the blessing was done."

John laughed.   " I heard the buzz," he said.
" I am sorry to hear that I caused it."

" Well, you did," Claude answered.   " I expected them to encore you once or twice, and
waited for them to call you back when the show
was over."

"Coming from a little country church, it did
seem something of a show."

" It is ; and to-day when you were real, it caused
a sensation.   I saw people standing up and kneeling down whose knees I have doubted until to-
day."

"Old Mrs. Badger was quite put out," Marjorie
said; "it was amusing to hear her. ' My dear
Miss Van Kuyster, that young man looked at me

quite severely because I sat during the Te Deum ;
does he not know that people like to be comfortable when they are hearing good music ?' It was
funny."

" Where did the old person sit?" John asked.
" I do not remember looking at anyone in par-
ticular."

" Just under your nose," Claude answered; "and
before service was over she looked like a boiled
lobster."

" It is a very handsome church," John said.

" And comfortable," Marjorie answered.
"The benches are well angled—if I may coin an
expression; the heating is good, the light well
tempered, the music bearable, and the sermons
short."

" But, oh, the voice!" Claude exclaimed. " Ratcliffe's voice is like a blank wall; I never realized
it until to-day."

" Church seems to have done us great good,"
Mrs. Van Kuyster said, rising; and Beatrice re-
tiring on the plea of a headache, the rest wandered into the study.

" Beatrice does not seem to be strong," Mrs.
Van Kuyster said when they were seated about
the fire.

" She has never been ill," John answered ; " but
her mother was extremely delicate; she seemed
to die chiefly of inability to live. The physician
diagnosed it as lack of vitality."

" We must put Beatrice on a tonic, mother,"

Claude said quietly, " and this climate will help her. It was old Ratcliffe's twaddle that tired her out."

"Why do you not change your parish?" John asked.

"Any other would fare just the same," Mrs. Van Kuyster answered.

"Yes, and there is not another building so comfortable," Marjorie said.

"Why do you go to church at all?" John went on.

"Because it is a good habit, and the correct thing," Marjorie answered. "Why do you go?"

"Because I believe in it as a divine institution."

"Really?"

"Of course; if I did not, I would not go near it."

Marjorie looked a little uncertain. "I do not think that I quite understand how it is you believe in it," she said.

"Why, only this, that the Christ came to earth to found his kingdom, the Church; and it was in pursuance of this work that he suffered and died. Must it not seem holy and of worth to me—to anyone who looks at it truly?"

"I was taught that Christ came down to die for our sins."

"He came to work, and died because of our exceeding sinfulness. Socrates said that if the perfect man ever appeared on earth, he would be put to death."

"You conducted the service as if you believed in it," Mrs. Van Kuyster said.

"How could you think otherwise?"

"I do not know that I thought about it at all; but your manner was unusual and struck me."

"I think I must tell on Claude," Marjorie said. "He was in such misery this morning, Mr. Paget, and all on account of your having to read the service. If you had fallen below his standard, he would have become suddenly ill, and have come away."

"Indeed I would," Claude answered so earnestly that John laughed. "I do not mind my people being failures if I can take them off by themselves, but it really hurts me to see the public stare at anything that is mine."

"Unless it be a stare of envious admiration," Marjorie corrected.

"Granted; and Marjorie never lets me alone about it. She says that I am not loyal—that ridicule could make me forego the love of my life; what else, Marjorie?"

"That if it were the fashion to admire bald-headed, cross-eyed women, Claude would never be contented until he possessed a wife with a head like a billiard ball, and eyes that lapped; but that if the fashion changed, he would persuade her into a sisterhood or a widows' home, even if it broke what he calls his heart. He cannot stand the criticism even of Waters, here."

"My word, Marjorie, you draw it strong! Now won't you give us a companion picture of Jack? If I am not mistaken, I have seen a very different criticism of him in your eyes."

"Quite different!" Marjorie answered. "If Mr. Paget loved a person, the opinion of the world would be to him as a wind that had blown itself away before this country was discovered. If he should meet a friend in rags on Fifth Avenue, he would walk with him to his tailor's and clothe him. If his friend failed in reading the service, he would go up to the chancel when the service was over, and shake hands with him and bring him home to dinner."

Mrs. Van Kuyster and John laughed; Claude's eyes flashed, but after a second's pause he answered amiably:

"I believe he would, Marjie; and nobody in the world admires that sort of pluck more than I do, but I haven't got it."

"You should cultivate it, my dear, seeing how patiently I have lectured you about it."

"There has been no lack of lecturing, but the process is disagreeable; and to what purpose?"

"The making of character. Don't you remember the sermon that stranger preached not long ago on character—the only thing worth having—the only thing that outlasts 'this world and the fireworks'?"

"Yes, it was a strong sermon, and if I believed in the kind of future that he believed in, why then that kind of supernumerary, supererogatory, superlative character would be worth striving for. But that future, if indeed there is any, is an unknown quantity, and the theological road to it is marvelously circuitous. What do you say, Jack?" Clasping his hands behind his head. "A moment ago you said something that had a strong, if a strange, sound; give me your views on the subject."

"On the future life, or on your attitude? I do not know where you stand. Tell me what you believe, and I will tell you what I know."

"Give me what you know for what *I* believe," Claude said; "a poor exchange, for I am certain only of my uncertainty. Better let me tell you what I think you would like me to believe."

"Very well."

Claude rested his elbows on the arms of his chair, put the tips of his fingers together, and leaning back looked at the ceiling. There was silence for a moment, then Claude dropped his hands together in his lap.

"It would seem blasphemous to you," he said.

John gave him a quick look. "What I want you to believe cannot be blasphemous."

"No, but my way of putting it—" and Claude passed his hand over his eyes.

"Do not put it that way, then. Since you do not look on me as a fool, and since I hold these views, there must at least be another side of the question; since there is a question, there must be a doubt—take the benefit of the doubt, then ; take it thankfully, and state your proposition as reverently as may be."

The quick color sprang to Claude's face, and the light to his eyes, but after a moment's pause he put the tips of his fingers together as before, and, once more looking at the ceiling, began quietly.

"You would have me believe in a personal God, who made man in his own image, pure and sinless, and intended that he should remain so. That this man was tempted by the devil, an unaccounted for being, and fell. This fall brought death. Humanity once having succumbed, sin was fascinating, and the devil frustrated the plans of the Almighty so entirely that the earth had to be purified by a flood. After a few ages, however, the human race was worse than before, and the anger of the Almighty could be appeased only by sacrifice ; and the only sacrifice that could satisfy the justice of this loving God, so that his mercy could be extended to the miserable creatures that he had created, was the incarnation, daily suffering, and death of his Son, the second person of a mysterious Trinity." Claude paused. "A moment ago you gave a different turn to that point."

"Of course !" and John, rising, rested one elbow on the mantelpiece, and looked down on his brother. "You have not stated Christianity at all. To begin. Man was created with a will, free to obey or disobey. You know this."

"*Know* it?"

"Yes, know it. What you cannot help thinking, that you know. You cannot think yourself an automaton, therefore you know that you are free. And these things that you cannot help thinking are revelations. Your own existence is one. Man was created free, then; anything else is unthinkable. Now take the exquisitely simple story of the fall; treat it as you will, and one fact remains—the law of righteousness was transgressed, and death came as it comes to-day to such transgressions. Transgress the law of righteousness to-day, and you are punished by the crippling or death of that much good in your nature. The law carries its own punishment. To say law, is to say obedience or disobedience. Disobedience is sin; sin means all the ills that flesh is heir to. The law of heredity brought the sin down to the third and fourth generation, and we say now, 'Man is born to sorrow as the sparks fly upward.' The cure for all this is obedience, and obedience is the one motive that the Christ ever gave for his coming into this world. He came to work. Was sent to establish this 'kingdom of obedience'—the Church, to bring us once more into our true relations with the Father."

"A personal God?"

"Yes."

Claude shook his head. " I cannot," he said.

" You believe such a thing as ' good ' ? "

" Yes."

" What is it ? "

" As I see it in you——"

" Thanks ; I do not want an imaginary portrait of myself, and you have granted my proposition before it is made—that you cannot think of good as something suspended in the air; you must think of it as inhering in something. Now you may doubt good if you choose, but you cannot make such a mistake as to doubt the existence of Claude Van Kuyster, for the very doubt proves that there is one who doubts. Claiming this revelation of self-existence for yourself, you must grant it to all the creatures in the universe, and hope that each has his little germ of good. Now the greatest good must reside in the highest Personality—call this 'the Unknowable,' call this 'The All-Being,' the 'First Cause,' the 'Stream of Tendency '—if you like ; for me there is but one name, God the Father. For that which satisfies the insatiable craving for a final cause—that which is the sum of all good, therefore of all that is true and beautiful—that is my God."

" Now to the next proposition," Claude said, " that He made man in his own image."

" Very well. Here we meet again those limitations—those things that we cannot help thinking, and those things that are unthinkable. We cannot help thinking 'Good'—we cannot think good apart from some form.   We have no celestial imagination by which to produce a celestial form, nor any celestial language in which to describe it, so we are forced to say in finite humility, 'in his own image'—the form he gave as highest, the best we know. You may protest against it as anthropomorphic, but you can *think* nothing else. And this 'in his own image' means free will— the sense of good and evil—the law of obligation, the immense 'Ought' that 'makes for righteous- ness'—that dominates the universe, and against which we so often beat out our little lives— the law that leads us, whether we will or no, to a lawgiver—your First Cause, my God. Now, just here, I will grant you everything that natural selection and evolution can prove. But the moment when the 'divine spark' that 'makes for righteousness,' came to the clod, or the ape, or what you will; at that immortal mo- ment, God made man, and 'breathed into his nostrils the breath of life.' Evolution only adds to the miraculousness and the glory of it all. The flood we will leave to the geologists; grant- ing, however, that the purification was needed."

"And the devil?" Claude said.

"Is evil personified."

"You hold to a personal devil?"

"Yes. A fallen angel. Angels are as free to disobey as we are, and this Prince of Evil, the founder of the kingdom of disobedience, had the splendid audacity to approach the son of God himself."

" I thought that was allegory."

" If one part of the Scripture is allegory, why not all? where will you stop? Because a thing is difficult for our finiteness to compass, are we to call it allegory? You cannot understand your own walking stick, and why it must have two ends, but you do not for that relegate your walk-ing stick to the realm of allegory. Impersonal good and evil are as unthinkable as a one-ended walking stick."

Marjorie laughed. " That one-ended stick will torment me forever," she said ; " I shall dream of sticks that stretch into infinity—I shall spend my life in extending them. What a horrid sugges-tion."

" And what do you do with the literary criti-cism of Scripture?" Mrs. Van Kuyster asked.

" I read it. It is plausible, poetical, and some of it is well done ; but no one mortal critic can decide spiritual things for me."

" I agree with you entirely on that point," Claude said. " I maintain always that there is no logical stopping place; you must believe all or none. After the best translation is made, after the canon of Scripture is decided, then, for a Christian, there can be no further tampering—all or none."

" And I hold it all," John said.

" Believe all the miracles as you believe that I

sit here?" Marjorie asked. "Take the stories of the Gospels as historical facts?"

"As every kind of fact," John answered. "Believe it as I believe in Christopher Columbus and George Washington."

"How *can* you!" Claude said as if involuntarily, rising from his chair.

"How is it possible not to!" and John's eyes flashed. "Give up the Scriptures, give up everything except the one central, incontrovertible fact that Jesus of Nazareth"—and he bowed his head reverently—"lived on earth, and then go to history and trace his work. Try again; reconstruct history without the Christ, give us civilization as we have it to-day, bad as it is, without his system of morals. You cannot; Christ and his kingdom, the Church, permeate the whole universe. The taking up of our humanity into his divinity has made man a different creature."

"And the ages before Christ?"

"God has never been without a witness in the world. All truth, all beauty, all good, wherever found, is a revelation of himself. God is immanent in his universe, and miracles cease to be miraculous."

Claude shook his head. "You put it well," he said; "but the faculty, or the sense, or whatever it may be that is required to grasp it, that thing I have not got. What is it?"

"There are several things required," John answered; "a little common sense to recognize your limitations ; a little humility to grant them ; a little reason to see that you cannot think effect without thinking cause, that you cannot think evil without thinking good, that you cannot think matter without thinking spirit. You need clearer eyes to see that the limited and the relative bring home to us the absolute, that the finite is outlined on the infinite, that death means life, and the universe shows us God. In the midst of all this mystery we grope and cry as a little child cries in the darkness, and our only hope is to grasp our Father's hand. Faith as a little child, and our eyes are opened."

"I do not know that I will admit that I lack all these other things," Claude said, " but on faith I lay no claim. I think I was born without it. As a child I was told that God made me; I asked Mr. Van Kuyster, ' Who made God ? ' "

"And what did he answer?" Mrs. Van Kuyster asked.

Claude shook his head. "I do not like to repeat it," he said; "but I laughed, and he gave me a gold dollar."

XII.

" The door was shut.   I looked between
　　Its iron bars ; and saw it lie,
　　My garden, mine, beneath the sky,
Pied with all flowers bedewed and green.

A shadowless spirit kept the gate,
　　Blank and unchanging like the grave.
　　I, peering through, said : ' Let me have
Some buds to cheer my outcast state.'

He answered not.   ' Or give me, then,
　　But one small twig from shrub or tree ;
　　And bid my home remember me
Until I come to it again.'

The spirit was silent ; but he took
　　Mortar and stone to build a wall ;
　　He left no loophole great or small
Through which my straining eyes might look."

WALKING to his club that afternoon,
Claude's step was slower, and when he
reached his destination his manner was more
preoccupied than usual.   After the briefest greetings, he took his seat near a window with his
back to the room, and a paper as excuse for
silence.

A new view of life had been presented to him,
a view he had known of, but that had never been
brought home to him until now.   Now he stood

side by side with a man he was bound to respect
and in a measure look up to; a man who had
tested life, and who was no "goody," for manli-
ness showed in every movement and sounded in
every tone, and yet he took this view.

Could he have taken John's training, and *would*
John have taken his? Would John have been
satisfied, even for a little while, with life as he,
Claude, looked at it? John seemed perfectly
willing that other people should take life lightly
and cheerfully, should laugh and see the farce of
it all; but for himself, John seemed to be forever
looking through the flimsy show to the tragic
background. That the background of life was
tragedy, everyone knew who thought at all; but
why live with this always in mind? The tragedy
was the part that lasted, and it was the earnestness
of John's nature that turned him to it. To him
the life and Christianity of the Van Kuysters'
world must seem like stucco work and ginger-
bread trimming. Already, this afternoon, he had
betrayed the scorn he felt for it. Soon this
scorn would extend to the people who could be
satisfied with such shams, for John really believed.
How strange that in this age a man like John
should hold as vital truths things which, if science
and literary criticism had not entirely destroyed
them, were at best held in mild solution; things
that had been spared only because they had
served so long as moral police that the world,
feeling some obligation to them, had pensioned

them off, as it were, or had turned them out to graze. Yet to John this old creed was a living thing—a thing for which he would give his life.

And after all, was he not wise? Was not life more worth living to him than to most people? He had, at least, something to strive for in the race—a crown that he believed to be incorruptible. And if all the crowns were alike of straw, and all who strove for them more or less idiots—the man who believed that his crown was imperishable gold might be the greatest idiot, but was he not at the same time the happiest man? How strange to have the strong belief of John, or the unquestion.ing faith of Beatrice.

He put down for a moment the screening paper he had not read, and lighted a cigar.

Should he go over to them, or bring Beatrice over to him ; or would it be better to stay where he was, and to leave her in the mystic dreamland that seemed to satisfy her? Win her he would, but could he do it and not touch her faith? How would it do to have a wife who looked on one with doubt? Did the child have any faith save in the people who had guided her life—had not the Mother been her religion, and was not John her religion now? She was in awe of John as she had been of the Mother, but it was the reverential awe that was the surest foundation in the world for hero worship. Could she have John for her ideal and Claude for her lover? And through the drifting rings of smoke rose up the soft eyes of the girl who had so disarranged his carefully planned life.

No. Whatever might be the result, he, Claude, must be her ideal, her crown, her religion. She was still asleep, and the vision that should waken her would be the dream of her life. John loved her, yet he seemed unconsciously to be fighting against the realization of the fact. Why, was a mystery. She would hamper him in his race, maybe? Claude laughed a low laugh. Which was the greater fool: he, who would put his life into the keeping of an undeveloped child, or John, who would put aside everything pleasant for the sake of an exploded idea? John, with youth, and strength, and beauty, and wealth, turning aside to be an ascetic. To live on a high moral plane where only highly moral and spiritual flowers would grow. Did he fight against loving Beatrice because he knew that she could not live there? She could not. She could be a nun and live in one long passion of religious ecstasy; or she could be a woman and make her life one long passion of devotion; but a cool love, a friendly affection, *that* would be death. Her mother had died from no known cause; perhaps she had been starved on a high spiritual plane—bleached out of life.

He looked out on the passing throng, all in holiday dress. Were they as contented as they seemed, as contented as he had been before the entrance of this new force into his life? But why should he be discontented; why could not he love Beatrice naturally and heartily, and ask the same kind of love in return? What was the necessity of all this introspection and discussion; why not ignore all differences and be comfortable? Was it Mrs. Van Kuyster or John who made all this to do, or was it his own questioning, dissatisfied self? He would go home at once, and make a new common-sense beginning. Beatrice would be rested by this, and be downstairs, and John would be gone to church.

He found Beatrice sitting alone in the study, looking through the open doors of the conservatory.

"Do you think it a sin to go into the conservatory on Sunday?" Claude asked as he entered.

Beatrice started. "No, oh, no!" she answered, "the Mother used to make Sunday the nicest day of all. I did not go in because——"

"Because?" Claude repeated, standing with his back to the fire, and looking down on her.

"Because the smell of the roses makes me homesick. I know it is weak, and ungrateful too, and I *am* trying to overcome it," looking up wistfully. "That is the reason I am sitting here."

"You are trying to be a ridiculous little martyr," and drawing a low chair close to her, Claude sat down.

"Now, listen to me," he began; "if the flowers

make you sad, the conservatory shall be closed
at once."

"Do you think me so weak as that? Why the
Mother would be ashamed, and John would be
mortified. We ought to fight against such things,
and be glad of the opportunity to learn self-control. Everybody tells me that."

"*I* do not," Claude answered. "We are put
into this world to be happy, and why not *be*
happy? If the conservatory makes you unhappy,
close it; I only opened it because I thought it
would please you."

"It did—it does! It would hurt me dreadfully
to shut it up."

"Why?"

"First of all, John would be——"

"Confound John!" Claude broke in, "I do
not care a straw about John's opinion; he prefers being miserable, and would rather enjoy
being roasted by a slow fire; but you were not
made for that sort of nonsense. You ought not
to cry any more than the flowers do; you ought
to have sunshine all the time, and you *shall.*
Martyrs are tough, rawboned dyspeptics, who
are not happy unless they are miserable, who go
about the world begging people to step on their
coat-tails. You are too young and too pretty for
any such folly. To-day you were tired out by
that stupid sermon, and now you are made sad
by the flowers. If you do not get better, you
shall not go to church, and the flowers shall be

banished. You may obey John in his house, but
I am master in this house and you must obey
me. I shall shut the conservatory."

"Oh, no!" Beatrice cried, springing up and
laying a detaining hand on his arm, "I beg
that you will not ; I had much rather that you
took me into it, and let me become accustomed
to it."

Claude stood a moment looking down into the
pathetic face so near his own, and a shiver ran
over him, and the afternoon's thoughts came back
to him ; how much better to go through life with
the little hands held close in his ! Only a moment he paused, then took hold of Beatrice's
wrist.

"Come, then, I will let you enjoy martyrdom
for a little while, I playing torturer. Come!"
and he led her down the one step that separated
the study from the conservatory. "Now, remember that I am going to try my best to hurt you,
give you such a good dose of misery that you
will never yearn to be a martyr again."

Beatrice laughed a little, but there was a puzzled look in her eyes. "You are so queer!"
she said, "I never seem to understand you."

"Of course not," Claude answered; "for you
are a provincial saint, while I am a metropolitan
sinner. But come, let us do the martyr act.
Cross your hands behind your back ; cross them
so that I can tie them at the wrists; you gesticu-
late a great deal when your feelings are excited,

and you must not have the relief of gesture, for that is weak," and with his handkerchief he skillfully tied the wrists that at his bidding she had crossed.

" Now, shut your eyes, for they might move me to mercy, and I must not be merciful. Christians must be strong. Now, you may sit down, for it is only morally that I wish to torture you, not physically," and he led her to the seat where the day before she had sat to try the guitar. " Now," he went on, picking a rose and taking his seat beside her, but with averted face, "keep your eyes close shut, and think as I tell you. Do you remember how the roses grew in the Convent garden? Smelling this rose I have purposely bruised will make you remember better. This is a Christian rose; it smells so sweet because I have bruised it, and I bruised it for my pleasure and your pain. How sweet it is! almost as sweet as the Convent roses that used to peep through the grating of the gate to see the rippling waters of the gulf. Do you remember how blue the sky was, and how the white clouds were blown this way and that, and lying flat on your back you used to watch them and wonder where they came from and where they were going? And how above you the roses nodded in the wind, and the jasmine seemed to be sweeter than all of life together? How softly the Convent bell would ring for the Sisters to kneel and pray by the lighted altar, how the oleanders peeped in at the chapel windows, and the mock-

ing-birds sang all the live-long night. Do you
remember? And the water was so blue, and the
curving beach so white, and in the hot, still summer days the whole wide land seemed dead—still
and dead, save when a bee drowsed from one
flower to another, or a bird fluttered in the leaves.
Do you remember how sweet it all was, how
peaceful? Do not you long to go back—long
for the simple love and the peace and the rest?
But now it would not be the same, for now you
have listened to the hum of the world, you have
heard far off the cry of pain that has no answer,
the echo of problems that none can solve; you
have put your lips to the cup of life, and nothing
would seem the same. Nothing will ever seem
the same again, for you are waking from the
dream of childhood. Do you believe me?"
His voice ceased and he waited for a sign, but
no sign came, and he repeated, "Do you remember—do you believe me?" Still no answer, and
turning quickly, he found the great dark eyes
wide open, and fixed reproachfully on his averted
face.

"You really wanted to hurt me," she said. "I
thought you were in fun, but you were not, for
you turned your head away; you meant to hurt
me, but you could not bear to see the pain. Untie my hands!"

"Not yet," Claude answered, "not until you
have learned your lesson thoroughly. Yes, you
are right," he went on gravely; "I meant to hurt

you, and I would not look because I could not bear to hurt one whom I love. You believe that John loves you, and you say John thinks that you ought to bear pain—useless pain like enduring these flowers—in order to grow strong. You believe that the Mother loves you, and you say the Mother thinks that you ought to control yourself —useless self-control—in order to grow strong. Now, *I* think all this is foolish, but my opinion has no weight ; you have no faith in me because I say, 'Be happy.' This afternoon I have hurt you unnecessarily for two reasons—to show you how foolish such pain is—to show you that though I wish for you nothing but happiness in your life, though I am so frivolous as to insist that this kind of self-denial is nonsense; in spite of this radical difference between me and John— that I love you too, and hurt you, and hurt myself in order to prove it to you. I hurt myself a thousand times more than I hurt you. It hurt me to tie your little hands—to bring you in here, and every syllable of every word I said held for me a separate pain. I can never forgive myself, but if it is only by paining you that I can win your faith, I will leave no kind of pain untried."

The girl rose quickly. "You are hurting me now," she said, her voice trembling, " hurting me more than anyone ever did before. Untie my hands ; untie them and let me go!"

Claude obeyed her. "You will not believe

me?" he asked, " well, I will not insist," and following her into the study, he shut and locked the conservatory doors, and put the key into his pocket.

"What is that for?" asked Mrs. Van Kuyster, who at the same moment entered the study from the hall.

"The flowers give Beatrice the blues," Claude answered, "and she must not have the blues, she must have a tonic."

"I begged him not, Aunt Claudia."

"I agree with Claude," Mrs. Van Kuyster said. " I would shut up a hundred conservatories rather than be depressed."

"It is weak," the girl insisted.

"Be weak, then. Anything is better than useless misery. There will be plenty of pain in your life ; do not adopt gratuitous suffering. Above all, do not be morbid and introspective; it is not wholesome."

"But self-examination is a duty."

"Not always. Where one has a vital decision to make it may be very well, but very few decisions are vital. We generally use the first as a weapon with which to commit either mental or moral suicide, and of course no following decision can be vital. But the shutting up or opening of the conservatory can scarcely be vital."

"John says that every decision either weakens or strengthens one."

"Perhaps, as a rule, but not always. Some

people stand very near to nature, and are very direct, very simple, very true. They believe implicitly, they love intensely ; and falseness of any kind is a pain to them. A nature like this does not need the religious training as represented by confessions, and meditations, and penances—all made for the intricate and false ; it turns to the truth naturally, and needs only room to grow and to expand—needs happiness and a tonic."

Beatrice started. "But, indeed, Aunt Claudia," she exclaimed, "I was happy at the Convent—from morning until night I was happy, for I had nothing to do but to obey. But ever since I left, things have been growing confused to me. Whenever I asked the Mother : 'Is this right,' or 'wrong'? she always answered : 'Yes,' or 'no'; but when I asked John, he would say : 'What does your own judgment,' or 'your own conscience tell you?' *My* judgment and *my* conscience ? Why, just as soon as I act on a decision, I am sure it is wrong."

Mrs. Van Kuyster laughed. "Poor child," she said, "'the divine right of private judgment' is wasted on you. But now that you belong to us, you need not use it; we will only require you to do what is pleasant, and be happy."

Beatrice looked doubtful.

"She has no faith in us, mother," Claude said.

"Indeed I have, Aunt Claudia, only your orders are different again. The Mother used to say : 'Only right things are pleasant.' Then

John said : ' Do it because it is right, and remember that right things are seldom the pleasantest.' Now you say," looking from one to the other, "' Whatever is pleasant is right.   Be happy.' "

"And happiness seems wrong ? "

" From Beatrice's standpoint, happiness and self-indulgence are one," Claude said gravely, " and I, for one, shall treat her very differently."

" I would rather that you left me to Aunt Claudia," the girl answered, with a gentle dignity that was quite new, but that became her wonderfully.

" You have quarreled with Beatrice ? " Mrs. Van Kuyster asked that night when they were alone in the study.

" Beatrice thinks we have quarreled ; in reality, I am just waking her up. Her unconsciousness is very fresh and sweet in the abstract, but not as applied to me."

"And you locked the conservatory to make her feel your power ? "   With an amused smile.

" No, I locked it because she was using it as a penance, compelling herself to endure the homesickness which the flowers produced. It was bad for her health, and I thought a little counter-irritant in the shape of anger would be wholesome. Her Roman Catholic ancestry comes out very strong in her ; she absolutely needs laws and infallibility ; before long I will be her Pope."

Mrs. Van Kuyster shook her head.   " Her

belief has been so ground into her," she said,
"that unless you adopt it, you will never wear
the triple crown of her respect, her faith, her
love."

"Well said!" and Claude bowed. "And I
would rather talk to you, as you show yourself
now, than to anyone I know; nevertheless, you
will see me Beatrice's Pope."

"You may make her love you," Mrs. Van
Kuyster said; "you may even lead her aside
from her beliefs; but the moment she discovers
that she has wandered, she will turn back, and
you will not be able to hold her. Religion is in
that girl's flesh and blood, and it is her Roman
Catholic and Protestant heredity that are at war;
one led by John, the other by the Mother; but
Protestantism is too free for her, and I think that
it would have been happier to leave her a little
nun in her beloved Convent."

Claude threw away his cigar and clasped his
hands behind his head. "What an awful lack of
principle and conviction your words show!" he
said. "John would preach you a sermon on the
wickedness of leaving a person in error in order
to leave him in peace. You are very clever," he
went on, "and read your fellows easily; but in
reading other women you leave out the greatest
factor in their lives; the factor that can lead
them aside from duty, faith, principle—everything; this greatest factor is love, and you
leave it out because it has had no play in your

life, my dear. Once win Beatrice's love, and she would die for one."

"I knew her father," Mrs. Van Kuyster said; "he would die for a friend, but he would not so much as entertain a wrong thought; no, not if it would save the life of the creature he loved best on earth."

"And you think Beatrice like him? Maybe, but with this difference; she is a woman, and love to a man and to a woman is as different as black and white. This is where you fail to make allowances for your own sex. You are reasonable, logical, magnanimous—the only magnanimous woman I have never known."

"Thanks."

"But all these qualities," Claude went on, "limit your understanding of your own sex. They do not limit your criticism, mind you, but they do limit your sympathy."

" Only for women who lack balance."

Claude laughed. " I rather think that takes in the whole sex," he said. " I grant you that a man always wants his wife to be reasonable and balanced, but, when he is in love, he wants quite another creature to that. The old pattern for women—the vine clinging to the oak—seems to be going out of fashion, but it is not in reality. It is the light weights who get married, or the women who for the time being pretend to be light weights. The women who love dress and luxury, who seem to have wistful eyes and appealing ways,

these win in the world ; while the women who
spend themselves on good works—on the higher
education—who go in for dress reform, and common sense, and spring-heels, and metaphysics,
they—well," drawing a long breath, " they are
allowed to spend their time that way."

Mrs. Van Kuyster laughed.

" One wants the woman one is in love with,"
Claude went on, " to be—— "

" A fool for the time being," Mrs. Van Kuyster
struck in, " but to recover her senses later on ; you
want her to revolve around you, to think your
thoughts, believe in your vagaries, kneel down
before your selfishness, and be a door-mat to your
digestion."

" Exactly ! " Claude answered. " You put it
beautifully ; that 'door-mat to the digestion ' is
really fine, and that belief in one's vagaries is
good too. A man can meet plenty of clever
women in society—the spring-heeled, high think-
ers, for instance ; but at home he wants a wife on
whom he can rest his mind, or a wife who is clever
enough to be everything at once, a wife like—— "
he paused.

" Whom ? " Mrs. Van Kuyster asked quickly.

" Marjorie," Claude answered. " She would make
an ideal wife : she could play the fool, being sensible all the while ; she could make one thoroughly
comfortable, and would always take life from the
calm, high ground of expediency."

Mrs. Van Kuyster looked at him gravely. " I

have often thought that you and Marjorie were made for each other," she said; "she knows the world and you, thoroughly; she is even-tempered and generous; she has her vagaries under perfect control, and has a clear appreciation of yours; she is what you call 'clubable;' she would allow your life to flow always as peacefully as it does now."

"It is all true," Claude said, then was silent, looking into the fire.

"She has money," Mrs. Van Kuyster went on, "and a fine constitution——"

Claude sprang up. "She may have it all—all—all!" he said, bringing his fist down on the table with a heavy thud, "but I *love* Beatrice—unreasonable—delicate—prejudiced—illogical—conscience-ridden—it does not matter; I love her with that love you do not understand—love her, if that love leads me into a seven-times-heated furnace! Good-night! Call me fool if you like!" and he left the room, followed by Mrs. Van Kuyster's light laugh.

The love she did not understand! and she put her hands over her face.

XIII.

"Young Love lies dreaming ;
But who shall tell the dream ?

.   .   .   .   .

He sees the beauty
Sun hath not looked upon,
And tastes the fountain
Unutterably deep."

THE next morning Beatrice missed the rose
that every day, since the opening of the
conservatory, she had found beside her plate.   It
had become a habit to fasten this rose in her
dress, and she looked for it almost unconsciously.
No one seemed to observe her after the first
greetings, and Claude and John went on with
their talk as if no interruption had occurred.

"Grant to humanity all it wants," Claude was
saying, "let all be clothed—fed—all with leisure,
and what would be the point of life?   We should
return to the condition of brutes, and vegetate.
I consider the inequalities of life, with all their
attendant turmoil and confusion, as boons to the
human race.   I consider it a great good that
charity has come down from its high moral plane
to be called a science.   Once let humanity agree
that it is a science, and there will be no end to
the refinements it will undergo—to the misery it

will not touch—to the strife it will arouse. It will look on itself as the Science of Humanity—the science that is to take the place of theology, and will serve as an exciting stimulus and problem to several generations."

"From your standpoint," John answered, "I confess that the whole thing does look rather useless. I cannot understand how you live."

Claude shrugged his shoulders. "As to that," he said, "life holds many things to be enjoyed, and there are interesting experiments and discoveries yet to be made, and many problems yet to be hammered at. I was only expressing my unwillingness to have the socialistic millennium come in my day. I was in fear that the time-old fact that 'men must work, and women must weep' would become extinct. Weeping and working make a variety—for the observer."

"As much as you seem to appreciate both," John said, "you do not seem to have done either."

"Indeed, not, and if I keep my senses I never will. My theory is that everybody's duty is to be happy, and, as far as it is consistent with his own welfare, to make others happy. The perfect man will find his happiness in the happiness which he produces. I know what you would say," holding up his hand to John; "' he that loseth his life'—I know it is the best we can do; still, there is another side. Suppose every man should do nothing but devote himself to his neighbor—what an awful bore it would be to the neighbor. Even the little I have seen of modern scientific charity has shown me how the poor are harried by their would-be helpers. Many are happier when they are dirty, and enjoy the excitement of stealing a meal."

John laughed. "A thousand years ago," he said, "our ancestors enjoyed raiding on their neighbors, but it would be no pleasure to you to steal Mrs. Slater's best silver teapot! Just this difference, we hope to make in the descendant of the present thief. Restrain him—force his children into a purer environment, his grandchildren will be purer, and in a thousand years they may even blossom into a Claude Van Kuyster!"

"Noble ambition!" Claude cried. "I will put on my dress suit and visit the police stations —I will say ' my brothers, cease from your evil ways, and in a thousand years you may be as I am!' Do you think they would cease?"

"No," Mrs. Van Kuyster answered; "it would be another case of pearls and swine. Show them some stoker who has made millions in oil, and is in congress—wears diamonds and broadcloth, and doubtful linen—he would seem the highest to them."

"My dear mother, you are charming! I am pearls, Beatrice; I must be handled gently and dusted with a rose-leaf."

"I have no rose-leaf this morning," Beatrice answered.

"Do you want one?" Claude asked so quickly

that it was revealed to Beatrice that the flower had been banished purposely.

"No," she answered, "you do not look dusty now."

Mrs. Van Kuyster laughed; John looked from one to the other, not understanding the situation, and Claude explained. "The flowers depress Beatrice, and I have had them banished; but she can have them again whenever she wants them."

"Of course she wants them restored immediately, do you not, Beatrice?" John asked quickly·

"Of course. I begged Claude not to shut the conservatory."

"Where do you go to-day, John?" Mrs. Van Kuyster interrupted.

"I am going on a tour of investigation. I shall cover my clericals with an ulster, and strive to see the real thing. I wonder if Claude will go with me. Will you?"

"Slumming? My dear Jack, impossible! Think of how it would unfit me for living up to the duty of being serenely happy? At best I could only go in a close carriage with all the glasses up, and all the curtains down, and lots of cologne. Any other method would wreck me!"

"Are you in earnest?" and John looked puzzled.

"Of course I am. I do not believe in slumming. I will build things, and support schemes; but to investigate the private residences of 'rounders' and barrel-pickers would seem to me indeli-

cate. You are different, it is a part of your profession."

"I will not be at home to lunch, Aunt Claudia,"
John said, and turned away. Then Mrs. Van
Kuyster followed Claude into the study, and
Beatrice went up to what might be called her
schoolroom.

It was a back room, cheerfully furnished and
bright with light from two large windows. The
outlook was not bad, for, it being a rich neighbor-
hood, the little courtyards were models of neat-
ness. One neighbor, whose lowest story pro-
jected back some twenty feet, had railed in the
roof, and every day two children and two dogs
were turned out there to play. It seemed pitiful to Beatrice, and yet they looked healthy and
happy. The children were in their "pen"
this morning, running about with the dogs, and
screaming with laughter. What would they think,
Beatrice mused, if they could be turned out into
the Convent garden ! Claude always spoke of her
youth as an imprisonment, yet how much freer
than that of these children. The children had
brought out their dolls now, numbers of them, and
were busy seating them on the stone coping with
their backs to the iron railing ; once more the
window was pushed open, and the maid put
out two doll carriages, and the children trun-
dled their dolls one by one round the inclosure. "How stupid!" Beatrice thought. "Poor
children !"

There was a tap at the door, and Claude entered.

"Idling?" he said; "what will Miss Grigsby say?" Beatrice was surprised: he had only been in her schoolroom once, on the day of installation, and she wondered a little. He came and stood beside her.

"Those children," she said, " I am so sorry for them. I am wondering how long they will play in that stupid way. I had only one doll," she went on; "so had Antoinette and Marie; droll dolls, Sister Térèse made them; but they had beds of rose-leaves, and swung in jasmine vines."

"See!" said Claude, "they are changing their play; reproducing their own nurses," as the little girls began shaking and slapping the dolls, and reseating them violently on the stone ledge.

"Poor things," Beatrice answered; "but what now?"

The children seemed at a loss for the moment, then stood talking earnestly.

"Some mischief," Claude said, "see how they watch. Ah!" as the smallest girl, taking hold of a doll, pushed it through the railings. "Little villains! how they enjoy it."

One after another the dolls were hurled to destruction; hurriedly, and with furtive watchings of the nursery windows. But interruption came from below. A footman ran out in the paved court and remonstrated; this only excited them the more, for the larger girl began to hurl them

over the railing. Then up went the windows
and the maids dashed out on the culprits, seizing
them and shaking them violently.

"See!" said Beatrice, "that is just the way
they punished their dolls; and they have not a
doll left. I wish I knew them."

"You shall," Claude answered. "We will
take them to drive, and get them a lot more dolls
to reward them for their originality. I am glad
they have had such a good murderous time.
But how are the lessons?" turning from the
window. "I came up to help you."

"It is German to-day, and I know so little that
it is hard."

"Let me see your task," and Claude drew a
chair to the table.

"A little poem which I have memorized,"
finding a place in her book. "I have picked out
all the words of it, still I cannot express it in
English. I think the person who wrote it must
have been unhappy. It is about a lonely fir
tree shut up in snow and ice, that dreams of a
lonely palm tree burning up in the desert sands.
It makes me feel lonely too."

"Heine," Claude said. "Yes, that poem
evades English. I often think it, but I think it
in German."

"I am so glad," and Beatrice looked relieved.
"I thought it was my stupidity, I am so often
stupid. I do not think I understood you this
morning. You seemed to be twisting right things

wrong. You said it was a duty to be happy, and yet, it would be a pity if people could stop working and weeping, for there would be nothing left to do. Don't you *know* that as long as people are wicked there will be trouble and want?"

"So the Mother taught you that people are poor because they are sinful? I know some good people who are poor."

"That is because other people are wicked. Besides, good people are contented, and content. ment is wealth."

"The Mother is a logician"—and Claude looked amused. "Then the way to rectify the ills of life is to make people good. Then what will be left us to do?"

"To grow better."

"I see. Good—better—best."

"Yes. Best is God."

"And when we reach the region of Best?"

The girl looked startled. "Of course we shall be satisfied," she said. "Perfectly satisfied."

"And if you loved one who had different ideas of right from yours," Claude went on, "what would you do?"

"I would try to persuade him to my views. If I could not, I would go away and leave him."

"But suppose he convinced you that his way was best?"

Beatrice was silent, looking out of the window. "Something always tells us 'do this,' or 'do that,'" she said at last, turning her face to his, "and if we obey we will be right. And if you tried to persuade me against that," she went on, innocently transferring his abstract proposition of "someone she loved" to himself, "I would go away and leave you."

"Leave me to grow worse and worse?"

"You could come with me and be better."

"But if I were so—what shall I say—so——"

"Obstinate."

Claude laughed. "So obstinate, then, as not to follow, would you still leave me?"

"Yes."

"If you loved me—loved me better than John or the mother?"

"Yes."

"Then you would be a hard-hearted little monster!"

"Still, I would have to go, for you are so clever that you would make me agree with you; so I would go."

"Might I not be 'righter' than John or the mother? Am I not as well educated, have I not as much sense, have I not seen more of the world? Why may not I be right and they wrong?"

"It seems to me that you laugh at everything," Beatrice answered. "Nothing seems important; you go by what is pleasant, and one thing seems as right as another. But John believes things. His eyes light up, and he looks strong and earnest to go out and face the world and die like the saints and martyrs!" her own dreamy eyes catching fire as she spoke.

"And I," Claude said, while the color crept up his face—"I am like the Roman youths who watched the bloody shows and turned a thumb down when the victim was to die? You think life is a show to me, and that I could turn the wild beasts of Poverty and Sin out on helpless humanity—and I could laugh, and be almost too lazy to turn my thumb down. Is it so?"

He paused, but the girl, drawing idly, did not look up.

"And you would have me spring down into the arena like the young monk and be torn to pieces?"

"But he stopped the awful shows, St. Telemachus did," she answered eagerly. "He was grand!"

"The wrong only changed its form," Claude went on. "The brute in humanity had to come out, and Christian persecutions took the place of the games. I think it had been better to let the brutality of the 'elect' come out in shows. But why not have life bright and happy, why insist upon being tragic and solemn—and why need I sit here and preach to you?"

"I should like to be gay and happy," Beatrice said, "but we ought to live to be good and to grow better."

"And I do not ask you to do anything else,"

Claude answered gently, putting his hand on hers to stop her idle drawing. "You have been through a great deal lately that is trying, and I only want to turn your mind away from sad things. I am not like John and never can be, any more than a butterfly can be like a lion ; and the butterfly cannot help brushing the flowers lightly with its wings—cannot help enjoying the sunshine and the sweet air. The butterfly could not crush the flowers as the lion can, even if it wanted to—crush them down to death as he makes his way into the dark jungles of life. And the butterfly cannot help your seeming a flower to be cared for tenderly —kept in the full sunshine and sheltered from the storm, and even from the lion's paw. The butterfly will do his best to keep the flower from the lion, but if the flower insists on coming to destruction in the pathway of the lion—the butterfly can only suffer. Isn't that a nice little parable?"

Beatrice laughed. "You are so clever," she said. "But it seems so useless to be only a flower."

"Did you think all these dismal thoughts when you used to watch the jackdaws stealing figs?"

"No," drawing her hand from under his in order to turn about curiously his cuff-button that struck her fancy. "No, I used not to think anything in those days. I did not know how to think until father grew ill, and I used to fan him and listen while he talked to John. And after Aunt

Claudia came, I stopped thinking again until you and John began to discuss things."

" And do you like to think?"

"I do not know," lifting her face to look out of the window, and resting her hand on Claude's. "I do not really know."

Claude rose quickly. "*I* know," he said, putting his hands into his pockets. " I know that you were meant to be a flower ; that your mission in life is to make people happy, and you must fulfill it. It seems to me that this is a high mission, and whenever you consent to be a flower and begin the serious work of making things bright and beautiful for me and John, we will tune the guitar and open the conservatory." And nodding gayly, he left the room.

XIV.

"Let us alone.   Time driveth onward fast,
And in a little while our lips are dumb.
Let us alone.   What is it that will last?
All things are taken from us and become
Portions and parcels of the dreadful Past.
Let us alone.   What pleasure can we have
To war with evil?   Is there any peace
In ever climbing up the climbing wave?"

MARJORIE came to dinner that day, sending
a note beforehand to say that she wanted to
escape a bore. "I am fleeing a philanthropic
terror," she said as they took their seats at table.
"I can never bring myself to believe in them
thoroughly, because I have the misfortune to be
a born skeptic. I am harmless," smiling at Beatrice, who looked startled, "I only mean that I
have the skeptical temperament. My Holy Grail
has been the '*ding an sich,*' which I translate
Reality, with a very big R."

"And you do not find it?"

"Not so far. I have 'carved the casques of
men' only to find them empty, and I have 'thrust
sure' at windmills until that now I am tempted
to pitch my tent in the desert of Agnosticism and
sink into Nirvana."

"Marjie, Marjie, what ails you!"

"Mr. Paget inspires me. He turns me into an Ancient Mariner, and makes me confess my sins. He is a glimpse of reality."

"My dear Jack," Claude said, "you had better escape at once. Think of being called '*ding an sich*' and idealized into a kind of Holy Grail. What an awful run you'll have for it."

"I have been after the '*ding an sich*' myself," John answered.

"Yes, by the way, your slumming?"

Waters appeared with a card on his waiter. "The gentleman says he will wait."

"Why, it is Martin Kinsey!"

Marjorie sank back. "It is from him I me hiding," she whispered.

"His sister would faint at the thought of his rushing in on us at this hour," Claude said. "And I will bring him in, mother; we will be here for ages yet."

"So glad to see you," Mrs. Van Kuyster said, shaking hands with the newcomer, "so nice of you to be so sociable."

"Thanks! You are awfully kind. I have so little time, and hearing Miss Van Kuyster was here, I was glad to catch you together."

"And I am glad that you should meet my brother Mr. Paget," Claude said. "He is a slummer, too."

"Indeed!" adjusting his eye-glasses and fixing his eager eyes on John, while his words tripped over each other with nervous quickness. "You are interested in charities, Mr. Paget?"

"I am in orders."

"Quite so—quite so! I am not in orders, not at all; but all that sort of thing is very near to me. But the clergy go in for that sort of thing; they ought to."

"And they do," John said; "I have been looking into the work to-day. In the provinces we read a great deal about the degraded poor in the cities, and the little done for them."

"Quite so, quite naturally so!" Mr. Kinsey interrupted eagerly, "quite naturally so, and you saw it to-day."

"From my cursory view, I almost think that too much is done in the matter of amelioration."

"Bravo!" cried Claude.

"You astonish me!" And Mr. Kinsey laid down his knife and fork.

"Strange as it may seem, Kinsey, I have looked into this thing myself," Claude said, "and was saying, not long ago, that it is fortunate that charity is leaving the region of the heart, and going to the head—is become a science."

"But I have gone into these things very carefully," Kinsey said. "I belong to a number of societies—the Audubon, and the Cruelty to Animals—and I am on several committees on lunatic asylums and station houses and many other things; and I assure you that not half enough is done."

"Grant all that," John answered. "I meant that to ameliorate is to prevent the eradicating that ought to take place."

" I have a cousin," Claude said, with a twinkle in his eyes, while the color crept up Beatrice's face, "who declares that the only cure for poverty and suffering is to make people good."

"And your cousin is quite right, whoever your cousin may be," John answered quickly. "A man, a gentleman, who lives down in those awful haunts, said to me to-day that the dishonesty of property holders and builders made the slums. I asked him why he did not 'stump' the country against these people; he answered that to do that would be to 'stump' the country against its whole corporate self. That the whole nation would have first to be lifted into a cleaner moral atmosphere. That as long as all offices could be bought and sold, money would be the greatest power in the land, and builders and property owners would be allowed to manufacture slums, would be *encouraged* to manufacture slums; for during the elections the power of the slums is immense, and their votes cheap."

" His assertion is rather sweeping," Kinsey said, more nervously than ever; "some property owners are very conscientious indeed, Mr. Paget. But you cannot know the impossibility of keeping houses for such people in repair."

" It is not impossible to prevent subletting and overcrowding," John suggested. "A man who owns property there ought to make it his life's work."

"Mr. Kinsey does a quantity of that sort of work," Margie said.

"Ah, thank you, Miss Van Kuyster, but really my work is all for helpless creatures—birds and beasts and lunatics and prisoners."

"It seems to me," said John, "that it would be a 'saving of time and money to go to work and destroy some of the causes of lunacy and vice. Wipe out the places where your lunatics and prisoners are manufactured. The destruction of your tenements would lessen your societies immensely."

"Is not that a rather large proposition?" Claude asked. "And as your friend says, it cannot be, as long as the city government, and the State government, and the national government are bought and sold. The only way would be the individual reform of landlords."

"Exactly."

"You will have to begin with us, then," Mrs. Van Kuyster said, laughing. "The Van Kuysters own a great deal of that sort of property. I used sometimes to write for Mr. Van Kuyster, and I know what those tenement people endure. They are slaves to high rents and 'sweater's wages.'"

"You have gone into the subject?" John asked.

"Yes, and have let it be. I remembered how

that in the South, when one master would free his slaves—some did it—it made all conditions worse; made slaves discontented, and, as a consequence, masters severe. A solitary slum iconoclast would have the same effect."

"Quite so," Martin Kinsey agreed quickly. "Turn the poor things out, and they could only crowd into the next tenement. More crowding, you see; and to stop their taking boarders would be to stop a source of income."

"Shoot the sweaters," John suggested quietly, "and lower the rents; then they would not need such large incomes."

"To lower rents is simply to insure overcrowding," Mrs. Van Kuyster answered. "It must be a concerted movement."

"And as landlords will not concert, and the state cannot destroy under the existing system," Marjorie summed up, "the only thing left to do is to join Mr. Kinsey's societies to soothe the lunatic, cheer the prisoner, and enjoy the punishment of keepers."

"It seems an awful conclusion," John said slowly.

"My dear Jack," and Claude held his wineglass up to the light, "you take things too desperately; you turn everything into a life-and-death problem. You, and all other philanthropists go on the supposition that these creatures and other beasts and birds suffer as we would suffer under like conditions. They do not because they cannot. For generations I, for instance, have lived a satin-lined life; my whole mind and body are adjusted to a satin-lined life. A loosely rolled umbrella is a pain—dust, a great trouble. I cannot even drive through lower New York to the docks without many shocks to my whole nervous system. A railway station is an abomination. I send my man ahead to buy tickets and bestow my luggage; I rush through the station and take my seat with my back, as far as possible, to my fellow-travelers. You cannot persuade me that a low-caste piece of humanity, or a horse, suffers all these delicate agonies, or requires this same satin-lined environment? My chief grievance is that I do not own enough tenements to possess myself of a private car."

"Do you really own tenements?" John asked.

"No, not really. The governor settled the tenement property on mother; mine is in shops and uptown houses."

"My father left me slaves; my husband left me tenements," Mrs. Van Kuyster said.

"I would not mind either," Marjorie answered. "Your slaves were freed. Probably the government, when sufficiently centralized, will pull down your tenements. Meanwhile, take time by the forelock, and invest the proceeds in something else. That is what you should have done in the case of the darkies."

"My husband *did* sell my slaves," and Mrs.

Van Kuyster smiled; "the price was invested in *uptown* tenements."

"Hard luck for a conscientious woman with cultivated tastes and 'flesh-pot blood,'" Claude said, laughing. "I am almost as sorry for you as for Kinsey, here; he is a born philanthropist, and yet owns tenements."

"My grandfather owned slaves too," Kinsey said hesitatingly.

"A Southern man?"

"No; oh, no! Massachusetts."

"So? then you burnt witches also," and Marjorie laughed. "You have more than your share of heredity, I think; a witch-burner, a slave-owner, and a tenement landlord; dreadful!"

Kinsey looked at her doubtfully. "It is really very bad," he said earnestly. "Our ancestors were queer."

"Very queer, to state it gently;" and Marjorie followed Mrs. Van Kuyster and Beatrice from the dining room.

"What are you going to do with Martin Kinsey?" Mrs. Van Kuyster asked, as she and Marjorie stood near the drawing room fire, Beatrice having gone into the study.

"Nothing," Marjorie answered.

"I was sorry for him during the tenement discussion," Mrs. Van Kuyster went on, "and amused when John asked if I had studied the subject. Mr. Van Kuyster used to collect the statistics for my benefit, and focus them and the ills of sla-

very for me ; then left the property so that I cannot possibly sell it."

"Then you are not responsible," Marjorie
said gently.

Mrs. Van Kuyster looked amused.

"You are sorry for me?" she asked. "Do you
suppose I am sensitive still? It would not be
possible. I have sounded so many depths that
I have reached the point where life seems a farce.
I assure you that I am very comfortable. My
teeth are sound, my digestion good, and I sleep
like a top. What more can anyone ask?"

XV.

"What of the end, Pandora ?   Was it thine,
The deed that set the fiery pinions free ?

. . . . .

What of the end ?   These beat their wings at will,
The ill-born things, the good things turned to ill—
  Powers of the impassioned hours prohibited.
Aye, clench the casket now ! Whither they go
Thou mayst not dare to think ; nor canst thou know
  If Hope, still pent there, be alive or dead."

THE gentlemen came in presently, and Claude missed Beatrice. He had to wait before going in search of her, however, and during that time she appeared. She pushed aside the *portière* and looked in doubtfully, and Claude waited to see what she would do—to whom she would come.

Martin Kinsey, seated near Mrs. Van Kuyster, was talking rapidly. John, leaning on the mantelpiece, was listening to Marjorie ; Claude was standing there too. At the first movement of the curtain, Marjorie knew that Claude's attention was gone, and instantly became more interested in him than in her own words. She still talked, however, and John still listened.

Presently Beatrice came forward, making directly for Claude. Marjorie's voice ceased, and John turned to see the cause.

"Are you very busy?" Beatrice asked, looking up at Claude.

"My dear child, how can you ask? Is not Marjie talking? Still, what is it?"

And Marjorie thought, "How well he does it!" for she had caught the flash of triumph in his eyes when the girl came to him.

"An English composition," Beatrice answered. "I know that I ought not to interrupt you, but I cannot even begin it."

"And the subject?"

"Modern Civilization."

The trio laughed.

"How simple," Marjie said. "Suppose we write it turn about? Miss Grigsby will think that she has unearthed a genius. Let us go to the study."

"No," Claude answered. "That will not help Beatrice in the least. You stay here and empty your vials of conversation on Jack; I can reduce modern civilization to a pulp in a few minutes, not to speak of Miss Grigsby."

John watched them go with a look of surprise in his eyes, and Marjie watched him. "Is he beginning to understand?" she wondered. But his expression had not changed when again he spoke to her.

"How kind Claude is to Beatrice," he said. "She seems to turn to him quite naturally."

"Do you think it hardship to be kind to a pretty girl?"

"A composition is always dull work."

"Would you have found it dull if Beatrice had come to you?"

"No; but then I love the child."

For a moment Marjie was speechless, then she went on:

"Claude is very fond of Beatrice too."

"*Fond* of her? He scarcely knows her."

"If Claude takes a fancy, he cannot be kept at a distance. If he should meet and like the Angel Gabriel, he would make the angel his friend in fifteen minutes."

"What you say is quite true," John answered, laughing. "I am glad he likes Beatrice; he seems nearer her age than I can feel myself to be. I think of her always as a child, and yet, she is seventeen. Her mother married at sixteen."

"Was the mother as beautiful as Beatrice?"

"Is Beatrice beautiful?"

"Are you blind?"

"When you live with a person always, you forget looks."

"You should go to Washington and Boston to see the sights; a fortnight would do it comfortably, even with your bad eyes."

"We were speaking of Beatrice."

"We were speaking of blindness."

John looked at her thoughtfully. "You are trying to tell me something," he said simply, "and I am too dull to see. I am awfully stupid sometimes."

"Yes, you are," promptly. "Go to Washington, Boston, and Philadelphia, if you like ; then come back, and you will be able to take a new view of us. There is nothing like absence for teaching one the value of things."

"You think I do not value my friends enough?"

" In bulk, yes; I mean relative values. Some one of us must be more necessary to you than some other of us. Away, you will be able to grade us; at present we are in some confusion. Your work stands first."

" As it shall do always."

" Perhaps."

" I will admit no doubt."

"Grant work the first place, then ; after work comes Claude ?"

" Yes."

" Then your aunt? "

" Yes."

"Then Beatrice and I in the background. Poor little Beatrice ! to think of that beautiful nose being broken, not to speak of her heart."

"You go too fast ; I did not grant this last proposition. Beatrice goes without saying."

" Ahead of your work ?"

" I feel her my most sacred duty."

" A duty ?"

"Of course : she has no one in the world but me."

"Cousin Claudia and Claude."

" Oh, that is temporary ! She belongs to me."

" Then you should take charge of her education."

John looked at her intently, a slow fire seeming to catch in his eyes. He moved away abruptly, upsetting with his elbow a little vase that stood on the mantelpiece. Marjorie caught it, with an exclamation that made him face about again.

"A most valuable bit of porcelain!" she said. "I have saved it. I shall demand it of cousin—mine by right of salvage."

"I shall add my entreaties," John answered, "and we will call it the reward of divination."

"And are you glad to have eaten of the tree of knowledge?"

"No; you have set my life in battle array against me. At least, so it seems to me now." He paused, looking down into the fire. "So it *is !* " raising his eyes to hers with a pain-stricken look in them—"So it is !"

In the study, Beatrice was working faithfully; somewhat mystified, but going on obediently, this being her only hope of getting her task done.

"In the beginning there was but one notion, self-preservation—but one determining quality, strength," Claude dictated, walking up and down with his hands behind him and a set look on his face that seemed out of all proportion to the work of the moment. " The strongest were best

able to survive—to seize and to keep. They inspired in their fellows fear and awe; from this
they became rulers—chiefs; after death were
deified. These strong ones demanded a certain
behavior from their fellows: this demand was
the beginning of law. The behavior was the
beginning of manners and customs."

Beatrice looked up. "Is this really true,
Claude?"

"Of course, dear; does it not seem perfectly
simple and reasonable? The awe these chiefs
inspired was the beginning of religion."

"But, God, Claude?"

"How do you think of God?"

"As my Father in heaven."

"Why do you think of God as a person, dear?"

"The Mother said it was a mystery. That
God said, 'Let us make man in our own image,'
so we cannot think of anything grander than
man. That is what she taught us."

"So in the beginning they deified man?"

"The Mother said that the Incarnation lifted
humanity up. From the beginning the spirit of
God was in man—the breath of life—and only
man himself can destroy the divinity within him,
and become a brute. You say man was deified.
I do not know just where the wrong comes in,
but you seem to lower God."

"While the Mother elevated humanity? Then
she is a greater civilizer than I am. Now, slavery
was an instrument for taming barbarous man.

The *Zeit-Geist* is the great regulator of manners, customs, laws, and creeds. The *Zeit-Geist* is the Time-Spirit," he added, in answer to a puzzled look from Beatrice. "It sweeps toys away from children and tribes—it sweeps trammels away from men and nations. In one age Might rules —in another Right must rule. We are in a transition state; we have neither Might nor Right, and the world knows not where to turn, for the false and the true seem to be inextricably mixed. This mixture can scarcely be called civilization, but it is modern without a doubt. Man is confused because his mental self has developed more rapidly than his moral self. Intellectual teachers have but one cry—' Advance, explore!' Ecclesiastical teachers have but one cry 'Walk in the old paths!' The old paths have become ditches like the path of the mill-horse about the mill. The wind of truth is blowing the dust from the road of progress into the ditches of the old path, and the *Zeit-Geist* is leveling them over. Soon the moral nature will be set free to progress; then Might, that is, Customs and Creeds, will be packed out of sight into the old path, and Right, because it is Right, will rule the world."

"Are the creeds wrong?" looking up with consternation in her eyes.

"The creeds are mighty," Claude answered. "See what Miss Grigsby will say," then he sat down beside her. Beatrice read the remarkable production, and Claude, reading it along

with her, showed her where a word was mis-
spelled.

"The Mother would be shocked, that of all
words you should not know ecclesiastical!"

"I am mortified," Beatrice said slowly, while
the blood stole up in her face. Claude watched
the changing color on the cheek so near his eyes
—a tide of tint, not color; up to the blue-veined
temples—up under the shadow of the drooped
lashes—down the soft curve of the throat it crept.
His hand, that lay on the back of Beatrice's chair,
closed on the top round with a sudden grip that
jarred her slightly. She looked up.

"I was only joking about the spelling," he said.
A simple speech to make his voice so breathless.
"You have been most carefully taught—drilled,
in fact."

She did not answer. Her eyes were fastened
on his wistfully, questioningly, like the eyes of a
child. His expression puzzled her. He looked
away, moving idly the pens and pencils that lay
on the table. He must not make a fool of himself and terrify her, he must waken her gradually.
He took up her hand that still held a pen—took
it up quite carelessly and looked at it.

"The hand of a musician," he said; "long,
slender fingers. Do you believe in palmistry?"

"Old Angela did," the girl answered, "and
she would never tell me what she saw in mine."

Claude turned her hand over, while the pen
dropped with a little clatter. "A very nervous

hand," he said, "and you have a very hard time introspectively. You are an idealist—and a mystic—and an æsthete, and all the rest of it—and—the life line is neither deep nor long—lucky girl! It is all nonsense, dear," raising her hand to his lips—"You have got a very nice little hand, built on purpose to make music, and gather flowers, and pull open purse-strings; and as far as I have the ordering of said hands, they shall never do anything else. What do you think?"

"Very nice, but rather useless."

"Think of the good you can do when you pull open the purses."

"I have no purses."

"My dear child, all our purses are yours! Besides," he added mendaciously, as he saw the color spring to the girl's face, "from your mother you have a little surplus of your own. Have you no check-book? John turned over everything of yours to the mater as your guardian, and as I am her business manager, I must see to this. You must have a bill at a book shop, a confectioner's, a florist's, and anywhere else you like. We will institute them to-morrow; then there will be some point to your walks with your very respectable woman Billings."

"And the tenement people they were talking about at dinner," Beatrice went on, her eyes shining; "there must be children there; might I give them things?"

"Of course, dear; we will make a pilgrimage

to all the nurseries, and orphanages, and children's homes and hospitals, and have a good time. Once you are interested, you will grow well and strong, and not be homesick any more; then we can open the conservatory, and tune the guitar."

"Do it now, Claude," laying her hand on his impulsively. "I am happy now—I am not homesick!"

"I am afraid; I am an arrant coward about people looking sad."

"Open it!" rising and moving toward the closed doors, "open it now. Please, Claude!"

Claude hesitated a moment, then followed her. "Will you promise me," he said, standing between her and the doors, "promise to tell me if it makes you homesick?"

"Yes."

"Promise to hunt me up whenever you feel blue?"

"Yes."

"Promise to come to me for everything you want?".

"Yes."

"To look on me as your Father Confessor and business manager?"

"Yes."

"Promise, as you hope to save your little soul?"

"Yes."

He stood looking down on her a moment, then

reaching the key from a bracket near at hand, he opened the doors. A wave of warm, sweet air—and a dim vision of moveless flowers.

"In a garden they would be nodding," the girl said. "Here they stand still and dream like the pine tree that dreamed of the palm. Does everything dream and long, Claude?" Then she turned quickly away.

"Homesick?" Claude asked, stopping her with a hand on the shoulder.

"Only a moment. Don't shut it up—can't you understand? I cannot explain. I call it homesickness because I know no better name; but I have felt it at home when the moon would rise over the water, and the waves reached longingly up the land. I have felt it because a guitar was thrumming in the street—because the mourning doves were cooing in the Convent garden. It seems to me that these flowers must be longing for the flowers that are blooming and blowing wherever it is warm and sweet. They are all Southern flowers. Don't you know how tears come into your eyes because you are happy?"

"I will not shut it," Claude said, and wondered how much longer he could keep up this "brotherly business." "You may have your little tearful joys as often as you like," he went on, "if you will promise to take your tonic, and to exercise faithfully. Tell me what you are thinking now; something unflattering, I am sure."

"You are a puzzle; you seem to have hard spots in you. I——"

"I did not think you would call me lumpy!"

"Of course I expressed it badly, but something seems missing in you. You can put a wall behind your eyes, as it were, and a slab over your feelings, and yet, you are always reasonable."

"It is reasonable, but unfeeling to mix tonics and tears. I agree with you entirely; but an excess of feeling is unwholesome and uncivilized ; it shows a great lack of culture, and a surplus of liver."

"But *you* have feelings."

"A headache now and then, a little fury for an ill-cut glove."

"I am not so silly as you think. More than once I have seen your heart in your eyes."

"*My heart in my eyes!* My child, do you know how the heart looks? It is large, and round, and red!"

"Please be in earnest. If you ridicule me like this I cannot keep all my promises. I cannot confess if you laugh at me."

"You are quite right; ridicule is death, and not for several universes would I murder one of your little thoughts or fancies. But I should like to make you so happy that you would not always see 'the tears in mortal things,' but sometimes the smiles."

"You do make me happy," looking up in a way that made Claude put his hands behind him, and long for some interruption from the outer world. "You are kinder to me, more thoughtful of me than anybody has ever been. You are constantly arranging pleasures for me. It does not seem to me that you can have time to think of anything else."

"I do not."

"I was afraid so. Please leave me alone. It worries me to think what a trouble I am. I assure you that I am not accustomed to so much spoiling, and I do not want to be a bore. I will understand that you are fond of me without all this."

"*Fond* of you?"

She drew back, the color leaping into her face. "You are so kind to me that I thought you must like me a little."

Claude laughed. "You are quite right, I am very fond of you. I repeated your words because 'fond' is rather a stranger to my vocabulary. I *like—I like awfully.* For instance, I like you awfully. You are 'fond' of things—you find things 'droll'—you ask for a 'bit.' It was only the phrase I was thinking of."

The door opened and Marjorie came in.

"I want to go home, Claude," she said, "and I do not want Martin Kinsey to go with me; get your hat and coat, please. How is the composition, Beatrice?"

"Oh, it was finished long ago!"

"And what have you been studying since?"

" Many things," Claude answered :

> " Why the sea is boiling hot,
> And whether pigs have wings."

> " ' I doubt it,' said the carpenter,
> And shed a bitter tear,"

Marjorie quoted.

"You were ever a skeptic, Marjie ; make your farewells, my dear, while I fetch my hat and coat."

XVI

" When the fight begins within himself,
A man's worth something. God stoops o'er his head,
Satan looks up between his feet—both tug—
He's left, himself, i' the middle ; the soul wakes
And grows. Prolong that battle through his life !
Never leave growing till the life to come ! "

MARJORIE'S teaching had a varying effect on
John. For a day or two he had put it away
from him, but, the scales having fallen from his
eyes, he could not help seeing. Even a retro-
spective glance proved the truth of Marjorie's
assertion that he was blind and stupid. He
laughed, remembering it. He thought that he
would have preferred hearing nothing of the matter until it was announced. It would be ; an un-
sophisticated child like Beatrice could not resist
a man like Claude ; and there was no reason why
she should resist him.

He was sitting alone in the study with a book
turned down on his knee and a paper knife in his
hands. A slightly wrought silver thing, and he
bent it slowly back and forth—bent it double
while he thought.

It would be a very good marriage for Beatrice,
and settle her beyond most of the ' chances and
changes ' of life. She would be his little sister.

He twisted the paper knife round and round, and looked at it reproachfully when it fell apart. What a fool he was! He must go down to the shops and replace it at once. Possibly his aunt might want something, or Beatrice; he would go up and see. He had not been into Beatrice's schoolroom since the first day.

Mrs. Van Kuyster smiled and said she wanted a gray gauze fan, if John would select it for her at Tiffany's.

Going up the next flight, he tapped at the open door of the schoolroom. Billings sat sewing near the window, and Claude and Beatrice were at the table with their heads together over a book. They looked up in much surprise.

"Why, where are the slums?" Claude asked.

"I cannot go every day, you know," approaching the table. "I have class work at the seminary."

"So you have."

"Just now, I am going down to the shops, and thought that Beatrice might want some errand done."

"Oh, thank you!"

"Don't you want the coupé?" Claude asked.

"Thanks, I prefer walking. Another composition, Beatrice? did the last win a prize?"

"Indeed not; Miss Grigsby was quite angry."

"Miss Grigsby is not advanced," Claude said. "I am waiting now to have a long and exhaustive discussion with her."

"I wish I might hear, but I must go. I am sorry I can do nothing for you, Beatrice—good-by."

Why had he been such a fool as to suggest doing errands for the family; they had regarded him quite as if he had lost his senses. Was he fool enough to think that he could enter the lists with Claude? Even if he had the skill, he had no right. His past life, that he was hating more and more each moment, bound him. Was Claude's past any better? Manifestly, this was not his affair; Mrs. Van Kuyster was the girl's guardian, and all his responsibility in the matter was with himself.

A gray gauze fan—silver-gray. He did not believe that Mrs. Van Kuyster wanted it really; she had a queer look in her eyes when she gave him the commission, for he had been idiotic enough to tell her that he was on his way to ask if Beatrice wanted anything. It was a perfectly new thing for him to do, and of course, if Marjorie could see through things, Mrs. Van Kuyster had seen, too; they had discussed it all, probably. Confound it! While he was flapping about like a bat!

He selected a fan and ordered it sent up; if she did not want it, she could send it back. The paper knife he matched exactly, and left the broken one to be mended. He would keep the mended one as a reminder of his temporary insanity. He hoped that it was temporary. He bought also a little pansy pin, with a diamond dewdrop in the center. It would be quite proper to give it to Beatrice; she was his little sister. And when he reached home the little brooch was locked away in his desk.

He read diligently until lunch, and at lunch declined to realize Claude's possessive way with Beatrice; but going out to walk after lunch, he reflected on it. Of course Mrs. Van Kuyster saw it, for it was ridiculously plain. Beatrice seemed to take it as a matter of course. She liked being watched over and directed. She had her mother's dreamy, dependent, ease-loving nature—weak, in short. And how could she help that, poor child? Was *he* weak enough to grow spiteful to Beatrice and jealous of Claude? He had no right to think of Beatrice in any way.

And Elizabeth? Since Marjorie had opened his eyes, how continually she had haunted him. Surely he had done right in forsaking that old life, so full of evil—a life that he now loathed! Was his memory playing him false, or had Elizabeth been as strong as she seemed to him now? Her father's degradation was a bitter thing to her, yet how she had stood by him, even to the extent of patiently enduring her stepmother, who was most obnoxious to her. And how earnestly she had tried to improve her half-brothers into something decent. What young devils they were! Of course, having determined to take orders, he could not herd with such people, and as they had lived far from the town, he had found no difficulty in avoiding them. In his contentment at being freed from them, it had not occurred to him how strange it was that he *never* saw Elizabeth after the day she helped him home. But now he wondered over it. She could have put herself in his way if she had wanted to ; was it possible that she had avoided him ?

Elizabeth had a steadfast face and level brows, and eyes that looked calm to the extent of coldness. He had been attracted by this quiet reserve and dignity that was so out of keeping with her apparent place in life, where the women were usually viragoes and worse. When he knew her better and found out how far her father had fallen, he put down the good qualities to heredity ; for as her mother had died at her birth, she had always been free to be the lowest of the low.

Why should she haunt him now ? He struck his stick on the pavement impatiently. Poor Elizabeth ! What had become of her and her little dog Wamba ? Wamba would be a big dog now. A sick setter puppy, a waif whose life she had saved. He remembered so well when she named the clumsy, tumbling creature. The men at Marsden's had tried to drive it away, but she had been kind to it, and in spite of everything it would creep back to her when night fell. At last they were about to kill it, when Elizabeth rescued it, and announced that, if they touched it, she would retaliate in kind. She took it out of the

house after this, and by the light of the moon
she bathed the poor bruised body and named it
Wamba.

"He is a fool in his faithfulness," she said,
looking up at John, and in the moonlight he had
seen the sneer upon her lips. It was pitiful that
a girl of her age could sneer at faith.

Again he struck his stick on the pavement.
What were her views of her kind now? how faithful had she found them?

The last time that he had ridden out to Marsden's, Elizabeth and Wamba met him on the edge
of the chaparral. The picture came before him
vividly. The world seemed to be all gray sky
and gray prairie that met far away; down in the
west a dash of red like a smear of blood; then
the line of leafless chaparral, and a white speck.
As soon as he descried that speck, he knew it to
be Elizabeth. He slackened his pace after he
saw her; his head ached, and he had come
against his will. He hated all the world that
afternoon, and was angry that Elizabeth should
wait for him. Had he given her unnecessary
pain when he met her? She had looked better
than usual. Her hair rippled back prettily, and
she had on a plain, dark frock, with a white kerchief about her throat. This was the white he
had seen so far away. Every circumstance of
that evening was as clear in his mind as if it had
just happened. How rough the loft was where
Elizabeth lived and kept her few belongings;

and how perfectly neat. He had been astonished
to find books up there; remnants of what her
father had once owned, and the Marsden coat-of-
arms pasted in under the old man's name! She
had studied each one of these books, and
" Wamba, the faithful fool " had appealed to her.

" I am a faithful fool," she said, " my dog is
another; we do to go together. I have named.
him well." John could hear her voice—he could
feel her close beside him as he bent to rebuke
her for her bitter words. His face burned, and
his breath seemed to come with difficulty. Was
he the same man as Elizabeth's " Jack ? "

It was nearly five years. She had loved him,
and for a time he had thought honestly that he
loved her. He had been sure of it, but love was
higher than anything he had given Elizabeth.
And if she had loved him truly, she would have
sent him from her, and from his evil companions.
He was quite sure that if he loved anyone, he
would put her good before his own happiness.
Elizabeth had not done this, and yet she was
coming back to him as the strongest woman he
had ever known.

Was it love for Beatrice that made him analyze
love ?

During these days when John was trying to
readjust himself with both past and present,
Claude watched him curiously. His unique
offer to shop for Beatrice was puzzling, especially
as nothing had followed. Since then he had

held aloof, scarcely seeming to observe the girl. Claude thought this a more dangerous sign than the effort to approach her; for to anything excessive there must come a reaction.

He wondered if John realized that he loved Beatrice, and was fighting the feeling; or was still fighting blindly against acknowledging the feeling.

In either case there would come a reaction, and Claude determined to be prepared.

XVII.

" How the world is made for each of us !
How all we perceive and know in it
Tends to some moment's product thus,
    When a soul declares itself—to wit,
By its fruit, the thing it does ! "

MARTIN KINSEY was a great resource to John at this time; so was Marjorie; and it was not long before the latter was going with the two men on some of their expeditions. "I am old and ugly enough," she said, laughing, "and sometimes it is almost exciting. One does not know Mr. Paget, Cousin, until one sees him at work. The whole man is changed and filled with magnetism, and the worst people heed him."

"And the smells, Marjie ? "

"They are pretty bad, but I carry my salts, and when no one is looking I take a sniff. Last night I persuaded Martin Kinsey to take me where I could see Mr. Paget at his rescue work. Of course this is a dead secret between you and me and Beatrice—not even Mr. Paget knows— for it was questionable. But I assure you it was far better than any play. Mr. Paget went to this saloon entirely alone, he will go alone; Martin Kinsey is so devoted to him, however,

228

that he follows and watches. We watched last night from the shadow of a shop awning. There was a screen across the entrance, but there was a group of men between it and the door. As Mr. Paget stepped in a man jostled him purposely, and Mr. Paget asked him why.

" ' Because you've got no business here.'

" ' This is a free country,' Mr. Paget answered, ' and if I have money to pay for a drink, I suppose I may come and get it as well as you."

The men all gathered round him and asked what office he was running for.

" ' I want to be a priest in the Church,' he said. You should have heard the awful groan they gave. Mr. Kinsey made me take my hand off his arm.

" ' They may hustle him,' he said, ' and I must be ready to run in.' Actually I began to tremble with excitement, but Mr. Paget stood there very quietly with his hands clasped behind him, until the same man jostled him again, then he turned and said :

" ' I have been a cowboy out on the border; I have had to fight for my life many and many a time, and possibly I can teach you something. Why, once '—and then he began to tell a story. I cannot pretend to tell it, but every man there listened, and when he was done three or four went away with him. Awful looking brutes, walking off so quietly. And to see Martin Kinsey's eagerness. This philanthropy business used to be a fad; now he is so desperately in earnest that at last he is interesting."

"But you must not go into the rescue work, Marjorie, that is going too far; suppose there had been a difficulty?"

"I should have run for the police."

"And have had the town agog over Miss Van Kuyster in the witness-box of the police courts! *I* would have had to go with you."

"Poor cousin, it would have been truly awful; Claude would have had convulsions."

"Unimaginably awful! Did you have on this frock?"

"No. You need not be afraid of me; that garment hangs in the trunk room. But does Mr. Paget go to Newport with you?"

"I am afraid not: I think he will only run up and down: he is absorbed in this work. You will come as usual?"

"I will, but not immediately; I will follow in in a week or two."

"Why do you wait?"

"Why do I go? Why do I do anything? Because there is nothing else to do. I think that I am entertained just now, so will remain where I am until that fallacy is exploded; then I will come to you in Newport."

"And you think that this delusion will last a whole fortnight?"

"A week at the outside; the second week will be consumed in preparations."

" Why do you not study? " Beatrice asked.

They had forgotten the girl, and now Marjorie turned to her, laughing.

" Is it possible you would have me pose as a bluestocking? "

" I thought it would entertain you, and——"

" And improve my mind? Say it out, dear, I like your little reproofs and suggestions. But to what purpose besides entertainment would all this mental effort tend? A few years of superior education for which my circle has no use, and then? Nirvana? "

" What is Nirvana? "

" It is the Buddhist heaven, which practically amounts to annihilation."

" But that is not true. When we die, we go into another life and carry all the best things with us."

" Languages and music and drawing? "

" Not the actual things, the Mother said; but all the true and the beautiful and the good that education introduces us to. Is it not so, Aunt Claudia? "

" Yes, dear."

" So I must study? Perhaps I shall. Which instructress goes with you? "

" I left it to Beatrice, and she has selected Miss Grigsby."

" The cross one? "

" She is so poor," Beatrice explained, " and I thought the change, and having enough to eat,

would be good for her. Claude said that he
would do German and French with me."

"So Claude is making use of his education. I
will assist in your music, perhaps. But what can
Sister Grigsby teach me?"

"Oh, she is awfully learned!"

"That sounds well. Perhaps I shall follow you
in ten days, cousin; this educational mania may
be interesting."

"It *is* interesting," Beatrice insisted. "Claude
makes everything so easy. I begin to think that
after all I am not entirely stupid. John used to
make me feel very hopeless."

"What did John teach you?" Marjorie asked.

"I used to read Church history aloud to him.
He said that the history of the Church was the
history of the world. Maybe it is; I do not
remember, but it was awfully dismal, and I used
to cry. You see, John had reason to think me
dull; he needs clever people like you, Miss Van
Kuyster, to interest him."

"Thank you. Claude, I suppose, is not so
exacting."

"Claude? Nobody knows how gentle and
patient he is. I have never had anyone so good
to me before."

"And you love him very much?" Marjorie
asked.

"How can I help it?"

Mrs. Van Kuyster's embroidery needle moved
more slowly, and Marjorie walked to the window.

"No one has ever been unkind to you?" Mrs. Van Kuyster suggested.

"Oh, no! but nobody ever troubled to ask if I were happy or not; nobody ever put me first before. It is nice to be first; don't you think so, Aunt Claudia?"

"Yes, child, if it be only a dog that loves you best, it is something."

"Cousin!" and turning from the window, Marjorie laid her hand impulsively on Mrs. Van Kuyster's shoulder.

"Thank you, dear," looking up with a serene smile; "you are a great deal to me."

The spring was growing into summer, and the annual move to Newport, which Beatrice had looked forward to as a great joy, was now in the near future, but she had ceased to think of it longingly, for the city life had become a charming thing. Very soon she had been promoted from the riding club to riding in the Park with Claude; besides, Claude had taken her on many expeditions, introducing her to art exhibitions and shops that were dreams of delight. Her wish to make poor children happy had been indulged in many ways, and Claude thought it worth a fortune to see her face when she was distributing toys in a day nursery. Always free from care and responsibility, her young life had been negatively comfortable; now it had become positively happy. Thanks to Claude, even her lessons had

been made pleasant, and all Miss Grigsby's sharp
criticisms were cleverly blunted before they
reached her.   Miss Grigsby, however, deeply
resented Claude's interference; she had never
forgiven the composition he had dictated, and
once had gone so far as to appeal to Mrs. Van
Kuyster, when she found a volume of Matthew
Arnold's poems in the schoolroom. Mrs. Van
Kuyster listened, then told her that Claude had
taken charge of his cousin's education.

Miss Grigsby was not agreeable, and Beatrice
knew that she could easily have her dismissed;
but she had seen that there were holes in the
good lady's gloves, and that on cold days she
looked quite blue, and she said in confidence to
Claude:

"I am sure she does not have enough to wear
nor to eat."

"And you think that is why she is cross?"

"I am sure it is; and since I have lived here I
have such a horror of people being cold and
hungry. In the South it is easy to keep warm
and not starve; but here the streets look so hard
and the houses so unapproachable, and the wind
is so sharp. I feel so selfish when I meet a
woman hugging herself in a thin shawl, and I all
wrapped in furs. Once I bought a shawl and
made Billings carry it until we met a poor woman.
Billings did not like it; she said people were
looking at us. Then the woman said such bad

words when I gave her the shawl—it was awful."

"Poor child!" and Claude laughed. "Did the woman put on the shawl?"

"No. Billings said she would sell it for drink. Do you think she did?"

"Probably. But I will send some shawls to Kinsey to distribute for you at one of his station houses, will that do?"

"You are so good to me, Claude."

"Pure selfishness, I assure you. You are 'something to do,' don't you know?"

"I keep you very busy, and make no return."

"Indeed you do. You sing for me every evening, making me feel myself a Spanish Hidalgo, owning the waters of youth in the far-off 'Land of Flowers,' and a private bull-ring at home; or a Mexican ranchero able to shoot my neighbor or steal his cattle, to ride like the wind across the prairies, or drink myself crazy. And this is a great boon to a poor man whose only resort is an extremely conventional club, a trot in the park, and the whole vista of the future blocked up by a bald head and an enlarged waist. You put a touch of the unusual into my days, with your unblunted sympathies and unique training."

"Aunt Claudia says that I must not be unconventional."

"My darling child, that is a woman's view. I

love you better than Aunt Claudia does. I think I may say that I care more for you than any-one else does. I would not tell you anything that was not for your good, and I am in serious earnest when I charge you on no account to change. Don't try to be like other women. If you do——"

The girl looked up wistfully.

" I will stop loving you without a moment's grace."

" O Claude ! "

" Indeed I will."

" But could you ? Can people stop loving all in a minute like that ? "

" I can."

" I could not. I could not even do the way John does—forget slowly."

" How do you mean ? "

" I mean that he does not seem to remember that I am in the world. He likes to talk to that Mr. Kinsey, though, and to Miss Van Kuyster; they seem to be together all the time."

" They are interested in the same things. If you want to interest John, now, you must be very wicked or very poor. To be pretty and com-fortable and good shuts you outside the pale of John's sympathies. But, of course, he cares for you just as much as he ever did—cares more for you than for anyone else in the world."

To himself Claude said : " Next to a dictatorial devotion, nothing interests a woman so much as a pronounced neglect." ·Unconsciously John had taken the strongest weapon that Claude had left him; and Claude, being a "child of this world," took pains to assure the girl of the mean-inglessness of John's apparent absorption in others.

XVIII.

" And if any painter drew her,
He would paint her unaware
With a halo round her hair.

. . . . . .

And all voices that address her,
Soften, sleeken every word,
As if speaking to a bird.

. . . . .

And all hearts do pray, ' God love her ! '
Ay, and always in good sooth,
We may all be sure He doth."

IF the life in New York had grown to be a
pleasant thing to Beatrice, the life in Newport
seemed a dream of happiness.

The beautiful, wide-spreading villa ; the shady
piazzas ; the lawns sloping down to the cliffs ;
the beds of brilliant flowers ; the beautiful drives,
the boats, the sea. The gray days with a light
wind that were devoted to sailing ; the long rides
and drives on brilliant days ; the walks in the fogs
that shut them away from the world, when all
was mysterious, and the booming of the sea grew
awful. It was like a fairy story—too strange and
too pleasant to be true.

Miss Grigsby and the solid studies were not in
much demand ; for from the beginning Claude

insisted that Beatrice's health must be the first
consideration, and that in their walks and rides
he was teaching her geology and botany and like
healthy things. In spite of earnest efforts on
Beatrice's part, however, Claude and Miss Grigsby
did not get on, and in the many discussions they
had Miss Grigsby generally came out the worse
for wear. It worried Beatrice, and one aftenoon
when she and Claude were walking in the fog, she
asked him not to have any more discussions.

"I cannot always follow them," she said, as he
helped her down a very slippery place, "and they
worry me for a long time afterward. They make
me feel uncertain about you."

"And why not about Miss Grigsby?" Claude
asked, as, landing her safely on the beach, he
took her tennis hat and gloves of which she
divested herself, and put them in his pockets.
She liked to go bare-headed and bare-handed,
and she used the dense fogs as screen for her
little unconventionalities. Claude drew her hand
through his arm, and pushed his last question—
"Am I so far below Miss Grigsby that I cannot
be trusted?"

"You do not strike me as being *safely*
religious."

"There you are mistaken; I am *very* religious,
and with what I think the highest kind of
religion."

"Are you, Claude?" stopping and lifting her
face to his wistfully. "If I thought that you

were religious, I should be absolutely, perfectly happy."

As they stood there Claude looked away through the dimness to where great waves rolled sullenly. Gradually he was coming to the conclusion that Mrs. Van Kuyster was right, and Beatrice's belief was in her flesh and blood. He could not sway her from these principles that seemed to be the foundation of her whole nature. He could not let her go. He had gone over this ground many times of late, and now that she pleaded with him for her happiness, he reached a decision quickly. He paused only a moment as he turned his face out to sea, then looking down into her eyes he said :

" You may be absolutely and perfectly happy, Beatrice."

" True ? "

" Have you ever found me false? "

" I could not stand it to find you false."

" But even though I am religious, your faith in me is not quite perfect? "

She turned away. " You are different from anyone I have ever known," she said; "you can argue from any side——"

" Beatrice ! "

" Wait a moment. I mean that you are not rigid except in what your station in life requires. Things are not right and wrong to you as a man, but only as a gentleman. Do you see what I mean? I have thought about it a great deal."

Claude's eyes were bright with surprise and amusement.

"You are an arch deceiver," he said. "Under your ' sweet simplicity ' you are dissecting ruthlessly my moral—immoral character. It is not fair."

" Well, you so often say 'a gentleman can't do that'—and once—' it is a waste to spend time on any low-caste people.' But they have souls and hearts, and right is right for a common man as it is for a gentleman, is it not ? "

" No. That is one of the great mistakes. The proposition that before God all men are equal, cannot be true. The Scriptures tell us of angels and archangels; and the Church shows us archbishops, and patriarchs, and popes, and bishops, and priests, and deacons; down to nuns, and women's auxiliaries, and fashionable guilds, down almost to the democracy of the Salvation Army. If Heaven and the Church are divine institutions, republics cannot be. And what might be quite proper for the highest official in the Salvation Army, could be highly improper for the Archbishop of Canterbury. And though proper and improper are not hanging matters, save in the case of women, they are degrees of right and wrong; and once you admit degrees, rigid lines become impossibilities."

" But the Bible *does* say that God is no respector of persons," Beatrice persisted.

"That only means that the Almighty does not

gauge man as man does. I give a rich man deference willingly, so long as he behaves as a rich man should. I salaam profoundly to a prince, if he behaves as a prince should. A gentleman may be as poor as 'Job's turkey'; I honor him as much as the prince, if he lives up to his blood. Now, the general rule is to pay deference to the money and the title, and to pass over the poverty-stricken gentleman. This is to respect persons. Don't you see that more is required of a prince, and living up to his station he does more than a rich man—who is only a rich man—can possibly do it if he lives up to every responsibility? Obversely, if a prince fails, he deserves to be kicked out to a much greater distance than the rich citizen would."

"But the poor creature who lives in the slums? Everybody in his class of life is wicked and dirty; so all that you could ask of him would be to stay wicked and dirty?"

"Your logic terrifies me!" Claude said, laughing. "But you are right. A creature who is content in the gutter deserves nothing better, save the penitentiary."

"There!" and she stopped and faced him again; "that is what hurts me—that is what I mean; it is a hardness that could become cruelty. Father and John think as you do about station, but they said that the higher one is, the more one ought to try to help up lower people."

"Shall I ask my tailor to dinner?"

" I did not mean socially—I meant in a Christian way."

" My child, the Christian way is grand in theory; practically,—where it meets the social question,—it shades off into social Pharisaism. ' I should like to save your soul, but I can't give you a seat in my pew or ask you to dinner!' Now the socialist comes to anarchy, and the humanitarian makes charity into a science that leaves the humanity of the pauper out of account, because it leaves love out of account. Mine is the only logical position ; live up to the requirements of your station, and be comfortable in believing that the law of 'the survival of the fittest' is the greatest regulator and adjuster possible."

" That is so unmerciful."

" Is Nature unmerciful ? It is her chief law."

" I wish I knew enough to argue further, but if you would only be less logical and more merciful, I think it would be better."

" If you will love me I will be anything"—laying his hands on her shoulders.

Something in his eyes made her look falter, and she drew away from him.

" I do love you," she said slowly.

" How do you love me?" Putting his hands in the pockets of his sack-coat, and looking down on her much as a cannibal might have done.

" With all my heart," she answered simply; " just as I love John."

"Do you love me enough to give yourself to me?" he went on.

"Do you mean to marry you?"

"Yes."

"You should ask Aunt Claudia that," with an access of dignity; "she or John must decide."

"Shall I ask them, then?" and in spite of himself he smiled. "And if they give you to me will you come?"

"Of course."

"And love me better than you love John?"

"I do not know if I can promise that."

"The devil!"

"I have loved John all my life, you see."

"But it is wicked to love anyone more than you love your husband."

"Oh! but many girls love their father and mother better than their husbands," and she looked curiously at Claude, who, equally divided between amusement and annoyance, was pulling his mustache rather savagely. "Sister Thérèse told me so; and when I asked the Mother she said that if I respected my husband, that would be all that any well-brought-up girl could do at first—that the love would come afterward."

"And if it did not?"

"There would be the respect."

"Suppose that after you were married you should meet someone you loved better than your husband?"

"That would be impossible—it would be wrong."

"And wrong is impossible to you?"

"It would be impossible deliberately to choose wrong, I think; just as jumping off that cliff would be impossible unless I lost my mind."

"I see."

They walked on in silence for a little while, then Claude said, "I will ask for you, then."

"Do you really want me?" Looking up and coloring like the inside of a sea-shell.

"I really want you," Claude answered quietly, while the veins in his forehead stood out like cords.

"I am so simple, Claude, and ignorant—I am so young—I am afraid you will grow weary."

"Will you come to me?"

"Yes."

"And after awhile you will love me better than all the world?"

"Of course; and you are so good to me, it will not take long."

Claude stopped still; he longed to shout with laughter; he almost wished that Marjorie were there to see the humorous side of the position—he longed to snatch up the girl and rush away with her to the ends of the world. Instead, he said:

"I asked the mater for you long ago, dear, and she said yes; but I wanted to win you for myself, so I did not tell you. I asked the very first evening after dinner."

Beatrice's eyes grew wide with wonder. "Before I knew anything, or had any good clothes?"

"Before you had been in the house twelve hours. But I wanted to win you—have I?"

She turned her face away, looking out to sea. All the while he had loved her! How kind, how gentle, how patient he had been; how he had watched over her! In all her life, no better thing had come to her—no better thing could come to her.

"Yes," she answered, looking up into his shining eyes—"yes, you have won me."

He drew her close to him and laid his cheek against her little wet face. "You will never be sorry?" he asked—"never lose your mind and want to jump over the cliff?"

"Never, I think."

XIX

" An unaccomplished destiny
Struck cold his forehead, it may be."

"CAN I come in, mother?" And Claude hammered impatiently on Mrs. Van Kuyster's dressing room door.

"Yes, come in. My dear boy, you are soaking wet!"

"Only fog; we have been out walking, Beatrice and I."

"Instructing her as to amphibious animals, I suppose."

"Anything you like. But do you know how nuns conduct betrothals?"

"Claude!"

"I am in earnest. I have proposed to Beatrice."

"Of course——"

"There was no 'of course' in the matter," Claude interrupted; "she was as proper and as simple as possible; but I see that if this thing is not done formally, as the Reverend Mother would do it, she will not be satisfied. A finished coquette could not have tormented a man into a finer frenzy than she did me."

"How charming! I wish I had been there."

" I wish you had. I longed for someone to enjoy it with me. I love her a thousand times better for it."

" You are positively beside yourself."

" Of course I àm. When a girl defers the whole matter to her guardian, saying coolly that once married it will not take her very long to love—that anything else would not be correct— it is enough to put a man beside himself."

" How remarkable ! " Mrs. Van Kuyster said. " Unconsciously that child has managed you as no wisdom could have done."

" True ; she binds me hand and foot by her simple passivity. If you should say no, I believe she would resign me cheerfully because it would be right."

" I told you so."

" Yes. But can you make this thing formal and solemn, as the Mother would ? "

Mrs. Van Kuyster laughed. " I can only send for the child and tell her how glad I am." Ringing the bell. " I am glad, since you seem really to love her."

" Seem ! " Claude repeated as Mrs. Van Kuyster spoke to the maid. "You do not understand."

" Perhaps I do not—perhaps that is why I am so contented and happy—no wrenching emotions."

The door opened and Beatrice came in. "You sent for me ? "

" Yes, dear "—turning and holding out her hand
to the girl. "Claude has just told me that he
has spoken to you. I gave my consent on the
first day of your arrival."

" Yes, I know, but "—and her voice seemed to
fail her.

" I think you will make him very happy," Mrs.
Van Kuyster went on, laying the little hand she
held in Claude's. " I am glad to give you into his
keeping. We will not make it public yet, however, you are so young. And now I must dismiss
you both ; I must dress for dinner."

Beatrice paused a moment, then looked up
wistfully. "Won't you kiss me, Aunt Claudia,"
she asked, " and say ' God bless you ? ' "

" Of course, child," kissing her gently, " and
God *will* bless you, you are so good."

Christine, the maid, entered, and Claude drew
the girl away. In the dusky hall he paused, and
took the little face between his hands. "You are
mine now," he said, " and must come to me for
all your love and blessings."

"Yes, I will ; but I had hoped that Aunt
Claudia loved me a little."

" She does; but the mater either used up all
her power for loving long years ago, or she has
none, I cannot decide which. But I love you
enough for two, dear ; will not that satisfy
you ? "

" You are very kind."

" But it does not satisfy you ? "

"Of course. I should be ungrateful indeed if I were not satisfied. I wish old Angela were here, or John. I will write to John—will not you?"

"Yes. Good-by until after dinner," and he kissed her gravely. She baffled him; perhaps she really meant it when she said she would have to learn to love him. She did not seem to love him now.

Writing to John was almost a sort of vivisection. Yet, John had not raised a finger to stop him, and he must have seen what was going on. He would simply announce the fact—the shorter the better; but it was not a pleasant job. And yet, if John knew, as he was beginning to realize painfully, how elusive was the prize, would he find much to envy? That Beatrice was capable of a great and absorbing passion of devotion he was absolutely certain. Why had not he wakened it? She was undoubtedly fond of him—he made her happy—she would miss him if he were gone, and yet, she eluded him at every turn. Was it the spiritual side of her—the religious, fetish-worshiping side of her—that evaded him? She was not satisfied, herself; the blessing she had asked for, the wish for the old servant and for John, showed it. When John came, would she turn to him and find the vacuum filled? Claude swore a little under his breath. He must keep John away until he had won the girl entirely.

This view of John's relations with Beatrice made the letter an easier thing to compose.

John found the letters on the hall table after a long day's work. The woman left in charge had lighted the lamps in the study and in the hall, but this evening he seemed to realize all the darkness in the great still house. In the day he did not think of his loneliness ; his work, as assistant in a down-town mission, occupied him fully, and his meals were taken in a restaurant, but this evening he was unusually tired, and things seemed dreary.

He had begun to think that the sufferings of the poor were as great, if not greater, in summer than in winter. The heat was so intense ; the crowded tenements were so insufferable. Why did not all die—men, women, and children ?

He had buried two little children that day—he was always glad to do it—to feel that they were at rest. The mothers did not regret it, either— "They are better off," was the formula. And now he was really glad of the property his aunt had settled on him, for there was so much to be done. Work enough to fill hundreds 'of lives ; and to do it properly the lives ought to be untrammeled. Nothing to hold one back, nothing to tempt one, not even sympathy that would say : "You are overworked ; you have done more than your share "—or " Your work is so noble, so high !" Human nature was too weak even for

this encouraging praise. The only way was to
lose self; to forget if one were tired or hungry; to
forget whether others worked or idled; to forget
that praise or blame existed. That was the only
way. Never to loosen rein; never to lessen the
spur; to drop in the race, and die on the roadside—
this was to live. And he, feeling himself weaker
than most men, must drive himself without
mercy, must never look either to the right or to
the left. He was too weak to dare the happy
mean.

He leaned back wearily in the deep chair, his
letters held loosely. Only one thing haunted
him—a doubt as to his duty. Had he not tram-
meled himself in the past? Those old ties that,
in his early zeal for a purer life, he had broken so
relentlessly; had he had a right to break them?
Legally, yes,—in the letter he was free,—but the
spirit? He closed his eyes, and the face of Elizabeth rose up before him. She had left him absolutely free, and he had used his freedom to drop
her out of his life. She had made no motion
to recall or to reproach him—she had never sent
him even a message. Could he have been as
strong as that? It was almost grand, for he knew
that she loved him.

He had never questioned his action with regard
to Elizabeth until he found that he loved Beatrice.

At the thought of the girl, a relaxing despair
seemed to sweep over him, and his head drooped

on his breast. He had never known what love
was until now, and now he knew how Elizabeth
had suffered ; and was suffering still, perhaps;
for Elizabeth would not forget. Was it his duty
to search her out? It could not be; it would destroy him heart and soul. He would never try to
win Beatrice, or any woman, but he could not
go back to the remnants of those days he had
learned to loathe. The Prodigal had not gone
back to the husks and the swine.

How hard he tried to deceive himself—he knew
Elizabeth was not that.

He drew himself together. This struggle beset
him whenever a quiet moment came—beset him
in his devotions—in his sleep. He was weary,
and looked at his letters. One from Claude—one
from Beatrice. Did it mean anything, their coming
together? Any letter might tell him the thing
he dreaded to hear. Day after day he told himself: " It is only a matter of time"—but he shrank
from it as he would shrink from putting a red-hot
iron into an open wound !

He read Claude's letter first. It was a plain,
clear statement of the fact that Beatrice had
accepted him, and he hoped that John, as co-
guardian with Mrs. Van Kuyster, would approve.
Then he went on to name the most liberal settle-
ment—a fortune, in short.

John read it through. A good letter from an
honorable gentleman ; what more could any
guardian ask? He opened Beatrice's note.

DEAR JOHN:

I am to marry Claude. He asked Aunt Claudia long ago, and she consented, but he did not tell me, because he wanted to win me himself. Do you like it? Claude is very good to me, and gives me all I can possibly want, except you, and I want to see you very much. You do not seem to care for me now as you used to do at home. You seemed to be fond of me then ; now you have put me to one side, and only your work interests you. . I am not jealous of the work, but I am homesick. I was happy and contented until I found that Aunt Claudia had given me away, but that has made things so irrevocable. I cannot keep house for you now as you promised. Do not think that I am unhappy ; I am not, and I love Claude very much, but Claude is not you, and there is no place like our shabby little home in Corpus. Why did we ever come away? When Aunt Claudia gave me to Claude she did not kiss me nor bless me until I asked her ; and then she kissed me on the cheek and said she was sure that God would bless me because I was good. I longed for father or you, or even old Angela — for somebody who loved me really. Have you not time to come down?

Lovingly,

BEATRICE.

John folded it carefully, returned it to its envelope, and laid it on the table. An involuntary thrill of exultation went over him. Claude had not won the girl yet! Dear little thing—so pure —so gentle. What a paradise he could make for her, now that he understood her! He had been mistaken in trying to train her; she needed no training, only love ; for her heart would always be a child's heart, trusting and unquestioningly faithful. She had keen observation, but never any harsh judgment. Evil puzzled her, and always

would. Claude had read her more quickly than
he, and of course would win her—unless! John
covered his face with his hands. How base he
was! He must not try to win her; he had decided
that; and he must even refuse her little prayer
to come to her. She had better believe him to
be selfishly absorbed in his work. Claude was
her future, and surely it was a good future. He
turned to the table; he would write at once and
destroy the temptation. God would help him to
find peace, once he had put this thing aside.'

A short note to Claude, and to Beatrice a long
letter. He sent his sympathy and blessing, and
showed her how bright her future could be. Then
he described his work, and told of the suffering
he witnessed day after day—of the sick and
dying, who needed him. " This is my work that
God has given me to do," he finished, "and I
must not leave it, even for you whom I love far
better than any except God. You must not
think for a moment that I have forgotten you;
your welfare lives in my heart; your work in life
will be to make the lives of those about you
brighter and happier by simply living and being
yourself. I only ask you to add to this work
some thoughts and prayers for your brother, that
I may be strong to resist temptation, and that,
however weak and sinful I have been or may be,
God will forgive me, and bless my work to my
fellows. I ask for nothing but work—His work.
When I go back to the South, wherever I may

be stationed, you and Claude will come to me. In spite of all the ease and luxury you find here I think you will never cease to love the South and your brother John."

He inclosed this letter in Claude's. It made a formidable looking missive, and Claude felt a little uneasy as he opened it. What in the world had John to say to him, that would require such a volume?

"From Jack," he said, as he tore it open. Marjorie looked up quickly. The engagement was no surprise to her, but she wondered a little how John would take it, and she looked with interest at the thick letter that Claude was opening. The thickness was all due to an inner, unsealed envelope. Claude turned it over.

"For you, Beatrice," he said. "I have only a note."

It was very short; but as Claude read his face changed. How he had mistaken this man in judging him by worldly standards. How ashamed he felt of the thought he had entertained that he must take Beatrice farther away. John was grand. He handed the note to Mrs. Van Kuyster. "It is the letter of an anxious father," he said lightly, feeling obliged to say something for his own relief. "You read it also, Marjie, then maybe Beatrice will let me have a look at hers."

Beatrice started and looked up; there was a suspicious moisture in her eyes. "May I read it first by myself?" she asked.

"Of course!" Claude answered. "I was only joking, dear"—and rising, he held the door open for her.

"John loves her better than you do," Mrs. Van Kuyster said when Claude returned to his seat.

"He cannot, my dear mother."

"He must; he is a better man."

"Oh! that sort of better; I grant you that; John is too good; he is going to make hash out of his life. He had a far better chance for Beatrice than I had, and why he did not take it I cannot imagine. Some religious fad, as I told you from the beginning. He has lived a wild life on the border, in his early youth, and his one idea seems to be to atone for it; or, he might have ties we know nothing of."

"For shame!" Marjorie cried; "I have never heard you make a really mean speech before, Claude."

"My dear Marjorie, you are hasty; you have lost some of your civilization lately. Listen: a man as chimerically conscientious as John would make ties out of words and actions that a man of the world—your humble servant—would not so much as remember; and I do not doubt but that some ridiculous youthful folly is the rock on which he will shipwreck his life. Now repent your attack on my innocent self!"

"Mr. Paget is the noblest man I have ever met," Marjorie said, "and I do not see where the line of conscientiousness can be drawn. It seems to me that, logically, it is all or nothing. The lines of right and wrong, of duty and obligation, have got to be clear-cut and rigid."

"Whew! My cousin, my comrade, my chum, have I lost you!"

"I'm afraid not," Marjorie said. "I realize it, but I cannot live up to it. Whether I would or not, habits, follies, weaknesses, have grown too strong for me. The low standards of my youth hold me away from the really high. I am even sorry that I have seen it."

"My dear Marjorie," Mrs. Van Kuyster said, "you have been always such a comfortable person, I beg that you will not grow morbid and moody. Really you are one of my chief dependences in life."

"Am I, Cousin? I am glad to know that. I am afraid that you may depend on me still; once I have confessed my sins, I will not change. We shall have to make a compact like the blind man and the deaf man; we will supplement each other and hobble through life as best we can."

Claude walked to the window impatiently. "I am sorry that John and Beatrice ever came," he said; "we were quite comfortable before, and now we are upset with all sorts of motives, and stupid introspection and moral indigestions and probings; and I turn hot and cold a dozen times a day because of a child who asks uncomfortable questions and has a hectic conscience. My dear Marjorie, come to your senses. Life is as good as ever it was; we 'have our nuts and teeth to crack them' and nothing special to repent of. I used to think that I yearned for earnestness—that if I could find a thoroughly conscientious Christian, I would permit myself to be convinced, and throw in my lot with his. Now, I begin to appreciate old Ratcliffe. He told me once that I was mistaken, that I and the whole parish would rather be comfortable. He was right; I will make a motion to increase his salary. If earnest, conscientious, consistent Christianity means John's way of doing things—John's standard of self-abnegation, John's rigid scrupulousness, I am not in it. I cannot rise to that height, and I will not try."

"'Fish we are that love the mud,'" Mrs. Van Kuyster quoted.

"Anything you please," Claude answered; "and my work in life will be to make Beatrice think that the mud is the sward of Paradise."

"You will never do it," Mrs. Van Kuyster said; "I told you so long ago."

"God forbid that you should!" Marjorie added. "It would be an awful sin. You must leave her in her own world, Claude, and save her happiness from shipwreck by never allowing her to realize your world."

"You speak as if I lived in the depths of degradation."

"Worse than that," Marjorie answered, "you

do not live at all—you exist in the lifeless desert of critical negation. Nothing sweet nor true can live there; nothing high can breathe there. It would kill Beatrice."

"By Jove! I must go until you people have recovered your tempers. I advise a mint julep to pull you together"—and he went out hastily.

"I told you that all would break their hearts their own way," Mrs. Van Kuyster said, as she threaded her needle. "Nothing else ever satisfies humanity."

"I do not call Claude's a heart," Marjorie answered; "it is a bundle of selfish desires and expediencies. I think that he loves Beatrice as much as he can love, but he cannot touch her on the spiritual side, for Claude has no spiritual side; it died of starvation. Whether one holds the Scripture divine or not, one must hold it as wise, and two things it says that I have watched working out in Claude; one is that spiritual things are spiritually discerned—so it is that Claude understands neither Beatrice nor Mr. Paget—the other is, that there is a spiritual death."

"Perhaps," Mrs. Van Kuyster answered. "But which shade shall I vein this leaf with?" holding up her embroidery. "Light or dark? my needle is threaded with dark."

"Light, then," Marjorie answered. "To unthread your needle puts a little bit of work into your life."

Mrs. Van Kuyste laughed. "You are saucy,"

she said ; " I will repay you by repeating to you
what I have been telling Claude ; that he would
be happier with you, if he could get you, than
with Beatrice."

"And what did he say?"

" He agreed with me entirely, but is infatuated
with Beatrice. I have always hoped that you
and he would make a match. I care for you
more than for anyone else."

"Thank you, dear. He might have, if Beatrice and John had not come."

"John?"

"I only mean that, until I knew Mr. Paget,
Claude was the best I had found. Not that I
am breaking *my* bundle of expediencies over
Mr. Paget; only that, relatively, my opinion of
Claude has lowered."

" It may come about yet," Mrs. Van Kuyster
went on. "For if John lifts a finger, Beatrice
would obey."

" I do not agree with you. John is now pos-
ing in Beatrice's mind as a fleeting blessing, and
so she imagines him to be the greatest good in
life. But in reality, Claude is more necessary to
her. One thing I am sure of, however: if she
realizes Claude's religious position, she will look
on him with horror. I must warn Claude."

" I think that he has found it out for himself,"
Mrs. Van Kuyster answered.

" He says, nevertheless, that Beatrice must be
won gradually to think with him."

" Still, he told me that what I had said about the girl was true—that her belief was in her flesh and blood."

" It is ; and in Mr. Paget's too. When Christianity comes to me as theological science, it is no more to me than any other science ; but when I see it incarnated, as Felix saw it in Paul, I tremble."

" My dear Marjorie, you are a clever woman ; you talk extremely well, but I prefer gossip to reasoning, and embroidery to feeling. I stopped thinking and feeling some time ago ; and when you harangue me on these subjects, I have a pre-existent sensation, as it were ; just as they say that after a man's leg has been cut off, he can still feel it, and have a shadowy rheumatism in it. It is not a pleasant sensation, and I see no wisdom in subjecting myself to it."

" You shall not have any pre-existent rheumatism, my dear," and Marjorie patted Mrs. Van Kuyster's hand gently ; " you have had your share of the real thing, and if ossification has ensued, why, so much the better. I will serve up Mrs. De Loren and her fascinating cousin Dick. Mr. De Loren left in his yacht last week, you know, for a year's cruise, and immediately Dick arrives from South Africa, via Paris, where he had paused to have all sorts of claws and teeth and tails set and trimmed with gold and diamonds; and last night at the ball the fair De Loren looked like a Fiji idol decorated with votive offerings.

Newport is divided between envy and amusement."

"Delicious! I must have them here; how can I manage it?" and Mrs. Van Kuyster leaned forward in an interested way. "It is such a bore, half mourning; the laws for it are so sketchy. But I must see them together. Dick has always been a favorite of mine, and now that he has made a fortune, he must be charming—his poverty made him melancholy."

"He asked after you last night. Had heard of all the changes in the family, of Claude's infatuation and Beatrice's beauty, and is coming over at once. Why not have a lilac lunch? It would be subdued and lovely; have a man for every woman—not many of any kind, and all clever. It would be charming. I could design exquisite costumes for the three of us, and it would pull me out of theology and slums more than anything else. Indeed, the memory of these, my latest fads, will season most charmingly the racy list I will make up."

"By all means," Mrs. Van Kuyster said. "You are yourself once more. Claude is right; we used to be most comfortable before John came."

"And I," Marjorie answered, "feel 'swept and garnished,' and ready to house seven other spirits worse than myself. We will head the list with Ted Dennis; he is the wisest, wittiest, worst, and most charming man I know. I had best realize my limitations as Claude has done. I cannot attain to Mr. Paget's heights, so I will not try."

Mrs. Van Kuyster smiled. "It is warmer down on the levels with the rest of humanity," she said.

XX.

"Be not mocked !
Life which ye prize is long drawn agony :
Only its pains abide ; its pleasures are
As birds which light and fly.

Ache of the birth, ache of the helpless days,
Ache of hot youth, and ache of manhood's prime
Ache of the chill gray years and choking death,
These fill your piteous time."

THE summer was a trying one, hot and damp ;
and all through the length and breadth of the
land people found fault with it. Even in Newport it was "steamy," and extremely detrimental
to crisp summer finery. Marjorie declared that
never in her life before had she spent so much
money on clothes ; and Beatrice wondered more
than once at the succession of costumes provided
for her. Claude kept a very critical eye on her
wardrobe, and Billings and the dressmaker had
much to do to please him.

"You make me feel like a doll," she said one
day, when Claude, after changing the flowers in
her belt, rearranged the bows of her sash. "A
useless puppet to be decorated at will."

"Did not Jack tell you in that letter that your
work in life was to be lovely ? " Claude retorted,
"and is not my effort to keep you 'trimmed and

burning' a worthy one? You are the light of my world, and I cannot allow your brilliancy to be dimmed by crooked bows or ill-chosen flowers. You must let me have my will in this."

"Of course, but I think so often of the difference between us and John; his life is so high and noble."

"Do you remember my parable of the lion and the butterfly? You are the flower, I am the butterfly; can we help it? It is fate, dear. Jack cannot flutter, I cannot roar. We had better acknowledge our limitations and be happy. I am free to say, however, that I prefer being the butterfly, with my sweet flower to make life one long joy."

"It is not right to love a creature so," Beatrice said gently. "God will not bless idolatrous love."

"A jealous God?"

"The Mother said that meant watchful over us."

"The Mother has a long head, and if I could be converted, you and the Mother would do it."

"How do you mean converted? You seem very good to me."

"This world is full of puzzling things, my dear, and of fine distinctions. There are moral men and spiritual men; and the typical moral man is seldom spiritual, being sufficient unto himself; and the typical spiritual man is not always moral, being mystically dependent on something outside of himself, that does not seem always to make him toe the mark. I consider myself a

moral man, but not typical ; and not feeling sufficient unto myself, I pray to the fetish of blood
and station to keep me straight. Now to convert me would be to make me into a spiritual
man. Maybe you will, in time ; so you can satisfy your little conscience by looking on me as
a missionary jurisdiction. I will get a little mitre
for you, and a little pastoral staff ; and I will go
so far as to say ' baa ' sometimes."

" You frighten me, Claude," laying her hand
on his arm and looking up wistfully. " If I did
not know the truth from your own lips, that you
are religious, I should think sometimes that you
were not a Christian. Do not be offended, " trying to look into his face that he had turned away.
" I know better ; I see how kind and gentle you
are, and how you give so much to help the poor,
and how you go to church. Of course I know
that it is only for argument and for fun that
you talk sometimes. You see I have been accustomed to only one kind of people—serious
people like father and John ; and you are so
different that I have to learn you. And now
and then a sort of terror comes over me—' suppose
Claude means all he says '—but I know that you
do not. Won't you look at me ?" putting her
hand on his cheek to turn his face to hers. " I
beg your pardon—I am sorry I blunder so."

Claude put her two hands together in his,
" Could you love me in spite of everything ? " he
asked, looking straight into her eyes,

"I must love you always."

"But suppose I should set you free, and tell you that I am a false, wicked man."

"I should not believe you."

"Suppose John proved it to you?"

"Willfully wicked—refusing the right?"

"In John's eyes, yes."

"It would break my heart, and I should die."

"You love me, then? better than you did when you were given to me?"

"Infinitely."

"Better than John?"

"Differently."

"How do you love John?"

"As you would love a saint to whom you could pray. I used to be bored when John would talk to me of the Christian life, for I had not learned to think then; but now—now I think it is the only life. I sit and think sometimes of all the Mother taught me—of father—of John. What high lives! I could adore them—so, I love John."

"And I am different; on a lower level—not adored—not looked up to?"

"You are unkind."

"Then truth is unkind."

"But you can be high and noble."

"What is it to be noble? I do not lie, nor cheat, nor traduce my neighbor. I am not stingy nor low in my tastes."

"You are like the young man in the Bible; who

kept all the law, but let the spirit of love go—he did not give *himself*. The Mother said that the only true life was the life lived for others—self-abnegation is true nobility. I think the reason that I am realizing it now is that I love you. To love anything better than one's self seems to make one understand so many things—to see so much more clearly."

Claude dropped her hands and turned away. Beatrice watched him with a pained look growing in her eyes. "Claude!" she called softly. "Claude, I beg your pardon."

He turned quickly and came toward her. "Beg my pardon, child? I have nothing to forgive. I went away because——"

"I had hurt you?"

"Because I felt so unworthy."

"If you let me go I will die," she said. "My life seemed all to go out of me when you turned away."

Claude drew her close to him. "You shall not die," he said; "but remember, I have confessed to you. I am not noble; my aims and my life are not high as you count high; I am of the earth, earthy, and in loving me you come down to the earth."

"Claude!" Mrs. Van Kuyster called, and Claude went to her, where she was in the study across the hall. She handed him a letter. "From Martin Kinsey," she said.

"Martin Kinsey? Is Jack ill?" Then he read:

I take the liberty of writing to you, my dear Mrs. Van Kuyster, because I think your nephew needs some good advice and some care. He is overworking himself. I have been away for a little while, and returning find the weather stifling and Paget working as if it were midwinter. This is not the worst. He hears rumors of fever in the South, and says that he will go if it be declared epidemic. I think that this resolution is partly due to his being run down and morbid. Send Claude after him. When you see him, you will forgive my interference.

"I shall fetch him myself," Mrs. Van Kuyster said. "It will have more weight, I think, than your going."

"I agree with you," Claude answered, folding the letter slowly. "What nonsense, to go South in case of fever! These very good people are so uncomfortable. When will you go?"

"To-night. I shall not tell Beatrice or anyone; I am simply going for a day on business. It annoys me. As you say, there is such a thing as being too good."

The change from Newport to New York seemed dreadful to Mrs. Van Kuyster. It was many years since she had spent even an hour in the city at this season, and she felt it a great hardship.

She drove first to the down-town mission and left a note for John; then, taking an early lunch at a restaurant, went to the house. How the bell echoed through the empty place; how desolate it seemed, and how very long the woman took to come! Inside, it seemed worse, for everything was packed up and dusty. It must be very dreary for John, she thought. The woman opened the study windows and asked if Mrs. Van Kuyster had come to stay. " Air my bedroom and some linen ; I may spend the night ; but you need not cook anything for me, I will go to a restaurant." The woman dismissed, Mrs. Van Kuyster looked about her while she took off her gloves and bonnet.

The table seemed not to have been touched since John had left it. The inkstand was uncovered, the stampbox open, and spread out on the blotting book was a letter in Beatrice's handwriting. It was unmistakable. Was it so he conquered himself?

She folded it and put it in its envelope; it would hurt him to find that he had left it open, and, if put away, he would at least be uncertain about it. Why had he not striven against Claude—could there be anything in Claude's suggestion of former ties? Not a book was out of place—not a magazine or newspaper in sight. Did he spend his time beating himself down with that letter as an instrument of torture? This was to be righteous! Would she ever have been righteous, even if she had married Carter Wilton—been a conscientious, self-sacrificing, devoted Christian like John? A clergyman's wife, overworked, badly dressed, tired out! Patching, turning, drudging—an upper servant, in short, with a lot of children at her heels. Dreadful! She would never have known how painful another kind of life could be, and would always have deemed herself something of a martyr. It was better as it was; things generally *were* better as they were—"might-have-beens" were delusions. She would not give up her experience, her suffering, for anything; for that would be to give up her development. Some people might not like the thing she had developed into, but that did not hurt her. She could have no deeper sensations now than annoyance, or perfect comfort; anything more poignant she was incapable of feeling. "The string o'erstretched breaks"—all the strings that used to vibrate to acute joy or sorrow had snapped, and she was glad. Acute joy? There was one verse in the Psalms that seemed to her the most exquisite description of joy:

Then were we like to them that dream ;
Then was our mouth filled with laughter, and our tongue
　　with joy.

Carter had read it to her long ago—before she knew anything but him. She had been perfectly happy once, and that ought to satisfy any creature who looked about with intelligent eyes. She had thought over every possible sorrow that could come to her, and there was not anything that could bring more than discomfort. Physical suffering might come, but there were narcotics that would let her sleep her life away, and she would use them. The thing that could annoy her most would be the dying out of the name of Paget, and that did not seem probable, for besides John, Claude had declared that his second son should take the name of Paget. And even if the name should die : what then ?

She would try to persuade John back to Newport with her, and avert this possible unpleasantness of his risking his life in the fever. He could torture himself more effectually at Newport, seeing Claude and Beatrice together. She would suggest it. According to John's code, it would be a good way of strengthening his spiritual muscles. How silly humanity was ! even Claude had been betrayed into exaggerated feeling. She wondered what he would do if Beatrice should ever turn from him. It was not an impossible thing ; she was quite capable of throwing over all the wealth and happiness for religious scruples. Under such circumstances Claude would be a study.

She heard the click of a latchkey, a step in the hall, and rose as John entered.

" Dear Aunt Claudia ! How nice to see you ! " And he kissed her more than once. She did not move from the circle of his arm, but looking up she laid her hand on his cheek.

" Do you love me ? " she asked.

" Aunt Claudia, you know that I do ! You know that I look up to you, depend on you, and think you altogether lovely. You are the nearest thing to a mother that I have ever known. Often I have wished that you were dependent on me ;

as it is, nobody really needs me, not even the slummites, for there is always somebody to take one's place."

"I need you," Mrs. Van Kuyster said, and there was a tone in her voice that John had never heard since her first recognition of him—a ring of something like despair. "I have come for you," she went on; "I cannot leave you here any longer. I know that it will hurt you"—looking him straight in the eyes—"but the best cure for a burn is to hold the burnt spot close to the fire."

John led her to a chair. "Perhaps you are right," he said.

"We will pack your things, then, and you will come home with me to-night."

"Not to-night. There are two people dying down in a stifling tenement—a blind, deserted old woman, and a young girl dying of wrong and neglect. Both are afraid to die, and I must not leave them. When they are gone, I will come to you. But you have not told me yet what brought you here?"

"Martin Kinsey wrote to me about you."

"And you came entirely on my account?"

"Perhaps. Martin wrote that there was a rumor of fever in the South; yellow fever, of course."

"Yes. Did Martin tell any more tales?"

"That you would go if it were declared epi·demic."

"Of course."

" I see no 'of course' in it. If you were down there as a clergyman or a physician, then it would be your duty; but you have positively no ties there, and I cannot see how it is your duty to go any more that it is mine."

" Except to humanity at large, I have no ties anywhere, Aunt Claudia; so that I am the one of all others to go. But there is no epidemic yet, so we will not discuss it, and I will come to you as soon as possible. You think that Beatrice and Claude are doing the right thing?"

" I think Beatrice would have been happier with you. Marjorie does not agree with me; she thinks that Claude is necessary to Beatrice's happiness."

" Then they will be happy; my only fear is that the girl is so young and undeveloped, and one cannot say certainly of a girl of her temperament that she will be this or that. Of course, with Claude always beside her, her development is apt to take place along such lines as he lays down for her."

" Claude is a selfish man," Mrs. Van Kuyster said, "and seeing him with Beatrice, I realize that he has never really cared for any creature before. He really loves Beatrice, however, and it is doing him good. Save for creature comforts, Claude has been absolutely careless all his life, and until now he has never wanted anything except what money could buy. I half way wish that he could be deprived of Beatrice."

"Aunt Claudia!"

"I mean it. It is a wonderful revelation to people such as we are, to find how powerless money is to procure the realities. Life would be a new thing to Claude. The effect would be curious."

"And you would study him in his pain?"

"What else have I to do in life save study my fellows and embroider tea-cloths?"

"And the world so full of sorrow and sin!"

"Would you send a leper out as a sick nurse? I am absolutely selfish, and selfishness is the very germ and root of sin."

"Is your religion nothing to you?"

"What is my religion? That it is not the same as yours is the only thing I am sure of."

"I do not believe you."

"It is true, nevertheless."

"Don't say that! I pray that you will not talk in that way; you may convince yourself in time. Won't you rouse yourself—do something for somebody?"

"My dear boy, I do not want to. For many years I have been striving to reach what Claude calls the height of civilization, which is to be absolutely without feeling. I can still be disturbed by an ill-fitting dress or a badly served dinner, but not much."

John walked to the window and stood looking out for a moment. "If this is so," he said at last, "why should you care if I work myself to death, or die of fever in the South?"

"You are the last of the Pagets," Mrs. Van Kuyster answered.

"You asked me a moment ago if I loved you," turning on her quickly; "what did you mean?"

"Exactly what I said. I want you to love me, for then you will fulfill my wishes. I want you to marry Marjorie Van Kuyster and re-establish the family."

John turned again to the window, a frown on his brow. He felt baffled, hurt. To fight this worldliness and unbelief was like fighting shadows. Life seemed one great negation. The poor wretches down in the slums were higher than this. He would hate these people presently; this superiority to everything genuine was maddening. Claude was right about his world; it *was* cheerfully cold and critical—almost bloodless. If these were the results of civilization, he would rather be a border barbarian.

"Marjorie is above the average in many ways," Mrs. Van Kuyster continued, "and has sense enough to know that her happiness will be in throwing herself into your work. She has not crystallized yet; she still has enthusiasms and impulses, but she can control them, which is an added charm. I wish you would think of it."

John turned from the window and began to walk up and down the room with his hands clasped behind him. "I scarcely think that you have the right to use Miss Van Kuyster s name in this way," he said gravely. " I admire her extremely, but she has done nothing to give you the right to speak as if she were simply waiting for a proposal from me."

Mrs. Van Kuyster leaned back with a smile creeping about her lips, and a look of amusement in her eyes.

" Miss Van Kuyster has been kind and pleasant to me," John went on. " She has been interested in my work, but I understood perfectly that it was only because it was a new sensation. If you had been with us on our expeditions, you would have understood this too ; and you must excuse me, but I cannot permit you to speak of Miss Van Kuyster in this way."

" My dear John, you are a survival, and *you* must excuse my being amused. I had no idea of answering for Marjorie, nor of suggesting that she had said ' snap ' before you had said ' snip.' Marjorie, however, is a child of this world, and, if she ever had the youthful, romantic notions of love has outlived them. In short, she is rational. You are handsome, you have position and some money. Marjorie has position and a great deal of money. All these things weigh with a rational being, and I have no doubt that if you have sense enough to ask her, she will have sense enough to accept you, and make you very happy."

John stopped in front of her. " Unless you withdraw all this, Aunt Claudia," he said, " I

cannot come to Newport while Miss Van Kuyster is there."

"My dear John!"

"I am in earnest."

Mrs. Van Kuyster looked up at him a moment.
"I withdraw it all, my dear. Please consider it
all unsaid, and the thought shall never cross my
mind again. In return, you must promise that
as soon as your inconvenient paupers die you
will come down. You really look ill; and if you
have any idea of indulging in a Southern epidemic
you had better get a little strength in order to
die comfortably. Now, where shall we go for
dinner?"

The return to Newport was very flat to Mrs.
Van Kuyster, and she felt irritated with herself
because she had indulged in an impulse. She
had taken a tiresome journey, and spent a hot
day in the city for nothing, for John would have
come eventually with only a letter for persuasion.
To add to her annoyance, she found that during
her absence a disagreement had arisen between
Claude and Miss Grigsby, the governess, which
she was expected to arbitrate.

"Miss Grigsby is meddlesome," Claude said,
having sought Mrs. Van Kuyster in the sacred
solitude of her dressing room. "I would send
her off to-morrow but for Beatrice."

"Does Beatrice object?"

"I have said nothing to her about it; if I did

she might ask inconvenient questions. She is actually fond of the old person."

" I am a little in the dark," Mrs. Van Kuyster said. " What has Miss Grigsby done ? "

" Well, Miss Grigsby sought a private interview with me yesterday, and had the impertinence to tell me that I was undermining Miss Wilton's Christian faith, and that as a Christian she thought it her duty to remonstrate."

" And are you not ? "

" If I am, it is none of her business.

" She will not agree with you there."

" She *does* not agree with me there. When I told her that seeing that Beatrice's future belonged to me, I had a right to train her to suit myself, she answered coolly that before Beatrice was my wife she was an immortal soul for whom she herself was in part responsible, and that she would leave no stone unturned to destroy my influence. It is no laughing matter," he went on more crossly, seeing a smile on Mrs. Van Kuyster's lips, " and I cannot see how it amuses you."

" My dear Claude, *you* amuse me. You have always posed as one who could not be moved or disturbed by any turn of fate, and here, at the very first opposition of your whole life, you are totally routed. It is rather unique, too, that the first person who tries to teach you the ' uses of adversity ' should be an insignificant, poverty-stricken little old woman, without influence anywhere in the world."

" I am glad that I furnish you entertainment."
Claude answered, after a moment's silence,
"though in seeking you I had no such amiable
intention. I want you to dismiss Miss Grigsby."

" I cannot without just cause and due warning."

" Pay her a quarter's salary, and let her go."

" You have yet to learn, Claude, that money is
not all-powerful. Miss Grigsby is a lady, and because of her poverty is more sensitively proud
than you are. She would not accept it."

Claude walked up and down the room impatiently.

"And surely," Mrs. Van Kuyster went on, "you
can hold your own against her for the little while
we are going to be here?"

" If she should tell Beatrice that I am what she
calls an infidel, I could not hold my own for a
moment unless I lied."

" Well?"

" I cannot lie."

" To one who professes to hold everything in
solution, truth must be a fluid where lines cannot
be drawn, and to which bonds cannot be set."

" That is nonsense ! "

"On the contrary, it is a logical deduction.
Remember that to assume the truth of your own
existence even, is to plunge yourself into endless
difficulties; so to make two assumptions, first
that Claude Van Kuyster *is*, and further, is an
agnostic, is rash in the extreme. I think that instead of losing my temper with Miss Grigsby, I

would explain my difficulties to her, and ask her to convert me."

"What has become of *your* morality?"

"I am logical, and keep that in solution too; but it seems to me that you have lost your head in this matter; and for a man who believes in nothing but intellect—who relegates all emotions, both spiritual and moral, to the domain of the liver—for such a man to lose his head is ruin."

"You will not dismiss her, then?"

"I cannot, any more than you can lie."

Here the maid brought a request from Miss Grisby for an interview.

Lifting a *portière*, Claude stepped into the next room, while Mrs. Van Kuyster smiled; then she sighed and said, "Bring her in, and as soon as she is gone, Christine, bring me a cup of tea. Tell Johnson I want the carriage at half after five. Ask Miss Van Kuyster and Miss Wilton to drive with me if they have no other plans."

Then Miss Grigsby came in.

"Please find yourself a comfortable chair, Miss Grigsby," Mrs. Van Kuyster said, looking about as if comfortable chairs were rare.

"Thank you, madam"—and Miss Grigsby took her seat on the edge of the straightest chair she could find.

"Do you wish to see me about anything important?" Mrs. Van Kuyster went on. "Has Beatrice been rebelling?"

"I consider it very important, Mrs. Van Kuyster, it concerns Miss Wilton vitally; and as I am partially responsible for her as her governess, I hold it my duty to speak to you, her guardian, on this subject. I do not know that you realize it, but Mr. Van Kuyster is a confirmed skeptic "— pausing expectantly.

Mrs. Van Kuyster bowed slightly.

"And is undermining, systematically, Miss Wilton's faith."

"You think that Miss Wilton is giving up her belief consciously?"

"Not consciously; Mr. Van Kuyster's attacks are too subtle for her to understand the force of them; but I see the leaven working, and it is a cruel sin," her voice trembling.

"You know, I suppose, that with my free consent Miss Wilton is to marry Mr. Van Kuyster?"

"Yes, madam."

"And that a woman is very apt to think with her husband? If Miss Wilton falls in with his views unconsciously, it will not be sin for her."

"With all due respect, Mrs. Van Kuyster, permit me to say that I cannot comprehend your attitude in this matter"—and Miss Grigsby's faded eyes were flashing.

"My experience, Miss Grigsby, has taught me that it is dangerous to dogmatize—that there is generally another view of everything than the view we may take. In this case there are many things to be considered. Miss Wilton loves Mr,

Van Kuyster, and I believe that her happiness depends very much on her spending her life with him. Point out to her his skepticism, and you risk all her happiness; leave her alone, and she will probably never find it out. And grant that she drifts into his mode of thought, she will do it unconsciously, and as I have just said, that will not be sin to her."

"And you feel no responsibility for yourself in this, Mrs. Van Kuyster?"

"It is not often I permit myself to be questioned as to my feelings, Miss Grigsby, but in this case I will answer you that I do not feel very much about it in any way. Further, I think that a great deal of what Christians call conscientious remonstrance, is in common parlance, meddling; in ecclesiastical language it might be called 'works of supererogation.' I do not think that I shall interfere—nor shall I permit you to interfere."

Miss Grigsby rose, a dull color creeping up her withered cheeks. "I am sorry that I disturbed you, Mrs. Van Kuyster," she said, "and as I will not mention the subject to you again, I consider it my duty to warn you of my intentions. I cannot permit my conscience to be stifled. I cannot think for one moment that any happiness which Miss Wilton may enjoy as Mrs. Van Kuyster can compare in value to the least spiritual loss. She has a pure and lovely spirit—she has a beautiful childlike faith—she *is* as a little child, and

so, fit for the kingdom. I am always remembering the words of the Master, ' Whoso shall of-
fend one of these little ones which believe in me,
it were better that a millstone were hanged about
his neck, and he were drowned in the depths of
the sea.' As a Christian I *must* interfere. I cannot see a soul wrecked, even unconsciously, and
not put out a hand to save it. The sin of the
loss would be mine, mine ! "—her voice breaking,
and her eyes filling with tears—"and I love the
child."

Mrs. Van Kuyster looked away out to sea. The
little old woman in her straight black frock was
touching the sublime. What a power it gave one
to believe absolutely in anything ! How could
this insignificant person dare to run the risk of
wrecking two lives.

" I should scarcely value the love that would
wreck my life for me," she said, turning her face
again to Miss Grigsby's.

"What she thinks of me, or feels towads me
must not matter, Mrs. Van Kuyster. Nothing
should come between a Christian and his duty."

"And will you go to the child and tell her this
thing that I warn you will break her heart—can
you do this ? Miss Wilton is extremely frail, and
the consequences may be serious."

The little lady laid her hand that was like a
bird's claw, on the back of a chair—she was
trembling from head to foot.

" I cannot say how I will do it," she answered,

"and I cannot at all weigh the suffering that it will cause me, but it must be done. I pray that I will be guided. I beg that you will pardon my intrusion, Mrs. Van Kuyster, and will now accept my thanks for the consideration with which I have been treated in your house. I say this now, for I may feel it my duty to leave your service—of that, however, I will give you due warning. I bid you good-afternoon." Near the door she paused. "I have forgotten to tell you that I have warned Mr. Van Kuyster, and that I may determine to appeal to Mr. Paget—though I have no wish to put the onus of this interference on any-one else. But I feel sure that Mr. Paget will act entirely for Miss Wilton's best interests—her spiritual interests."

"That will be to make things very disagreeable, Miss Grigsby. Mr. Paget is Mr. Van Kuyster's brother, and to make strife between brothers would not be true Christianity, would it?"

"'I came not to bring peace, but a sword,'" the little woman quoted sadly, then shut the door.

In a moment Claude entered from the next room, followed by Christine and the tea-tray. While the table was being arranged near Mrs. Van Kuyster's chair, he walked up and down the room impatiently.

"You heard it all," Mrs. Van Kuyster said when the servant was gone.

"Of course."

" And you realize that to dismiss her would be only to precipitate matters?"

" Yes."

" Is not discretion the better part of valor? Why not go to Miss Grigsby and assure her that you have no intention of tampering with Beatrice's faith? I have told you many times that it will be useless for you to try to make Beatrice as you are. Why not compromise, and avoid this disagreeable fracas, that may possibly work much ill to you both? I think Miss Grigsby would believe you if you promised."

Claude stirred his tea sullenly. " I should much prefer killing the little viper," he said.

" I have an infinite respect for Miss Grigsby," Mrs. Van Kuyster answered. " As she stood there she looked a relentless little Fate, ready to clip the thread of any number of lives."

" Damn her ! "

" My dear Claude, do not descend so low as to fight the inevitable, and to use bad language ; recover your temper and judgment, and compromise. Take a little run off somewhere, and think it over. If you are gone, Miss Grigsby will let matters rest for a little while. Think of the complication if she rouses John. It would be a curious study."

" You would make a study of it ? "

Mrs. Van Kuyster smiled as she remembered that she had aroused John on this same point, and she answered in the same words: " What else have I to do in life save to study my fellows and embroider tea-cloths!"

"Good God! when a woman lets go, how far out she swings!"

"Quite true; it is all or nothing. The feminine nature is essentially concrete; drive it to the abstract, and it is lost. To keep its balance it must hold on to something. I have, as you say, let go. Life had to beat on my hands a long time before they loosed their hold. You helped to do it, and dealt your strokes most skillfully."

"And you hate me for it?"

"No; it is you who seem to disapprove of me. You see you have learned to love of late, and that changes every relation in life, and throws a new light on every person, and thing, and thought."

Claude looked at her curiously, sipping his tea slowly from the spoon. "Your life must have been slow torture," he said, dropping the spoon in the saucer, "and I have added to it—I see it now."

Mrs. Van Kuyster laughed. "Tears and spilled milk are an abortive mixture," she said, "and as I am thoroughly comfortable on my desert island of life, you need not worry yourself with posthumous sympathy. Love is making you maudlin."

Claude rose. "I will take your advice," he said, "and go away for a few days." Then he left the room.

XXI

"Oh, the Jew findeth scholars! certain slaves
  Who touched on this same isle preached him and Christ ;
  And (as I gathered from a bystander)
  Their doctrine could be held by no sane man."

LITTLE Miss Grigsby's frame of mind was not
enviable. She had never trusted Claude, and
had combated his influence from the first, hoping
that something would occur to divert him from
his fancy for Beatrice. To her dismay, however,
she saw Claude's influence growing, then was
asked to give her best wishes for the engagement.
Day by day she seemed to see the girl drifting
further and further away from the teachings of
her childhood, and becoming more and more
absorbed in the life about her. Miss Grigsby
would have deemed herself presumptuous if she
had called the life of this favored class pointless.
Since it was permitted, it must be of some use in
the universal plan ; but she did not hesitate to
say that it was far from being a high life.

Claude had said to her one day : " You would
not treat us with so much contempt, Miss Grigsby,
if you would reflect that there must be results as
well as purposes—we are a result ; just as the
foam on top the wave is a result. You could

not have the foam without the wave, nor the wave without the foam. Be a little more tolerant." He was so plausible and handsome, he was so courteous, that it was a great temptation to let things be. Who could say that it was her business to interfere? Only her own conscience, which through all her straitened life she had obeyed without question. No pain to herself could have made her hesitate for a moment; but before she brought pain on others, she must weigh matters well. Her wrestlings had ended in her appeal to Claude, which he treated as an impertinence. She then went to Mrs. Van Kuyster, and retreating baffled, she cast about for some better plan. John Paget was her last hope, save the girl herself. He was a clergyman, and from what she could gather, was considered by this family to be absurdly strict, and morbidly conscientious. After a fashion he was Beatrice's guardian, and an appeal to him might result in something definite.

She lay awake most of the night after her interview with Mrs. Van Kuyster, trying to settle on some plan. That John was coming down later, she had heard them say. Should she wait, or should she write? And morning came .before she had reached any decision.

Early in the day, Beatrice came to her to say that as Claude was leaving in the afternoon to be gone some time, she would not have any lessons at all, but drive with him instead.

" Will Mr. Paget be here soon ? " Miss Grigsby asked.

" I hope so," the girl answered ; " he is just waiting for an old pauper woman to die."

Miss Grigsby gave a little shiver ; she was an old pauper woman herself. " He must be a noble man," she said, " to wait to help an old pauper."

" Noble ? " the girl repeated, her face lighting up. " No one *can* know how noble he is."

" You love him very much ? "

" As one does a saint."

" And would heed his advice ? "

" I would heed his least look. But you shall know him when he comes." Then she went away.

Claude's absence, and the hope of John's coming, was a reprieve to Miss Grigsby, and she composed herself for a little rest.

When Claude went away that day he was very far from a compromise, and his last word with Mrs. Van Kuyster was that he saw no reason against an immediate marriage ; and Mrs. Van Kuyster answered wisely that she would think about it.

" Cannot you take a little tour, Marjorie ? " she said later, " and persuade Miss Grigsby to go as your companion ? "

" You wish to get rid of her, Cousin ? "

" Claude does."

" Claude is afraid of her, is he ? " Marjorie

asked. "He may well be; she is keen and obstinate, and I am afraid that under the circumstances nothing will persuade her away. I will try, however."

She was as good as her word, and, telling Miss Grigsby that she had given her own companion holiday for the summer, asked her to go with her to Mount Desert for a little while.

Miss Grigsby gave her a keen look, which Marjorie answered by saying:

"I will be willing to give you whatever you may think it worth to you."

A dull color crept into Miss Grigsby's face. "I do not doubt that for a moment," she said, "but there are other considerations, Miss Wilton."

"Of course I have not asked you without my cousin's knowledge," Marjorie answered, "and she is quite willing."

An obstinate look came over Miss Grigsby's face. "My own conscience is involved," she said. "Perhaps you have not heard, Miss Van Kuyster, that I have appealed against Mr. Van Kuyster's influence over Miss Wilton."

"Yes, I have heard it, and considered your duty in the matter done. Besides Claude does not intend to interfere with her faith."

"He has done it already."

"If this is so, you have warned him."

"He laughed me to scorn."

"Only because no man likes to seem to take

advice, especially from a woman; besides, he was angry."

" I think he was determined, too."

Marjorie looked out of the window for a moment. Miss Grigsby *was* irritating. She could understand perfectly how she had worked Claude into a rage.

After a moment, Marjorie went on:

" You know that Mr. Paget is perfectly aware of Mr. Van Kuyster's religious position, Miss Grigsby, and yet gave his free consent to the marriage. Surely it is more his affair than yours?"

" I cannot believe that Mr. Paget realizes the state of things."

" But Mrs. Van Kuyster does."

" She seems to be of her son's way of thinking."

Marjorie rose. " If you will not go, you will not," she said coldly. " I thought that I was giving you an opportunity of ending your engagement here pleasantly, and possibly of making another among my friends at Mount Desert."

" You are very kind, Miss Van Kuyster; my engagement here can be ended any day that suits my employers, and—I have saved a little money."

" You think I meant to bribe you?" Marjorie said hotly. " I assure you I had not such a thought. I appreciate your scruples, and feel very sorry for all parties. My disinterested advice is that you come with me, and leave things to Mr. Paget."

Miss Grigsby held out her hand. "Please shake hands with me, Miss Van Kuyster, and forgive my momentary misjudgment. If you will allow me, I will give you my answer to-morrow."

"I am afraid we have made a bad move," Marjorie said, when a little later she and Mrs. Van Kuyster drove down to the shops to match some embroidery silks.

"I do not think so," Mrs. Van Kuyster answered. "I am sure she will go with you."

"When does Claude return?"

"Not for a week or ten days, I hope. I wish he had compromised with Miss Grigsby before he left, but she had irritated him too much."

"Being thwarted is a new sensation to Claude. How strange it is that insignificant little Miss Grigsby should grow to so great importance."

"It is the strength of fanaticism; I have met it before. If I am not mistaken, John has a great deal of it, and I want very much to prevent a meeting between him and Miss Grigsby. We stand some chance of managing either one alone, but allied, I do not know what may not happen. When will you leave if Miss Grigsby agrees to go with you?"

"By Friday, certainly. This is Tuesday; won't that do?"

"It *must* do. I cannot understand," Mrs. Van Kuyster went on, "why I have permitted myself

to become involved in this affair. I suppose because there is an element of intrigue in it."

"And because you love them a little?"

"I am not so sure about that. Claude has
never cared for my love, Beatrice has never got
further than my pity—and it would not be safe to
love John; he would be always allowing his duty
to trample on me, and expect me to enjoy it.
No constitution could stand that, you know. I
believe you are the best thing in my world,
Marjorie; you are satisfied to give and accept a
rational affection."

Marjorie laughed. "It is the best I can get,"
she said, "I must be satisfied."

"It is the best that anyone can get," Mrs. Van
Kuyster answered; "desperation does not pay."

After a moment, Marjorie said: "Do you
know, I think it will be wiser for me to tell Miss
Grigsby the state of things between Claude and
Mr. Paget: she might write to Mr. Paget."

"Scarcely, Marjorie; she would not presume."

"There can be no presumption in writing to a
clergyman, you know, and she is very determined
about this thing. I think I will tell her on my
own responsibilty; it will at least save Mr. Paget
from a painful position. If she writes to him, he
can scarcely help investigating, and loving Beatrice as he does, how will it look for him to interfere? It would be agony to him."

"Doubtless; but in saving John, you expose
Beatrice. Miss Grigsby has already appealed to

me and to Claude. If you tell her not to go to
John, the only person left is Beatrice. If Beatrice
only had a little strength of mind—just enough
to pass the thing over—there would be no trouble.
But her training and her blood are against it. I
am afraid that, at the first intimation, she will
look on Claude as a lost soul."

"Claude's soul *is* dead to the higher things,"
Marjorie answered, " so is yours—and mine. Do
you remember reading how Darwin lost all his
love and appreciation for poetry? That was a
sort of spiritual death. The law is inevitable—
that which is not cultivated and used, dies."

"You will soon induce an attack of that pre-
existent rheumatism of which I told you the other
day, Marjie; pray change the subject, and tell
Miss Grigsby anything you please."

Reaching home, Marjorie went straight to Miss
Grigsby's room, and found her writing.

"In speaking to you about Miss Wilton,"
Marjorie began at once, " I suggested that you
should leave the matter to Mr. Paget. Thinking
it over, I became afraid that you might have
taken my words to mean that you should tell
Mr. Paget—I did not mean that."

" I am writing to Mr. Paget now," Miss Grigsby
answered.

" Then I am just in time. I want to tell you
that Mr. Paget is much more in love with Beatrice
than Mr. Van Kuyster is, and that this is known
to everyone except Beatrice. If you write to

him and compel him to interfere, you will give him untold pain. You will not want to do this?"

Miss Grigsby was silent.

"Have you ever loved anyone, Miss Grigsby? Can you realize for one moment the dreadful position of having to break the heart of the creature you love best in the world? One would far rather break one's own heart. And yet this is what you may drive Mr. Paget into doing." Again Miss Grigsby made no answer.

"Mr. Paget will not dare to comfort the child; he cannot take her away, he cannot avoid the enmity of his brother. Think of all this pain you will make him suffer."

"Someone must suffer it."

"If Claude should promise you that he would not influence Beatrice?"

"I could not believe him."

"Miss Grigsby!"

"I do not mean that Mr. Van Kuyster would break his word willfully, for I believe the only creed he has is that a gentleman cannot lie nor steal—I have heard him say so; but I mean that he is so absolutely without faith of any kind that it seems silly to him, and he cannot help laughing at it, and leading Miss Wilton with him. He cannot be trusted, and she must be warned. No one regrets it more than I do, Miss Van Kuyster."

They were silent for a little time after this, while Marjorie was asking herself if she could undertake the horrid task. Should she alienate these only friends and kinsfolk she had, in order to save John Paget? Claude would hate her for-ever, and John would never understand why she had done it. She could not plead principle as a reason—she could not say, 'I did it to save Mr. Paget.' No one would understand, and yet some would *think* that they understood, and smile. The color burned in her face—this was self-abnegation!

She looked up and found Miss Grigsby watch-ing her.

"Will you trust me to do it, Miss Grigsby?" she asked.

"I would trust you most implicitly, Miss Van Kuyster," Miss Grigsby answered quickly, "but you would be misunderstood all round. In ap-pealing to Mr. and Mrs. Van Kuyster, and to Mr. Paget, I have only thought of saving Beatrice; as between Beatrice and Mr. Paget the simplest and least painful way is to tell the girl herself; how-ever it comes, it will hurt her, and I see no rea-son to hurt Mr. Paget by the way. As for me, pain should not matter to old people"—and tak-ing up the letter she had been writing, she tore it into small pieces and dropped it into the waste basket.

"And are you determined, Miss Grigsby," Marjorie said, making a last appeal, "determined to plunge us all into this pain that we cannot possibly gauge beforehand?"

"I can only obey my conscience, Miss Van Kuyster, and leave the rest to God. I have seen

a great deal of Mr. Van Kuyster; he is often present at Miss Wilton's recitations, and is directing
her private reading into dangerous channels. If
my faith is anything to me—if my Christianity
is worth anything at all, I must strive to save
this child. I love her, no one knows how dearly.
My heart was very cold and lonely when she came
into it, and by some instinct she seems always to
divine just the kind of sympathy I need. I love
her too much to let her drift into spiritual death.
Whom our Heavenly Father loves, he chastens;
perhaps this necessity I am in to wound this love
that is so sweet to me is a part of my chastening;
perhaps the pain I will give Beatrice is a part of
her chastening. She will believe me when I tell
her that God sends it for her good; she will nail
this worldly love to the cross when I tell her that
the Master asks the sacrifice; she will know that
those wounded hands will lead her, and bring her
peace at the last. In hesitating to tell the girl
myself, my faith faltered. It is a just punishment
to me, that you, who do not believe in the power
of this faith, should have witnessed my weakness.
I will not falter again."

Marjorie rose and left the room.

The next morning Miss Grigsby sought her.
" I will not be able to go with you to Mount
Desert," she said. "I think it my duty to stay
here and bear the results of my action until Mrs.
Van Kuyster sees fit to dismiss me. I thank
you very much for your offer,"

"When will you tell Beatrice, Miss Grigsby?"

"I do not know, I shall await an opening."
Then she went away, and Mrs. Van Kuyster,
coming in, found Marjorie sitting there alone, with
her face hidden on her arms that were crossed on
the table.

"Marjorie!" she called from the doorway,
"Marjorie, are you ill?"

Marjorie lifted her head slowly. "No, Cousin,"
she answered, "it is only Miss Grigsby. It seems
to me that I am waiting for the ax to fall—that
I am waiting to see the thread of that young
life cut. I am so anxious, I am so nervous, it
seems like a horrid dream! I do not even know
when she will do it. Will Beatrice come to us
and tell us—will she hate Miss Grigsby and defy
her? I should, but then I am not a Christian.
I used to think I was, but not now."

"Take a dose of aromatic ammonia, my dear,
and when Beatrice comes in, we will give her a
dose, and in addition a dose of common sense.
I shall ask for Miss Grigsby's resignation at once;
she is too irritating," and Mrs. Van Kuyster rang
the bell. When Christine came she gave her
orders promptly. "Bring me a dose of aromatic
ammonia," she said. "Tell Johnson I want the
carriage at once. Tell Waters to put up a lunch
for six, with champagne and the tea-kettle. Tell
Miss Wilton that she will not go to Miss Grigsby
at all this morning, but will prepare at once to
go out with me. Give the messages to the men;

then look after Miss Wilton yourself. We go to the country for the day." Then she took her seat at the writing table.

Marjorie had not spoken, but was leaning back looking quite pale ; and when Christine brought the ammonia, she drank it silently.

" Now prepare for the picnic," Mrs. Van Kuyster said, " and it will help you as much as the lilac lunch did. We will stop for Ted Dennis, and tell Dick and the fair De Loren to follow," and taking the note she had written, she went away to her own room.

Very soon she heard the carriage drive round to the front, and Beatrice and Marjorie questioning Waters as to the contents of the hamper. She only waited long enough to inclose a check in the note she had written, and giving it to Christine told her that as soon as they were gone, she must give it to Miss Grigsby. She was also to tell Waters that Miss Grigsby was to leave for New York that day, and he must see to her comfort and pay all expenses. He was to order a cab for her and go with her himself to the station or the boat, whichever she preferred.

" And if she gives you or Waters any note or message for Miss Van Kuyster or for Miss Wilton, you are to bring it to me."

She went downstairs, smiling, and they drove away.

XXII.

" They told me she was sad that day
(Though wherefore tell what love's soothsay
Sooner than they, did register),
And my heart leapt and wept to her,
And yet I did not speak nor stir.''

THE picnic was a grand success. Marjorie was restored to her usual cheerful self, and Beatrice declared that she never had had such a pleasant time before in her life.

"Once you are married to Claude, your life will be one long picnic," Marjorie said in answer to Beatrice's ecstasies. "Claude is having a brand-new steam yacht built; it is a secret, but I tell *you*. It is to be named the *Jackdaw*, and we will cruise all over the world, next year."

Beatrice's eyes sparkled. "After the jackdaws in Corpus! how good Claude is to me"—and she ran away upstairs.

Mrs. Van Kuyster's first question to Christine was:

"Did Miss Grigsby leave any note?"

"She did not go, ma'am."

Mrs. Van Kuyster frowned and looked at the clock. She had barely time to dress for dinner, to which four or five friends were bidden. She could not see Miss Grigsby now, and to lay any command on her not to see Beatrice would be as useful as to tell the wind not to blow; besides, in any event, Miss Grigsby could make her revelations by letter. After a moment's thought she said: "Go and tell Billings not to leave Miss Wilton alone for one moment until she comes down to dinner."

It was all she could do, and Billings, who had not been rung for yet, put down her paper in a leisurely way, and went in search of her charge.

As Beatrice ran upstairs, she met Miss Grigsby.

"I wish to speak to you in the schoolroom for a few minutes," she said.

"Before I dress for dinner, Miss Grigsby? There is such a little while."

"Immediately. I will not keep you ten minutes." And leading the way into the room she closed the door. The lamps were not lighted, and Beatrice walked to an open window.

"I asked you to come," Miss Grigsby said, "because I must leave in the early morning train, and will not be able to see you. Mrs. Van Kuyster does not need my services any longer. Indeed, I begin to feel that her bringing me down at all was a piece of charity."

"I assure you, Miss Grigsby——"

"I know all that you would say, my dear," Miss Grigsby interrupted. "And you must not think that I have not the kindest appreciation of you, for you have made my life very pleasant to me, and I trust that you have learned to care for me a little."

"Indeed, Miss Grigsby," catching the little lady's hand impulsively, "I have grown very fond of you, and Claude says that you may live with me always if you will, just to read with me."

Miss Grigsby shook her head. "Mr. Van Kuyster does not want me now," she said ; "we have had a very serious difference, and it is this that I wish to tell you about. Mr. Van Kuyster is an infidel, and hopes before long to persuade you to think as he does. I have combated his influence as well as I could, hoping that his fancy for you would fade. It has not, and all I can do is to warn you. To Mr. Van Kuyster there is no hereafter; this world is all that he believes in, or wishes to believe in. He has no code of morals except what is proper or improper for a gentleman. He is selfish through and through, and gives his money to the poor only to save himself from being bored. To him," pausing a second, "Jesus Christ is a self-deceived man !" Her voice was low and tense; her hands were locked together, and even in the dusk light Beatrice could see how her eyes were burning. "They have done everything to keep me from telling you—they took you away to-day, and dismissed me in order that I should not speak with you. But I trampled underfoot all my sense of delicacy—I risk all your affection—everything, in order to frustrate their schemes and warn you.

I could not see your soul destroyed and lift no
hand to save it. By your trust in the holy
woman who trained you—by the memory of
your dead father—by the love and suffering of
Jesus Christ, I beseech you to nail this unholy
love to the cross—to turn from this death-in-life
before it is too late. Farewell!" and she left the
room swiftly.

The blackness of darkness seemed to have fallen
on Beatrice, and through it came the sullen thun-
der of the waves.

"You have only fifteen minutes before dinner,
Miss Wilton," and Billings stood in the doorway.
Beatrice started ; this at least was real—Billings
at least was sane ; and she went immediately to
her room.

The guests were already assembled when Beatrice entered, looking lovelier than usual, for her
cheeks were flushed and her eyes were shining
with a startled look in them. An abyss of plots
and counterplots and falseness seemed to have
opened at her feet. All that had seemed simple
had become complex—all whom she had trusted
had failed her. Or had Miss Grigsby lost her
mind ?

" I think Miss Wilton is one of the most beautiful girls I have ever seen," Ted Dennis said to
Marjorie, "and this evening she has just that
touch of brilliancy which she needs to make her
perfect. Van Kuyster is lucky."

Marjorie looked at the girl critically, then gave

one quick glance at Mrs. Van Kuyster, who answered it with the slightest possible movement of one shoulder. Mr. Dennis smiled. "Has she put on the wrong gown," he said, "that you telegraph Mrs. Van Kuyster?"

"No, only the wrong mood," Marjorie answered with a laugh; "see how preoccupied she is. She is such an absent-minded child."

The whole evening seemed a dream to Beatrice, and that night, when she laid her head on her pillow, the only conclusion that had drifted up and lay stranded on her consciousness was that, if Miss Grigsby were not crazy, and had told the truth, everybody in her world was banded together to take away her faith, and she must trust no one. She had not realized any consequences yet, and had come to only one determination: she would write to John the first thing in the morning.

After that one communication which Ted Dennis had detected, Mrs. Van Kuyster and Marjorie had no opportunity for a word together until the guests were gone, and after a quiet good-night Beatrice had left them looking at each other in a state of foiled vexation.

"Shall we telegraph for Claude?" Mrs. Van Kuyster asked.

"What good will that do?"

"His presence will counteract Miss Grigsby's revelations."

"Would it not be better for us to keep the

girl amused, and let the revelations grow dim before Claude returns?" Marjorie suggested. "Let her come out a little more; drop the farce of half-mourning; immerse her in a round of gayety, and drown the disagreeable impressions."

"Perhaps; at least I will try the experiment, though I have little faith in its efficacy. Beatrice is morbid by nature and introspective by train-ing, and it will all come to the front now. I look for developments that will seem very extraor-dinary to civilized people. She has taken the first news quietly, however, and your morning's apprehension of a furious tragedy was a useless strain on your nerves."

"I think I am more afraid of the quiet," Mar-jorie answered, "but do you think she will say anything to us, Cousin?"

"Scarcely; she will take it out in probing Claude through and through. I am curious to see how he will stand it; whether his temper or his civilization will triumph."

The next morning Beatrice wrote to John:

DEAR JOHN:

Something very strange has happened : Miss Grigsby has been dismissed, and before she left she told me that Claude is an infidel; that he is trying to destroy my faith, and that she was being sent away because she had threatened to warn me. Do you think it *can* be true? You have said that I might marry Claude, and surely you would not let me marry an unbeliever who looks on the Christ as a *self-deceived man!* I have never heard such an awful thing before. Sometimes Claude has said strange things, but

I thought that it was for argument's sake. O John, it seems too awful! The Mother said that the sin of Judas was unbelief. Do you think Miss Grigsby can be crazy? Cannot you come down? Everyone else is in league against me, Miss Grigsby said, so I cannot talk to them. Please come; it is your duty to help me.

BEATRICE.

As she wrote, things seemed to become clearer, and the truth of Miss Grigsby's assertions seemed borne in on her. Presently, the question of her duty loomed up, and one after another, like the waves on the shore, the possible consequences.

"Some gentlemen have called, and Mrs. Van Kuyster says, please to come down, Miss Wilton."

Beatrice looked up in surprise. " I will be down in a moment," she said, "and please see that this letter goes at once."

Was this being called down a sign that her schooldays were done? Was she to be a young lady now? Having lost much of her timidity, she felt a little thrill of pleasure. Miss Grigsby *must* be crazy.

John was going down town; he was a little late, and in his hurry he almost ran over a woman at the foot of the steps.

"You scarcely remember me, Mr. Paget," she said; " my name is Grigsby; I was Miss Wilton's governess."

"Why, of course I remember you. Have you just come up from Newport? "

"Yes. I have left Mrs. Van Kuyster's service, and if you can spare me a few moments in the house, I should like to tell you why."

"Certainly."

John led the way up the steps, and opening the door with his latchkey, ushered Miss Grigsby into the study. He placed a chair for her, then, sitting down opposite, waited for her to speak.

"Of course you are aware of Miss Wilton's engagement to your brother," she began rather tremulously, "but I do not think that you *can* know that Mr. Van Kuyster is trying to undermine her faith. I thought this before I left New York, but was not sure enough to speak. In Newport I became sure, and warned Mr. Van Kuyster that I would interfere. He treated my warning as an impertinence. I appealed to Mrs. Van Kuyster, who declined to have anything to do with the matter. My next thought was you, but I was afraid of making a difficulty between brothers, so I went to Miss Wilton and told her the whole truth."

After the first moment of surprise John sat perfectly still, looking down into the waste basket. There were some pieces of a very ugly yellow envelope on top, and some bits of a blue bill— then the page of a sermon torn in half. He would remember the appearance of that waste basket to the end of his days. Presently he became conscious that his companion had ceased speaking, and looking up found her eyes fixed on him.

"You warned Miss Wilton yourself?" he said hastily.

"Yes."

"And what did she say?"

"I had no time to wait for an answer."

"And what do you want me to do?"

"Whatever your conscience directs"—rising. "In warning Miss Wilton of Mr. Van Kuyster's views and intentions, and of her danger, I feel that I have done all my duty in the matter. She will doubtless appeal to you for advice."

"And you think I should advise her not to marry my brother?"

"As you would forbid her marrying a savage African or a leper," her eyes flashing. "Tell her to turn away from this false life, and to nail this unrighteous love to the Cross!"

John sighed deeply. "I must wait until she appeals to me," he said; then looking suddenly at his companion he asked: "Do you believe that a man should crucify his own life in order to live up to a promise made in his wicked youth?"

"Not if it be a wicked promise."

"It was not wicked—but it was not a promise in the letter either, only in the spirit."

"Keep it, then, at all costs."

"Thank you."

At the door Miss Grigsby paused. "Remember, I leave Miss Wilton in your hands." Then she was gone, and John not remembering to open nor to close doors for her, or to say good-by, sat holding fast to the arms of his chair, with his head bowed on his breast.

Why had Elizabeth's face come up before him in that moment of wicked joy—looked at him from the *débris* of the waste basket so distinctly that he almost spoke to her. And that woman, that ugly little woman, had said that he must keep his promise at all costs. It was no business of hers. Beatrice would not marry Claude now, he felt sure of it. He had not connected Claude's unbelief with her before—he should have done it; he should have taken better care of the child. God forgive him!

But in any case *he* could not marry Beatrice; he must go and hunt for Elizabeth and marry her! Perhaps she was dead.

He rose quickly; until now he had never dreamed how vile he was. And he had *never* really made any promise to Elizabeth.

His work was waiting, he must go. All through the long sultry day he worked and fought. Beatrice would turn to him for advice, for comfort; how cruel! Perhaps she would not; she might disregard the advice of Miss Grigsby—then what would be his duty?

Before these developments, things had seemed hard enough; now they seemed impossible. Who could have dreamed that Claude was a traitor? Yet, nothing was true to him—how

could anything be false ! He was going to marry
the girl, and it would be extremely inconvenient
to be obliged to consider her prejudices in favor
of Christianity—to have to live up to a standard
that meant nothing to him, and that yet would
involve a good deal of personal comfort. But
how awful to take away the faith of a child ! and
she, poor clinging thing, could not live without
it. To drift into unbelief one's self was one
thing, but to persuade a child's soul away from
the truth—how awful ! And these people in this
gilded world were consuming with moral dry rot
—their hearts were worm-eaten, and they did not
realize it. Spiritually dead, what a farce their
religion was ! why did they not throw off the
mask and come out in their true light ? The
vagrants in the slums were better material—the
wickedness out on the border was more hopeful.
Yet, until he had kept his promise as that ugly
little woman had told him he must, how much
better was he than this world he affected to despise ? By *being* false, had he not sapped the
foundations of faith more surely than could be
done by any teaching ?

He must go in search of Elizabeth—go at once.
But what should he do about Beatrice ? How
was it that he had not foreseen just this state of
things ? The answer was simple enough—he had
been too much occupied with himself, and a
stranger had had to lay the truth before her.

How long the day was, and how hot ! He was

so tired he was not fit to think or to decide anything. The old woman he had been caring for
had died two days before; the young girl died
this hot afternoon. He had prayed with her—
had heard her say she forgave all who had
harmed her—had stood silent under her gratitude
and blessings. He seemed to be able to look at
himself as at another person, and to loathe this
other man as false—as a hypocrite—as self-deceived and self-righteous. How had he dared to
criticise; dared to despise; dared to pray or to
teach! would God forgive him?

He took a cab up to the house, and found
Beatrice's letter; he read it, and put it in his
pocket. He wrote a letter to the mission—spent
a half hour over a railway guide, then packed a
valise, and told the woman that he was going
away for a few days.

He was going to a little place he had never
heard of before; but it was by the sea, and far to
the north. It would be quiet and cool.

He had better not decide anything until he
had rested and changed his environment.

XXIII.

"A little while a little love
   The hour yet bears for thee and me
   Who have not drawn the veil to see
If still our heaven be lit above.
Thou merely, at the day's last sigh,
   Hast felt thy soul prolong the tone ;
And I have heard the night wind cry
   And deemed its speech mine own.

"A little while a little love
   May yet be ours who have not said
   The word it makes our eyes afraid
To know that each is thinking of.
Not yet the end : be our lips dumb
   In smiles a little season yet ;
I'll tell thee, when the end is come,
   How we may best forget."

FOLLOWING Marjorie's advice, Mrs. Van Kuyster put aside her half mourning, and though it was the very end of the season she opened her house gradually to larger companies, and Beatrice was brought forward imperceptibly.

But however gay the day the night would always come, and with it to Beatrice the memory of Miss Grigsby's last words. Claude had not come back yet, and from John she had had only a note, dated at a little place far up on the coast of Maine. He had gone there for a few days' perfect rest and quiet thought, and from there would come to Newport and talk with her. She had never spoken to Marjorie or Mrs. Van Kuyster about Miss Grigsby, although they had led up to the subject by talking of the ex-governess and her peculiarities. She remembered Miss Grigsby's warning, and would not discuss anything. They might overpersuade her, or, all Miss Grigsby had said might have been her imagination, and so need not be mentioned. She broke the Mother's command, however, not to write to her, and poured out all her troubles. She was not at all sure that the Mother would answer, for letters except in the strictest business sense were against the rules of her order. She had written to the Mother on the same day that she had written to John, quite a week ago; but it was so far, and such an out-of-the-way place, that it would take a fortnight and more, to hear. In her letters to Claude she had made no allusion to anything, except to say that Miss Grigsby had gone. She had begun to dread his return, and to hope that John would come first. Often she felt a deep anger against Miss Grigsby that she had not let things alone; they had been so happy. Yet why was it necessary that this interference should make any difference? She need not think with Claude; surely she could hold her own faith and maybe convert him; and she would hug this thought to her heart, and fight valiantly against other conclusions,

Meanwhile she made friends with Mr. Dennis; he was of Claude's world, and she turned him into a moral effigy of Claude, asking him numerous and unusual questions, so that he voted her not only beautiful, but piquante.

"You are not a Christian, are you?" she asked him quite frankly, and he answered with equal frankness:

"Of course not. What made you think so?"

"Nothing. But would you marry a Christian?"

"If she were very pretty, and would not bore me with religion, I would not mind much."

"And you would allow her to continue a Christian?"

"I do not think I would bother my head about it, one way or the other."

"Are you afraid to die?"

"I don't think so."

"And what do you think comes after death?"

"I have never thought about it; and as nobody has ever come back to tell us, nobody can know."

"Jesus Christ came back again; and the Bible is full of the happiness and glory of the future."

"So!"

"I believe it"—looking up wistfully.

"Then you must be very happy."

She shook her head. "I ought to be," she said.

"But you are troubled about those who do not believe?"

She nodded assent.

" I don't think that is your concern."

" It must be my concern about those I love.
And don't you see how it would be if your wife
were a Christian ?   She could not help talking to
you about it ; and it would break her heart if you
did not believe.   On the other hand, if you persuaded her over to your way of thinking, she would
die of misery and remorse.   Don't you think so ? "

Dennis looked at her curiously.   " If she were
your kind of Christian, she would," he said ; " but
Miss Van Kuyster would not mind much, do you
think ? "

" I do not know.   I do not know if she be a
Christian at all ; is she ? "

" Upon my word, I don't know, either.   As far
as I can see, we all do the same things—we all
seem to be pretty much alike.   You see it is not
a general topic of conversation, and one cannot
tell.   Charity organizations, now, are boringly the
thing ; but that has come to be a science, and
science and religion are opposed, are they not ? "

" I do not know."

"And are you miserable about Claude's soul ? "

She looked up quickly.   " Is he——" she
stopped.   " Do not tell me anything—I must ask
Claude himself.   But you are very good to let me
talk to you as I please."

" You may say whatever you like," Dennis
answered kindly, "and be sure I shall always
understand you."

"Thank you. Now tell me honestly, what would you think of a Christian who would marry an unbeliever?"

"You must tell me first how Christians regard unbelievers."

She drew a long sigh that caught like a sob. "Don't ask me that," she pleaded, and her voice was so low he could scarcely distinguish the words. "What we *must* think of them seems so awful. Won't you please believe?"

"I cannot, any more than you can let it go. But do not let us be so gloomy; come, take a turn at tennis. I see Dick Leveret and Miss Van Kuyster idling about the court." She acquiesced gently, and Dennis, looking at her critically, thought that she grew more fragile and pathetic every day.

Mrs. Van Kuyster and Marjorie, also, saw that Beatrice grew paler and more languid, else she was unusually gay and with a brilliant color. But the calm, childlike happiness that had a smile always ready, that made her songs and laughter involuntary, and movement a pleasure—that had gone.

"I have followed your advice, Marjorie," Mrs. Van Kuyster said one day when they were driving, "but the revelations of Miss Grigsby are not fading from Beatrice's mind. I shall write for Claude, and speak to her."

"Perhaps it would be as well," Marjorie answered. "She has taken it quite differently to what I expected, and keeps me at a distance with the ease of an old worldling."

" Her father had that faculty of impassable silence ; I shall find difficulty in breaking it down."

She wrote to Claude, advising his return, but she put off from day to day the talk with Beatrice. She had no fancy for the possible storm, and as it was Claude's affair, thought that he might just as well be there to bear the brunt of it.

In his turn Claude began to feel averse to meeting Beatrice. He knew that she would question him unerringly, and that it would be all but impossible to turn her aside. He had almost determined not to try, but to declare his position openly and depend on her love. He dreaded this test, however, and, like Beatrice, was willing to defer the evil day. For Miss Grigsby he had only the most condemnatory words in three languages, and agreed with himself that if ever there were an honest hatred in the world, it was his for that ugly, meddlesome little woman. In short, things were becoming decidedly difficult, and he felt provoked and impatient. Why in the world was Beatrice such a bigot ! she should be more considerate. Then he would remember a tone—a look—a touch—and a great gulf would open in his life. He would swear ten thousand oaths not to touch her faith !

One day a letter came from John.

My Dear Claude:

I inclose a note from Beatrice to me, which will explain itself. When will you return to Newport? I do not wish to be there before you, and yet I feel that I must go very soon. I am going South shortly, and wish to see Beatrice first. There is no need to tell you what Beatrice is to me, nor yet what the Faith is to me—you can see how, to a certain extent, my hands have always been tied, and still are. Heretofore I have looked on your unbelief as negative— certainly not as positive and proselytizing. I have not touched on the question with Beatrice; she has been carefully trained in religious matters, and the question is one that only she can decide; but I am afraid that the breach is irremediable. Please let me know as soon as possible when you will go to Newport.

Claude read this letter twice. It seemed impossible that he should ever gauge either John or Beatrice, or foresee at all what they would do under any circumstances. Six months ago he would have expected John to rush to Newport, and snatch Beatrice as a brand from the burning; he would have said that Beatrice would fill her letters with pleadings and persuasions. Now, John left the matter in Beatrice's own hands, trusting to her training; and in her letters Beatrice avoided the subject. It was strange. But one thing was certain, the time had come for action; and he telegraphed both John and Mrs. Van Kuyster.

"Claude comes to-morrow," said Mrs. Van Kuyster as she handed the message to Beatrice.

They were having afternoon tea, and, as usual

of late, Ted Dennis was with them. He saw Beatrice start a little as Mrs. Van Kuyster spoke, then watched the color rise and fade, and a pathetic look come into her eyes. This was surely not the look of a girl expecting her lover; were they putting force on the child? The engagement had not been formally announced, but a few understood it, and until now, he had never seen a happier looking girl, especially when she was with Claude. Did those very candid religious questions she had put to him have any bearing on the case?

That night was the worst that Beatrice had had, and morning found her very pale and languid. After breakfast, out on the veranda, Mrs. Van Kuyster said:

"I hope you will be happier, now that Claude is coming, Beatrice."

Beatrice looked at her gravely. "I hope that I may be, Aunt Claudia," she answered, "but I do not know; I must try before I can tell. It seems to me now that we have drifted very far apart."

"Is it possible, Beatrice, that you will allow Miss Grigsby's sensational reports to influence you?"

"That is what I cannot tell. I must wait until I see Claude. I am so weak, you see, and I love Claude so much, that I would almost surely come to think with him after a while, and that would be death, Aunt Claudia. You are strong, you see, and so can live with unbelievers and still keep your faith. I am afraid of myself."

"So you believe Miss Grigsby?"

"Sometimes I have been wicked enough to hope that she was false or crazy, Aunt Claudia, but Miss Grigsby was so settled in her ways, and so good, that I am afraid she was right. I must ask Claude."

"And if what she told you be true?" Marjorie asked.

Beatrice looked out to sea. "Then I will have to decide what I can do," she said.

Marjorie moved quickly to the steps where the girl was, and sitting down beside her put her arms about her.

"Will you break our hearts, child?" she pleaded —"ruin Claude's life and destroy our happy circle? Have we not loved you—have we not been tender and gentle to you—have we persuaded you to any wrong word, or thought, or deed?"

Beatrice was still as a stone in her arms.

"*Can* you leave us—leave Claude and all his loving care? His eyes are always on you, his voice cannot be soft enough for you, his love spreads all over your path to make every step smooth. Don't you love him?"

"Yes." The voice was very tense and low, and a tremor ran through the girl. Marjorie drew her closer.

"Are we so wicked that you cannot live with us—will contact with us wreck your soul?"

Beatrice drew away a little so as to look into Marjorie's eyes.

"That is not it," she said. "That is not it—not *my soul*, but my loyalty, my honor! How can I live with those who would have laughed the Christ to scorn—who would have betrayed and crucified him?"

A look of wonder grew in Marjorie's eyes. Mrs. Van Kuyster rose. "I hear Claude," she said; "he has come by the early boat."

In a moment Claude stood among them, fair and handsome, with a new light in his shadowy blue eyes that were hunting for Beatrice.

"Well, mother; well, Marjorie"—kissing them lightly. Then he put his arm about Beatrice. "Are you glad to see me?" he said, "and must I charge this pale face to the account of that brier of a woman, Miss Grigsby? Could not you and Marjorie have taken better care, mother?" drawing Beatrice to him, and turning to them with his eyes full of pain.

. Beatrice laid her hands on his lips. "Everybody has been very good to me, Claude," she said, "even to Mr. Leveret and Mr. Dennis."

"The mischief!" laughing delightedly at the turn of her speech, "what have *they* to do with you?"

"She and Ted Dennis have become tremendous chums," Marjorie said; "you will have to look to it."

"I will, indeed. Just wait until I have had my

bath and breakfast—don't run off, Beatrice."
Then he went away, and they heard him going
upstairs three steps at a time.

Picking up a hat, Beatrice stepped down on
the lawn and walked toward the lower end that
stopped abruptly on the cliffs. There was a brisk
wind, and a booming high tide, and the great
waves were racing toward the land in gigantic
glee—dashing against the stolid cliffs, and fling-
ing themselves toward the sky in glittering
showers of spray. The sky was blue, the sun
was bright; a bed of mignonette near sent up a
faint perfume. What a wonderful world and life
these people had! she thought; at the Convent
the sky and the water were just as blue—the wind
as fresh, the flowers as sweet—the love as true.
But nothing would seem the same.

Claude had said, " You have listened to the hum
of the world—you have heard far off the cry of
pain that has no answer—the echo of problems
that none can solve—you have put your lips to
the cup of life and nothing will seem the same."
Of course nothing would be the same. Could
she play with her doll again? Could Marie and
Antoinette understand so much as one word of
her story—the words she would say to them
would seem like a strange language. "The cry of
pain that has no answer." It had come close to
her—close. Her heart joined in it. Why had
they not left her to be a nun? She would never
have known anything; she would have been only

a grown-up child. But the fruit of the tree of knowledge was always pain, the Mother had said, even though the flower might be joy. She had gathered the flowers and held them to her breast, and the thorns had pricked the blood from her heart; and the fruit was bitter on her lips. The waves were not satisfied until they dashed themselves to pieces on the rocks. The flowers were not satisfied until the sun had burned the life out of them. The heart could not be satisfied save by the knowledge of death. Faith satisfied it— religion? This was the only one of the Mother's lessons that had failed her. Nothing could satisfy her now save love or death!

She clasped her hands until they hurt her. Had she lost her faith, that it could not satisfy her? Then why not take love that came to her in such beautiful guise?

She got up hurriedly. She must go to her room, where she could fight this temptation on her knees, as she had been trained to fight all her little trials. And her training had been good.

In the hall she was stopped by Claude, who drew her into the unoccupied study, closing the door. "I have millions of words to say to you, dear," he said, "and I want to begin, for fear that life will not be long enough to say them all unless I begin at once. This divan is comfortable, we will sit here," drawing her down beside him. "First, you are pale; second, you are sad; third, you are silent. Render an account. You need not look at me while you confess your sins—you may hide your face here close under mine; but you must confess. You have gone away to nothing but eyes, and your hands are like two little icebergs. Talk, don't sigh like a high-pressure engine. I wish I had followed my impulse the day that little viper came to me, and strangled her ; but her throat was all in strings, don't you know, and I did not like to touch it. I assure you that was the only thing that restrained me. If I had thought, I might have broken her up with my walking-stick—she looks brittle." He lifted Beatrice's face. "Cannot you raise even the ghost of a smile, sweetheart? You used to laugh at all my nonsense. I would not hurt the little Grigsby for the world; I will endow her if you say so; I really feel grateful to her. That fetches you, does it? Why you are blushing—you are almost as red as a piece of mother-o'-pearl! You may hide your face again now, for I see that you are going to speak."

"Why are you grateful to Miss Grigsby?"

"Because she has opened the way for me to say some things that I wanted, yet dreaded, to say. I was afraid to touch my happiness; but since she has made an explanation imperative, I am glad to speak, for it will only make my happiness secure. You know that my education has been altogether different from yours and John's. Mr. Van Kuyster was an atheist, and mother was not permitted to have any influence over me. Do you see how I was trained?"

Beatrice raised his hand to her lips, and the mute gesture seemed to make the whole world spin about him. "I had no Christian training," he went on, drawing a long breath, "and I would not become an atheist, so the best I could do was to hold all things in solution. I hold them so still, dear; will not you crystallize them for me? You are the highest I have known; will you not lift me up? I will never say a word or think a thought against your faith; until I can rise to it, I will reverence it. Will you not trust me?"

Beatrice made a motion to draw away, and his arms dropped from about her. She looked into his eyes that did not flicker—looked until her own grew dim.

"It is I who am weak and wicked," she whispered at last, putting her hands each side his face, "I who love you more than I love God!" Then she broke into convulsive sobs.

"That's right," drawing out his handkerchief, "we will cry it out and be done with it. Put your head down and sob as much as you like. This handkerchief is not meant as a preventive, dear, but only as a sort of breakwater. I think I heard a little smile then? You must forgive my nonsense; it is born of hilarity, which in its turn comes of the immense relief of hearing that you, and not I, are the chief sinner in this matter, and that the sin is what it is. But love like yours is never a sin, my darling, no matter where it is placed. And even Calvin's God would not hurt *you*. I think you must have been an 'elect infant,' little one; what do you think? Here comes the mother "—looking up, " Come in, mother, we have told all our secrets, and Beatrice is going to bathe her face, then help me with my breakfast."

" Oh, how hungry you must be!"

" It is truly awful," putting her hand in his arm, and leading her into the hall; " but I thought that I would have to vituperate the little Grigsby, and I could have done it better hungry, don't you know; as it was, I had to use a good deal of self-control not to eat you." Then Beatrice went upstairs, and Claude and Mrs. Van Kuyster into the dining room.

" Well? " she said.

" Well! " And taking his seat at table, Claude leaned back wearily. " I have been having a beastly time, and it is not quite over." Then to Waters, who was leaving the room, " I want everything you have in the shape of food; I have not had anything decently served or cooked since I went away. As for me," turning again to Mrs. Van Kuyster, " I have come to the conclusion that you are the wisest woman I know; and after much thought and introspection, which have been a useless bore, I have taken your advice. I have sworn a thousand oaths not to touch the faith of anybody, not even a twenty-wived Mormon; and further, I am willing and ready to have my latent faith developed, and my fluid hypotheses crystallized into immovable beliefs. In short, I am waiting to be converted."

" If it can be done"—and Mrs. Van Kuyster smiled.

"That goes without saying. My conversion will be good spiritual exercise for Beatrice."

" You will get very tired of that."

"She will get tired first, I fancy. The next trial will be Jack: he is going South—the fever, I suppose—but will come here first."

"You think he will be difficult about Beatrice?"

" No; he is consistently Protestant and leaves the decision to her private judgment; and beyond that, he may be as easy to convince of my amenability to religion as you are."

" I am nearer feeling contempt for you, Claude, than ever in my life before."

" Thank you; in a mild degree I am enjoying the same feeling myself. Yet, I have not done anything intrinsically false or illogical. I profess to hold only what can be proved absolutely; and on careful examination I find that I cannot prove so much as my own existence. And as an unprovable existence cannot give bond for the existence of anything else, there is no truth—hence there can be nothing false. And it will be hard to sustain a solid contempt for a fluid nothing—*nicht wahr ?* "

" What was Marjorie's fine phrase about you the other day?"

" Marjorie has been using so many fine phrases since Jack has become the inspiration of her life, that I cannot possibly remember any special one."

"That you do not live," Mrs. Van Kuyster went on calmly, "but only exist in a lifeless desert of critical negation—it was good."

" Marjorie says a great many things that are good according to the modern standard—that is, introspective analytical things. I am tired of them: I should like to be transported back into the good old days when squires of high degree could neither read nor write, and ladies became excited over tapestry work ; when knights rode forth and killed anybody who did not agree with them. By which token I am going to reread Sir Walter and Fielding. There is no science or religion there, thank God. Nothing but good old stories where black was black, and white was white, and introspection an unknown word. I am worn out with modern infinitesimalness."

" Literature has taken a wide sweep," Mrs. Van Kuyster answered, "but we are coming back to stories. Presently the machinery of introspection will be kept out of sight, and only the results given in the action, this action being most delicately adjusted, and every word necessary."

" Why do not you write a novel ? "

" Why do not you go out as a day laborer ? "

" That answer is the result of concealed introspection, I suppose, and you would call it delicately adjusted."

Mrs. Van Kuyster laughed. "As you like," she said ; "but you are answered."

"Granted. What have you on hand for to-day?"

"The usual round of rides, and drives, and tennis; a few people to dinner this evening, and to-night, cards. By Marjorie's advice I have been bringing Beatrice forward, in order to divert her thoughts from Miss Grigsby's revelations."

"Good ; has it succeeded at all?"

"We cannot tell; she has never opened her lips on the subject until we put the direct question to her this morning. Marjorie asked her what she would do if she found what Miss Grigsby said of you to be true ; and she answered that she did not know, she would have to try herself and see."

Claude stirred his coffee reflectively. "She is all right now," he said, "but I dread Jack a little. He wrote that it was a question that Beatrice must decide for herself—still——"

"You are afraid?"

"A little ; Jack seemed so sure that Beatrice would be true to her training."

"I am sure of it, too."

"I wish I had obeyed my instincts and dismissed Miss Grigsby long ago."

"Do not blame Miss Grigsby too much, Claude ; if she had not made the mischief, time would have ; and it is better for it to come before things are irremediable. You will suffer, but neither long nor deeply."

"In the name of common sense, what do you mean!" he said, and his eyes were flashing. "Do you dream for one moment that I will be defrauded of Beatrice? to keep her I will sacrifice everything—truth—honor—all!"

Mrs. Van Kuyster helped herself to a bunch of grapes. "The only trouble is that with all your sacrifices you will not be able to deceive her," she answered quietly; "absolute truth is an unfailing touchstone. Have not you observed how in the person of John it has touched all our motives and lives to their infinite detriment? Have we not felt ourselves 'sounding brass and tinkling cymbals' beside him? Your protestations may shine like the silver of truth, but they will turn black when tested. I am not making myself agreeable, I know, but I want you to take hold of yourself in time, and look at this thing in a calm way. I do not want you to let go the only thing you have that is worth having—your self-respect. You have no faith outside of yourself, therefore you must be self-centered, and the core of your life is your self-respect. If you let go 'truth—honor—all,' as you threaten, you will have to despise yourself and be miserable. You believe in nothing, therefore there is nothing to which you can make confession—that can absolve and reinstate you. Christianity turns even sins to account—trampling them into steps on which to rise. Your only hope is to trample your desires underfoot, and be what you call civilized. In short, *refuse* to feel ; it is all you can do. It is the same process as petrifaction, and it hurts, but not as losing your self-respect would hurt. Here is Beatrice—come in, dear."

XXIV.

IN a few days John arrived, meeting the family first as they came down to dinner. After dinner Beatrice slipped her hand into his.

"Sit by me on this sofa," she whispered, and John obeying her, she still clung to his hand. "I feel as if I had been all by myself in the dark," she said, "and I am so relieved to find you."

John smiled kindly. "I am glad to find you too, dear, but it is not quite the thing for me to keep your hand in this roomful of strangers, even if they cannot see it."

"It cannot matter with one's brother," she said; "can it, Claude?" Turning to him as he approached, "Is it wrong to hold one's brother's hand in company?"

Claude looked at John and smiled. "It is wrong to hold one's grandmother's hand in company," he said; "don't you think so, Jack?"

"Just what I have been telling her," John answered, giving her hand a little pressure, then letting it go. "And Aunt Claudia is signaling me—see!"

The light died out of Beatrice's eyes as he

334

went away, and the color from her cheeks; and as Claude slipped into John's place, she rose quickly.

"Let us play cards," she said. "I do not want to think, please, Claude."

"Very well, we'll never think again, if you say so; but before we agree to stop, let me express one thought, dear—that I make a better return for your affection than Jack does."

"You are looking worn," Mrs. Van Kuyster said, as John drew a chair near hers; "you make life too much of a struggle."

"I do," he answered. "I should long ago have reached that point where doing my duty would not be an effort."

"You know very well that I did not mean that. I think that you do too much duty. What is this I hear about your going South?"

"Only that I am going. The fever is epidemic, though not yet declared so."

"And this is the duty that requires effort?"

"Not at all, I am glad to go."

"John!"

"It is true: I am sinfully glad to go; my death there would be almost a case of suicide. I am so tired."

Mrs. Van Kuyster was silent, opening and shutting her fan slowly.

"Beatrice held my hand and called me brother," John went on.

Mrs. Van Kuyster's fan shut with a snap. "How do you think she is looking?" she asked.

"Pale. She seems troubled, too. Miss Grigsby —came to see me."

"And what will you do?"

"That depends on what Beatrice does. She has been carefully trained, and Miss Grigsby warned her. She should decide for herself; but if she appeals to me, I must tell her what I think."

"That it would be a sin to marry a skeptic?"

"That I should be afraid to trust myself to do it. But I did not dream that Claude's unbelief was positive."

"It has grown with his growth; but he will not touch Beatrice's faith."

"There is great analogy between faith and muscle. A prize-fighter, for instance, has to live very carefully; so has a Christian: and a prize-fighter would never dream of living in a bad atmosphere."

"You are too good, John; it is not practicable."

"My dear aunt, I ought to be kicked. If it would do any good, I would confess my sins to you."

"Beatrice holds you a saint, and adores you accordingly."

"That hurts me more than I can tell. If I could only reveal myself—could make people realize me as I am, it would be a marvelous relief. Just as the Ancient Mariner told his story everywhere."

"And the world would 'beat its breast' and vote you a bore. I assure you that the world only cares for results—it prefers to make its own estimates, and is not in the least grateful for revelations unless they be spicy. That the roots of the vine were wrapped around forgotten bones, does not matter if the fruit be sweet and the wine strong. And if the world, grubbing about, found the bones—found even the sunken headstone saying that its faithful friend Smith lay there, the world would drink his health and say 'Smith succeeded better as a vine than as a man!'"

John laughed. "I have no intention of putting the dry bones of my past on exhibition," he said, "but I have a perfect loathing for shams."

"Rest quite sure, my dear, that you will get your deserts. The world never overestimates an *honest* man, though she sometimes worships brute beasts. Moses might have been inspired, but he was mistaken in thinking that he had destroyed the golden calf."

There was a moment's silence, then John asked, "Where does Claude stand religiously?"

"Nowhere."

"Is he open to conviction?"

"About as much as you are to carefully premeditated sin."

"Aunt Claudia," looking at her earnestly, "how do you live? how can you do without hope—without the comfort and strength that Christianity gives one? How can you bear to have your horizon bounded from winter to summer, from New York to Newport?"

"We go to the Adirondacks sometimes," she answered, smiling. "We meditate a trip there in a week or ten days. Then Claude is having a new steam yacht built, and after his marriage we will go on a long cruise. Our horizon will be immensely widened, don't you see?"

"Yes," John answered quietly; but he was pale down to his lips, and his eyes were flashing.

"Are you bent on going South?" Mrs. Van Kuyster went on.

"Yes."

"How soon?"

"As soon as possible."

"Your living without common sense is as enigmatical to me as my living without faith and hope is to you."

"Let us hope that we misjudge each other," John answered, "and while I think of it, I want to ask you a question: In case I never marry, how would you like the Paget property left?"

"Claude's second son is to take the name, he says."

"Leave it in trust to Claude, then."

"Don't you think it would be better for you to marry?"

"I may be married very soon," John answered.

Mrs. Van Kuyster leaned forward. "You have someone in view?" she asked.

"Yes; in the South."

" Good blood, John ? "

" Her father is an Englishman with a coat of arms; and she is the strongest woman I know."

"Are you engaged to her?"

" No, but I intend to give her the opportunity of accepting me."

"Will you tell me her name ? "

"Yes, when we announce our engagement."

" Meanwhile, you are bent on committing suicide in a fever epidemic. I would not accept you."

"Until I have made other duties for myself, I consider that all humanity is my duty."

Mrs. Van Kuyster leaned back in her chair.

"I repeat that your ability to live without common sense is an enigma," she said.

"Is this the gray gauze fan you let me select for you last spring?" John asked, taking her fan from her.

"Yes, on the one occasion that you instituted yourself errand boy for the family."

John laughed. "I must make a confession about that," he said; "I had broken one of your paper knives and wanted to replace it before you knew—I was afraid of you. This is honest."

" It is too ridiculous to believe."

" Nevertheless it is true."

" I never understood that freak ; as you never repeated it, it seemed a freak."

" I never broke any more paper knives. Do

you think Miss Van Kuyster will ever accept
Kinsey? He is a fine fellow."

"I think Marjorie will marry Claude."

"Aunt Claudia!"

"I really think so; I have not the remotest
expectation of Beatrice's doing it."

"Then what will become of the child?"

Mrs. Van Kuyster shook her head. "I cannot
tell—I cannot even surmise. Do you think it
right to go and kill yourself first, and marry a
stranger afterward? Do you owe no duty to
Beatrice?"

John's face had a grayish look, and his eyes
that were turned on Mrs. Van Kuyster were filled
with despair. "Surely she loves Claude," he said
in a low voice; "surely you will not let her heart
be broken."

Mrs. Van Kuyster shrugged her shoulders.
"What can anyone do but wait, and watch, and
help gather up the fragments?" she said. "We
are never satisfied until we have broken our hearts
and maimed our lives in our own way. I tell you
that nothing else satisfies humanity. Save people
against their wills, and they hate you forever;
the mirage you held them from takes ever more
and more beautiful colors, and you grow ever
more and more obnoxious. Beatrice and Claude
fancy that their love is a life-and-death matter;
but this question of religion will make shipwreck
of it all. What can I do? Only wait, and watch,
and help gather up the fragments. This is life."

"It is *not!*" John said. "We may maim
our lives, we may break our hearts, we may descend into the blackest sin, yet even of sin we
can make steps on which to rise. I will not
think but that there is glory and joy in life. I may
not reach it—that is my fault; but it is there
for those who live aright; and whatever befalls, I
will not let go my hope, my faith. The God-
Christ lives and loves us, and is with us; do not
dream that I doubt it for one second—no, not
even if you find that I touch the lowest depths
of degradation." Then he left her. As he
passed around the card tables, he paused a moment beside Beatrice because he had caught a
wistful look. Mrs. Van Kuyster watched him as
he stooped a little to see her hand; how deathly
white he was! He smiled and nodded, and went
his way out into the brilliant night; the only
comfort for his pain was to be where none could
see.

The moon was touching every shrub and tree
into light; the wind was laden with the perfume
of flowers, and every wave was turned to silver as
it came. It was a help, this tumultuous sea; its
movement seemed to still him as he walked on
slowly, thinking of the problems that lay about
him.

Somehow this gilded luxury, the highest reach
of civilization, touched hands in its effects with
the brutalizing slums. Both extremes seemed to
smother heart and soul; but in these higher

ranks the death seemed more complete, for the
death was so slow and so sweet. Down yonder
they fought it, for the death was bitter.

Must he leave Beatrice to this slow, sweet death?
It would surely come to her, that or the bitterest
struggle of all. What was his duty to Beatrice?

He sat down on a rock and covered his face
with his hands. Must he tell Claude all his humiliation of the past as well as the pain of the
present in order to convince him that there was
no selfish motive at the root of his interference,
if he must interfere?

He rose and walked on hastily. Even this he
would do, if necessary. A little humiliation more
or less, what did it matter in the light of what he
had already suffered and might avert from others?
After a time pain numbs one.

He turned again to the house. It was well
this trial had come into his life, to show him
what a coward and hypocrite he was.

They were still playing cards, and he drew a
chair near to Beatrice.

Her face lighted up. " Do you know how?"
she whispered.

"Yes, but I must not advise."

Watching him, Marjorie felt her heart ache,
Mrs. Van Kuyster analyzed his pluck, and Claude
grew uneasy. The sooner he made his position
clear to John, the better; there was no counting
on these conscientious scruples, or what they
might persuade a fanatic into doing.

" Are you going South ? " Claude asked, when, the guests having gone, they were standing about preparatory to separating for the night.

" Yes."

"South, John ? " and coming close to him Beatrice laid her hands on his arm, and lifted a distressed face to his. " What for—when ? "

" To my work, child, and now."

"You promised, John," she faltered.

" That I would never go without your full knowledge, and that I was sure you would let me do my duty—you will ? " taking her hands and holding them together in his. " And remember," he went on, " that things have changed since then. Then you belonged to me, in a measure ; now you belong to Claude." Turning to his brother, " I have never ceded my guardianship formally ; will you let me give it up now ? " And he put the girl's hands into Claude's. " Remember, it is a soul you take, not my little sister only."

" It is twelve o'clock ! " And Mrs. Van Kuyster held out her hand to John. " Come, help me upstairs, I am so tired. And, Claude, do not take too long to realize Beatrice's soul ; the child looks pale."

" I am coming too," Beatrice said quickly. " Wait for me ? "

"One moment "— and Claude detained her. " I promise not to keep you long."

She looked at him appealingly. " Not tonight, Claude," she whispered, " not to-night."

"Yes, to-night: it is a secret I want to tell you."

By this time they were alone, and letting Beatrice's hands go, Claude put his own in his pockets, and stood facing her.

"What I am going to say, Beatrice, must be absolutely sacred—will you promise?"

"Yes."

"You know that you are my faith—my religion—my life; that apart from you I have no hope. You told me three days ago that you loved me more than you did your God. To-night you have avoided me, and turned to John. Have you deceived me? Have you, a Christian, told me, an unbeliever, an untruth? This is not polite, is it? It is even a little brutal—I should be more civil and say ' Have you been mistaken in your feelings?' But when a man's whole life is at stake, he cannot mince matters. I do not want an answer now, you are not fit to give it— you are trembling and angry because I have hurt you; but I want you to think it over calmly and carefully, and tell me to-morrow. My darling!" drawing her close to him; " be careful, do not fasten your affections on John, it would only annoy him. Will you forgive me this plain speaking?"

Beatrice's eyes were flashing, and she tried to push him away; but he took her hands and clasped them fast in one of his, and with his other arm he held her still.

"Do you think I will let you stand off and quarrel with me?" he said, and his voice was wonderfully sweet. "You must speak where you are—where you can feel each throb of my heart, and use them to punctuate your words. I have hurt you."

"Cruelly! how could you hurt me more than to think that I have told you an untruth—that I would love John against his will—that I *could* love him save as a brother! I almost hate you for it; and you must let me go."

"Not yet; not until I have told you one more thing. I know that I am not worthy to approach you—that you are far above me in every way—in all the best things in life—but I know, too, that no being in all the universe can love you as I love you. There is no wrong you could do—no sin you could commit that I would not forgive; and loving you in this way—a sinful way, you think— I will yet rather set you free, than cause you one moment's annoyance, even. In short—I lay my life down before you—what will you do with it?" Beatrice's head had drooped, and her hands were clinging to his now, instead of being held.

"What will you do with it, dear?" he went on. "Will you drop it in the roadside dust to perish?"

"O Claude, you *know* that what I told you the other day is true! It is *my* love that is sinful; and that is why it is a pain—that is why I can find no rest in it."

"How is it sinful?"

"It is not true to my Faith. Loving you, how could I also love your bitter enemy and give him my life? You are Christ's enemy, and I am not loyal. All the time I feel that there is a bar between us—that there is something missing from you and your love. It troubles me, it pains me; and John is the only one I could have asked about it."

"If John should tell you to give me up, what would you do?"

"I should die."

"And what good would that do, save to make me a castaway?"

"You could solve it all by simply saying I believe."

"I believe," Claude said quietly.

The girl's whole being seemed to stand still as he spoke; her hands grew cold in his, and he could not feel that she even breathed.

"I believe," he repeated.

She pushed him from her. "Honest unbelief is better than blasphemy!" she said, while her eyes flashed.

Claude smiled. "I only wanted to 'solve it all' for you, dear," he said, "in order that you might sleep. I take it back, and am an honest unbeliever still. You must go to bed now. You will remember all that I have said, and will you forgive me sufficiently to say goodnight?"

"Yes."

"Good-night, then." And ringing for the servants, he led her to the foot of the steps.

"Good-night," she said gently, but her hands and her lips were as cold as ice, and her eyes looked far away.

XXV

" Between two worlds life hovers like a star,
'Twixt night and morn, upon the horizon's verge.
How little do we know that which we are !
How less what we may be ! The eternal surge
Of time and tide rolls on, and bears afar
Our bubbles ; as the old burst, new emerge,
Lashed from the foam of ages."

CLAUDE had put an insuperable barrier between Beatrice and John, and John now waited in vain for any appeal from the girl. He had written her in answer to her letter that he would come, and that she then could talk to him of her troubles, but she sought no interview. Instead, Claude came to him and said that all had been arranged ; that he had no intention whatever of touching Beatrice's faith, and that if he took any steps in the matter, it would be in the direction of Christianity.

"You may trust her to me," he finished, " feeling that you have left her to do missionary work."

And John did not answer.

Very gradually it dawned on Beatrice that John's sudden move South was to meet an epidemic. She had heard the talk of fever as in a dream at first ; then she began to read the papers and connect it with John. The reports were very meager, and the hope was that, beginning so late, it would not do much harm. But her eyes once opened, she went to Marjorie.

"Is John going South on account of the fever?" she asked.

"He thinks that he may go to offer his services, that is, if anyone is needed," Marjorie answered cautiously.

"That must be what he is going for," Beatrice insisted; "because he did not intend going South until he had been ordained priest."

"He may prefer being ordained in his own diocese," Marjorie suggested. "But why do you not ask him?" She followed this advice, and at lunch that day she asked John when he would go.

"On next Wednesday," he answered. "I have agreed to wait and go with the family from here to New York, on your way to the Adirondacks. Aunt Claudia thinks that she must see to my outfit herself."

"And are you going because of the fever?" looking him straight in the eyes.

By tacit consent they had kept this from her, and there was a moment's pause before John answered:

"Yes, Beatrice."

"Not truly, Mr. Paget?" And Ted Dennis, who was there at lunch, looked up in surprise.

"Fever does not seem so bad to a Southern man as it does to you, Mr. Dennis," John answered; "but I do not know that I would feel so careless about your diseases of diphtheria and pneumonia. They seem quite awful to me."

"Are your family down there?"

"All the people I have in this world are at this table," John answered, "save some distant cousins, and they are not in the fever district."

"I think he is very foolish," Mrs. Van Kuyster said. "I see no duty in it."

"Save the duty of helping my fellow-creatures. My ties are so slight, my duties so few, that I am the very one who ought to go. I have given no hostages to fortune, you see."

"Still, life is rather a nice thing to have," Ted Dennis suggested.

"I count it a great blessing," John answered.

"And yet you throw yours away?" Marjorie said.

"Not necessarily; and even if I succumb, you could not say that it was thrown away, Miss Van Kuyster. Life is a loan that we ought to use for the benefit of our fellow-creatures, and if we let it go in the service of humanity, then it has been honestly spent. To look on it as a thing that belongs to us—as a thing to be only enjoyed, and to be spent only as we like, is a great mistake. For me, I am strong to help the sufferers physically, and commissioned to help them spiritually. I have no one dependent on me. There is no glory in my going, for I can see no escape for myself. Now, Kinsey——"

"Does *he* want to go?" Mrs. Van Kuyster asked.

"Very much indeed, but I have persuaded him that it is not his duty. He is responsible for a great deal, and must look to it. An epidemic in the tenement district, now, would be his duty."

"And mine?" Claude asked, raising his eyebrows.

"Yes."

"You think my life has been lent to me to be spent on the scum of foreign nations?"

"They are human—immortal."

"They may be all that, but not my duty; and I think I should go to the Adirondacks all the same. I would have ties, you know."

"It puts matrimony in quite a new light," Ted Dennis said; "I must think it over."

"It gives a new meaning to the name 'a man of the world,'" John suggested. "You belong to the world, Mr. Dennis."

"Thanks; I think I must hunt up a Mrs. Dennis, and belong to her. Anything, even matrimony, is better than epidemics and slums. And you, Miss Van Kuyster, they'll be roping you in next; will you not turn in the direction of matrimony?"

Marjorie laughed. "Knowing men, I believe I prefer slums and epidemics," she said. "There is a certain amount of glory in fighting death; and if you die, there is peace; neither of these obtain in matrimony, for I have watched carefully."

"I do not believe that I yearn for glory," Dennis answered; "and, for peace, there is the club."

"Does your brother mean what he says?" Dennis asked of Claude later.

"Every word."

"No hereditary ansinity?"

"Not a bit."

"Money?"

"Plenty of it, and a beautiful place in the South."

"What has made him so peculiar?"

"He is a clergyman."

"I saw that; but clergymen, even, do not usually kill themselves in this wild way."

"My brother is either a survival—or a new type."

"God forbid!" Dennis said earnestly. "I could stand one—a survival; but to have a new type like that to come into the nineteenth century—it would be—well, it would be *unusual.* You know what I mean, Van Kuyster—that it would interfere with a great many pleasant things, don't you know?"

"No one better."

"Think of Martin Kinsey wanting to go South," Marjorie said, as she and John and Mrs. Van Kuyster took their seats on one of the broad verandas.

"He is a fine fellow," John answered. "And

you cannot know him all in a moment ; there are depths in Kinsey that surprise one."

" I think that you have developed him," Marjorie said ; "he was only a kind-hearted crank when you took hold of him."

" I do not agree to that; Miss Van Kuyster ; still, if it were so, it is in his favor that he allows himself to be influenced ; not many people will go even that far, especially if it means the least self-denial."

" Granted !" And Marjorie held up her hands, laughing. " I would not argue with you for the world, Mr. Paget. You destroy the most carefully arranged and comfortable systems by some quixotic thrust that no one expects. Things that we weak mortals think essential, you ask us without the least hesitation to put aside. Fancy living on the plan that life is lent us simply for the benefit of others—why it would destroy the very foundations of social life. If you should bring me to believe that, I should return the loan immediately from the top of Brooklyn bridge."

John looked at her for a moment. " I think you could be trusted to lend your life out," he said, " and that without any interest. If you will forgive me, I will say that I think you could be very noble. I have found you to be unselfish, you see ; and that is a rare quality to come to one naturally."

" Thank you, but you do not know me," Marjorie answered, while the blood crept up her cheeks. " I am good on a spurt—I might even get excitement out of the danger and work of an epidemic ; I might even nurse lepers, if the world looked on ; but to sacrifice myself day after day— to plod through a level round of uninteresting duties without any audience ; to live what might be called a gray life—a monotonous life—I could not do that ; a month of it would send me to the bridge.   Therefore, you see, I am neither unselfish or noble even potentially."

" A gray life *would* be the hardest to live," John said ; " but I have faith that you could do it. A gray day has a very brilliant close, some- times."

" That is poetry," Mrs. Van Kuyster said ; " the actual thing is prose—dismal prose.   For me, I would not dream of attempting anything of the kind.   I see no use in it ; I see no use in any of this hunting for work, these humanitarian fads. What I cannot get out of doing, that I accept as a duty ; but nothing short of necessity can make me do it."

" I may be very rude, Aunt Claudia, but I do not believe you.   I will insist that you always do your duty as you see it ; I will not allow you to destroy my ideal aunt, who is as good as she is beautiful "—and leaning over, John raised her hand to his lips.

" It is well you have only four days more with your ideal," Mrs. Van Kuyster answered.   " I may keep up the illusion for that length of time."

" Four days," Marjorie repeated. " I am sorry
to go—I love the sea."

" You have said that you love the Adirondacks
too."

"Yes; but it will be bad to think of Mr. Paget
down in the heat, fighting a pestilence," Marjorie answered. " It will make us feel so poor,
and mean, and low ; even the prospect makes me
uncomfortable."

"John is positively unkind," and Mrs. Van
Kuyster rose hastily, spilling all her embroidery
things; " where is the Christianity in making
one's whole family miserable ? "

John picked up her things putting them carefully into the little silken-lined basket, then
looked after her vanishing figure sadly.

" She loves you," Marjorie said, as if in excuse.

" She knows perfectly well that I go gladly,"
John answered. " It is no sacrifice to me ; I want,
to go. I will confess to you"—looking straight
into Marjorie's eyes—" I am running away from
the gray life, and this epidemic is my Brooklyn
bridge. Do not think of me as a martyr, but
pray that, if it be God's will that I live, I may
live up to what I know to be my duty. You
believe me ? "

Marjorie shook her head.

"You ought to," John went on ; "you opened
my eyes."

" And was a fool for my pains."

" On the contrary, I shall always be grateful

to you. And you will love Beatrice and be kind to her, and you will put some love into Aunt Claudia's life; her heart is starved, that is what ails her. And above all, do not think of me and the epidemic. I am sorry Beatrice found it out."

"So am I; I am afraid she will do something desperate."

John shook his head. "She is too timid and sensitive for that. I think she could stand still and die without one plea for mercy, but she would never dare Brooklyn bridge. However, we are taking trouble on trust. She loves Claude, and my letters shall be disarmingly cheerful, and carefully fumigated. Don't be afraid."

Beatrice, meanwhile, sat alone in the deserted schoolroom, with her hands locked together, looking straight out to sea.

"I think it a good idea, our going away to-gether," Mrs. Van Kuyster said to Claude when they were settled on the boat. "To have told John good-by in cold blood, here, would have been most uncomfortable."

"You put it mildly," Claude said. "I have come to the conclusion, however, that in order to live in peace there must be similarity—all must be Christian, or all must be heathen. There was a most comfortable and rational unanimity among us and our circle of friends, until this eruption of early Christians. Marjorie and I were drifting

into a placid alliance, when I fell violently
in love, and she had a new standard of excel-
lence set up before her that made it necessary for
her to read just all her valuations. It was un-
fortunate."

"You are still violently in love, however?"

"Of course; but moods are difficult—religious
moods impossible. Grant Christanity one proposition—less than that, one possibility—and death
is the only thing that will end the turmoil and
struggle into which one is plunged."

"Are *you* struggling?"

"Only with Beatrice. God forbid that I should
touch Christianity. Beatrice by her lone self is
enough to keep me busy for years. Damn Miss
Grigsby!"

"I hope that this change will help Beatrice to
settle down to common sense once more," Mrs.
Van Kuyster said with a yawn. "I must confess
that for me the play has not been worth the
candle."

"My life would be a dreadful blank without
the child," Claude answered, pulling his mustache
gloomily.

"Do you contemplate letting her go?"

"Not for a moment, actually; but she eludes
me now: I suppose I must say, spiritually. She
has never, since I have known her, looked at me
without a question of doubt in her eyes."

"At all events, it has been a valuable experience," Mrs. Van Kuyster said.

" As valuable as a sword-cut given to teach you how a wound feels."

New York was not very hot, but it was dusty, and the fashionable part of it, being still uninhabited, looked dreary. Nobody said so, but the whole party felt immensely depressed.

For the few days that they were to be there, Marjorie was to stay at Mrs. Van Kuyster's, and at Claude's request she made it her business to keep Beatrice employed, and if possible, interested. Claude went so far as to suggest an immediate marriage, but Beatrice looked so distressed and terrified that he withdrew the proposition instantly.

John's outfit was of course the great object, as he was taking all sorts of supplies ; and the talk was all about those who were going, for both Protestant and Roman Catholic Sisters were under orders to go, besides several nurses. Martin Kinsey followed John morning, noon, and night, in a faithful, doglike way that was touching, and that was encouraged by John, as his presence prevented any possibility of confidential talk with anyone. But in spite of all precautions, the last of the three days of preparation was a great strain, and John and Claude agreed that the farewell should be brief to the verge of neglect. The plan was simple. Instead of leaving by the night train as he had intended, John would leave by the afternoon train, and go from the lunch table without telling of the change in his plans. It was carried out, and Claude came back with the news that John had been obliged to go without coming home again. It was a little blank, but Mrs. Van Kuyster and Marjorie agreed privately that the arrangement was wise.

"I have caught the enthusiasm at last," Marjorie said to Martin Kinsey, who had breakfasted with them the morning after John left. "I am almost longing to follow Mr. Paget's example."

"It is much harder for me to stay here," Kinsey answered simply.

"Let us go," Beatrice said quietly; "do not let us ask anyone, but just go—I am sure we could help."

"You bad child," Marjorie said, laughing. "Could you reconcile it to your strict little conscience to run away?"

"I do not know—I might."

"I think it would be very wrong," Kinsey said gravely. Waters entered with a letter for Beatrice.

"What a portentous looking missive"—and Marjorie took it from the waiter. "What a lot of purple wax is in the seal of it!"

For an instant Beatrice looked at the letter without touching it. "From the Mother!" she said in a breathless undertone.

"Do not you want it?" Marjorie asked, "or is the honor enough?"

Beatrice sprang up. "It is more than life

to me," she said, and taking it quickly, she left the room.

Locking her door, she knelt down by the bed and laid the letter down in front of her. She clasped her hands, and lifting her face she prayed:

" Father, give me strength to obey, and patience to endure, for the sake of Jesus, Thy Son."

Then she laid her face down on the letter, and sobbed as if her heart would break. She knew that the Mother had sent a decision.

The sobs ceased gradually, and still on her knees she opened the letter. It was very short.

My Child : for whom I have never ceased to pray, in the name of God I command you to flee from temptation—from certain spiritual death. Have all my love and teaching gone for nothing, that you hesitate ? Will your life be lonely— think of Christ in the desert. Will you suffer—think of Christ on the cross. Would you give your life to an unbe- liever ? would you commit the sin of Judas and betray your Master ? My child, come to me; your place is here in my heart. The dove has no safety among the eagles of the world ; birds of prey have no mercy. Oh, little dove, come home ! Here is love, and peace, and life eternal.

MOTHER.

The girl stretched her arms out across the bed and laid her face down on the open letter. "You have listened to the hum of the world," she whispered. "You have heard far off the cry of pain that has no answer, the echo of problems that none can solve—you have put your lips to the cup of life, nothing will be the same."

The whisper ceased. She seemed to be looking into Claude's shadowy blue eyes.

At lunch Beatrice asked many questions about John's route—about when they could hear from him, and many other things of which she had never seemed to think before; and after lunch, when Claude had gone to make some final purchases for the Adirondacks, she asked Mrs. Van Kuyster if she might go for a walk with Billings.

"Of course, my dear," and Mrs. Van Kuyster looked at her in a relieved way; she was taking John's going so quietly. "And, Billings," to the woman, "when Miss Wilton seems tired call a cab; do not be out later than six o'clock."

"We will go to the bank," Beatrice said when they were in the street. At the bank they took a cab and drove down to the shops; here Beatrice gave Billings some money.

"You said that you needed aprons, Billings; you had better get them here, for we go away the day after to-morrow, you know," and Billings being occupied, Beatrice made her own purchases and had them put into the cab. Next they stopped at a bric-à-brac shop near the junction of Fifth Avenue and Twenty-third Street; and Beatrice told the woman that she need not get out. Once in the shop, Beatrice walked through to Broadway and into a railway ticket office. She asked many questions, and bought a ticket and sleeping berth for the next evening's train. If her ticket's time ran out before the end of her journey, she could pay the rest of the way. She hurried back to Billings.

After dinner, she seemed to Claude to have gone back to her old self of the days before Miss Grigsby's revelations, and he felt that with John's departure all trouble had ceased. Mrs. Van Kuyster had been mistaken in thinking that Beatrice's creed was in her flesh and blood—and he had been right in thinking that love would hold her.

"If I should die, Claude, would you think that I had been annihilated?" she asked, as they sat together in the study.

"I would rather think that than anything else, dear."

"But it would hurt me if you thought that," she went on; "for then you would not know that sometimes I might be near you. I should ask to come back as your guardian angel; and whenever you did a good deed I should be happy."

"I will believe that, then," he answered; "anything in the world to make you happy."

"And your unbelief is honest, Claude?"

"Perfectly honest, dear."

"Then God will find some way to give you light. After all, to be true is the great thing." Then more slowly, "You said once that I had some money—have I spent it all? I drew a lot this afternoon. Were you in earnest about its being really mine?"

"In the soberest kind of earnest."

"Have I as much as one thousand dollars a year?"

" Much more than that."

" May I give Miss Grigsby a thousand dollars every Thanksgiving Day? You said that you would endow her "—moving so as to look into his face—" but she would not take it from you, you know ; may I do it ? "

" Of course, my darling, anything in the world to make you happy."

" And may I give a little, whatever you think, to the nurseries ? "

" Yes."

" Thank you. You have always been so good to me, and have made me so happy." She was silent for a moment, then she said as if to herself, " God will forgive me for loving an unbeliever, for I did not know it."

" Child," and Claude lifted her face to look in it, " it is foolish to think that you have sinned in loving me ; if your God is a God, he himself must love me, for he made me."

"Of course he loves you ; but that is quite different from my having loved you better than him."

" ' Having loved,' " Claude repeated ; " is your love for me in the past ? "

" I am afraid not ; but God will forgive me if I do my best to yield it up to him."

Claude drew a long breath. " We will talk it all over, dear," he said, " and I will do my best to think with you ; " but in the sacred recesses of his own room he said more than once, " Damn Miss Grigsby ! "

All night long Beatrice was busy; at dawn she went to bed, and when Billings came she was sleeping like a little child. All day she went about as usual, save that she sought Claude more than she had done of late, much to his contentment. Then in the dusk, when Waters and Buttons were busy in the pantry, when Billings and Christine were gossiping until they should be rung for, when Marjorie and Mrs. Van Kuyster were taking a little rest before dressing for dinner, and Claude smoking quietly in the club—a nun stole down the broad stairway and out of the front door. The bag she carried seemed rather heavy, but at the corner she got a cab, and gave the order, " Desbrosses Street Ferry."

Christine was putting the finishing touches to Mrs. Van Kuyster's hair, when Billings appeared with a sealed note.

" I found this on Miss Wilton's table, Mrs. Van Kuyster," she said.

"The catastrophe has come," was Mrs. Van Kuyster's instantaneous thought—but she opened the note quietly.

DEAR AUNT CLAUDIA :
The Mother wrote me that I must come away. My own conscience said the same. I am safe ; do not hunt for me—do not let any trouble be made. In the late mail Claude will get a letter.

BEATRICE.

She put the note back into the envelope, then looked at herself critically in the glass.

" This puff of my hair is a little too high, Christine," she said. Then as she sat down that the defect might be remedied, she said to Billings : " Finish Miss Wilton's packing, and bring me her keys. After dinner Waters will pay you up to date, and one month's wages extra, for I will not need your services after to-night."

Downstairs she found Claude alone in the study, and gave him the note to read.

" She has done it as quietly as possible," she said, " and there must be no talk. She has gone to the Convent, of course."

" She has gone to John——"

" Hush ! she *must* be gone to the Convent—she is our kinswoman."

XXVI.

"Go from me.   Yet I feel that I shall stand
Henceforward in thy shadow.   Never more
Alone upon the threshold of my door
Of individual life, I shall command
The uses of my soul, nor lift my hand
Serenely in the sunshine as before,
Without the sense of that which I forbore,—
Thy touch upon the palm.   The widest land
Doom takes to part us, leaves thy heart in mine
With pulses that beat double.   What I do
And what I dream include thee, as the wine
Must taste of its own grapes.   And when I sue
God for myself, he hears that name of thine,
And sees within my eyes the tears of two."

DOWN in the desolation of the fever-stricken
city, when in the dead silence a footfall
sounded like the tramp of doom, and the rumble
of the dead-wagons echoed ceaselessly, a
little band fought desperately, hand to hand
with Death.   Through the burning days when
the arching sky looked hard as adamant, and
the round, red sun glared down without the
shadow of a cloud—through the long, close
nights made lurid with the light of cleansing
fires, those faithful men and women strove
against relentless death. Now and again one
dropped, and another paused to dig the hasty
grave; then without a word the ranks closed up,

and the awful war went on. Shoulder to shoulder they fought and died, bound close by a common cause, led on by a cross held high in wounded hands.

How small and far away the world seemed now, when a day stretched into a lifetime, and the murky nights were endless, and the angel of death so busy !

In the dusk of the evening, on a doorstep near one of the red tar fires built up and down the empty streets, a woman was seated. She was known in the city as the " Gray Sister," because of the dress she wore. By her side crouched a large red setter, who watched her with brown, wistful eyes, begging with his paw on her knee, sometimes, or licking her tired hands. She looked very weary as she leaned against the railing of the steps, with the gray hood of her cloak fallen back from her head, and her strong white hands dropped at her sides.

A long way off she heard a step approaching— quick, decided. How strange it seemed that any-one lived in this death-hole who was not worn and weary. It must be one of the newcomers. Did she know that step ? Surely something in it spoke to her as it came nearer and nearer, echoing up and down in the empty cellars, thrown back and forth by the desolate houses. She was too tired to turn and look ; if the step was seek-ing her it would find her.

It was close beside her now ; it stopped, and

the dog growled. She must turn and see who it was that she felt staring at her in the flaring light of the tar fire.

As her look traveled up she saw that it was a clergyman; then her eyes met the eyes looking down on her.

"Elizabeth!"

Her look did not waver. "John Paget," she said, and rose. John steadied himself with one hand on the railing of the step, and put out the other to stop the woman, who seemed to be moving away.

"Wait, Elizabeth."

"Not now, I am too weary."

"Where shall we meet again?"

"If you have come to fight this death," she said, "we shall meet everywhere. Come, Wamba."

"Wamba?"

"Yes, the faithful fool." Then she went away, and John stood and watched her until the shadows swallowed her up.

Swiftly and surely the struggle absorbed the newcomers; no change from day to night was heeded, and time seemed to cease. There were headquarters for food and coffins, and lodgings where the workers slept whenever a spare moment could be taken. A young physician shared John's quarters, a kindly fellow, who would pursue John and drag him in for a little rest, and brew for him tea or coffee.

" It is all very well to help the poor creatures,"
he said, " but I doubt if there is one in the whole
city who is worth your dying for. If you are
anxious for a job, however, there is an awful
case at 210 Fourteenth Street," he went on as he
poured John's coffee into a tin cup and gave him
a crust of bread to stir it with. " It is hopeless,
and I left him raving and blaspheming. I
promised Father O'Bryan I'd send help; he is
worn out. You go, and I will hunt for the Gray
Sister; she has a wonderfully quieting way with
her."

" You call her the Gray Sister; does she belong
to any order? "

" No, she explained that she did not; but as
she has never registered any name, and as she
dresses in gray, everybody calls her the Gray
Sister. She came alone, and if she died this
minute her grave would be nameless. She is
wonderful. She has the care of half a dozen
orphan children whose parents have died in the
epidemic, and who cannot be sent out of the city
now. I have never even found out where she lives.
I begged her to tell me in case she should fall
sick, but she would not. She has a big dog, and
this is all that anyone knows; so she goes by the
name of the 'Gray Sister.' "

In the midnight John knelt by the dying man.
He had had a struggle to keep the poor creature
from self-destruction, and now with his hands
gripped hard by the hands made strong by fever

and death, he felt almost too weary to say the
prayers that had been asked for. The words
came slowly, and with staring eyes the dying
man watched him, and now and then repeated a
word. The door opened, and looking up John
saw Elizabeth.

"You are worn out," she said. "I will finish
this," and loosing John's hands, she raised the
sick man so that he breathed more easily.

John stood aside and watched her. What skill
and tenderness and strength she showed, and
how gentle her voice and words!

"His soul is passing," she said—"is gone."

She closed his eyes, and folded his hands, and
straightened the bed. "Somebody in the world
has loved him best," she murmured, "God comfort them." One moment she stood looking
down on the dead face. "So often I watch
them," she said; "no muscle moves; there is not
the twitching of a nerve even, yet a change
comes. Sometimes a light comes as if they saw
a vision. So often I watch them, I know it is
only this body that dies—and its woes die with
it." She turned to John. "Is it not true?"

"God grant it!" he answered.

She drew the sheet up over the dead man's
face.

"Will you report this death, or shall I?"

"We will go together."

Outside the door Wamba joined them. "It is
a dreary life you lead now, old dog," she said, as

he shoved his head under her hand, " always waiting and watching for death."

For some time they walked in silence, then near one of the tar fires John paused.

"I have much to say to you," he said ; "will you come to my lodgings, or take me to your place?"

" Neither; we will sit here on these steps. There is no need to report that death until daylight."

She took her seat, leaning her head back wearily against the railing, as when John first found her, and fixed her eyes on the leaping flames. John sat facing her, lower down, with his elbow on the step above him, and his forehead on his hand. If Elizabeth looked down, his face would be shaded from her eyes. " You remember the night that I tried to kill Manuel," he began, " and you made the boys tie me?"

" Yes, I remember ; it was for my sake you tried to kill him."

" And afterward I told you that I was ill, and in the morning you rode with me to the edge of the town to see that no harm befell me? I did not want to leave you then, Elizabeth, and you made me. You said that there were no comforts, and that it would ruin my character to be found in your father's house. You sent me away Elizabeth."

" And it broke your heart?"

John looked up, but her eyes were still on the

fire, and her lips were shut close as he remembered
them so often of old. What a strong face it was!
Too strong for a woman, and handsomer than he
remembered it. "You were good to me," he
went on; "nobody in all the world has ever been
as unselfishly kind to me; and for strength of
mind and character, I admire you more than any
woman I have ever seen. Don't think for one
moment that I have forgotten any of your goodness, Elizabeth, nor your strength under tempta-
tions. It lives, and will ever live in my heart."

"Thank you."

"I left New York to come and hunt for you,
and I am telling you all this because it is a new
realization to me. I—Elizabeth, I left——"

"Let me tell it to you," Elizabeth interrupted,
her eyes still fixed on the fire. "Let me be kind
to you once more; you will not like to say the
disagreeable things that must needs be said.
You left me at the edge of the town with a scant
good-by because your head ached, you said. I
did not heed that much, for my whole life had
been scant; but I watched you go, knowing by
some strange prescience that you were gone. You
were ill for weeks; you stood at the gates of
death. I stood with you, for I went there as a
nurse; it was well, for you called on me incessantly. I waited outside your door during the
sleep that meant life or death : you waked to life,
and I left you. In the sight of God you were
mine, but I loved you. I left you to a pure life

under the influence of Mr. Wilton. So strong
he was, so true, that only to know that he believed,
saved me from shipwreck. God keep him ! From
behind the hedge I watched you the first day you
came out to lie in the hammock under the trees.
I saw Mr. Wilton sitting near you, and suddenly
you reached out your hand to him and he took it.
You remembered me and the old life in which you
had thought you loved me, with loathing then.
I could almost hear you abjure that pitiful past.
You looked quite different after that, and you
were always with Mr. Wilton. You looked a
Pharisee then, Jack."

John's head sank a little, but he made no
answer.

" I watched you riding and boating," she continued, "always alone, and always with the look
that I am sure the Prodigal Son had when, having left the swine and the harlots, he was comfortably reinstated. But your old face had been
honester and truer, Jack, even when you tried to
murder Manuel Planco. Of course you were
right, I knew that—right to live a higher, better
life, even if built on the foundations of a broken
faith. It was only a faith, you know; there was
no promise. But you did not trust me enough to
tell me. I watched you for three years. Your
cousin came home from the Convent. She was
beautiful, and I saw you with her constantly.
You used to ride with her to a certain bluff—
there was a view there—and hidden in the cha-

parral, I heard you trying to train that simple child. I laughed, for I knew that you would never win her in that way. You loved her; but you did not know it. I used to see you reasoning with yourself. You sitting inside with a book, and close under the lamp, as if you studied; I outside in the darkness, watching through the open window. I used to read your very soul, for it all shone out when you thought you were alone. 'I have made Elizabeth no promise,' you would say, 'it would be impossible to marry her; all would think me a fool. We are worlds apart, and she would not let her people go. I cannot fall so low again. Her people are debauched; and her own past—who can vouch for that? I have sinned; I have been low and debauched myself; I must turn and repent; God will forgive me.' You were in earnest, Jack, for your nature is essentially true; and you suffered. It was the strength of the reaction that made you loathe me. I was there when you were ordained deacon, and I thought how much that white robe covered. I laughed to think of the one doctrine of which you had convinced me. We used to have theological discussions sometimes, do you remember? and because of my father and his sins I had let go what I had learned of eternal punishment. You used to argue with me on this point. After that you put me in hell. That was your first doctrinal teaching.

"Mr. Wilton died. That was a grief to me.

I went in at the study window and saw him dead. His face spoke to me, and I promised to live as he would have me live. God keep him! I kept that vigil with you the night that he lay in his coffin. I was close to you in the shadow; if you had loved me, you would have felt my presence.

"You and your cousin came away with a beautiful woman. I saw her—I saw her at the funeral, and again the day you left. I was at the station the day you came away; I was dressed as a boy, and stood quite close to you. You gave me a half-dollar for putting your things in the train. As the train moved I said, ' Good-by, Jack.' You turned your head, and your face went quite white. You thought it was a ghost.

"I wanted to follow you and watch how the rich, luxurious world would lay hold on you— watch how you would strive to make that child love you. I knew she never would. I could not go, for I could not leave my father. He had got shot in a mail robbery, and was crippled for life. He is dead now. Of my two half-brothers, George is dead; Jim disappeared in Mexico. My step-mother and Manuel took the place. Have I told your share truly?" looking at John for the first time.

John's eyes met hers, and he laid his hand on hers. "It is all true," he said; "I was a Pharisee. Now I will finish the story. I loved my cousin; but, as you say, I did not realize it; not until I realized that my brother loved her.

Women call Claude beautiful, and he is ; and the child became fond of him at once ; he was kind and gentle to her, and did not try to train her. At the moment that I realized my love for Beatrice, you stood before me, and looked straight into my eyes. I could not even try to win the girl. Day after day I realized more and more what I had made you suffer ; realized the wrong I had done you, and loathed myself. There is no pain in life, Elizabeth, like the loss of self-respect. I lived in misery, trying to help my fellows. One day a dying girl, a pauper, said to me ; ' My death has been caused by falseness and desertion ; I hated all humanity until you showed me what a true man could be. God will bless you for it.' And I so false ! So I came away to hunt for you—" Elizabeth laid her hand on Wamba's head—"you who had let me go without one reproach—whose unselfishness has made me selfish—whose gentleness had let me be cruel."

"And in the eagerness of your quest you stop by the roadside to play with Death ? "

" Elizabeth ! "

" It is true, Jack, and you know it ; but you are honest in it all—brutally honest. Let me read you to yourself once more ? Your cousin is debarred you forever ; you are too true to preach truth, having been false, without attempting restitution ; you know at last what you made me suffer, and you think I am suffering still. Love has clear eyes to read, Jack, and, loving you, I

read you. Remember, I love you ; whatever I
may say, I love you ; so it seems to me that in
my turn I can be brutally honest, and with a better grace than you. Having argued it all out
with yourself, you come to the conclusion that
the nearest thing to happiness that you can attain is the restoration of your self-respect. You
must seek me, restore to me my faith in humanity, *my* self-respect, soothe my broken heart,
and convince yourself of your own sincerity by
sacrificing your life to me. You set out on your
quest honestly determined to carry it out to the
bitter end. Still, you counted two chances. I
might have died, or in this epidemic death might
find you. If you lived, you would seek me ; if
you died, a death died for others *must* be sufficient atonement. But you did not want to find
me ; I saw that in your face the other night.
Still, I count what you have done as more than
sufficient atonement, for not one man in a thousand would ever have remembered a woman in
Elizabeth Marsden's position. And you made
me no promise."

" No, but I won your love deliberately and
intentionally ; I took it all ; I took your life,
then dropped it in the roadside dust because I
had become so good, and had such high and holy
work to do ! "

There was silence for a moment ; then Elizabeth said : " It was a natural reaction. If I
had been as true to you as I should have been, I

would have sent you away before. But my life was so empty! Nor does that past seem sin to me. By keeping true to it, it is true and pure to me still. And my life is not so spoiled but that the Crucified will use it. There are plenty of people down in the mire who will not mind if a little mud be on the stepping stone that helps them on to higher ground. You have done all you can; you have found me, and would offer me your name and protection; a man can do no more. It is I who have refused restitution—have refused to be the altar on which you sacrifice your life. And in refusing, I give you back that life, and free you of that past forever." She rose and held out her hand to him. "May we meet and work together many times as friends, and whenever my love or my life can help you in your work for the Master, remember that they are yours. Good-by."

John laid his brow on her hand for a moment, then she turned and went away.

XXVII.

"Hast thou not sung? and is not song enough?
  Hast thou not loved? and is not loving all?
Art thou not weary of the wayfare rough,
  Or is there aught in life thou wouldst recall?
    Ah, no! ah, no!
The life came sweetly—sweetly let it go!"

IN the dusk one evening Elizabeth went to the
train to get a package of clothing that had
been sent for the little children. Waiting at the
door of the office until the one overworked man
could serve her, she felt her cloak pulled gently,
and turned to find a nun at her elbow. Something in the face made her feel faint, as if an old
wound had been opened afresh and her life were
ebbing away. Then swiftly it came to her who
this nun was. That beautiful face was painted
in lines of fire on her heart; and now how came
she here looking so pale and worn?

"Will you help me to lodgings for the night?"
the nun asked.

"Yes," Elizabeth answered, "you may come
with me," and taking the bundle the man
handed her, she led the way out of the station.

Presently she slackened her pace.

"I go too fast for you," she said.

"No, I like to walk fast."

" Then your bag is too heavy ; here——" And giving to Wamba the bundle she carried, Elizabeth took the nun's bag.

" Indeed, I am quite able."

" No, you are not, and Wamba likes to be useful. You are too delicate for this sort of work."

" Oh, don't say that ! I can fan sick people at least, and in the papers I read of the little children left desolate. I can mind them."

" Yes," Elizabeth answered, " you can do that. But who let you come to this death-hole ? "

There was a moment's pause, then the little nun looked up wistfully.

" I ran away," she said.

" Is there anyone here whom you know ? " Elizabeth went on, " whom you have come to join ? "

" Oh, no ! That is, there *is* someone here I know, my cousin ; but I would not have him see me for the world ! "

" What is he here for ? "

" He is a clergyman ; he has come to help—to give his life. He is so good ; so wonderfully good and strong ; so far above me that he would despise me if he could know how deeply I have sinned."

" *Sinned*, child ? "

" Yes, sinned." Then laying her hand on Elizabeth's arm : " You look a sort of Sister yourself ; you look so kind and strong ; I will tell you all my story if you will help me ? "

" I will," Elizabeth answered, and turning into a new street where the houses stood far apart with dismal empty lots between, she went up the steps and opened the door of one that seemed never to have been opened until now.

As they entered they heard children's voices, and cries of " Elizabeth—Elizabeth!" Then down the narrow, barren hall where the walls were of a new and ghastly whiteness, and the floor still stained with lime, came pattering feet. Seven little children in all, watched over during Elizabeth's absences by the eldest of them, a child of ten with the expression of a woman of fifty. They all crowded round Elizabeth now— all save one that was too young to walk, but was creeping with all its little strength to meet her.

She put down the bag and lifted the child from the floor, and as the little arms stole round her neck, and the little head nestled close to hers, a light like sunshine came over her face. The other children retreated behind Wamba—who, having put down his bundle, licked their faces with indiscriminate patronage—looked with some awe at Elizabeth's companion, and took her outstretched hand very carefully.

" She has come to take care of you," Elizabeth said—"ask her what you must call her ? "

" My name is Beatrice," the little nun said, "but you must call me Sister."

" Say it," Elizabeth ordered, " say ' Sister.' "

" Sister ! " came in chorus, and the less timid ones left the shelter of Wamba's broad back, and began a closer examination of the newcomer.

" If you will take off your cloak and hood," Elizabeth said as she removed her own, " they will be more friendly." Then as Beatrice obeyed, taking off her cap as well, Elizabeth smiled scornfully at herself, because the girl's beauty struck her heart to pain.

Had she been such a fool as to let her heart stir ?

After this, Elizabeth, with the child still on her arm, busied herself about supper. Bread and milk was all, but that was as much as a feast would have been at any other place or time ; for the milk alone was " above rubies." For herself and Beatrice there was hot tea in addition, and for Wamba a bone saved from dinner. Elizabeth patted him gently ; he was growing very gaunt.

Beatrice helped to put the little ones to bed, and when all were safe, save the child that was asleep in Elizabeth's arms, Elizabeth said to Beatrice, " Will you tell me your story now, or to-morrow ? I have until eleven o'clock to rest ; after that I shall be gone for the night."

" I will tell you now," Beatrice answered, " but may I not put that child down for you? He will tire you."

" No ; it rests me to hold him, I think. He is the first one that came to me, and I believe I love him. I shall have to send him away before long, when the fever is done, to his grandmother. Meanwhile I am a little foolish about him. But suppose you put some of those blocks on the fire before we begin. It is healthy to have a little fire, you know; besides it is cheerful."

If a fire could be dismal, that little fire was. It was made of bits of laths and boards left from the building of the house, and built on the hearth where as yet there was no grate.

Beatrice went to work carefully, not being an adept, and Wamba, watching, signified his approval when she was done by stretching himself before the blaze.

Then, without moving from where she knelt, Beatrice began.

She told of her childhood at the Convent, and of the Mother, with a lingering love as if she did not wish to leave that peaceful time—then her life at home, her father's death, and the removal to New York.

She told it very simply, as a child might, and Elizabeth saw that the thought of John, except as a brother, had not entered the girl's mind up to this point. Over the life in New York, however, she hesitated a little, while Elizabeth watched every shade of expression, and listened to every doubtful tone.

Was John coming in now; was she going to hear now, how, that, deceiving everyone, even John himself, the girl yet loved him enough to follow him to death ?.

But presently like a pent-up flame the truth burst forth. "Claude! oh, I loved him so!" and there was a catch in her voice like a sob. "Oh, yes; I loved him more than life—more than God! That was my sin. I told you I had sinned; but I did not realize it. Life was like a dream then, such a beautiful dream. Have you ever loved anyone, Elizabeth? Loved him—loved enough to sin? You look too strong. I beg your pardon, it was a wrong question—almost an insult. But I am so weak, you see. Then Claude went away for a few days, and while he was gone my governess told me dreadful things about him. She said he was an infidel; that it was sin for me to love him; that I must nail my love to the Cross, and leave Claude.

"I was so wicked, Elizabeth, that I tried to persuade myself that Miss Grigsby had told lies; then I hoped that she was crazy. Do you think God will forgive me? Then I wrote to the Mother, and I wrote to John and begged him to come and help me."

Elizabeth's eyes had a far-away look in them, and she drew the sleeping child close to her breast.

"And did John come?" she asked.

"Not for a long time. I asked him to come in my joy, and I asked him to come in my sorrow, and he did not come either time. He was absorbed in his work, you see, and my joys and sorrows could not seem much to him."

Elizabeth sighed. "But of course he loved you?"

"I think he thought me rather weak and foolish; and Claude said that my affection would annoy him. When Claude came back," she went on, "there seemed to be a mist between us. We had an explanation, and he said that he would try to think as I did; but still the mist was there. At last John came. O Elizabeth, John is so high! He is so strong, so noble; he seemed so far away from me always, and he dwarfs everyone who comes near him. He did not tell me; I found out that he was coming to this dreadful place to work, to suffer, perhaps to die for the love of his fellows. And we were going to the Adirondacks for love of ourselves. All the time I seemed to see the face of the Christ on the Cross, and to hear him say 'Father, forgive them, for they know not what they do!' Claude, who does not believe in Him, did not know; and all who were going in search of pleasure did not care. Only John was going to pain and death for Christ's sake. But *I* knew, and the Christ would not ask forgiveness for me if I did not care; if I stayed willfully for love of one who was Christ's enemy. Knowing all this, I longed to stay; I tried to stay; and hated Miss Grigsby for telling me, and John for coming away. You see how wicked I was; how I sinned, Elizabeth!"

Elizabeth stooped and kissed her brow. "But you came away," she said.

"Not of my own will. John came, and I took his departure as quietly as a brute; then, after he left, I got a letter from the Mother. She said I was committing the sin of Judas, and betraying the Master afresh; that I must leave all, and come to her at the Convent. As I read, I faced my sin fully. I had known it all along, but had turned my back on it. In my heart I had been more false than Judas, and I knew that I must try to atone. So I came here. God knows how my life is bound up in Claude, and maybe God will forgive me, now that I have come away to this awful place to show my willingness to follow Him. In my letter that I left for Claude, I did not tell him once that I loved him. I wrote a cold, calm letter, and told him I was coming here to help. It was very hard, for I knew that it would hurt him. So often he asked: 'Do you love me better than John?' Now he will think that I love John best. It was the hardest thing I could think of to do, for it hurt Claude, and made him think ill of me, too. You think God will forgive me now, Elizabeth?"

"There is no doubt of it, child, even without your coming here to die. Will you not tell John?"

"Oh, never—never! I must not tell John, for that would make it easier for me. Besides, I promised Claude that John should not know that I was here; I wrote him that in my letter; but I did not say that I did not love John best.

He will think that I would rather die for John than live for him. If I live, I will go on to the Mother. If I die, Elizabeth, I will leave a letter for you to send to Claude, and this last farewell will tell him how I loved him all the while. When I am dead there will be no harm in comforting him. And you can tell John why I came, and tell him to pray for my soul."

"I think your cousin ought to know of your being here at once," Elizabeth said. "I know him, and I think I ought to tell him."

Beatrice sprang up. "You promised you would not."

"I promised I would help you," Elizabeth answered. "If you should die, he could hold me to account."

"And you are afraid of a little responsibility?"

Elizabeth smiled. "No, I'm not afraid, but it would not be right. Do you not see that you are almost committing suicide? You ought to be sent away from this place; and your cousin would do it."

Beatrice stood looking down into the fire.

"Where could I go?" she asked at last. "Who would receive me now?"

"There are stations outside where you could be taken care of until it would be safe for you to go on."

"And if I die there?"

"There is no reason why you should die."

"Yes, my heart is broken. I feel life going from me every hour."

Elizabeth looked up quickly, and once more was struck with the frail, worn appearance of the girl.

"My mother died of nothing," Beatrice went on, "and so will I; old Angela told me so." Once more she knelt by Elizabeth. "I am safer with you than anywhere else," she said; "why not leave me in peace? Already I love you and the little children. If you insist on telling John, I must go away and hide even from you."

"I do not insist," Elizabeth answered, "but I must think about it before I can make you any promise. Now I must sleep, and you must, too. See, it is eight o'clock; by eleven I must be gone. Sleep quietly for to-night, and I will tell you my decision in the morning."

She showed the girl a bed in the next room, · and Beatrice took her bag and her wraps from where they hung, and carried them with her.

Presently she came back half undressed, and with a pair of scissors in her hand.

"Will you cut off my hair?" she asked; "it is so hard to get under my cap."

Elizabeth looked at her a moment. "No," she said, "I will plait it very tight for you instead."

Beatrice sighed. "Nobody believes that I am dead to my past!" But this was all her protest, and she sat quite still while Elizabeth brushed and braided her hair. When it was done, she took Elizabeth's hand.

"You have been very kind to me, Elizabeth, and I thank you very much. Would you mind kissing me for good-night?"

And Elizabeth kissed her. "Sleep well," she said; "you need it sadly."

But when Elizabeth looked in at eleven o'clock, the room was empty. While she slept the heavy sleep of exhaustion, the girl had gone. On the table there was a letter sealed and stamped, addressed to Claude Van Kuyster, and a note to Elizabeth begging her to mail this letter when the fever was done. "It will not make any difference then for him to know how much I loved him, for I shall be dead, or in the Convent. You will not see me again, nor will John. Good-by. God bless you."

Putting the note and letter away, Elizabeth hurried out. She must find John at once. At the bread depot she found several calls awaiting her, but could get no news of John. Mr. Paget had not been in for twenty-four hours, and no one could say where he was.

Elizabeth left a note for him with several addresses where he might find her, her own first, and begged him to come to her at once. She then went on to her night's work—a family of four, all ill, and two dying. In the morning she went again to the supply office, and from there to John's lodgings; but he had not been in the office since the morning before, and his lodgings were locked tight. Her only resource was to slip a little twisted note into the keyhole.

She did not wish to institute any systematic search for Beatrice, even if it were feasible, but she looked for her herself; asking for her at the houses of both Protestant and Roman Catholic Sisters, without success. The girl seemed to have vanished.

It was useless to regret that she had told Beatrice her intentions, for she would in no case have acted without Beatrice's knowledge; and she could not blame herself for the girl's rashness; but she was deeply troubled. She might be in some empty house—there were many such, emptied by fever—where it would be certain death. She might be working beyond her frail strength; she might fall into other serious dangers, she was so beautiful and simple.

At her own lodgings that evening the children gave her a note, and said the Sister had left it. It was only a line—" I am safe."

Again Elizabeth went out on her night rounds. She had done her best by the girl, and until she could see John, she could do no more.

Toward dawn her charge for that night died, and she was taking her way slowly homeward, when a voice called her:

"Elizabeth!" By the light of the fires John recognized the dog across the street, and came over to her. He took both her hands.

"You want me, Elizabeth?" he said. "I have your notes and have been hunting for you. I am so glad that you want me."

The voice, the words, the strong grasp of his hands, shook her as no pleading could have done. The calm that had come after years of struggle was swept away, and she trembled like a leaf in the wind. Some words she had read once came back to her—"There is no love so tender as an old love renewed."

"What is it?" John asked, looking down into her eyes.

She drew a long breath. "I am so tired," she said, "that I believe my mind is leaving me."

"Please take care of yourself, Elizabeth; you are one of the people we cannot spare from this world."

"Hush!" she answered quickly, "I do not matter; but there is someone here who needs your care, and it is for that I sent for you; your cousin."

Then she stood alone in the dead world. Her brain, her heart stopped; even the fire hardened into one tall flame as she watched the man before her.

"You mean——"

"Beatrice. She has run away, and is here disguised as a Sister of Mercy."

"Beatrice!" he whispered.

Elizabeth turned to see if the growing day had yet risen over the house-tops to touch his face.

"Beatrice!" he said again.

"I met her at the station by chance," Elizabeth went on, smoothing one hand over the other as if to smooth away the marks of the grasp in which they had been held. "I took her home with me. I intended to keep her there with the children, but I told her what I thought you ought"—she stopped abruptly, then after a second went on, "You would send her back to her friends. When I looked into her room again, she was gone."

"When was that?"

"Night before last—before this one."

"Nearly forty-eight hours! What shall we do—what must we do, Elizabeth? She is so young, so frail, so beautiful! Can you not help me, Elizabeth?" laying his hands on her shoulders. "Can you not help me? She will die! And she *loves* me. She would not have come else; would she, Elizabeth?"

"I have hunted for her already," Elizabeth answered, turning her eyes away from his. "We must describe her at the offices, and ask everyone to keep a lookout for her. It is all we can do."

A step approached, and both turned. It was the young physician who stayed with John.

"Tell him," John said.

So Elizabeth described Beatrice.

"I parted with her an hour ago," Dr. Rogers answered. "A woman had died, and the nun, Sister Dolores she called herself, took away the little child. She said that she knew where it would be safe."

Elizabeth stretched out her hand to John.

"She will bring it to me, Jack; come!"

Rogers watched them away in silence, too surprised to ask a question.

In the dusk of the day that was dawn when they parted, John and Rogers met at their lodgings.

"You did not find Sister Dolores?" Rogers said.

"No, but she had left the child there."

Rogers lighted the spirit-lamp and put on the little kettle; he brought out some bread and cold meat, and from his coat pocket a bottle of milk.

"I met the Gray Sister," he said. "She told me, and gave me this milk."

John did not seem to hear him.

"You know the Gray Sister," Rogers went on.

"Elizabeth? Yes; but I have not seen her in nearly five years."

"She is wonderful!"

John turned and looked at Rogers curiously.

"If for nothing else, she would be a wonder of physical endurance; but to-day she looks worn out; quite as if she might break down. In twelve hours she has changed dreadfully."

"She is worried about Beatrice," John said, just as if Rogers knew it all.

"Does she love this Beatrice very much ?·

"Elizabeth love Beatrice?" John repeated slowly. "No—I think not. No."

"Then I wish Beatrice, with her pretty baby face, had kept away from here——"

John rose quickly.

"I mean no offense. I know nothing of this young woman or her relations to you," Rogers went on; "only I adore the one you call Elizabeth. She is worth a stack of ordinary women, and this young person seems to have broken her all up."

"Beatrice—Miss Wilton is my cousin," John said, "and I *must* find her." He picked up his hat.

"You won't go until you have had your supper, however," and Rogers locked the door and put the key in his pocket. "Pull yourself together, Paget; remember, you will need strength. The Gray Sister and I are hunting, too; street by street we go : and two friends of mine are on the watch. I think that Father O'Bryan knows more than he will tell."

John's eyes were gleaming. "She was educated in a Convent," he said quickly, "and if the Romanists get her——"

"Shall I offer to help build Father O'Bryan's new church?" Rogers asked.

"To *any* extent."

There was a knock at the door, and Rogers unlocking it, Elizabeth entered.

"Just in time for supper," Rogers said.
"And you can help me manage Paget, too."

"I came to ask if you have heard anything,"
Elizabeth answered. "I have had my supper."

"Another cup of tea will not hurt you ; and
if you will help us consume this beef, your dog
here, shall have the bone. As a physician I pre-
scribe this second supper; sit down comfortably,
and in twenty-four hours we will have Miss
Wilton safely locked up."

Elizabeth obeyed him, so did John, and both
felt it a good thing that he rattled on cheerfully without waiting for an answer to anything
he said. When supper was over, Rogers gave
John a list of names.

"I do not think that any of those people will
live until morning," he said, "and all want to
see a clergyman. I have numbered them ; the
highest numbers having the longest chance of
life. At seven o'clock in the morning we will
meet here. For you," turning to Elizabeth, "I
have three moderate cases, which please make
comfortable before you go on to the fourth case,
which is very bad. This fourth case will need
all the time you can spare. I will send relief to
you at six in the morning, however, and you can
be here by seven. Of course we will search as
we go, and at any moment we may meet Sister
Dolores."

After this they said good-night and went their
several ways.

But morning found them unsuccessful still, and night and morning, and yet another evening, found them without word or token.

The children were all in bed save the one Elizabeth loved most, and he lay asleep in her arms where she sat by the little fire. It seemed a month since Beatrice had knelt there telling her story; such a pitiful, innocent story as it was. She would have been wiser to grant the girl's prayer not to tell John, but she could not have foreseen the sequel. Her own sympathies were all with Claude; his case seemed so hard.

That morning she had mailed the letter to him which Beatrice had left, inclosed in a note from herself, telling him the story of Beatrice's meeting with her, and the reason why she had again run away. She finished with a promise to telegraph him as soon as Beatrice was found. It was all she could do for him, and having done it, she felt more at rest. No one could know better than she how much he needed comfort. John was happy in thinking that Beatrice had come for love of him; happy even through the misery of not finding her, and Elizabeth did not un-deceive him. She could not help admiring the faithful way in which he did his work in spite of everything. He never flagged, but his whole being seemed ever on the alert; he seemed to be always looking and listening, and turned to Elizabeth for sympathy and help as confidently as a child would turn to its mother.

"You taught me to depend on you long ago, Elizabeth," he said one day, "and so it seems natural to come and ask you to help me bear my burden. Do you think me very weak?"

"No," she had answered, "men were born to strive and to suffer; women—to sympathize. At least that is the theory which men have formulated."

She had done her best to help him. For herself, she was too tired to feel anything save a vague pity for all.

While she sat by the fire thinking wearily over the same course her mind had followed for days, there was a knock at the door, and opening it she found young Rogers. In the hunt for Beatrice she had given him her address in case of news.

"I have come for you," he said. "Father O'Bryan is down. I do not think there is much hope for the old chap; and as I strongly suspect that he knows where Miss Wilton is, I want you to be with him. I found him sick in the street, so carried him where I pleased."

Elizabeth put the child in his bed; made the fire and the lights safe, then, buttoning on her cloak, followed the young man. It was a long walk, all across the town, and when they arrived the priest was unconscious.

"He may come out of this just at the last," Rogers said; "watch by him."

So all night long Elizabeth watched, and to-

ward morning she was startled from a doze by.
the voice of the priest.

" Tell Rogers," he whispered, " that the girl is
at the Sacred Heart, sick.   She is always calling
for Claude.   Is Rogers' name Claude ? "

Elizabeth raised him quickly, but there was
only a gasp—then he was dead.

It had rained a little in the night, and the
morning was cold and damp, and Elizabeth
shivered as the outer air struck her.   The change
would kill all the sick, she feared.   She must find
Rogers and John, and tell them at once where
Beatrice was.

The clouds were flying low, and the rising day
touched them to exquisite opal tints.   Even in
her haste she looked up more than once to the
growing light and beauty, and drank in gratefully
the freshened air.   It was so sweet after the close
room of death.

A sharp bark arrested her, and she turned to
see Wamba, who had been with her the moment
before, standing on the steps leading up to a re-
cessed porch.   She called to him because she
was in haste, but he did not come.   She turned
away, and he whined.   She turned back toward
the steps; then Wamba retreated into the porch,
still whining.

He had found something; a forsaken child,
maybe, and she mounted the steps with a little
curiosity.   But it was not a child; a woman in
black was lying there.   Her feet and the hem

of her dress were wet with the rain that had driven in.

Elizabeth paused, overcome by an unaccountable dread. The feet looked so dead.

Wamba whined appealingly, then broke into a long, low howl. She could not move ; that cry of unreasoning misery seemed to have frozen every drop of blood in her body. How long it was ! how it reverberated in the desolation !

Again the dog lifted up his head, and the long, low howl—longer and lower it seemed this time —crept through the silence.

A shudder passed over Elizabeth, but she could not move. She heard a step approaching, and struggled with herself as a person in a nightmare.

" Somebody sick up there ? "

It was Rogers' voice, and his step that came up quickly. " What is it ? Your hands are like ice ; are you ill ? Don't stare so !" shaking her slightly.

" Thank you," Elizabeth gasped. " See there, it is Beatrice, and she is dead. I knew it the moment I saw the little wet feet——" and she moved toward the prostrate figure.

" Good God ! "

" Father O'Bryan said that she was ill at the Sacred Heart, crying for Claude. She must have slipped away." She raised the girl in her arms. " How lovely she is—look," pushing back the disguising veil and bands from the brow.

Rogers stooped over them. " Is there no sign of life ? "

For answer, Elizabeth lifted Beatrice's hand and let it fall. Rogers drew back.

" Paget is just behind me," he said, " we were going to his lodgings to meet you for news. I must stop him and prepare him ; or take her away."   .

" It is too late," Elizabeth answered, " he is here."

" Rogers ? " and John came quickly up the steps. " Oh, God ! " he said—" oh, God ! " and Wamba's howl seemed to finish the wail.

One moment he stood quite still ; Elizabeth, worn and white, looking up at him, and on her breast Beatrice's dead face, smiling like a child in its sleep.

" She is mine," he said in a low voice, as if to himself. " At last she is mine—mine ! Give her to me—give her to me. How dare you keep her—touch her ! *You !* Mine—mine ! "—lifting his hands to heaven. " At last she is mine ! "

He took the girl from Elizabeth's unresisting arms, and folding her close to his breast, he laid her head on his shoulder, and drew her cloak and veil about her.

" You know she is mine, Elizabeth ; she came because she loved me. How dare you try to hold her from me ? Mine—mine. No one must touch her now ; go away ! "

" Paget ! "   .

"Go away! Death has given her into my arms. Go, leave me with my dead. You will not? Then I will go. Do not follow—do not follow!"

And as he went away from them Elizabeth, still kneeling on the wet stones of the porch, looked up into Rogers' face, while something like a smile crept round her white lips.

"He loved me once," she said, "and now I go to send a message to the man *she* loved."

XXVIII.

"Then they left you for their pleasure : till in due time, one
   by one,
   Some with lives that came to nothing, some with deeds as
   well undone,
   Death stepped tacitly and took them where they never see
   the sun."

"BY all that is pleasant, how came you here,
Mrs. Van Kuyster?"

"By ship and by rail," Mrs. Van Kuyster
answered, holding out her hand to Ted Dennis,
who leaned over the carriage door. It was in
the Corso in Rome, and Mrs. Van Kuyster's
carriage was waiting for Marjorie, who was shopping.

"Is Claude with you?"

"Yes, he is in there with Marjorie."

"You had not planned this when I left you in
the Adirondacks last autumn, had you?"

"No; I think your coming over made us
think of it; and Claude was rather upset about
his cousin, you know."

"Little Miss Wilton; she still sticks to her
Convent, I suppose? It was hard on Claude, but
she would have tried him dreadfully, I think."

"Of course; their training and views of life were
so different."

" Her training was very bad."

" Bad ? Surely, Mr. Dennis——"

" You misunderstand me. I only meant so hopelessly religious, don't you know."

" Yes, what you say is true ; it was hopeless to expect her to adapt herself to our mode of living or thinking. Life was a very serious business to her."

" Did she have any effect on Claude ? I mean, her taking it so seriously as to leave everything that was pleasant and worth having, to go into a Convent ? "

Mrs. Van Kuyster paused a moment. " He has never talked to me about her once—but he says that his children shall be Christians—that, if he will, his brother shall train them."

" My word ! " and Dennis pulled his mustache reflectively. " His brother—that very striking looking fellow who went down to the fever ? Do you know I really thought for a little while that he was wrong in his head—a fellow like him throwing his life away so utterly. What has become of him ? "

" He is quite well now, I hope. He is on his plantation in the South, resting. He had a dreadful time in the epidemic, and was desperately ill, but he had a good nurse and physician, and so pulled through. Claude actually wanted to go down to him, but both the nurse and the physician wrote him not to think of such a thing, that he would only do harm. I was very thankful that they had so much common sense. The physician ordered six months' rest for John, before he took any work. Claude sent his yacht down for him, and he has cruised about a little, I believe. The physician is with him, and Martin Kinsey. Martin wrote me that John was in every way the most perfect man he had ever known. His hair has gone quite white, he says. Martin is such an enthusiast!"

"Yes, he is another incomprehensible. I always thought that he and Miss Van Kuyster would make it up."

"Oh, no! I have quite other views for Marjie. Just between us, remember, not a word to a living soul about it! I have always thought that she and Claude were made for each other."

Dennis looked up quickly. "So? You give me light. That is what reconciled you so readily to the Convent scheme. I wondered, last autumn, at your taking it so easily. You remember I happened to go down to New York with Claude just a few days after Miss Wilton left you, and you had settled in the Adirondacks; well, he found a letter at the Club that seemed to tear him limb from limb, as it were, and he dragged me about in a frantic way to lawyers and things, to get a little old woman endowed. She was to get a thousand dollars every Thanksgiving Day from Beatrice Wilton. She had been Miss Wilton's governess; I had to witness the papers,

you know. It was a horrid wet day. I made
him pay up, however, by rushing over town with
me; I was to sail that afternoon, you know—I
actually dragged him down to the steamer. But
honestly"—lowering his voice—"he frightened
me. Claude is usually such a quiet fellow, you
know, but about three hours after he got the
letter, we had just finished lunch at the Club,
when a telegram was handed him. He looked at
me a minute and said: 'Would you believe it,
Dennis, she is dead!' That was all; he would
not say another word. He was very quiet, but
I was afraid to leave him, so I took him to the
ship, and at the last I turned him over to Tilly,
who promised to see him safely back to you.
Tilly joined me two weeks later in Paris; he said
that you and Miss Van Kuyster had taken it very
quietly, and he supposed it only meant that the
girl had taken the veil. He wondered a little,
but now I understand."

Mrs. Van Kuyster nodded. "Claude was
'hard hit' as you men say, but he seems quite
right now, poor fellow. And soon it will be
with him as it is with all of us; this—episode—
will fade into a lovely 'might have been,' to
dream over when he smokes his after-dinner
cigar. Meanwhile, Marjie will see that the said
dinner will produce only dreams, and not night-
mares. *Voyez?*"

"Capital! Ah, how do you do, Miss Van
Kuyster," lifting his hat and shaking hands, "and

Claude, my dear fellow, it is balm to weary eyes to see you."

"Thanks. Where have you dropped from?"

"I have just come back from the East. Been reading 'Omar Khayyam' under a palm tree in a garden of roses—delicious, don't you know."

"It sounds well. Jump in, we are driving to 'the hill of gardens,' will you come?"

"I will; old friends are a boon. You ought to go to the East, though, Claude. Things are so slow and easy over there, every day is a little eternity."

"I believe time is enough for me," Claude answered.

"In this part of the world, quite enough; but houris, hookhas, palms, and roses make a very good perspective for eternity."

"And yet, you have come back," Marjorie said.

"Well, a winter of eternities is quite an addition to a man's life, don't you think?"

"Quite"—and Mrs. Van Kuyster laughed.

They stopped at the bank for letters. Claude brought out a bundle, which he distributed as they drove.

"A half dozen from your 'dearest friends,' Marjie," handing her several. "Yours, mother, are from Jack and Kinsey. Mine is from Miss Grigsby; thanking me for the furs, I suppose. Will you read it and answer it, Marjie?" And he handed it to her.

He took very little part in the talk for the rest of the drive, and his shadowy eyes seemed deeper, and the lines in his face more hopeless as he looked out over the magnificent view that spreads below the watcher on the Pincian Hill.

It was not the fashionable hour, and the place was still, save for some children playing near, and a peasant leaning against a tree in the sunshine, thrumming on a guitar. He hummed in a rich low voice the gay fandango he played, with its pathetic minor falls and broken chords.

A woman passed with a basket of roses ; Claude bought them all. And the roses and the music swept him away from the immortal scene·before him to commonplace New York—to a conservatory full of forced flowers. " In a garden they would be nodding," he heard her say, " here they stand still` and dream—like the pine tree that dreamed of the palm. Does everything dream and long, Claude ? " Away to a sullen gray sea, breaking against gray cliffs—to trailing mist clouds and a little wet cheek pressed close to his, and a low voice whispering, " Yes, you have won me."

" That guitar is dreadfully twangy," Mrs. Van Kuyster said. " Drive on."

Claude leaned out and gave the musician a gold piece.